Conn made slow, sweet love to Elizabeth. All the while his deep voice murmured in her ear—erotic things, exciting things, beautiful things—things that made her heart pound and her blood run hot and her body tauten and tremble. He told her how beautiful she was, how wild she made him feel. The words, whispered in that deep voice, were raw and shocking . . . and wonderful. He told her how much he wanted her, how much he needed her, how much he would miss her.

But he never told her the one thing she longed to hear.

QUIET FIRES

GINNA GRAY

HarperPaperbacks

A Division of HarperCollinsPublishers

This is a work of fiction. The characters, incidents, and dialogues are products of the author's imagination and are not to be construed as real. Any resemblance to actual events or persons, living or dead, is entirely coincidental.

HarperPaperbacks   *A Division of* HarperCollins*Publishers*
10 East 53rd Street, New York, N.Y. 10022

Cover illustration by Jim Griffin

First printing: May 1991

Printed in the United States of America

HarperPaperbacks and colophon are trademarks of HarperCollins*Publishers*

10   9   8   7   6   5   4   3   2   1

A special thanks to Patricia Smith for believing in me—
then and now.

Prologue

The Rocky Mountains—late October 1833

Riding single file, the two men picked their way cautiously down the slope toward the shallow creek. Since noon they had crossed the trails of two small bands of Indians— Indians traveling without their women and children.

They could be hunting parties, but they could also be raiding parties. Young bucks after horses and hair. Either way, the trappers were taking no chances.

Out in front, Conn Cavanaugh scanned the ground for more signs while his partner kept watch on the surrounding area. Each man carried his rifle in front of him across his saddle.

Pike, the rough-looking mongrel dog that traveled with them, had swung far out on their left flank and was trotting down the slope with his head up, sniffing the air.

The only sounds were the soft thud of the horses' hooves and the creak of saddle leather. The sun was still angled high, but low clouds were moving in and the air held a damp chill that promised more snow.

Conn set a zigzagging course, keeping mostly within the shadows of the trees and using every bit of cover he could. He drew up at the bank of the creek and signaled Taw to halt. For several minutes he just sat there, listening.

The dog crossed the creek downstream, came up the bank on the opposite side, and stopped, waiting, his ears pricked.

Except for the gurgle of the swift-running water, all was quiet. Overhead a hawk soared, and a small furry animal darted away into a clump of juniper. High above timberline, the jagged peaks of the surrounding snowcapped mountains glistened in the sun.

One of the horses bobbed its head and blew, impatient for a drink. At a nod from Conn, Taw came forward.

"I 'spect they was jist Ute huntin' parties." The old man worked over the wad of tobacco in his cheek and stared at the stand of pines on the opposite bank as the horses plunged their muzzles into the clear, icy stream.

Conn didn't answer immediately. Squinting against the sun, he searched downstream, his gaze sweeping over every rock and bush on both banks. "Could be. Or they could be Cheyenne or Arapaho."

He hoped Taw was right. For the past few years the Utes hadn't given them too much trouble. But Conn had a bad feeling he couldn't shake.

Across the stream, the big brute of a dog crouched to drink. The next instant his head came up sharply, his muzzle dripping water.

"Damn." In unison the trappers hauled back on their reins and made a dash for the cover of the trees . . . but it was too late.

Five Pawnee braves came around the bend, one in front and the others riding two abreast down the middle of the shallow creek. Their faces were painted, and the big one in the lead had a fresh scalp of long black braided hair hanging from his saddle.

The Indians' startled hesitation when they spotted the trappers lasted only an instant. Then they charged, weapons raised, yipping their blood-chilling war cry.

Conn got off a shot and saw a brave jerk and tumble from his horse. Another, the one with the fresh scalp, let out a yell and came at him with a lance. At the last possible instant

Conn lunged to one side. He felt a rush of wind and heard the hum of the staff as it whistled past.

Behind him, Taw's Hawkin boomed. On the other side of the river the dog had an Indian down and was hunched on top of him, ninety pounds of snarling, vicious fury.

Conn pulled the pistol from his belt and whirled his mount.

The big Indian turned back and galloped toward him with a tomahawk in his raised hand, yipping obscenely, his face savage beneath the hideous paint. Conn waited until he was at point-blank range and pulled the trigger. The ball struck the brave in the chest, knocking him backward and arresting the downward arc of the tomahawk.

Conn stuffed the empty pistol back under his belt. He heard the twang of a bowstring and felt the sorrel jerk under the impact of the arrow. As the horse went down, Conn rolled free.

He hit the snow-covered ground on his shoulder and kept rolling. He didn't stop until he was behind a log, half-buried in the small drift that banked it.

At once it was deathly quiet.

Breathing hard, Conn pressed back against the log and grabbed for his powder horn and shot bag. His eyes moving constantly, he poured powder down the barrel of his rifle, dropped in a ball, and rammed it home. Finished, he looked cautiously around the butt end of the log and eased his rifle into position.

His jaw clenched. Thirty feet away Taw lay on his back on the creek bank, half in and half out of the water, an arrow in his shoulder.

There was no sign of Pike, but the Indian he'd brought down was dead, along with three others.

Where was the fifth?

He wanted to go to Taw, but he didn't dare. Not yet. He knew well the patience of an Indian. A man who couldn't match it didn't live long in this country.

Conn waited.

The temperature hovered at freezing, yet sweat beaded his forehead and trickled down his spine. He wiped his damp palm against his buckskins. In the dive from his horse he'd lost his hat, and snow covered him, clinging to his heavy beaver pelt coat, his hair, his face. Little clumps stuck to his eyebrows and lashes. Mud from the creek bank caked his moccasins.

He studied the area with care. No rock, no tree, no stand of brush, went unexamined. He saw nothing, heard nothing, save the rush of water over rocks and the soughing of the wind through the pines. Still, he waited.

The dank smells of damp earth, snow, and rotting wood filled his nostrils. A gust of wind sent a shower of pine needles drifting down. A furry mouse scampered along the top of the decaying log. Halfway across he spotted Conn and froze, whiskers twitching.

Conn lay still, alert for any sound. After a while his foot began to cramp.

There had been no movement of any kind for a half hour. Had the Indian gone?

Conn had almost decided he had when a rabbit darted across the bank for the cover of some bushes about thirty yards away, then veered off at the last second and streaked into the woods. He watched the small clump. There was no sign of movement, but Conn raised his rifle and took aim.

The *whop* of the striking bullet was followed by a faint gasp. Conn quickly reloaded and fired again at the same spot. He scrambled on his belly to the other end of the log and peered around it. At the edge of the clump of brush he saw a brown hand claw the earth. Then it went limp.

In an instant Conn was up and running. He moved with catlike grace, long legs flying over the ground, silent and swift, his Hawkin rifle in one hand, his moccasined feet churning through the snow in a blur of motion.

Breathing heavily, he dropped down beside Taw and felt his neck for a pulse. Conn slumped and closed his eyes. It was thready and weak, but it was there, thank God. But it wouldn't be for long if he didn't get Taw back to the cabin, where he could keep him warm and tend to him properly. Taw Pruett was as tough as an old grizzly, but he was well past seventy.

Conn worked quickly. Gritting his teeth against the old man's tortured moan, he removed the arrow. He packed the wound with snow to stop the bleeding and bound it as best he could with a strip of rawhide.

As he worked, the dog came out of the woods. He was a big brute, rangy and muscled from running, his yellow eyes fierce and intelligent. Hackles up, walking stiff-legged, he circled an Indian, growling low in his throat.

"Pike." Conn's voice was sharp and commanding, and the growl changed to a whine as the dog approached Taw's prone figure.

There was a gash in the animal's side and his rough coat glistened red with blood, but Conn didn't have time to deal with his wound then. At a word from him, Pike went and rolled in a nearby snowbank.

Conn caught Taw's mount, the pack horses, and the three Indian ponies that hadn't spooked during the skirmish. When he'd rigged a travois out of saplings and beaver pelts, he lifted the old man onto it and covered him with more furs. He took the reins of the pack horses and swung into the saddle, then paused to take a last look around, his lean, hard-boned face grim as he surveyed the carnage.

"No more, by God," he swore with soft violence. "No damned more."

He put the buckskin into a slow walk and headed east. The big mongrel fell in behind.

It was almost dawn the next morning when Taw's crepey eyelids finally fluttered open.

He looked awful. Pain glazed his faded brown eyes, and his long white hair and beard were matted and scraggly. Beneath the leathery skin his seamed face had an ashen hue. During the long night's vigil he seemed to have grown smaller and older before Conn's eyes.

Hiding his concern, Conn sat forward and met his partner's bleary gaze and shook his head. "It's about time you woke up. I swear, old man, it's getting to where I can't even turn my back without you getting into trouble."

"Izzat so?" Taw wheezed. "Well, I may be gettin' . . . old . . . but I've saved yore bacon a time er two. An' I 'spect I'll . . . do it agin' 'fore I turn up my toes." His voice was weak, and when he tried to shift positions on the narrow bunk, he winced and gave up the effort.

The teasing light went out of Conn's eyes. "No, you won't. Because I'm going to see to it that you never have to. As soon as you're well enough, we're leaving."

"Leaving? Jist 'cause of that little set-to?" Taw paused to draw several deep breaths. "Why, shoot, boy, it was jist . . . plain old bad luck we run into them Pawnee. They was way outta their territory. Weren't nothin' but a . . . raidin' party, lookin' t' take a few Ute scalps. They been bitter enemies fer years." He lifted his hand, then let it fall back onto the blanket covering his chest and closed his eyes. "'Sides, ain't no point in leavin' here. There's Injuns all over this country."

"I'm talking about leaving the mountains, Taw. For good."

The old man's eyes popped back open. "You mean quit trappin'?"

Conn nodded. "I'm tired of wading in icy streams, and fighting Indians and wolves and god-awful winters. I'm tired of spending months away from my family. Besides, it's past time I quit. I only intended to trap for a few years. Just until I could save enough to give Millie and me a good start. I figured three, maybe four would do it. Five at most." He shrugged, his mouth twisting. "I've been at it almost seventeen."

Seventeen years. Merely saying it aloud depressed him. Where had the time gone? Conn wondered. What had happened to all the plans he and Millie had made so long ago?

Leaning back in the crude chair made of saplings and hide, Conn stretched his legs out in front of him and studied the shiny toe of his moccasin. "When I left Charleston last fall on my way back here, I swung through Texas for a look-see. There's some prime land there at a price that can't be beat."

"Ahhhh. So you didn't jist git a burr under yore saddle 'cause of them Injuns. You been thinkin' on this fer a spell, ain'tcha?"

"Yeah, you could say that." For several years now he'd been thinking about settling in Texas, but it had been merely a tempting idea until his visit home the previous summer. Since then he'd thought of little else. The brush with the Indians the day before, Taw getting wounded, had merely been the final push he'd needed to make his decision.

"Texas is a big land, Taw. Wild and free. A man could build a future there."

He waited for his partner to say something, but the old man remained strangely silent.

"I went with the idea of maybe staking out some prime wilderness land, but while I was there I heard about a plantation for sale—a place called Riverbend. So I took a look at it. The owner's a middle-aged bachelor. He's in bad health and wants to return east to his family. The place could use some work, but it's well set up."

"So . . . yore set on givin' 'er up, are ya?" Taw cleared his throat and looked at the wall. "Well, I'll miss you, boy. I surely will, an' that's a fact."

"What's the matter, are you losing your hearing in your old age? I said *we* are leaving the mountains. As soon as you're fit to travel, we'll take our beaver to St. Louis, then head for Texas. Once I've settled the deal we'll go to Charleston and fetch Millie and the kids."

"You mean you want me t' go with you? Live with you an' yore family?"

"Of course. Hell, we've been together too long to split up now. Besides, I've gotten used to looking at that ugly face."

The look of joy that flashed in the faded old eyes brought a lump to Conn's throat. Though Taw had tried to hide it, Conn knew that the old man's most cherished dream was to be part of a family. He yearned for a home and a few comforts in his old age, someone to care about him—all the things he'd never known. Until that moment, Conn hadn't realized just how much it meant to him.

Taw sobered and pursed his lips. "Does yore missus know what yore plannin'?"

"Not yet."

"She ain't gonna like it, I'm thinkin'."

"Maybe not at first, but Millie will come around once she gets used to the idea."

Conn rose and added another log to the fire. The blaze crackled and popped and sent a shower of sparks up the chimney. Lying beside the hearth, his snout on his paws, Pike watched him, his yellow eyes alert and glittering in the firelight.

Conn hunkered down before the stone fireplace, braced an arm on his knee, and stared at the dancing flames.

Texas. It pulled at him like a lodestone. There, in that vast land, he could finally have what he'd been working for all those years. It was his chance. He had to take it.

He sighed and gave the logs a poke with a metal rod. Taw was right about one thing, though: Millie wasn't going to like it. Not one bit.

Chapter 1

Charleston—January, 1834

"I do declare, Elizabeth Stanton, for such a sweet, unassuming woman you can be so stubborn at times!"

Elizabeth merely shrugged and lowered her gaze to the nightgown she was embroidering, her dark lashes shielding her eyes from her cousin's irate glare.

"Drat! Now I've got a knot. Oh, the devil take it!" Millie flung aside her own hopelessly butchered needlework and bounded to her feet.

A smile tugged at Elizabeth's mouth. Millie had never developed a liking for sewing, nor had she mastered the necessary skills for it. She was simply too full of life and gaiety for such quiet pastimes, and she used any excuse to avoid them.

Not that she wasn't truly vexed. From the corner of her eye, Elizabeth watched her volatile cousin flounce back and forth across the room, her quick, agitated movements betraying her impatience.

Millie came to a halt in front of Elizabeth. The toe of her dainty satin slipper tapped soundlessly against the luxurious rug. "Don't you understand? You have no choice!"

Glancing up, Elizabeth smiled, her soft gray eyes filled with gentle humor. "Of course I do. People always have choices, Millie."

"Not women. Certainly not a woman in your position. Single ladies of good family simply do not live alone. Not when they have a relative who can provide them with a home."

"I have a home." A spasm of grief squeezed Elizabeth's chest so hard, she could not breathe for a moment. She blinked back a rush of tears and blindly made a French knot in the center of a pale pink flower. The needle pricked her finger as she jabbed it through the fine lawn, but she scarcely noticed.

The house on Mulberry Street was small and a bit shabby, and certainly not in the most fashionable part of town, but it was hers now. Along with the meager furnishings and the pittance that represented her father's life savings, the house was her inheritance, all there was left to show for Dr. Edward Stanton's long years of selfless devotion to his patients.

"Honestly, Elizabeth. How can you even consider returning to that old place when you could live here?"

Elizabeth looked around the roomy parlor. It was exquisite in every detail, from the pale gray watered silk that covered the walls between white pilasters, to the marble fireplace and the twin brocade sofas flanking it. Oriental carpets, dotted with mahogany and rosewood tables and Empire gondole chairs, formed islands on the wide-planked glossy oak floor. Graceful swags of velvet and sheer, billowing silk draped the tall windows. An ornate silver tea service sat atop the center table, and exquisite bisque figurines, japanned boxes, small ivory and jade carved animals, and beautiful vases adorned the others.

"I know my father's house isn't as big or as grand as this, Millie, but it's been my home for as long as I can remember," Elizabeth replied quietly. "As it was once yours."

"Oh, dear. Now I've hurt your feelings, haven't I? I didn't mean to. Truly I didn't."

Sitting down on the sofa opposite Elizabeth, Millie placed her hand on her heart and widened her magnificent hazel eyes beseechingly. Combed straight down from a center part and caught just above her ears, her black hair hung in clusters of tight sausage curls on either side of her round face, giving it a childlike appeal that belied her thirty-three years and was impossible to resist.

Elizabeth sighed. She could never stay upset with Millie for long. No one could. Her beautiful cousin was a fairy creature, a combination of imp and seductress who could always tease, coax, or charm her way out of any situation, no matter how awkward or difficult.

"I know, Millie. I know."

Strangely, she did. Because Millie was special, she had been pampered and indulged all of her life by those who loved her—her own parents, Elizabeth's, Conn and his father, even Elizabeth herself. Millie was, as Edward Stanton had affectionately put it, "a thoroughly spoiled, self-centered little madam." Even so, Elizabeth knew that her cousin loved her—in her own way. And the feeling was more than mutual.

Satisfied, Millie smiled brightly and forged ahead. "You know, dear, even if your house were a mansion, it wouldn't matter. It would still be improper for you to live there alone. So you see, you simply must move in here with us."

"Aren't you forgetting something, Millie? This is Dr. Cavanaugh's house, not yours. I appreciate the thought, but dearest, it really isn't your place to invite me to stay."

"Oh, pooh!" With a flutter of her hand, Millie dismissed the paltry matter of ownership. "I've lived here for sixteen years, ever since Conn and I married. This is my home. Besides, Papa Joe wants you to come live with us as much as I do. After all, he and Uncle Edward were best friends."

"I know, but—"

"Really, Elizabeth! It's not as though we're talking about forever, you know. Only until you marry."

Elizabeth looked up from her embroidery so quickly, a pale blond curl dislodged from the cluster atop her head and tumbled across her cheek. This time she made no attempt to hide her amusement. "At my age marriage is a very remote possibility, cousin," she replied dryly, shoving the errant lock back into place and securing it with a hairpin. "I resigned myself to being a spinster years ago."

"I don't see why. You're still attractive, and it's not as though you haven't had plenty of chances. What happened to that nice Mr. Claxton:? I thought he was absolutely perfect for you."

But that didn't stop you from flirting with him, Elizabeth thought, flashing her cousin an ironic look from beneath her lashes.

Millie was a born coquette to whom flirting came as naturally as breathing. It was all innocent and harmless, Elizabeth knew. With her vivacity and sultry, little-girl beauty, Millie had been attracting male attention ever since she'd left the schoolroom. She was simply accustomed to being the center of attention whenever there was a man around. She expected it and could not abide anything less.

Not that Elizabeth had minded. William Claxton was a nice man, but he had not touched her heart in any way.

Turning over the fine lawn material, she snipped off the pink thread. "I haven't seen William in weeks."

"Oh, pooh! And I was so sure he was going to propose."

"He did."

"He *did*?"

"I turned him down."

"Why?" Millie wailed.

"Because I don't love him."

"Is that all?" Her cousin's voice reeked with disgust. "For heaven's sake, Elizabeth, you're thirty-one, not seventeen. I would think by now you'd be past all that romantic nonsense. You'd better settle for what you can get, my girl, and forget about love. Mercy me! You've never even been in love, so after all this time I doubt that it's going to happen."

Elizabeth shrugged and threaded her needle with a strand of pale green silk. Millie was mistaken. She had been in love for as long as she could remember . . . with a man she could never have. She loved him still, though God knew she had tried not to. To Elizabeth's sorrow, she had long ago accepted that she was one of those women to whom love came but once. Forever.

Her love was a secret that she had kept locked in her heart, a secret that, thankfully, she had not shared with her cousin all those years ago.

When Elizabeth didn't reply Millie rolled her eyes and made an aggravated sound. "Honestly, Elizabeth! Sometimes you make me so mad! You simply must listen to reason. I tell you . . ."

Conn made his way toward the parlor from the back of the house, his moccasined feet making no sound on the polished wood floor of the central hall.

His wife's words were unclear, but not the strident tone of her voice. Conn frowned and stepped into the doorway. The scene that greeted him dissolved his worried expression immediately. Leaning his shoulder against the frame, he paused to admire the lovely picture the two women made.

Slanting rays of weak winter sunshine filtered through the gauzy curtains and filled the elegant room with a pale golden glow that enhanced their exquisite femininity. Slowly, avidly, Conn took in the delicate profiles, the graceful little movements, the tender curve of a cheek, the saucy tilt of a chin. Like a thirsting man drinking his fill, he noted each tiny detail; silky curls shining in the sunlight, fragile lace against soft skin, full skirts gracefully spread out on the matching sofas, dainty slippers peeking from beneath.

He drew a deep breath and felt something ease deep inside him. At that moment the two women represented all that was soft and good and gentle in the world, all the things that were absent from his life too much of the time.

Each was beautiful in her own way, yet they were a study

in contrast, one dark-haired, voluptuous, and vivacious, the other wand slim and willowy, with a sweet serenity about her that matched her angel fairness.

A throaty chuckle drew his eyes to the blonde. He'd been surprised when Isaac and Jemma had told him that Elizabeth was there—surprised and pleased. He'd known her since the day she was born, and they'd been friends for almost that long, but for some reason he seldom saw her during his visits home.

His gaze switched to his wife, and he shook his head, his hard face softening with affectionate exasperation. Fairly crackling with ire, she was haranguing her poor cousin unmercifully about something. Whatever it was, it was obviously important to Elizabeth, for her to dig in her heels. Usually she couldn't resist Millie's coaxing. On the few occasions when that tactic failed, his wife switched to pleading. It was rare, indeed, that she had to resort to anger to get her way.

Millie's voice rose another notch, and Conn decided it was time to make his presence known.

"Don't tell me you two are fighting?" he drawled.

Both women gasped, looked around, and shot to their feet. "Conn!"

They spoke his name in unison, their voices soft and breathy with surprise. For an unguarded moment their emotions were plain to see, and the mellow feeling Conn had been experiencing turned to bitterness at the stark difference in the two women's reactions.

Joy lit Elizabeth's eyes and gave her face a glowing softness, but it was his wife's expression that held his attention.

First shock, then dismay flickered across Millie's doll-like features. Both emotions were gone in the blink of an eye, so fast Conn could almost believe he had imagined them. Almost.

To her credit, Millie recovered quickly, and with a glad cry she hurried toward him, her hands outstretched. "Conn, darling! You're home early!"

As he had countless times before, Conn pushed aside his

disappointment and hurt. It was as much his fault as Millie's that things were the way they were between them, he told himself. Forcing a smile, he held out his arms. "Yes. So I am."

When Millie reached him she grasped both his hands and offered her cheek for a kiss.

Conn's jaw clenched. Determinedly, he hooked his arm around her waist and pulled her close. Capturing her chin with his other hand, he tipped her face up and brought his mouth down on hers for a long, devouring kiss.

Elizabeth bit her lower lip and turned away. Her heart boomed painfully, and she pressed a hand against her breast. Her other hand went to her throat as she closed her eyes. *Conn. Oh, God, Conn.*

His sudden appearance, after she had just been thinking of him—something she tried so hard never to do—was as though she had somehow conjured him up.

Elizabeth glanced over her shoulder at the embracing couple and quickly looked away, pain slashing at her. She sank down on her knees and with shaking hands began to gather up her embroidery and thread from where it had tumbled, unheeded, to the floor.

She took her time, staying bent over on the carpet between the two sofas as the telling silence stretched out. At last she heard her cousin gasp and exclaim in a flustered, slightly irritated voice, "Really, Conn! Whatever will Elizabeth think?"

Elizabeth got to her feet in time to see Millie pull out of her husband's arms and brush fussily at her grayish blue day dress.

Conn gave her a long look. He captured an ebony curl and gave it a tug. "Probably that I love my wife, and that I've missed her."

He turned his head and looked across the room, and Elizabeth's heart lurched as their eyes met.

He looked so big and rugged and vital, even a bit savage,

standing there in his fringed buckskins. And so very dear. His black hair was overlong, almost touching his shoulders, and his deep-set eyes glittered that familiar, startling blue in his weather-darkened face.

Conn Cavanaugh was not the most handsome man Elizabeth had ever seen, but he was certainly the most uncompromisingly masculine. There was strength and character in that angular, square-jawed face, and the combination of sharp cheekbones, an aquiline nose, and a hard, thin mouth held an odd, craggy appeal. There was about Conn Cavanaugh a compelling aura of toughness and command that earned him the respect, sometimes the fear, of other men and made women feel all warm and shivery inside.

Elizabeth stood motionless, her hands clasped over her midriff. "Hello, Conn." Her voice came out soft, a trifle shaky.

"'Hello, Conn'? That's all the greeting I get from an old friend?" He held out his arms. "Come here, Elizabeth."

She had no choice. In any case, she could not have resisted that soft command had her life depended on it. Filled with dread and longing, she crossed to where he stood. He gazed down at her warmly, his stern face transformed by a slow smile into stunning masculine beauty, and when he pulled her into his arms she went willingly.

"Welcome home, Conn," she choked out in an aching little voice, rubbing her cheek against the soft buckskin shirt. "We're so happy to have you back."

"Thank you, Elizabeth. God, it's good to be back." He hugged her to him and rocked from side to side. "I've missed you all so much," he declared fervently. "So much."

It was both heaven and hell to be in his arms. Elizabeth's throat tightened. Her chest ached so she could scarcely breathe. He smelled of woodsmoke and sunshine and sweat. His big, powerful body pressed warm and hard against hers. Folding her lips together, Elizabeth squeezed her eyes shut and returned the fierce embrace with all her might. When he released her she swiped at her damp eyes and tried to smile, but her lips were trembling too much.

"Hey, little one, don't cry," Conn said gently, and raised a hand to touch her cheek.

Elizabeth stepped back out of reach and drew a lace-edged handkerchief from the skirt pocket of her black bombazine dress. She sniffed and managed a shaky smile. "Don't mind me. I'm . . . I'm just happy that you're back safe. That's all."

Behind Conn, Jemma and Isaac hovered in the hall. Happy grins split their faces as they watched the reunion. When Millie spotted them she immediately began to issue commands.

"Isaac, Mr. Cavanaugh will need a bath and a haircut. Please see to it. Jemma, find the children and tell them that their father is home."

"Yes'm." The tiny black woman turned and flapped her apron at her husband, shooing him ahead of her. "You done heard Miz Millie. You fetch the slipper tub whilst I put the kettle on to boil and round up them young'uns. Then I'm gonna cook that boy up a mess a chicken'n dumplin's, just the way he likes'm."

Still grinning, Isaac walked away with his customary slow dignity, impervious to his wife's clucking. Jemma was about to follow him when the front door opened. Immediately her face lit up and she exclaimed, "Dr. Cavanaugh! Dr. Cavanaugh! Come quick! Mister Conn, he done come home!"

"Conn? He's here? Already?" Hurried footsteps sounded in the hall. "Where is—" Joseph Cavanaugh halted in the parlor doorway, his distinguished face lighting with joy at the sight of his son.

Conn grinned. "Hello, Dad."

Joseph's black medical bag dropped to the floor with a solid thump, and he covered the distance between them in one long stride. The two men caught each other in a fierce bear hug that eloquently expressed the deep love between them.

Physically, there was a strong resemblance. At sixty Dr.

Cavanaugh had more silver in his hair than black, and his strong face lacked the rough-hewn look that years in the mountains had given his son's, but the features were the same. Both were arresting men, tall and slender, though Dr. Cavanaugh was an inch or so under Conn's six feet three inches and lacked his rangy strength.

Watching as they thumped each other on the back, Elizabeth felt her chest tighten with emotion. Joseph's face betrayed such heartfelt relief, she wanted to cry.

Dr. Cavanaugh had always been understanding of his son's restless nature. From the beginning, when a hunger for excitement and adventure had resulted in Conn's first trip to the mountains, he had sent the bold nineteen-year-old off with his blessing. In all the years since, his support had not wavered, but Elizabeth knew that he worried constantly about his son's safety.

"We didn't expect you for months yet." Still clasping Conn's shoulders, Joseph stepped back at arm's length and looked him over. "Are you all right? You're not hurt, are you?"

"I'm fine. I had some business to attend to, is all."

"Business?" Millie gave him a curious look. "What business?"

"Never mind. We'll discuss it later."

It was a command, soft but quelling, delivered in a tone that Conn rarely used with Millie. Ignoring the indignant lift of her eyebrows, he turned to Elizabeth and winked. "Right now I want to know why you were tearing a strip off poor Elizabeth when I came in. I didn't think you two ever quarreled."

Diverted, Millie shot her cousin an exasperated look and snapped, "Only when she won't listen to reason. Now that you're here, maybe you can talk some sense into her."

"Millie, please," Elizabeth protested, but no one paid her any mind.

"What seems to be the problem?"

Joseph placed his hand on his son's arm. "My boy, I'm afraid we have some sad news." Dr. Cavanaugh's kind gaze touched Elizabeth, and she looked down at her hands and the handkerchief she was twisting. "Elizabeth's father passed away a few weeks ago."

Shock, then compassion flooded Conn's face. He didn't hesitate but stepped forward quickly and pulled Elizabeth into his arms.

"Oh, God, little one, I'm sorry. So sorry." He held her tight and rocked her as though she were a small child, exactly as he had done years ago whenever she had been frightened or hurt. "I know how close you two were. And for this to happen so soon after losing your mother . . ."

Conn shook his head, his arms tightening around her. He maneuvered her to the sofa, and as they sat down he pulled her close once more. She pressed her face against his broad chest and briefly allowed herself the sweet comfort of his embrace.

But such self-indulgence was foolish, as Elizabeth well knew, and after only a moment she gathered what little inner strength she still possessed and pulled back. Sniffing, she sat up straight and dabbed at her eyes and nose.

"Thank you, Conn. I . . . you're very kind."

He smiled at her tenderly and fingered the dainty lace edging on her white collar. "I apologize, little one. I should have realized you were in mourning as soon as I saw my two favorite ladies wearing such somber dresses."

Elizabeth glanced at her cousin, and a weak smile tugged at her mouth. The gray-blue wool challis dress that Millie wore was subdued compared with the gay colors she preferred, but it was hardly somber. Still, for Millie, it was a concession. She flatly refused to wear black, claiming it made her look sallow.

"Elizabeth has been staying with us since Uncle Edward passed away. But lately she's been talking about leaving. I've been trying to convince her that she must make her home with us, but she just won't listen. She has this wild notion that she's going to live in her parents' old house all alone. Can you imagine?"

Conn's vivid eyes darkened with concern. "Millie's right. Your place is here. After all, she's your only living relative. When she was orphaned your parents took her in. Now you must allow her to do the same for you. It's only right. Besides, you know that we care for you. We wouldn't think of letting you fend for yourself."

"Absolutely not." Joseph sat down at her other side and took her hand, patting it gently. "Elizabeth, your father was my dearest and oldest friend in the world. Even if Millie weren't your cousin, I'd still consider it my sacred duty to look after you. Besides, you know that I've always loved you like a daughter."

Deeply touched, Elizabeth regarded him helplessly. "Thank you, Dr. Cavanaugh. I appreciate your offer. Really I do. But . . . well, you see . . ."

As Elizabeth groped for words, a shrill "Papa!" sounded from the hall, cutting off her explanation.

Fourteen-year-old Rachel Cavanaugh burst into the room like a small whirlwind, only to skid to a halt scarcely three feet inside the door. Breathing hard, her clothing and hair askew, she simply stood there awkwardly and gazed at her father, her blue eyes filled with a mixture of delight and uncertainty.

Like a little ghost, three-year-old Ian slipped into the room and hid behind his sister. With his thumb stuck firmly in his mouth, he peeked warily around her skirt at Conn.

"Honestly, Rachel," Millie snapped. "How many times must I tell you to slow down? A young lady does not charge into a room like a rampaging bull. And what on earth have you been doing? You look like a street urchin."

Rachel flushed. "I'm sorry, Mama. I was in the attic—"

"The attic! For heaven's sake, child, whatever for? It must be freezing up there."

Oh, Millie, Elizabeth thought sadly. You pay so little attention to your children, you don't even know them. Even she was aware that the attic was Rachel's special place. The child spent hours up there, trying on the old clothes in the trunks and dreaming a young girl's daydreams.

"Leave her be, Millie." Conn smiled at his daughter. "She looks fine to me."

The look of abject adoration on the girl's face tugged at Elizabeth's heartstrings, reminding her poignantly of herself when she had been Rachel's age, before she'd learned to guard her feelings.

Conn's love for his children was plain to see, but even so there was an awkwardness between them. He had spent too much time away from them, and his visits home were never long enough to allow a comfortable relationship to develop. Every year when he returned they had to get to know one another all over again.

Though she obviously worshiped her father, Rachel stiffened and held back when Conn hugged her close, and it took five minutes for him to coax Ian out from behind his sister's skirt.

By the time the greetings were over, the question of where Elizabeth would live seemed to have been forgotten. She knew that they all assumed the matter was settled.

Chapter 2

 He's different, Joseph decided, observing his son.

Every year he'd noted the changes, watched Conn grow steadily harder. There was no softness left, nothing of the exuberant, devil-may-care youth who had struck out in search of excitement and adventure all those years ago. Conn's toughness was ingrained and deep, without meanness or cruelty, yet quick, unyielding, even dangerous when necessary. Whatever gentleness remained was well guarded, and reserved for those few he loved, especially the two women seated at the table.

Joseph regretted the changes, but he supposed they had been inevitable. In coming to terms with the rugged land over which he had roamed, a man grew strong and hard . . . or died.

He did not regret, however—could never regret—giving his son his blessing when he'd announced his desire to go west. He never wanted Conn to know, as he had, the deep sadness and nagging sense of loss that came from abandoning your dreams.

Joseph understood the restless yearning that had sent his son to the mountains, just as he empathized with Conn's need for independence and space and shared his desire to build something strong and lasting. As a young man, he'd had much the same dreams.

Joseph glanced again at Elizabeth's bent head, and a wistful smile of remembrance tugged at his mouth. When he and her father had been in school together, they'd been full of ideals and hungry for adventure themselves. They had figured they could satisfy both by becoming frontier doctors and had planned to go west together.

Then he had fallen in love with Francis Glissard.

A silent, mirthless chuckle shook Joseph's chest. He picked up his fork and cut a dumpling in two. Lord, he'd been so naively confident when they'd wed that she shared his dreams and ambitions.

As it turned out, Francis had had her own ambitions, and a husband with wanderlust was not something she'd been prepared to tolerate. She had wanted a prominent place in polite society, a fine home, money, possessions—none of which she felt could be attained in the uncivilized West, nor by doctoring the poor and indigent, as Edward had been prone to do.

Because he'd loved her so desperately, he'd eventually conquered his restless spirit and settled down to the humdrum, genteel life of a prominent physician whose practice included only the cream of society.

By then Edward had been so caught up with his work among the poor that he, too, abandoned his plans to go west.

Joseph had been afraid when Conn married Millie that history was repeating itself. It had been obvious to him from the start that Millie, like Francis, craved a different way of life than that which her husband sought.

Joseph's attention switched to his daughter-in-law, and he felt a spurt of reluctant amusement. All evening she had been charming and vivacious, utterly enchanting, and as transparent as glass in her attempts to wheedle out of Conn his reason for returning home early. The little minx, Joseph thought with affection, watching her bat her eyelashes provocatively at her husband. At times she was like an impatient child.

Conn indulged her shamelessly, as they all did, but tonight Joseph doubted that her efforts would be rewarded.

Earlier, during a private talk, Conn had told him what he'd

done. They both knew that Millie wasn't going to be pleased. Unless Joseph missed his guess, she would do everything in her power to dissuade Conn.

Frowning, Joseph took another sip of wine. Year after year he'd watched in silence as his son's plans had been pushed back for another season, and another, and another. He'd almost given up hope they would ever be realized. Joseph was genuinely fond of Millie, but he did not intend to sit by idly and let her spoil this chance for Conn.

Millie ran her fingertips down the sleeve of Conn's black wool cutaway coat and gave him a sultry look. "Conn, darling," she purred. "Won't you please tell me what brought you home so early?" She leaned toward him, the action causing her voluptuous breasts to swell above the low-cut neckline of her gown. Her fingertips slipped down to trail over the back of his hand and play with the sprinkling of crisp black hairs covering it. She blinked slowly, an enticing smile curving her lips. "Pleeeze. I shall just expire if you don't."

Conn followed his wife's every move with a dark intensity that made Elizabeth's chest tighten. She watched as he swallowed a bite of chicken and calmly took a sip of wine. When he returned the fluted glass to the table, his callused fingers toyed with the fragile stem.

"I said I'd tell you all about it tomorrow, Millie. "Tonight I just want to relax and enjoy Jemma's cooking, and being home with my family." Warm indulgence glinted in his eyes, but his deep, quiet voice held an unmistakable finality.

Millie pouted prettily, but to no avail. Conn merely shot her an amused look and cut another bite of chicken.

Seated across from Conn, Elizabeth squirmed on her chair and tried not to watch the intimate byplay. She was impressed, even a bit awed, by the ease with which Millie could captivate. Tonight she was at her most beguiling, using every feminine wile at her command.

Millie had abandoned her mourning clothes in favor of a ruby red velvet gown trimmed with blond lace that bared her plump white shoulders and the rounded tops of her breasts. "In honor of Conn's homecoming," she had explained earlier, smiling sweetly as she patted Elizabeth's hand. "I knew you wouldn't mind."

As always, beside Millie's vibrant beauty, Elizabeth felt plain and insipidly pale, but especially so tonight in the drab black dress. Millie leaned across the corner of the table to whisper something in Conn's ear, and Elizabeth felt a little pang as she gazed at the two heads bent so close together.

They looked so good together, both dark and striking and yet so different. They were a perfect match; Elizabeth had known that from the beginning—Conn with his intensity, Millie with her sparkle, her vivid beauty. Though it had hurt, she had never blamed Conn for choosing her cousin.

Elizabeth fought the temptation, but she could not keep her gaze from straying to Conn time and again.

He was stunning in his black cutaway and embroidered blue satin waistcoat, she thought, peeking at him as she picked at the food on her plate. His broad shoulders and lean, fit body filled out the gentleman's attire in a way that put other men to shame.

In the soft light from the candelabra, his hair had the blue-black sheen of a raven's wing. Isaac had trimmed it, and now the thick mane curled neatly over his ears and the back of his collar. Against the crisp white linen his skin looked even darker.

But despite the haircut and the civilized clothes and the polished manners that had been ingrained in him since child-hood, there was still something tough and untamed about Conn. Something elemental and unbearably exciting.

Stop it, Elizabeth! Stop it right now, she told herself. You have no right to be thinking such thoughts. Instead of wallowing in self-pity you should be pleased that Millie is so happy, she scolded, wistfully noting her cousin's dreamy expression.

Millie's sweet smile never wavered, but inside she seethed with impotent anger. What was Conn doing back in Charleston in January, anyway? When she had looked up and seen him standing there in the parlor doorway, she had wanted to shriek. Drat the man. He was going to spoil the entire spring social season for her. She just knew it.

Beneath the table a satin slipper tapped against the rug, and her small fist clenched in her lap. What could be important enough to cause him to leave the mountains before spring trapping had even begun?

Uneasily she recalled the argument they'd had just before he had returned to the mountains the previous fall.

Perhaps she should not have broached the idea quite so directly. Conn wasn't as amenable as he'd once been, she thought resentfully. Usually he'd indulged her every whim. Sometimes it took a bit of coaxing and wheedling, but he had always come around before. But last fall, for the first time in their sixteen-year marriage, she had not been able to persuade him to go along with her wishes.

Millie watched her husband talking quietly to their children, and she felt a little thrill, despite her anger. He really was a deliciously striking man. All her women friends were positively pea green with envy on those rare occasions when she managed to persuade him to attend a social function. Perhaps it wouldn't be too bad when he gave up trapping and returned home for good.

Of course, she much preferred their present arrangement. It was marvelous to be able to enjoy the protection of marriage without having a husband constantly underfoot.

Millie's smile grew smug. When Conn was away she was free to go wherever she pleased, whenever she pleased. And to flirt without ever having to worry about pacifying an irate husband. If one of her admirers became tiresome and expected too much, a sharp reminder of her married state brought him back into line quickly enough.

Still, she had always known that the pleasant arrangement couldn't last forever. Each year it was becoming more and more difficult to convince Conn to return to the mountains for another season. And she was running out of arguments. Over the past seventeen years he had amassed a modest fortune, so she could no longer even claim they needed more money.

Millie sighed. If only she could talk him out of this foolishness about farming, she wouldn't mind so much. Why, the very idea of living miles from nowhere, cut off from all the gaiety and social whirl of Charleston, made her shudder.

The more she thought about it, the more unfair it seemed, and the more her ire and sense of ill use rose. Grasping her fork tighter, she struggled to keep her expression benign. She enjoyed her life exactly as it was. She did not want give it up.

If Conn weren't so stubborn and selfish, he wouldn't ask her to.

After dinner they sat before the fire in the parlor and talked, but before Elizabeth knew it the time she had been dreading was upon them.

The children had long since been in bed when everyone began to yawn. Dr. Cavanaugh stood and banked the parlor fire for the night and replaced the brass screen in front of the hearth. A trembling ache began deep inside Elizabeth as she and Dr. Cavanaugh and Conn and Millie climbed the stairs.

In the upstairs hall they paused. Smiling warmly, Conn kissed Elizabeth's forehead and murmured, "Good night, little one," and with his arm about Millie's waist, he led her into their bedroom and closed the door.

Elizabeth stood motionless.

"Good night, my dear."

Dr. Cavanaugh's soft voice penetrated her painful stupor,

and she dragged her gaze away from the door. "Good night," she murmured woodenly, and turned and went into her bedroom.

The banked fire had burned down to a few tongues of flame and a pile of glowing coals. A candle flickered on the table beside the four-poster bed, and Jemma had turned down the eiderdown covers and laid out her flannel nightgown. Ignoring them, Elizabeth walked to the window on legs that felt like wood and stared out into the darkness.

The weather had worsened, and sleet mixed with snow clicked against the small panes.

Elizabeth glanced back over her shoulder at the closed door and bit her lower lip until she tasted blood. She could not swallow for the painful constriction in her throat. Oh, Lord, she could not bear this. She could not. All these years she'd tried never to think of Conn in bed with Millie, making love to her, holding her close in the darkness against his warm, naked body. It had simply been too painful.

Elizabeth was a maiden lady, but she was also a doctor's daughter. She had spent too many years assisting her father not to know about the physical side of marriage.

It hurt. Dear God, it hurt so much. Why did she have to love him so? It was foolish and futile, but she could not seem to stop. She had tried. Oh, how she had tried.

Her eyes filled, and one by one the desolate tears spilled over and streamed down her cheeks. They dripped from her chin and fell like rain onto the bosom of her high-necked dress, making darker blotches in the black bombazine.

There was not a time that she could remember when she had not loved Conn Cavanaugh with all of her heart. As a child she had worshiped him quietly. As a young girl on the brink of maturity she had clung to the dream that one day Conn would see her as a woman and return her love. That dream had been all that had sustained her through that terrible year when Conn had gone to the mountains for the first time.

Before it could come true, however, her cousin Millicent had come to live in the Stanton household.

Elizabeth pressed her lips together and shook her head as she recalled how sorry she had felt for her orphaned cousin, how she had welcomed her with open arms.

She had been almost fifteen at the time, Millie just seventeen. For eight months it had been wonderful having another girl in the family, someone with whom she could giggle and gossip and share her deepest thoughts. Despite the two-year age gap, despite their opposite personalities, or maybe because of them, they had gotten along famously, and a deep and lasting affection had been forged between them.

Then Conn had come home.

Elizabeth pressed her hand against her knotted abdomen. After being sick with worry and pining for him for so long, she had been almost beside herself with excitement at the thought of seeing him again. At the thought of him seeing her.

He had been gone for almost a year, and during that time she had at last begun to blossom with the first promise of womanhood. Elizabeth's trembling lips curved in a watery smile as she recalled how she'd spent hours studying her reflection in the mirror, so pleased that the gawky angularity of adolescence had finally been replaced by subtle curves, by the way her thin features had taken on a new softness.

But Conn had not noticed the changes. He had taken one look at Millie and fallen head over heels in love.

Even now the memory was almost more than Elizabeth could bear. Clenching her jaw, she fought the terrible ache in her chest. She felt as though a giant hand were squeezing her heart.

No, she could not live with Millie and Conn and bear constant witness to their love. It had been precisely to escape this sort of pain that she had tried to avoid Conn whenever he came home. No. She loved them both and appreciated their kindness, but she could not do that to herself.

It had been bad enough, all those years ago, when she'd had to sit back helplessly and watch, her heart breaking into a million pieces, as Conn had courted and wed her cousin. How much worse it would be now, to live in their home, the poor spinster relation, an object of charity and pity, always, *always* aware of the love they shared.

Elizabeth leaned her forehead against the frigid window pane and closed her eyes. Oh, God, she could not bear it. She could not.

Slouched in the wing-backed chair, Conn swirled the brandy in his glass and stretched his slippered feet out to the small blaze he had stirred back to life in the fireplace. He took a sip of the fiery liquid and pursed his lips as it slid down his throat. Turning his head, he cast a thoughtful look at the bed, where Millie was burrowed beneath the covers, already asleep.

Had it been wrong of him to want this one night? A few hours of peaceful homecoming? Conn's mouth turned up wryly at one corner, and he looked back at the fire. Hell, face it. Months of celibacy had a way of making a man damned single-minded. What he'd wanted was a chance to make love to Millie before he broke the news to her.

He knew well enough that once he did, it would be days, maybe even weeks, before she tolerated his touch again.

Conn took another sip of brandy. Tolerate. That described perfectly Millie's attitude toward lovemaking. To her it was a wifely duty, nothing more, an act to be endured and gotten through as quickly as possible.

He knew that; he'd known it for years. So why, each time he returned, did he always hope for a warm response? For passion? By now he ought to know better.

Hell, he'd received a more enthusiastic greeting from Elizabeth than he had from his wife. He thought about that for a moment, his hard mouth curving in a reminiscent smile.

But then, Elizabeth had always been a warmhearted little thing.

Conn's face grew somber once again, and once again his glance strayed to the mound of covers on the bed. The quick, unemotional coupling he and Millie had just shared had temporarily eased his physical need, but inside . . . inside he ached for something more.

His callused thumb rubbed over the faceted surface of the fine crystal glass. The amber liquid sparkled like a brilliant jewel in the flickering light refracted through the cut prisms. What the hell had happened to them? Where had the fire gone?

With a sigh, Conn rubbed his hand down over his face. It was not all Millie's fault. She had not changed; he had. Life, the passing of years, the subtle molding of experience, had not touched Millie in any way. She was still the willful, charming coquette he had married, as pampered and spoiled as a precocious child. Hell, there were times when he felt a hundred years older than Millie.

The trouble was, he was no longer a blindly besotted youth. He loved her still, but not with the same depth of feeling, the same unquestioning devotion, of sixteen years ago.

Guilt pierced him at the admission. They'd simply been apart too much, he told himself. Hell, his own children didn't know him. How could he expect to have a normal, loving relationship with his wife when he was home only three months out of every year?

And whose fault was that?

The instant the insidious thought came creeping in, Conn's jaw clenched. Bitterly he recalled the arguments Millie had trotted out year after year, whenever he'd mentioned giving up trapping.

"Conn, darling, if you'll just trap for a few more years, we could buy a really nice place.

"I know you miss us, sweetheart. We miss you, too, but I'm afraid,

what with the price of land these days, we just won't be able to afford a decent-size place if you don't trap for a while longer.

"*Conn Cavanaugh, how could you even think of quitting? We may have enough to buy the land, but what about a house? You know I have my heart set on having an elegant place. And we'll need furnishings and servants and a carriage and . . . oh, just all kinds of things!*"

On and on it had gone, time and the dream inexorably slipping away.

He was equally to blame, of course. He had allowed himself to be convinced, at first because he had been such a lovesick fool that he couldn't bear to upset her, but also because, deep down, trapping had gotten into his blood. Later, on some level, at least, he had realized that he and Millie wanted different things out of life, and it had simply been easier to rock along they way they were than to face that unpleasant truth.

Dammit! When had the dream become his alone? From the beginning, before they had even married, they had talked of buying a place and moving to the country.

He needed freedom and space. After only one year of living in the mountains, he had felt stifled by city life, confined, and he had known that he could never return to it permanently. Millie had vowed that she understood and wanted the same.

Conn sighed. But every year for the past ten, whenever he'd broached the subject of giving up trapping, she had argued against it. Last fall he had braced himself for more of the same, but this time the thrust of Millie's arguments had taken an alarming new direction.

"*You know, darling, I've been thinking. Maybe, instead of a farm, we should start a business here in town. Of course, for that we're going to need more capital. Now don't look at me that way, darling. It would only be for a little longer.*"

He had known then that Millie had no intention of leaving Charleston—ever.

He supposed he should be grateful. They might have drifted along exactly as they had been had it not been for her revealing suggestion. That had been the spur that had sent him to Texas.

Conn drained the last of the brandy and stared into the fire, his jaw set. From now on, whether Millie liked it or not, things were going to be different.

The next morning Elizabeth awoke with a start to the sounds of raised voices. At first she thought it had been a dream, but then she heard an anguished wail and realized the voice belonged to Millie. Alarmed, she jumped from the bed and hurried for the door, pulling on her old blue flannel robe as she went.

A knock sounded as she reached for the doorknob. She jerked the door open, took one look at Isaac's puckered brow, and knew that something was terribly amiss.

"Isaac! What is it? What has happened?"

The normally unflappable houseman wrung his hands. "I don't rightly know, but Miz Millie, she's powerful upset. She said for me to fetch you quick.

"They're all in the parlor!" he called after Elizabeth as she dashed past him and down the hallway.

Fear lent wings to Elizabeth's feet, and she flew down the stairs with a total disregard for ladylike decorum, her gown and robe billowing out behind her. Her long night braid bounced against her back and hips like a thick golden rope.

In the parlor she found Millie sitting on the sofa, sniffing and dabbing at her eyes with a lace-edged handkerchief. Joseph sat opposite her on the matching sofa, and Conn stood before the fireplace, his rigid body and wide stance radiating cold anger and unyielding determination.

"Elizabeth! Oh, thank God you're here!" Millie jumped up and flung herself into Elizabeth's arms, sobbing hysterically.

"Millie! Millie, dearest, whatever is the matter?" Alarmed, Elizabeth patted her cousin's heaving shoulders and looked at Conn and his father.

"C-Conn is . . . b-being so . . . cruel!"

So accustomed was she to cosseting her cousin, Elizabeth shot Conn a look of mild reproof, forgetting for an instant who it was that Millie was accusing.

Conn returned the look steadily. "She's upset because I've bought a plantation."

"In *Texas!*" Millie wailed.

"Texas?" Shock rippled through Elizabeth. "You're . . . you're going to move to Texas?"

"Yes."

Elizabeth's first thought was that when they left she would probably never see Conn again, and the prospect brought such stabbing pain that she almost cried out. Drawing a shuddering breath, she managed to get a grip on her emotions and staunchly told herself it was for the best.

"He expects me to go to that godforsaken wilderness and live among savages," Millie accused tearfully against Elizabeth's shoulder. "We'll probably all be killed!"

"For God's sake, Millie. There'll be plenty of men around to protect you. It's not as though I'm taking you to a crude cabin on the frontier. Riverbend is an established plantation on the Brazos River, an area that has quite a few settlers. You've always said you wanted a gracious home. Well, now you have one."

"I don't care. I don't want to leave Charleston." She lifted her head from Elizabeth's shoulder and looked at Conn beseechingly, her beautiful hazel eyes swimming with tears. Her chin wobbled, and with a little catch in her voice she pleaded, "Please, darling. I'm sure Mr. Munson would buy the place back if you just explained that—"

"No, Millie." Conn's deep voice cut through her plea, implacable as granite.

Millie spun around and glared at him, her face flushed and tight with impotent rage. "Fine, then. Go to that godforsaken wilderness!" she screamed. "But don't expect me to go. I'm staying right here."

"I'm afraid that won't be possible, my dear," Dr. Cavanaugh put in pleasantly. "You see, I've decided to sell this place and go to Texas with you."

The calm announcement had the impact of a cannon shot. Conn started and flashed his father an incredulous look as Millie shrieked:

"*What!*"

"Dad," Conn began, his voice softening with cautious concern. "You don't have to—"

"Unless you don't want me tagging along, that is."

"No, of course it's not that. My only regret about making this move was leaving you behind. But—"

"Good. Then the matter is settled."

"Papa Joe, you *can't* be serious!"

Joseph directed a complacent smile toward his daughter-in-law. "Oh, but I am, my dear. Perfectly serious."

"But . . . but . . ." Millie looked around frantically. "You have this lovely home. You're a respected physician with a place in society. How could you give all that up to move to that wretched wilderness?"

"Quite easily, actually. This may surprise you, my dear, but I've always had a yen to go west and see the frontier for myself. I've suddenly realized that there is no reason why I can't."

"But—"

"The matter is settled, Millie."

His firm voice brooked no argument, and Elizabeth looked at him in surprise. She had always thought of Dr. Cavanaugh as a gentle, dignified, rather malleable man. Certainly Millie had been able to wind him around her little finger all these years. But for the first time, his tone, his implacable expression, reminded her sharply of Conn.

"Mr. Munson, the former owner, has agreed to stay and run Riverbend until we arrive," Conn announced into the taut silence. "My partner is there now. In a month or so, as soon as the planting is done, he and the overseer will be here to help with the move and the purchase of new equipment. Since there is safety in numbers, I intend to advertise for other emigrants to join us. If all goes well, we should have a wagon train organized by late April."

"Taw Pruett is coming here?" Millie shot her husband an outraged look. At his nod, she clenched her fists at her sides. "Oh! Ohhhhh! This is just the final straw, Conn Cavanaugh. I will not have that illiterate, uncouth old man in this house."

"Millie! Dearest, you don't mean that," Elizabeth rebuked gently. Once, years ago, Taw had accompanied Conn home, and though she herself had not met him, Elizabeth knew that her cousin had taken a violent dislike to the old trapper. Still, that did not excuse bad manners.

Conn's eyes grew glacial. "You will not only put up with his presence here, but in our new home as well. Furthermore, you will treat him with respect and make him welcome." Each clipped word carried the sting of a whip, but Millie did not seem to notice.

"You don't mean he's going to *live* with us?"

"That's right. May I remind you that if it hadn't been for Taw, I would have died the first year I went to the mountains? I was damn near starved and half-frozen when he found me and took me under his wing. As long as I'm alive, Taw Pruett will have a home with me. Do I make myself clear?"

"Oh, Millie." This time Elizabeth's voice held shock, disappointment, and censure. It was the first she had heard that Taw had saved Conn's life, and she looked at her cousin reproachfully, appalled by her lack of gratitude.

Millie had the grace to look abashed for an instant, but then she lifted her chin in sullen defiance, her gaze sliding from Conn to Elizabeth. When there was no softening in either, she sank down on the sofa and promptly burst into tears.

At once Elizabeth's anger dissolved. Sitting beside her, she put her arm around her cousin's heaving shoulders. "Now,

now, Millie. Don't cry so, dearest. You'll make yourself ill. Things aren't all that bad. Really."

"How . . . how can you s-say that? You know you're . . . going to h-hate it . . . j-just as much as . . . I . . . I will."

"Me? But, Millie . . . dearest, I'm not going to Texas."

Millie's head jerked up, and her tear-drenched eyes widened on Elizabeth in horror. "Not going? Of c-course you're going. You live with us now. We settled all that yesterday."

"No." Elizabeth shook her head, her look gently chiding. "You all merely assumed it was settled."

"But you must go."

A frown tugged at Conn's black eyebrows. "I took it for granted you would be going with us, Elizabeth. You're family, as well as a dear friend. We can't leave you here, with no one to care for you."

"My dear," Dr. Cavanaugh put in kindly. "I don't mean to be indelicate, but I don't believe that Edward could have left you much money. Isn't that true?"

Elizabeth self-consciously adjusted the folds of her worn robe and looked at the floor. She wanted to deny the statement, but they all knew it was true. "No, Father didn't leave much," she admitted grudgingly.

"Then, my dear, if you stay here, how will you live? Who will take care of you?"

"I'll take care of myself."

"How?"

"Well, I'm hoping to get work assisting one of the other doctors here in town." It had been her plan to rise early, before the others awoke, and make the rounds of her father's doctor friends. However, she had been so upset the night before that it had been the early hours before she had finally dropped into an exhausted sleep, and as a result she had overslept.

The look Dr. Cavanaugh gave her was pitying. "I doubt seriously if that will happen."

"But, why not? They all know that I helped my father with

his patients. I have since I was fifteen."

"Yes, I know. But, my dear, it is one thing to accept the assistance of a daughter, and something else again to hire a female, one who is no relation. It just isn't done."

Elizabeth lifted her delicate chin. "Very well. Then I shall just have to support myself as a midwife. Or as a seamstress. I saw a sign in a milliner's shop window just the other day."

"A seamstress!" Millie exclaimed. "A common seamstress! Elizabeth, you can't do this to me! Everyone will think that I abandoned you. That I refused to take you in. I'd never be able to hold my head up in polite society again."

A small, sad smile curved Elizabeth's mouth at her cousin's total self-absorption, but it fled the next instant when Millie began to cry in earnest. Covering her face with her hands, she hunched her shoulders and wept as though she hadn't a friend left in the world. Elizabeth bit her lower lip and touched her back hesitantly, and at once Millie turned into her arms.

"You h-have to come . . . w-with me, Elizabeth," she sobbed. "Oh, p-please. *Please!* I shan't . . . I shan't be able to b-bear it without you."

"Oh, Millie." Elizabeth's chest ached with emotion. She folded her lips together to keep them from trembling and stroked her cousin's back. She didn't want to lose Conn or Millie, but dear Lord, she could not bear to live out her life in the shadow of their love. She couldn't.

Over Millie's shoulder her eyes sought help from Conn, but he merely watched her expectantly.

Please don't do this to me, she implored silently. You don't know what you're asking. I can't come with you. I can't. I love you too much. It would kill me, little by little.

Millie's tears soaked through the shoulder of Elizabeth's robe, hot, wet tears that plastered the blue flannel against her skin. Her cousin's shoulders shook. "Oh, p-please, Elizabeth. Please."

A crushing weight bore down on Elizabeth's chest. She

closed her eyes and bit down hard on her bottom lip. She tried to steel herself, but she was not proof against that piteous cry.

"Very well, Millie." She drew a long breath and released it in a defeated sigh. "You win. I'll go to Texas with you."

Chapter 3

May 1834

The long line of groaning, creaking wagons lumbered along the dirt track. Wheels rumbled and harnesses jingled. Canvas tops rocked and swayed like sailing ships on a rough sea.

Holding tight to the wagon seat with one hand, Elizabeth pressed the other to her stomach.

"You feelin' poorly agin, missy?" Taw spat a stream of tobacco juice over his left shoulder and shot her a sidelong look, his faded brown eyes warm with sympathy.

Elizabeth sat up a bit straighter. "No. No, I'm fine."

The words were barely out when the wheel beneath her seat dropped into a shallow hole and the wagon lurched, drawing a helpless little moan from her.

"You want me t' stop so's you can git down an' walk fer a spell?"

Shaking her head, Elizabeth swallowed hard.

Poor little thing, Taw thought, sneaking another quick look at her pale face. She was sick as a mule but just wouldn't admit it. He wasn't surprised. They'd discovered the first day out of Charleston that Elizabeth became queasy after a few hours in the pitching wagon. Two weeks on the trail had not improved her tolerance.

Taw shook his shaggy head. She was a game little thing,

40

he'd give her that. She hadn't said a word to anyone about the problem, and she'd asked him not to, either. Said she didn't want to be a bother.

He snorted and spit. Unlike some people he could name.

Shoot, it just didn't seem possible that Miss Elizabeth could be blood kin to that snooty, highfalutin female Conn was hitched up with, he told himself for perhaps the hundredth time.

Taw heaved a sigh. Conn was the closest thing to family he had, and he loved him like a son. He wanted, more than anything, to live out his days sittin' in a rocking chair, surrounded by the boy's young'uns, but, Lord a'mercy, sometimes that woman purely did try his soul.

Since arriving in Charleston two months before, Taw had given Millie a wide berth. She managed to be civil—barely— at least, whenever Conn was around, but she'd let him know well enough that she couldn't stand the sight of him.

Not so the little missy, Taw thought. She, bless her, had gone out of her way to be friendly.

When Conn had introduced them, she'd smiled and walked right up and put her dainty hand in his horny ole paw. He'd almost been afraid to grip for fear he'd hurt her.

"How do you do, Mr. Pruett. I'm so happy to meet you at last," she'd said in that soft, sincere way of hers, and he'd found himself staring, awestruck, unable to believe the vision before him.

With her pale gold hair and rose-and-ivory skin and those big, soft gray eyes, she'd looked exactly like the picture of an angel he remembered seeing in his ma's Bible when he'd been a lad.

Told her so, too, he recalled with smug satisfaction. She'd blushed real purty, but he could tell that cousin of hers hadn't been at all pleased. The woman's mouth had drawn up like she'd been eating green persimmons.

Taw clucked at the mules and absently scratched his whiskers. It had been so many years since his ma had died that he'd lost track of them, but he could dimly recall her saying that "pretty was as pretty did." That being true, the way he figured it, Miss Elizabeth was beautiful right down t' the bone.

He'd grown fond of her during the months they'd spent preparing for the trip, regarding her as the granddaughter he'd never had, and in the past weeks his opinion of her had only risen. She was a real genteel lady, but from the first she'd accepted the hardships of travel and pitched right in to do her share.

More'n her share, if ya ask me, Taw thought, giving a disgruntled snort. Helps Jemma with the cookin' an' the washin' an' whatever else needs doing. Even gives the doc a hand whenever anyone's ailin'. Why, jist the other day she helped patch up Harve Sillsby after the danged fool shot hisself in the foot. Fact was, a lot of the women'd rather have the little missy see after them than Doc Cavanaugh.

'Course, the doc was always gallivantin' off somewheres, Taw ruminated. Ridin' out with ever' huntin' party, or scoutin' ahead with Conn ever' chanct he got. Durned if he wasn't the beatenest man. Acted like this trip was the most fun he'd ever had.

A movement beside him brought Taw's thoughts back to Elizabeth, and he glanced at her out of the corner of his eye. Yessir, she was a mighty fine woman.

Perplexed, he shook his head and spit again. He would never understand why Conn had married Millie when Miss Elizabeth had been right there under his nose all the time. It was enough to make a body plumb doubt the boy's good sense.

Elizabeth tried to focus on a distant point, but the thick woods crowding in on either side of the road obstructed the view. All she could see was the backs of the four mules pulling her wagon and the rig just ahead of them, rocking drunkenly. She averted her gaze and sighed. Since Conn was bent on settling on the frontier, it was a good thing he'd married Millie instead of her, she told herself.

For all that she had led a pampered life, Millie was blessed with a splendid constitution and a sturdy build. To Elizabeth's knowledge, her cousin had never known a sick day, not even when she had been expecting Rachel and Ian.

As always, the instant the memories arose, Elizabeth's mind shied away from them. It had been devastatingly painful for her to be around Millie during those times, to listen to her complaints, be the unwilling recipient of her confidences, particularly as her cousin had detested being in a family way. That knowledge had been like a thorn piercing Elizabeth's heart; she could not imagine anything more wonderful than being Conn's wife and bearing his children.

"I 'speck we'll be noonin' purty quick now," Taw said, giving Elizabeth's arm an awkward pat. "You'll be fit as a fiddle oncet you plant yore feet on the ground and git some cold cornbread an' coffee in yore belly."

Though she knew he was right, Elizabeth's stomach clenched at the suggestion. Holding tight to the rough plank seat, she concentrated on taking slow, deep breaths.

"Did I tell you 'bout the time me an' Conn got treed by a mama grizzly?"

Despite her discomfort, Elizabeth smiled at the sudden question. "No. I don't think so."

Taw let loose another stream of tobacco juice. Taking his time, he leaned forward and propped his elbows on his knees. "Well now, 'twas the winter o' twenty-eight, best I recall. We was up on Fat Woman Creek when this pair o' cubs . . ."

Elizabeth watched the old man fondly as he launched into the tale. Since leaving Charleston he had spun her one yarn after another, mostly, she knew, to take her mind off her queasy stomach, and his kindness touched her deeply.

She was grateful that Conn had assigned Taw to drive her wagon. By Charleston standards she supposed he was rough and uncouth, but she liked him all the same. What Taw Pruett lacked in polish and book learning he more than made up for in kindness, common sense, and practical experience.

He did cut a startling figure among the simple emigrants, though, she admitted, glancing at his fringed and beaded buckskins. Though his shoulders were slightly stooped, Taw was a big man, tall and rawboned, with a shock of shoulder-length white hair and a full white beard, two sections of which hung in narrow plaits at either side of his jaw. He wore a short billed fur hat with three feathers dangling from one side, a powder horn slung over his shoulder, an Indian amulet around his neck, a knife, two pistols, and a wicked-looking tomahawk stuffed into his leather thong belt.

During their talks they had told each other their life stories, and she'd been shocked to learn that Taw had been fending for himself since he was a child.

"My pa got hisself kilt in a Injun uprisin' back in Pennsylvanie when I was still in small clothes," he'd told her matter-of-factly. "Don't remember him a'tall. Me an' Ma, we eked out a livin' on that ole rocky farm till she took sick an' died. I was ten er there 'bouts. Couldn't work the place alone, so I took off fer the nearest settlement."

"But how did you live?" she had asked, overwhelmed with pity for the lonely, frightened little boy he must have been.

"Oh, I got by. Did odd jobs mostly—mucked out horse stalls, swamped in saloons, ran errands—anythin' I could git. On the side I did me a little trappin'. All the while I was workin' my way west. By the time I was a man growed, I'd ended up in the mountains."

After hearing Taw's story, Elizabeth had better understood Conn's determination to include the old man in his family, and the helpless love she felt for him had deepened even more.

As he rambled on, Taw adjusted the reins wound between his fingers. The action drew her attention to his hands. Age spots dotted them like splattered brown paint, but they were big as hams, scarred and ridged with calluses, powerful enough to break a man in two. Yet she had seen those hands touch a child's cheek with such exquisite gentleness that the sight had brought tears to her eyes.

Taw finished his story just as they emerged from the woods. There the road began a curving sweep across an open meadow. Elizabeth's heart gave a little skip when she spotted Conn up ahead, astride his horse at the front of the train. At his side trotted the big brute of a dog that Taw had brought with him when he and the overseer had arrived in Charleston two months before.

When Elizabeth had asked Taw how long he'd had the dog, he'd replied, "Oh, Pike ain't mine. He don't belong t' nobody. Jist showed up in our camp one day. He looked us over an' I guess he figured we was toler'ble, 'cause he's been travelin' with us ever since."

Elizabeth believed him. Though he obeyed Taw's and Conn's commands, the animal remained aloof from the others on the train.

"Pike does the choosin'," Taw had explained. "If he takes a shine t' you, you got a friend fer life. If he don't, you'd best leave him be."

Which was precisely what everyone did, though the advice was hardly necessary. Pike was such a fierce-looking beast, no one quite had the nerve to approach him. Even the other dogs with the train gave him a wide berth.

At Conn's signal the lead wagon turned off the road and began to form a wide circle in the open meadow.

"Time t' noon, I reckon," Taw announced as he followed the others. Elizabeth's wagon was fourth in line, tucked in among the twenty belonging to the Cavanaughs. By the time all fifty-two rigs were in place, they had almost come complete circle.

So anxious was she to get on solid ground, Elizabeth lifted her skirt and climbed over the side the instant the wagon stopped. She had no sooner planted both feet on the wheel than Garth Lathom, Conn's overseer, appeared beside it.

His dark eyes swept over her boldly. Grinning, he raised his arms and offered smoothly, "Please. Allow me to help you, Miss Stanton."

Poised atop the wagon wheel, Elizabeth hesitated. Garth Lathom made her uneasy. She wanted to refuse, but without being rude, she couldn't think of a single excuse for doing so. "Thank you," she said finally in a cool, flat voice, and reluctantly released her grip on the wagon bow.

As he swung her down she had no choice but to place her hands on his shoulders, but the instant her feet touched the ground she snatched them back.

Garth's grin widened.

Elizabeth didn't care for the look in his eyes, and she took a quick step backward, breaking free of the hands that lingered improperly at her waist. "If you'll excuse me . . ." She started to walk around him, but Garth sidestepped in front of her.

"What's your rush?"

"I must go help Jemma. Everyone's hungry." She started around him again, and again he sidestepped. His insolent smile sent prickles of alarm over her skin.

"I'm sure she can get along without you."

All around them the camp was a hive of activity. Men were unhitching the teams, women were busily hauling out the cold food for the midday meal. Squealing children chased one another around the enclosure. Elizabeth told herself that she had nothing to fear, but when Garth took a step closer she flinched.

"Mr. Lathom, I must insist—"

A low growl cut off her protest, startling them both.

A few feet away stood Pike. Hackles up, teeth bared, his yellow eyes glittered a warning at the overseer.

"Get away, you mangy mongrel," Garth snapped.

The growl grew more menacing, and Pike edged closer.

Furious, Garth glared at the huge dog. He looked as though

he wanted to kick him but didn't quite have the nerve. Before he could decide on a course of action, Taw called out from the other side of the wagon.

"Lathom! Come over here an' help me unhitch these mules!"

Garth scowled in Taw's direction, but when he looked back at Elizabeth he shrugged. "Ah, well. Duty calls. Perhaps we can talk some other time, pretty lady."

A shiver rippled through Elizabeth as she watched him walk away, and she pulled her shawl tighter around her shoulders.

She looked back at the crouched dog, surprise, gratitude, and healthy caution mingling in her eyes. "Good boy, Pike," she murmured. "Good dog." Warily, keeping her eye on him, she edged past the animal and hurried around the circle of wagons.

On the other side of the camp, Agatha Guetterman was already haranguing their hired girl, her biting voice cutting through the din like the crack of a whip. Standing at the tailgate of the wagon behind the Guettermans', Doris Maybry jiggled a crying baby on her hip and poured milk into tin cups with the unruffled calm of a mother of eight.

Farther down the line, Patrick Conlin bellowed a threat at his wife. At once the cowed woman scurried away to do his bidding. Elizabeth spotted their eight-year-old daughter, Faith, huddled beneath their wagon, her dirt-streaked face a pale, pinched oval peering through the spokes of the wheel.

Averting her gaze, Elizabeth sighed. Many of the emigrant families were poor, but none were as poor as the Conlins. All three were gaunt and worn, their drawn faces etched with hopelessness, their clothes little more than rags. Conn had almost refused to let them join the train, fearing their shabby rig and scrawny mules wouldn't last the trip. Elizabeth suspected he'd relented merely out of pity.

She knew that kind of soul-destroying poverty could turn a man bitter, even violent. God knew she had seen the evidence among her father's patients. Still, she could not excuse Mr.

Conlin's treatment of his wife and daughter. Margaret was a pathetic, browbeaten creature who lived in fear of the brooding man she had married, and little Faith was a sad wraith who did her best to stay out of his way. Elizabeth could not once remember hearing the child laugh, or even seeing her smile.

"Elizabeth! Elizabeth, wait for me!"

Turning, Elizabeth saw her cousin hurrying toward her, picking her way gingerly over the rough ground. Behind her, Isaac, looking absurd in his dusty livery, was unhooking the team of matched bays from Millie's carriage. The elegant vehicle looked ridiculously out of place among the covered wagons, but Millie had flatly refused to ride in one of the cumbersome rigs. Since his return in January, Conn had been unusually stern with Millie, but on this matter he had yielded.

As Elizabeth waited for her cousin to catch up, a childish squeal drew her gaze to the Grimeses' wagon, and she smiled.

Holding her five-year-old son, Jeremy, in a tight embrace, Hester Grimes was gleefully tickling the squirming child, her husky chuckles blending with his joyous shrieks.

When she sat the boy down she ruffled his red hair and gave his bottom a swat. "Off you go, now, boyo. And if I catch you in the sugar again, I'll tan your hide," she admonished with mock severity. Jeremy scampered away, trailing laughter.

Millie caught up with Elizabeth just as Hester spotted her. "You walking after we noon?" Hester asked, smiling.

"Yes. For a while, anyway."

"Good, I'll join you then. My rump's plumb numb from sitting on that wagon seat."

"Fine. See you later." Laughing at Hester's bluntness, Elizabeth waved and walked on.

"Honestly, Elizabeth. I don't know how you can tolerate that awful woman. She's so . . . so . . ." Making a sour face, Millie gave a delicate little shudder. "so . . . common."

"Hester is really quite nice, once you get to know her."

"Huh!"

"Really. She is." Elizabeth knew that she was wasting her breath. Millie had taken an instant dislike to the earthy, plain-spoken woman.

Millie gave a disdainful sniff. "I don't know why you walk so much, anyway. When I persuaded Conn to let me bring the carriage, I assumed that you would ride in it with me. But you never do."

"That's not true. I rode with you yesterday."

"For only an hour."

An hour was all Elizabeth could take. She had discovered that prolonged jostling in the closed carriage had an even more disastrous effect on her stomach than riding in the wagon.

"Obviously you prefer the company of that disgusting old trapper or that low-bred woman to mine."

Elizabeth's eyes widened at her cousin's sulky expression. Why she was jealous!

At once her tender heart melted. Slipping an arm around Millie's shoulders, she gave her a hug. "Oh, dearest, no. You mustn't even think that. It simply isn't so. Since Taw is nice enough to drive my wagon, I feel the least I can do is keep him company part of the time. I walk to stretch my legs, and because I enjoy it." She smiled coaxingly and gave Millie's shoulders another squeeze. "You're welcome to join us, you know."

Millie seemed somewhat mollified. "Well, perhaps I will. But just for a little while. I don't think I could stand to be around Hester for very long. Honestly, I find it positively amazing that such a crude person could have a brother like Ben Whitelaw. The man is charming and polite and ever so handsome. Don't you think?"

"I suppose so," Elizabeth agreed, fighting a smile. Bless her, Millie would never change. It wasn't charm or manners that made Ben Whitelaw acceptable to her cousin, but his masculinity, and his elusiveness.

Conn had needed men to drive his wagons and the loosely

herded bunch of milk cows, horses, spare oxen, mules, and other livestock that followed the wagon train. Since Ben was planning to move to Texas with Hester and Liam and their family, Conn had offered him the job. Ben had accepted eagerly, but he opted to take his meals with his sister and her family rather than with the Cavanaughs, as the other hands did, a circumstance that afforded Millie little opportunity to captivate him.

Drawing near the cook wagon, Elizabeth saw that Jemma was already hard at work, and she picked up her pace.

"My goodness, cousin. Slow down. What's your hurry?"

"I have to help with the food. Remember?"

In addition to Ben, Conn had hired twenty other single men. With so many people to feed, Jemma needed assistance, and since Millie had never cooked a meal in her life, the job fell naturally to Elizabeth.

"Oh, that." Millie flapped her hand. "Never mind. Jemma can get along fine without you for a few minutes. I want to talk to you." She cast Elizabeth a sly look. "I saw you with that handsome Mr. Lathom."

Handsome? The men were returning from watering the stock at the creek, and as they drove the animals into the enclosure formed by the wagons, Elizabeth's gaze went to the blond overseer. She supposed you could call him handsome, though he didn't appeal to her. His thin mouth had a cruel twist to it, and his hard black eyes were cold and crafty. Around Conn, Garth was always polite, even deferential, but she didn't like his insolent tone whenever he caught her alone or the bold way he had of looking at her.

"What were you two talking about?"

"Nothing. He helped me down from the wagon, that's all."

"Oh."

There was such obvious disappointment in that one word, Elizabeth had to laugh. Putting her arm around Millie, she gave her an affectionate hug. "Dearest, you're so transparent.

Are you really so anxious to marry me off?"

Millie's chin lifted, and her mouth set in a pout. "I'm only thinking of you," she said in an offended voice. "As for myself, I would be perfectly happy if you lived with Conn and me forever. You know that."

Elizabeth's smile faded. "Yes. I know."

"Of course, if you should happen to marry Conn's overseer, that would be perfect. Then you would not only have a husband, we would still be together."

Oh, Millie, Elizabeth thought, both amused and saddened. Even when you're trying to be thoughtful there's always a self-serving motive.

No fires were lit at midday. The break lasted only about an hour, and it was more to rest the stock than for the benefit of the humans. As always, their noon meal consisted of food left over from breakfast: cold cornbread spread with butter, thick slabs of ham, fresh buttermilk, and cold coffee.

When Conn finished eating he took his plate to the cook wagon and replenished his cup from the blue-speckled coffee-pot on the tailgate. He ambled to the front of the wagon, leaned against the wheel, and sipped the bitter leftover coffee without tasting it. Over the rim of the cup his brooding gaze settled once again on his wife.

All through the meal he'd watched her, sitting on a stool beneath a nearby shade tree, surrounded, as always, by the single hands. Like a queen holding court, he thought with a trace of bitterness.

She tossed her head and laughed merrily at something one of the men said. The action made her side curls dance and showed to great advantage the graceful curve of her throat, both of which Conn suspected Millie was fully aware.

The men vied for her attention, and she happily obliged them, batting her lashes and smiling coquettishly at one and all. Conn took another swig of cold coffee, his eyes narrowing as he watched Millie give one of the men a playful tap on the wrist with her lace fan.

The flirting had begun their first day out of Charleston. At first he had ignored it, telling himself that she was simply getting even with him for uprooting her life. But now . . . now he wasn't so sure. He had the uneasy feeling that Millie was too good at the game to be a novice, too practiced.

He didn't want to believe it. The ugly suspicion created doubts where before there had been none, made him question just how Millie had spent her time while he'd been away all those years.

Strangely, her behavior didn't arouse jealousy as much as anger. He didn't think for a minute that she would ever be unfaithful. If nothing else, her dislike of the marriage act would see to that. But no man wanted to be made to look a fool.

Up until now he had tolerated her behavior because he hadn't wanted to make things any worse between them than they were already, but his patience was wearing thin. Unconsciously he gritted his teeth. Lately he was seeing several sides to Millie's character he'd never seen before. Or perhaps he'd just never noticed.

A movement drew Conn's gaze to the end of the wagon and to Elizabeth, who was helping Jemma with the dishes. He watched her for a moment, then his gaze switched back to his wife, and he felt a fresh spurt of irritation. He set his jaw and pushed away from the wheel. Slamming his empty cup down on the tailgate, he headed across the camp with long, determined strides.

The men saw him coming and scattered. By the time Conn reached Millie she was alone.

"Heavens, Conn. Must you come storming up that way?" she demanded crossly. "No wonder the men left. You look positively savage." Looking away, her expression closed and petulant, she snapped open the lace fan and whipped the air in front of her nose.

"Maybe I am."

"Oh, don't be tiresome. Just tell me what you want. I know you didn't come over here to keep me company."

"You're right. I came to tell you that if you can pry yourself away from your admirers for a while, Jemma and Elizabeth could use your help."

"What?" The fan halted in midflap, and her head snapped around. "You can't be serious. You expect me to work like a . . . like a scullery maid?"

"No. But I do think it's about time you started lending a hand with the cooking and the other chores. Don't you?"

"I most certainly do not!" Millie could not have looked more horrified if he had suggested she dance around the camp stark naked. She sprang to her feet, bristling. "I do not do menial work. I have servants for that. And furthermore, I am insulted that you, my own husband, would even suggest such a thing."

"These are special circumstances, Millie. On a trip like this everyone has to pitch in and pull his own weight."

"Well, that's just too bad. If you will recall, I did not want to come on this trip."

Conn looked at his wife for several seconds, his chest tight with unwelcome feelings. "Neither did Elizabeth, but she doesn't seem to mind doing her share."

"If my cousin wants to act like a drudge, that's her business, but you needn't expect me to. Besides, you know perfectly well that she's led a different life than I. Uncle Edward was not a wealthy man. Elizabeth is used to doing domestic work."

Before Conn could reply, Ian ran up, knuckling his eyes and whining. The child had begun to get fussy even before they'd stopped to noon, and now his face was flushed, his eyes droopy with exhaustion.

"Ma-maaaa," he wailed in that grating tone only small children could achieve. Before Millie could stop him, Ian latched on to her skirt with his grubby little hands and buried his sweaty face in its folds.

"Oh, for mercy's sake! Ian, stop that! You're soiling my dress!" She grabbed the boy's arm and snatched him loose. Ian's whines escalated to the piercing screams of a full-blown tantrum and caused his mother's face to tighten with vexation.

"Jemma!" she shrieked. "For heaven's sake! Come take this child to the wagon and put him down for his nap! At once!"

"Yes'm, Miss Millie." The tiny black woman dried her hands and gave Elizabeth an apologetic look.

As she walked away carrying the fractious child in her arms, crooning to him softly, Conn turned a stern face on his wife. "You shouldn't snap at the boy that way, Millie. He's only three years old."

"Don't you dare tell me how to raise my children, Conn Cavanaugh!" Millie flared back. Her eyes flashed affronted ire. "You don't have the right, since you've been gone most of their lives."

Conn's head thrust forward. "And whose fault is that?" he demanded through clenched teeth.

But the barb had struck home, and they both knew it. He had missed his children's births and most of their childhood, and no matter the reason or who was to blame, or how much he himself had suffered at the loss, he would always feel guilty about it.

As Conn glared and Millie seethed, Rachel returned from answering nature's call in the nearby woods. Unaware of the tension between her parents, she rushed up to them and turned a hopeful look on Millie. "Mama, may I ride in the carriage with you this afternoon?"

"Certainly not."

"But why can't I? You're always asking Elizabeth to ride with you."

"Of course I ask Elizabeth, for all the good it does me. She's my cousin and my best friend, and I enjoy her company."

Rachel opened her mouth to argue further, but Conn intervened.

"Why not let the girl ride, Millie? There's plenty of room in the carriage."

"You stay out of this, Conn," Millie snapped. "The carriage is for my comfort. I did not insist that we bring it in order to amuse the children. Nor do I intend to spend the afternoon listening to childish prattle."

"Mama! I'm not a child! I'm fourteen years old. Soon I'll be fifteen."

"Rachel, that is quite enough. The answer is no."

When Millie used that tone Rachel knew better than to argue further. Her mouth compressed and her young face seized up in a sullen mask that refuted any claim to maturity.

Assuming a pained expression, Millie pressed the fingertips of one hand to her forehead and wielded the fan with the other. "I do declare, all this bickering has given me a dreadful headache." The resentful glance she flashed Conn's way said he was clearly to blame. "Now if you'll excuse me, I'm going to lie down."

As she marched away, Conn studied his daughter, his concern growing. "Don't fret about it, Rachel. Your mother and I had quarreled, and that put her in a bad mood. That's all. It had nothing to do with you. Give her a little while to get over her pique and I'm sure she'll change her mind."

"No, she won't," Rachel said in a flat voice. She watched her mother for several seconds before switching her gaze to Conn. Her eyes were as cool as winter frost. "But that's all right, Papa. It doesn't matter. I would rather walk with Sally, anyway."

Conn's hands balled into fists as he watched her walk away. Damn! He'd always assumed that mothers and daughters shared a special closeness, but there was a gulf between Millie and Rachel that seemed to be growing wider every day. It worried him more than a little, but damned if he knew what to do about it.

Chapter 4

As she finished up the dishes Elizabeth kept her head down and pretended she hadn't heard the quarrel.

Around her the camp grew quiet as everyone settled down for a rest before the afternoon march began. As always, when they had finished eating, the hired men had wandered off to seek a quiet place to doze. After the clash with her mother, Rachel had left, presumably to find Sally Dawson, a girl of about her own age with whom she had struck up a friendship. Conn, too, had wandered off somewhere. Isaac was stretched out on a pallet beneath the Cavanaugh children's wagon, where he and Jemma slept every night. Except for Taw and Joseph, who were playing a game of checkers, the area around the cook wagon was deserted.

Elizabeth returned the tin cups to the utensil box. She tossed out the dishwater and hung the pan on a hook attached to the hindmost wagon bow. As she gathered up the tablecloth spread over the tailgate, Conn joined her.

She glanced at him uneasily and tried to quell the helpless excitement that always assailed her whenever he came near.

"I didn't bring you along on this trip to work yourself to death."

Surprised by the hint of irritation in his voice, Elizabeth looked up and found that he was studying her intently, a slight frown creasing his brow.

"I don't mind. Really." Murmuring a quick, "Excuse me,"

she stepped over the wagon tongue and walked a few feet outside the camp circle into the meadow. To her dismay, Conn followed.

"Between helping Jemma and giving Dad a hand with the sick, you're wearing yourself out. You're pale right now."

Elizabeth shook out the tablecloth, giving it a pop and sending crumbs flying in the brisk breeze. As Taw had predicted, once she had gotten her feet on the ground and put food in her stomach, her queasiness had disappeared, but no doubt the outward effects had lingered.

"You seem to forget. I've always been pale. Next to Millie, I'm practically colorless."

"No, you're not." Conn stepped close and cupped her face with his hard palm. Elizabeth caught her breath as her heart jerked and a tingling heat spread over her skin from the point of contact. "You're very pretty," he said softly. "A golden-haired angel. That's what Taw calls you."

He shook his head. A bemused smile crinkled the skin at the corners of his eyes and kicked up one side of his mouth. "Somewhere along the way, that skinny, towheaded kid who used to follow me around turned into a lovely woman. I don't even know when it happened."

Too late to matter, she thought in silent despair. Her heart ached so it felt as though it would surely rend in two. For years she had yearned to have him say those things to her, but to hear them now was almost more than she could bear. *Oh, Conn. Conn.*

She struggled with the bittersweet pain, unable to meet his gaze for fear her thoughts, all she was feeling, would be there in her eyes. As his rough fingers caressed her cheek, she focused on the enticing tuft of dark hair visible through the lacing at the top of his buckskin shirt.

It was a mistake.

A pulse beat in the hollow of his throat, strong and sure. Mesmerized, Elizabeth stared at that flutter of brown skin. Her lips parted. Her eyelids grew heavy. Her eyes glazed. Every nerve ending in her body tingled with delicious, forbidden heat, and a trembling yearning wafted through her. For a reckless moment she let herself imagine what it would feel like to put her lips to that vulnerable spot, feel the throb against her tongue, taste the salty tang of his skin.

Heady and enticing, his warm, musky scent invaded her being with each shallow breath she drew. Mingling with it were the pleasing, fecund smells of spring that surrounded them: sprouting grass, rich earth, sunshine.

The wind whipped around them and toyed with her hair, tugging soft, curling wisps from the coronet of golden braids and making them dance around her face. Her brown linsey-woolsey skirt billowed about her legs. The capricious breeze lifted the hem of her white apron and snatched at the tablecloth, making both snap and flutter. Elizabeth clutched the checkered cotton so tight, her knuckles whitened.

"You're very dear to me, little one." Conn captured a cavorting curl and tucked it behind her ear. "I worry about you."

Elizabeth's lovelorn heart leaped with helpless excitement at his words, but when she looked up she felt like a fool. He was smiling at her tenderly, but his vivid blue eyes held merely the warm regard and affection of a friend.

Fighting tears, she gave him a wan smile. "You have enough to deal with without worrying about me. I'm fine. Really." Before he could object, she stepped away from his touch and headed back to the camp. Her heart felt like a lead weight in her chest.

"Elizabeth, wait!" When she paid him no mind, Conn came after her. His long legs quickly closed the distance between them. "I don't want you working so hard," he insisted, shortening his steps to match hers. "When we reach the next town I'm going to see if I can hire a woman to do the heavy work."

Elizabeth stopped short. "Don't be silly. I know I look fragile, but I'm a lot stronger than you think. Besides, since you're saddled with me now, the least I can do is earn my keep."

"Dammit, Elizabeth! I don't consider looking after you a burden!" he roared, startling her. Conn grimaced. His voice softened to a caress. "You're part of the family, little one. We all love you. Lord, don't you know that?"

What Elizabeth knew was that if she didn't get away from him soon, she was going to burst into tears. God, she shouldn't have come! No matter how much Millie begged, she shouldn't have come!

"Yes, of course I do. I didn't mean to sound ungrateful. But please, don't hire anyone. I can handle the work. Truly. I don't mind at all." Oh, Lord, now she was babbling.

"I'm sorry, Conn, but I really don't have time to talk about this right now. I . . . I have to look in on the Hilliard baby before we start again." Elizabeth quickly stepped over the wagon tongue and began to edge away. "She's teething, and . . . and I promised her mother I'd bring her some oil of cloves to rub on her gums."

Conn's heavy eyebrows knitted in a frown. Watching Elizabeth scurry toward her own wagon, he wondered why he felt as though she were running away from him. The idea was absurd, but all the same it filled him with a terrible sense of loss.

"Somethin' wrong?"

He had been so preoccupied that he hadn't heard Taw approach, but a quick glance found the old man leaning against the wagon wheel, just a few feet away.

"I'm not sure. Has Elizabeth said anything to you, Taw? Complained about anything?"

"Nope. But then, I don't 'spect she would. She's game as they come, that one."

"Well, something sure as hell is bothering her. I'm not sure what, though." Conn sighed. "Keep an eye on her for me, will you?"

"Sounds like you're worried 'bout that little gal."

"I am. To tell you the truth, I have been ever since we started. Elizabeth hasn't got Millie's stamina. She's delicate. Maybe too delicate for the frontier."

"Shoot, boy, she may look like a prairie flower, but you mark my words, there's steel in that little missy. You ain't heard her complainin' none, have you?"

A reluctant, somewhat weary chuckle broke from Conn at Taw's oblique dig at his wife. Since leaving Charleston, all Millie had done was complain. There had been times, like today, when he'd been sorely tempted to turn her over his knee. If he hadn't known that her childish behavior was as much his fault as anyone's, he would have. But he had indulged and pampered Millie for years. It was going to take time for her to accept the changes, in their lives and in their relationship.

Conn shot his friend a crooked grin. "No, I haven't heard a word of complaint out of Elizabeth. But I'd probably feel better if I had. A squeaking wheel I can fix."

Heads down, the teams strained against the rattling harnesses and hickory yokes. With each footfall a puff of dust rose, adding to the cloud that coated the mules and oxen, the wagons, the skirts of the women trudging along beside the train.

Walking between Hester and Millie, listening to her cousin's chatter with only half an ear, Elizabeth tried not to think about the blister on her heel, or how much her back ached, or the copper slipper tub in her wagon and how delicious it would feel to sink down into steaming, scented bathwater.

On Millie's other side, Agatha Guetterman marched along with them, her stout body jiggling with every heavy step. She had never walked with Elizabeth and Hester before, and Elizabeth suspected that she had condescended to join them today merely because of Millie. Agatha and a few of her friends, conscious of Millie's status as the wife of the most prosperous man in their group, had been currying her favor assiduously.

Had they still been in Charleston, Elizabeth had no doubt that Millie would have scorned the viperous woman's obvious attempts at social climbing, but loneliness had altered her cousin's tolerance level. Millie's unfortunate tendency to put on airs and look down her nose at the simple emigrants, coupled with her constant complaining, had made most of the women leery of her. Agatha and her cronies were about the only ones who would talk to her, and she was flattered by their attention.

Throughout the afternoon Elizabeth's companions had been an ever-changing group. Most of the women walked for only a short while to stretch their legs, then returned to their wagons. Elizabeth had kept up a steady pace for almost five hours and was so bone weary she could barely put one foot in front of the other. Still, walking was a lot better than being jostled in the wagon.

All along the line men cursed and goaded recalcitrant animals, lashing at them with whips. Pots banged and clattered. Somewhere near the back of the train an axle shrieked from want of grease.

Above the din Agatha's sharp voice droned on, mercilessly shredding the character and reputation of an absent female.

"Truly?" Millie exclaimed, her eyes alight with relish over a bit of juicy gossip. "You actually saw them together?"

"Yes indeed. Bold as brass they were, too. Her with twigs and grass in her hair and her clothes every which way." Agatha's voice and double chins quivered with righteous indignation. "Thank the Lord my Lisa's not a fast piece like that Darla McBain. Why, if that girl were my daughter, I'd take a hickory switch to her."

Hester snorted. "If Lisa Guetterman were any faster, this train would have to go at a gallop to keep up with her," she murmured so only Elizabeth could hear. "The little baggage is just itching for a chance to drop her drawers."

"Shh." Elizabeth tried to give her friend a stern look, but she had to bite the insides of her cheeks to keep from laughing. Seventeen-year-old Lisa was Agatha and Karl's only child. Though she was pretty enough, the girl was spoiled rotten and bolder than was good for her.

Behind them, they heard Patrick Conlin curse his wife. A sharp cry followed.

The four women glanced back and saw Margaret staggering along beside their wagon holding the side of her face. Feeling sick, Elizabeth exchanged an uneasy look with the others. They all knew he'd probably struck her with the whip he was using on the mules. He'd done it before.

"Bastard!"

Millie and Agatha gasped at the word, but Hester jutted out her chin.

"Well, what else would you call a man who treats his wife that way? And her in a family way to boot. Why, it makes my Liam so mad when he sees the marks on that poor woman, he wants to stomp the weasel into the ground."

Elizabeth had to hide a grin. Liam Grimes was only a little taller than his wife and slight of build. Elizabeth doubted that he was capable of thrashing Patrick Conlin, despite the man's gauntness. Still, she supposed that it was the thought that counted.

At that moment, looking like a scared little rabbit, Faith streaked past them, greasy braids and grubby bare feet flying.

Agatha sniffed and twitched her skirt aside. "Humph! If you ask me, Conn ought to kick those people off the train. They're nothing but trash. And they breed like animals."

Anger did not come easily to Elizabeth. Her nature was too gentle, and she'd spent too many years controlling her emotions. But the cruel words caused her temper to flare like a struck sulfur stick. She regarded the hatchet-faced woman coolly. "May I remind you that Faith is an only child."

The censure in her soft voice merely put the woman's beak of a nose a notch higher. "Humph! No doubt there's been a miscarriage every year since her birth."

"So?" Hester challenged. "Babies are gifts from God. Liam and I have five ourselves, and we'll probably have more. Besides, you can't expect folks to deny themselves the pleasures of the marriage bed."

"Huh! It's only pleasure for men," Millie scoffed.

"Oh, I don't know." Hester's lips curved as she smoothed her hands over her generous hips. "I think lying in my man's arms is just about the sweetest pleasure there is."

"*You* would."

Millie took no pains to hide her loathing, but the other woman merely regarded her with a touch of pity and laughed, the earthy sound rich with sensuous secrets and wicked delight.

Millie sniffed. "I really don't think we should be discussing such things in front of Elizabeth," she said primly. "After all, she is a maiden lady."

Color bloomed in Elizabeth's cheeks, but she was given no chance to protest.

"You know, I have to admit, I've been curious about that." Hester cocked her head to one side and pursed her lips. "How in tarnation is it that a woman as pretty as you never married? Are all the men in Charleston blind and stupid?"

"Some people have high standards," Millie answered for Elizabeth with quelling superiority, conveniently overlooking her own scathing opinion of her cousin's reason for remaining single. "Though I doubt you would understand."

"Millie, please."

Ignoring the gibe, Hester's eyes narrowed on Elizabeth's delicate profile and the becoming flush that stained her cheeks. "Well, she'll soon have her pick of men. There's a shortage of marriageable women in the West, and one as beautiful as Elizabeth will create quite a stir. Why, in no time she'll have more proposals than she can shake a stick at. You mark my words."

"Now, Hester. You really mustn't build false hopes, you know. I think you'll find that most of the men will prefer a young woman like my Lisa to someone of Elizabeth's age. No offense intended, of course," Agatha added hastily with an insincere smile for Elizabeth. "I'm quite sure that you will eventually find a husband, my dear."

Millie bristled. "Now, see here, Agatha!" she began heatedly in Elizabeth's defense, but her ire was forgotten as Ben Whitelaw rode up beside them and reined in his horse.

Bobbing his head, the big sorrel sidestepped twice before settling down to a plodding walk. The smell of warm horseflesh, leather, and male sweat drifted on the slight breeze. Ben tipped his hat and leaned forward, resting his forearm on the saddle.

"Afternoon, ladies." His hazel eyes skimmed over his sister and the two married women and homed in on Elizabeth. "Miss Stanton."

Elizabeth smiled, her murmured greeting blending with those of the other women.

She liked Hester's brother. At twenty-six he was younger than his sister by thirteen years, but the resemblance between them was strong. They had the same thick brown hair, the same steady hazel eyes, the same wide, sensuous mouth and well-defined features. But strangely, the combination that in Hester resulted in merely a strong, interesting face was stunningly attractive in its masculine version. Ben also possessed, in a more subtle way, perhaps, the same earthy appeal as his sister. Already all of the unmarried girls over the age of fifteen had set their caps for him.

More appealing, though, than good looks or personal magnetism, there was a quiet strength about Ben, a rock-solid dependability. They were qualities that reminded Elizabeth strongly of Conn.

Millie smoothed her hair and smiled up at him coquettishly. "Why, Mr. Whitelaw, how sweet of you to stop and chat."

Reluctantly Ben's gaze left Elizabeth. "Afraid I just stopped by to give Miss Stanton a message, ma'am." He favored Millie with a polite smile and returned his attention to Elizabeth. "Charlie Wyler wanted me to ask if you'd look in on his wife. She's not feeling too good."

"Certainly. Tell him I'll be right there."

"Yes, ma'am." Leather creaked as he straightened in the saddle. He started to ride away, then turned his horse back again. "Oh, by the way. We're coming up on a river crossing about a mile or so ahead. There's no bridge, so we'll ford, but first Conn wants to swim the cattle across. We'll be driving them up to the front soon, so maybe it'd be best if you ladies got back in your wagons."

His eyes crinkled beneath the broad-brimmed hat, and with a nod he turned his mount and put the big sorrel into a lazy lope toward the back of the train.

Ann Wyler had a fever and a touch of dysentery. Elizabeth dosed her with herbs and castor oil and told her to remain in bed until she felt better. By the time she left the wagon they were approaching the ford and the train had begun to slow.

The river was swollen from the spring runoff. Conn and several of the men whose opinion he valued surveyed the swift-running water and conferred on whether or not to attempt a crossing. Conn was doubtful, but one of the men rode his horse across and back without too much difficulty, and they decided to go ahead. To wait for the water level to go down could mean a delay of days.

Preparations got under way at once. Loose items were secured. Children were rounded up and put into the wagons with strict instructions to behave themselves. The beds of the wagons were raised several inches by putting blocks under them. Two medium-size trees were felled, and after the wheels were removed from Millie's carriage, the trimmed trunks were lashed to either side to act as pontoons.

When all was in readiness, Ben and the other drovers herded the reluctant bunch of mixed stock into the water. At once the banks of the quiet river erupted in a startling mélange of sights and sounds and actions.

Whips cracked the air like gunshots. Men raced about on their horses, waving their arms, shouting and cursing and yipping at the balking animals. Cattle bawled. Goats bleated. Horses whinnied and rolled their eyes in fear. Upset by the cacophony, the caged chickens set up a terrible squawking. Chains rattled as nervous teams shifted in their traces. Pigs squealed. Dogs barked. Small children began to cry.

Heads up, the protesting animals in the river struggled against the current. In the middle, where the water ran deepest, a few tried to turn back, but the men drove them on relentlessly.

Perched on the high wagon seat beside Taw, Elizabeth took in the spectacle with awe and growing trepidation.

Since leaving Charleston they had crossed many rivers and streams. At first there had been bridges, but the farther west they'd come, the fewer such conveniences they had encountered. A couple of times they'd had to raft across, paying enterprising ferrymen a dollar a wagon. The only rivers and creeks they had forded up till then had been shallow and fairly placid, nothing at all like the fast-flowing, wide expanse of water before them.

As soon as the last of the stock struggled up the opposite bank, Millie's carriage was floated across. Using a guide rope one of the drovers had stretched across the river, the task was accomplished quickly without mishap.

The driver of the lead wagon, on a signal from Conn, flicked the reins and urged his nervous team into the water. Ian, Rachel, and Jemma peeked out through the rear opening in the canvas, their eyes round with fear and excitement.

Elizabeth gripped the seat with both hands as the line of wagons began to edge forward. Her gaze fixed on the murky brown river. It smelled of mud and decaying plant life. Floating on the shiny surface, twigs, leaves, even an occasional tree branch raced by. Already the water lapped and sucked at the bottom of the second wagon.

For an instant, in the middle of the stream, the lead team floundered and the terrified mules brayed in terror. On the bank just ahead of Elizabeth's wagon, Conn stood up in the stirrups.

"Keep their heads up! Keep 'em moving! Willowby! Barnes! Dammit, get in there!"

On either side of the panicked team, cursing and shouting, outriders swam their horses in close enough to grab the bridle straps of the lead pair and urge them over the treacherous spot. The brown water churned with their efforts.

As the rig just ahead lumbered into the river, Conn reined in his horse alongside Elizabeth's wagon. He cast a concerned glance at her white face but directed his comments to Taw. "It's fast, but not quite deep enough to swamp you, except for a spot in the middle, a yard or so wide. Hit it at an angle and keep 'em moving, and you'll make it."

"I'll do 'er," Taw said, and clucked the team into motion.

Mind-numbing terror enveloped Elizabeth as the rushing water surrounded them. At the first slap against the bottom of the wagon she whimpered.

Taw sent her a sharp look. "You all right, Missy?"

She didn't answer. She didn't even hear him. Not that it would have mattered. Speech was beyond her. She sat as though turned to stone, frozen with fear, staring at the swirling current, her heart knocking against her ribs. Her hands clutched the wagon seat so tight, her fingers were bone white.

"Missy?" Taw's worried glance sliced her way again, but he had his hands full with the team. He slapped the reins over their backs and cracked the whip. "Giddyup there, you dad-burned mules! Go! Go, blast yore hides!"

They were almost to the halfway point when someone on the bank spotted the submerged log.

"Deadhead! Deadhead! Look out!"

"Christ a'mighty!" Bracing his feet against the edge of the

wagon, Taw laid into the mules with the whip. "Move, you lop-eared bastards! Move! Give us a hand here, dammit!" he bellowed at the outriders.

Shouts went up from both sides of the river. Ears flat to their heads, the frightened animals strained. The men in the water turned the air blue with obscenities and fought to do the impossible.

Beneath the surface of the water, the long dark shape glided straight for them—swift, silent, ominous.

"Get in the back, Missy! Get in the back!"

Taw's urgently roared command fell on deaf ears. Caught in the grip of paralyzing fear, Elizabeth clutched the seat and stared, wild-eyed, at the water, not even aware of the menace bearing down on them.

"It's gonna hit! Look out!"

The log slammed into the side of the wagon with a jarring impact that sent Elizabeth flying through the air like a rag doll.

"Elizabeth!"

For a stunned instant she heard Conn's anguished shout and her own piercing scream. Then both were cut off abruptly as she hit the water and the muddy torrent swallowed her up.

Chapter 5

Conn had never known such heart-stopping terror. He dug his heels into his mount's flanks and sent the animal lunging into the swift current. A second later Pike hit the water beside horse and rider.

"Hang on, Elizabeth! Hang on, I'm coming!"

He was only remotely aware of the shouts and frenzied efforts of the outriders, of the dog swimming somewhere off to his right, of Ben Whitelaw, on the opposite bank, jerking off his boots and diving in. Conn's entire being was focused on reaching the treacherous flow in the center of the river.

Pandemonium reigned. The log had jammed a wheel, and Elizabeth's wagon sat askew just beyond the deepest point, rocking dangerously as water buffeted the side of the bed. The terrified team fought to escape the rushing current, but they were unable to budge the heavy rig.

The wagon in line behind Elizabeth's, already committed to crossing when the accident occurred, had no choice but to swing out around the stranded vehicle and keep going or risk being swamped. The driver whipped the team and yelled blistering curses as he struggled to avoid the flailing mules, men, and horses in the river. The tumult turned the water into a muddy froth.

"I don't see her!"

"Where'd she go?"

"Dammit to hell! Don't jist sit there, you gawldurn fools!

Keep looking!" Taw, standing up in the wagon, fought to control the crazed team and at the same time shook his fist at the hapless outriders.

Reaching the spot, a few yards downstream of the wagon, where he calculated the current should have carried Elizabeth, Conn kicked his feet free of the stirrups and dove in.

The murky depths were cold and impenetrable, but he waved his arms and searched until his lungs nearly burst. Surfacing, he gulped in a deep breath and dove again.

The river was not deep. Except for the narrow trench in the middle, the water reached only to Conn's chin, but the swift current made standing impossible. It was over Elizabeth's head, however, and he knew she couldn't swim.

Not that it would have made any difference if she could, weighted down as she was by a long skirt and innumerable petticoats and hampered by a corset. She might as well have a damned anvil tied around her neck, Conn thought grimly, sweeping his arms through the swirling water. With each passing second fear squeezed his chest tighter and tighter.

When he broke the surface the second time, Pike was barking his head off, the sounds sharp and agitated.

Taw waved his arm. "Conn! I think he's found her! Down here!" he shouted, pointing beneath the wagon. Already one of the outriders was diving, and Ben had changed course and was headed that way.

Conn swam upstream against the current like a man possessed. Muscles straining, he assaulted the water with every ounce of strength in his powerful body. With every stroke he mentally cursed his slow progress, but surely, steadily, the distance grew smaller.

A few feet from the stern of the wagon his foot struck something. He sucked in a deep gulp of air and dove.

The deadhead had caught in the back wheel. Groping along the log, Conn discovered there were several branches still attached to it. He felt along the first one, found that the end was stuck in the muddy river bottom, and moved on to the next. Pike joined him beneath the water and bumped his side insistently over and over.

Conn's lungs were on fire. He started to go up for air when something soft brushed his hand and wrapped around it. His fingers closed around the stuff, and his heart gave a jolt. It was hair—long, silky strands of hair!

Elizabeth! Oh, God, Elizabeth!

He grabbed a fistful of the waving tresses and pulled, but succeeded in lifting her only a few inches before meeting resistance. He went deeper, wrapped an arm around Elizabeth's limp body, and hauled her close. Running his free hand down her side, he discovered that her skirt had snagged a jagged branch and was caught fast.

Cursing silently, he tugged the cloth. When it did not turn loose, he yanked it with a savage fury that rent the skirt from hem to waist.

Ben appeared at Conn's side as he pulled Elizabeth free, but when the other man reached for her, Conn waved him off. With an arm around her waist, he held her cradled against his chest and kicked them upward.

When they broke the surface a cheer went up from the tense crowds on the banks and the men in the water, but Conn barely heard it. He was aware only of Elizabeth hanging on his arm like a rag doll and the terrible bluish tint of her complexion.

Gulping air into his burning lungs, he hooked his hand under her chin and struck out for the west bank. Without a word, Ben came up on her other side and did the same. Pike paddled behind in their wake.

Millie stood waiting on the bank, wringing her hands when Conn waded from the river with Elizabeth. She hung lifeless in his arms, head back, her arms dangling. Water streamed from her waterlogged clothes and from her hair, which trailed almost to the ground in long wet ropes.

"Stand clear," Conn barked at the drovers when they rushed forward to lend a hand. They backed off at once, Isaac among them. Worry lines furrowed the elderly servant's brow, and there were tears in his eyes.

"Isaac, go get a blanket. And be quick about it!"

"Yessuh, Mister Conn!" Dignity forgotten, he took off for the wagons at an ungainly lope, his skinny legs bobbing up and down like a granddaddy spider's.

At the first glimpse of Elizabeth's pallor, Millie's clenched fist went to her mouth. "Oh, my God! Is she dead?"

"No," Conn growled, laying Elizabeth on the grassy bank. Pike dropped down at her feet, and Conn felt Ben standing behind him looking over his shoulder, but his eyes never left her. She couldn't be dead. He refused even to consider the possibility.

With shaking hands he smoothed back the heavy strands of hair plastered to her face. Mud streaked her delicate features, and bits of river debris clung to her skin. A nasty bruise was beginning to form on one cheek and another on her forehead where she had struck something. Probably the wheel as she was swept under the wagon, Conn thought. She looked so frail and helpless, and she lay utterly still.

Conn laid his ear against her sodden breast, but his own heart was thundering so, he couldn't hear a thing.

"Is she breathing?" Ben demanded.

"Yes," Conn snapped back, but he didn't really think so.

"Oh, you poor, poor darling." Sinking down on her knees on the other side of Elizabeth, Millie lifted her cousin's cold hand and chafed it between her own. "You poor—Conn! For God's sake! What are you doing?"

Ignoring his wife's distressed cry, Conn roughly rolled Elizabeth over onto her stomach. Planting his feet on either side of her thighs, he grasped her waist and lifted until her inert body hung from his hands in an inverted V. Holding her suspended, he jostled her almost angrily, lowered her, then lifted her again. Over and over he repeated the action, lifting and lowering, lifting and lowering, his face grim and set.

He blocked out everything but Elizabeth. The noise made by the men struggling to free the stranded wagon, his wife's soft sobbing, the clusters of somber spectators on both sides of the river—none of it existed. None of it mattered.

"Come on, sweetheart," he urged in a hoarse whisper. "Come on. Spit it out. You can do it."

Working ceaselessly, he pleaded, cajoled, commanded, and cursed. All the while, in his mind and heart, he alternately reviled and beseeched the powers that be.

This was Elizabeth. Sweet, gentle Elizabeth. Dear God, he couldn't let her die!

His own tears were mingling with the muddy river water dripping from his hair when at last the first strangled cough erupted from her throat.

A glad cry went up from those standing around them and was echoed by the people waiting on the other side of the river. Conn was so relieved and overjoyed, he wanted to snatch her close against his heart and rock her in his arms like a baby; but he knew she wasn't out of the woods yet.

She coughed again and again, harsher, deeper, the racking spasms running together until she began to gag.

"Conn, stop!" Millie cried. "You're hurting her!"

Without bothering to reply, Conn continued to lift and lower her in a rhythmic pumping action.

Elizabeth began to retch terribly, her upper body jerking with dry heaves, and Millie's protests grew more strident.

"Conn, for God's sake!"

Muddy river water gushed from Elizabeth's mouth and nose. She choked and gasped, but another torrent followed. She retched repeatedly, her abused body purging itself of the foul water along with the contents of her stomach. When at last the ordeal was over, she went slack in Conn's hands and moaned.

Gently Conn lowered her to the ground. Still standing astraddle her body, he braced his hands on his knees and released a long sigh. As his shoulders slumped he hung his head and closed his eyes. "Thank God."

Consciousness came slowly, painfully. A searing constriction in her chest, the terrible nausea, the clammy cold that made her aching body shake—all dragged her from the darkness with merciless insistence.

Her nose burned, and her throat felt raw. Remotely Elizabeth knew that she had been sick—violently sick—but she could not figure out why or even where she was.

Her eyes fluttered open. As her vision began to clear humiliation added to her discomfort. She was lying on the ground in a pool of her own vomit, and there were people standing all around, looking at her. She heard moaning, and her shame deepened as she realized the pitiful sounds were coming from her.

Gentle hands grasped her shoulders. She tried to resist their pressure but lacked the strength, and she was rolled onto her back.

The face hovering above hers was Conn's.

He brushed her uninjured cheek with his fingertips. "How are you feeling, little one?"

Concern roughened his voice, and his rugged face was taut with strain, ashen beneath the darkly tanned skin. As they searched her face, emotion darkened his beautiful eyes to a deep, azure blue. Dimly it registered that he was as wet as she was.

His soaked buckskins clung to his powerful body, and his black hair lay plastered against his head, except for the wet ringlets dangling over his forehead. A drop of water fell from one and splattered against her neck. The tiny action produced a cold sensation that jogged something in her mind, something she knew instinctively she didn't want to think about.

Wanted or not, remembrance came in a flood, sending a violent shiver rippling through her body.

"Dammit, Isaac! Where's that blanket?"

"Here 'tis, boss. Here 'tis."

As Conn tucked the patchwork quilt around Elizabeth, she recalled with stark clarity that awful moment when the brown water closed over her . . . blinding her . . . suffocating her. It had swept her along, slamming her against something hard again and again. And then . . . oh, God . . . out of the murk, gnarled fingers had grabbed her! She had kicked and fought to free herself, but they had refused to let go, and as silent screams reverberated through her head, the darkness had closed in.

Her heart began to race, and she made a panicky sound. At once she felt again the gentle stroke of Conn's hand.

"Easy, little one," he murmured. "Easy. You're safe now."

Even in the grip of hysteria, she responded to that deep voice. Her fear quieting, Elizabeth gazed up at Conn's beloved face and saw the worry he could not hide, and she knew then that he had somehow saved her.

Emotion clogged her throat. Her chin began to wobble and her eyes filled. She bit her quivering lower lip, but the salty tears spilled over and streamed down her cheeks. Then reaction set in, and she began to shake in earnest, her teeth chattering.

"Oh, C-Conn."

She barely managed to choke out the words in a raspy, raw whisper before the wrenching sobs overtook her. Her face crumpled, and the agonizing sounds tore from her throat, so piteous and heartrending that the men began to shuffle their feet and avert their eyes.

"Elizabeth, dearest, please don't cry so," Millie pleaded tearfully. "Please. I can't bear it."

Neither could Conn. As well, he knew how mortified she was to have everyone witness her loss of control. "She should be in bed," he said gruffly, reaching for her.

"Here, I'll carry her for you."

"No, I'll do it." Once again brusquely rejecting Ben's offer of help, Conn scooped up Elizabeth in his arms, quilt and all, and strode for the wagons.

"Millie, go round up more blankets," he ordered over his shoulder. "And bring her one of your nightgowns. Jemma, you heat some water. She needs a hot bath."

Inside the children's wagon, when Conn placed Elizabeth on Rachel's bed she clung to him, sobbing hysterically. "It's all right, little one. You're safe now. It's all over." His voice, which only moments before had been firm with command, was now raspy and low, not quite steady. He sat down on the side of the bunk and gathered her close. Rocking her gently, he rested his chin against the top of her head and stroked her back.

She wept uncontrollably, like a hurt child, the sounds choppy and harsh. "That's it, sweetheart. Let it all out. There's no one here to hear you but me," he crooned, stroking her heaving shoulders.

Her hair hung in a sopping mass that fell past her hips, the curling tips touching the mattress. He was struck by how small she felt in his arms, how delicately she was built. He felt her shaking as though in the grips of a hard chill. The tremors were echoed deep inside his own body at the thought of what a close call she'd had.

Gradually she quieted, her cries turning to hiccuping little sniffles. When those ended also she pulled away, and he eased her back down on the bed.

"I'm s-sorry. I d-didn't mean to carry on like that." She wiped her eyes with her fingertips, then plucked at the soggy quilt wrapped around her legs. Her lowered gaze followed the restless movement.

"Elizabeth, this is me, remember? We've been friends too long for you to worry about a few tears. Especially after what you've been through."

He ducked his head and tried to make her meet his eyes, hoping to coax a smile from her, but she kept her gaze lowered. Spiked with tears, her lashes lay like dark fans against her cheeks. For the first time he noticed how long they were and how they curled up at the ends.

Though she didn't move, he could feel her withdrawing from him. He frowned, not liking it a bit but no longer able to tell himself he was imagining things.

The wagon rocked as Millie stepped up on the tailgate, followed by Jemma and Isaac carrying a copper bathtub and pails of steaming water.

Leaving Elizabeth to the care of the women, Conn stepped from the wagon. Soon, he promised himself, he and Elizabeth were going to have a talk.

The rest of the wagons forded the river without incident. The task took up the remaining daylight hours and was accomplished amid much shouting and cursing and cracking of whips; but Elizabeth slept right through the hubbub.

Exhausted, physically and emotionally, she had begun to doze in the tub as Jemma shampooed her hair. She had barely been aware of the gentle hands assisting her from the warm water and had stood swaying on her feet, her heavy eyelids drooping as the two women patted her dry and eased her into the flannel gown. Before they had finished tucking the quilts snugly around her, she was sound asleep.

She slept straight through the night, missing dinner and breakfast, not stirring until she was awakened by the movement of the wagon when the train pulled out at daybreak.

Barely able to see in the dim light seeping through the opening in the canvas, she was disoriented for a moment, then realized that she was back in her own wagon and that Millie was sitting beside her in the old Boston rocker that had belonged to Elizabeth's grandmother.

"Ah, so you're awake at last." Immediately Millie laid her

hand against Elizabeth's brow. After a moment she pursed her lips. "Well, at least you didn't take a fever. Lord only knows why, falling into that nasty river."

"What are you doing here?"

"Taking care of you, of course. Jemma sat up with you last night. She's resting now, so I'm taking over."

Elizabeth was touched. To her knowledge, Millie had never even looked after her own children when they'd been ill.

The morning passed in a pleasant haze of dozing while Elizabeth pretended to listen to Millie's gossipy chatter. By midday her cousin had tired of playing nursemaid, and when they stopped to noon she abandoned the task happily. Elizabeth was just as happy to see her go, as she had begun to experience the familiar queasiness. She knew if she remained in the wagon, she was going to be violently ill.

Sitting up, she threw her legs over the side of the bed and rummaged through a trunk for a clean chemise and pantalets. She had pulled on the soft cotton undergarments and was lacing up her stays when the wagon rocked under someone's weight. Snatching up a petticoat, she held it to her breast and whirled around guiltily as Rachel loosened the pucker string securing the back opening in the canvas and stepped inside.

"Oh! You're up," she said, blinking to accustom her eyes to the dim interior. She shifted back and forth from one foot to the other and fiddled with the folds of her skirt, her eyes not quite meeting Elizabeth's. "Mama told me to sit with you."

Rachel's discomfort was obvious. Watching her fidget, Elizabeth experienced a stab of regret over the lack of closeness between them. But, she reminded herself, she had kept her distance from Rachel and Ian deliberately, not merely to guard her own heart against more pain, but for their sake as well. And for Millie's.

Had she allowed her love for Conn's children free rein, it would have been much too easy to unintentionally usurp Millie's place in their lives. Her cousin had an unfortunate tendency to shift her responsibilities to anyone who would shoulder them, and she had never cared for motherhood and all its demands. Even without Elizabeth's interference, the relationship between Millie and Rachel was sadly lacking.

"I see." She smiled politely. "Well, thank you, Rachel, but that won't be necessary. As you can see, I no longer need anyone to stay with me." Letting the petticoat drop, she reached back and jerked the corset strings tighter and tied them with quick, experienced fingers.

"But . . . I mean . . . Are you sure?"

"Of course. I feel fine." Elizabeth pulled the petticoat over her head, tied it securely about her waist, and reached for another. "So good, in fact, that I'm going to walk for a while."

"But Mama said—"

"It's all right, Rachel. Honestly. I'll explain to your mother that I didn't need you. Why don't you just run along and find Susan. I'll be fine."

After settling the fourth petticoat over the others, Elizabeth paused and debated adding more, then shook her head and closed the trunk. The five or six deemed proper were so heavy that they made walking difficult.

The wagon rocked a bit. Outside, Taw let loose a stream of colorful oaths, and she realized that he was hitching the team. Quickly she took a navy calico dress sprigged with tiny pink roses from a trunk at the front of the wagon. As she turned back from slipping it over her head, she was surprised to find Rachel still standing there, biting her lower lip.

"I, uh, maybe I'd better help you dress before I go. Mama will be mad if I don't do something for you."

The sharp note in Rachel's voice brought Elizabeth's head up. She studied the girl's closed expression and felt a sinking sensation in her stomach. It wasn't the first time Rachel had used that tone with her or made cutting remarks. Elizabeth was fairly certain of the reason behind them. More and more lately, she had sensed that Rachel resented the closeness and affection that she and Millie shared.

Considering how little attention Rachel received from her mother, her resentment was understandable, but it saddened Elizabeth all the same. She felt even worse for Rachel. She had long ago accepted that her cousin simply was not maternal, but that was small comfort to a child.

"Well, I suppose I could use some help with these." Elizabeth held out her arm, and Rachel stepped forward to fasten the row of tiny buttons on the tight-fitting, six-inch cuff. When she had finished she stood back and waited expectantly while Elizabeth adjusted the garment's dropped shoulders and full, leg-o'-mutton sleeves.

Giving the hovering girl an uncertain smile, Elizabeth sat down on the side of the bed and picked up her hairbrush.

"Here, let me do that for you," Rachel offered.

Too surprised to deny the request, Elizabeth handed over the brush and shifted sideways on the bed, giving her access to the fall of hair cascading down her back.

"Your hair is so pretty."

The compliment, though voiced grudgingly, surprised Elizabeth even more.

Rachel stroked the brush down the silky tresses all the way to the curling ends that lay on the mattress about Elizabeth's hips. "It's so thick and long. And it shines just like gold, even in here." The girl sighed heavily. "I've always wished I had blond hair."

"Why? Your hair is lovely."

"It's black," she stated, as though the reason for her dissatisfaction should be evident.

Biting back a smile, Elizabeth glanced over her shoulder. "I'll tell you a secret. When your mother and I were girls, I envied her her black hair. Actually, I still do."

"Really?"

Rachel's expression brightened instantly, her eyes eager and hopeful, and Elizabeth felt another pang of regret as she realized how ridiculously easy it would be to win the girl's affection. She was starved for a mother's attention and guidance, for simply another female with whom she could talk.

At fourteen Rachel looked about ten. She had inherited her father's startling blue eyes, but in every other way she favored her mother and would someday be a beauty. But at present, Millie, either out of benign neglect or maybe even jealousy, kept her daughter in pigtails and dressed in drab, uncomplimentary clothes more suited for a child than a young lady.

Elizabeth itched to give her advice on clothes and hairstyles, be her confidante, but she didn't dare encourage the girl. Millie wouldn't like it, and it really wasn't her place.

"Yes, of course," she answered briskly. "Now if you're through, I really must hurry. The train is about to move out." Taking the long tresses from Rachel's hands, she twisted them into a loose bun at the back of her head and secured it with what remained, after her dunking in the river, of her ivory hairpins.

For an unguarded moment disappointment flickered over Rachel's face, but she quickly schooled her features into the cool look of indifference she habitually wore.

It was all Elizabeth could do not to fold the girl in her arms and offer affection and friendship, but she forced herself to remain aloof. Much as she might wish otherwise, there was nothing she could do. Ignoring Rachel as best she could, she donned a pink sunbonnet that had a long *bavolet* to protect her neck and tied the ribbons under her chin in a saucy bow.

"There. All set. Thank you for your help, Rachel. And don't worry, I'll be sure and tell your mother that I wouldn't let you stay."

Taw wasn't surprised that Elizabeth was up and planning to walk.

"I was wonderin' when you'd git enough of that wagon." He scratched his whiskered jaw and pursed his lips, considering her. "Sure you feel up to it?"

"I'm fine. Really."

"I gotta admit, you look mighty fine. Purty as a rose in that bonnet." He grinned at her fondly, showing the gaping hole where he'd lost three upper front teeth. "Conn prob'bly ain't gonna like it, but go ahead. Only stay by the wagon, would ya? As a favor t' me?"

"I will. I'll walk right beside you so we can talk."

At first Elizabeth felt a bit wobbly, but the farther she walked the more her strength seemed to return. Everything went just fine for about an hour. Then Conn spotted her.

Riding in his customary lead position a hundred yards or so out in front of the train, he twisted in the saddle to look back, his eyes skimming over the long line of wagons for any signs of trouble. Suddenly he stiffened. At once he whirled his mount and rode back at a gallop. He brought the horse to a skidding halt a yard or so from her.

"What the hell are you doing out of bed?"

Elizabeth's eyes opened wide. Conn had never spoken to her in that tone of voice before.

He glared down at her, his face dark with anger. He looked dangerous. His horse did a sidestepping dance and bobbed its head nervously, reacting to the tension in the man on his back. Elizabeth could only stare.

"Answer me!"

She jumped and her steps faltered briefly, but she somehow regained the pace and kept going. "I . . . I . . ."

"Dammit, woman, you nearly died yesterday. Now get the hell back in that wagon. Now!"

"But . . . I'm tired of being cooped up."

"Son of a bitch! I don't give a go—" He bit off the curse. A muscle twitched along his clenched jaw. "What is this, Elizabeth?" he asked finally in a dangerous, grating voice. "Your sweet, quiet way of protesting? Of telling me that I should have left you back in Charleston like you wanted me to? Well, if so, it's a wasted effort. I've known ever since we started that you don't belong on this train."

The pain was stunning. It hit her like a fist to the heart and took her breath away. Elizabeth halted as though she'd hit an invisible wall; her legs simply stopped moving of their own accord. She stared up at Conn, her face white as chalk, the livid bruises on her cheek and forehead standing out starkly.

"Whoa, mules! Whoa now!" Taw stomped on the brake and hauled back on the reins, bringing the team to an abrupt stop. The bellowed command, embellished with searing curses, was repeated down the line as the wagons behind them were forced to do the same.

"Now jist a gawldurn minute," the old man barked, turning on Conn aggressively. "You ain't got no call t' be talkin' t' the little missy that'a way."

"Butt out, Taw," Conn snarled.

"No, I ain't a'gonna. I've backed yore play fer years, an' been glad t' do it, but not this time. I ain't gonna stand by and let you hurt her feelin's that'a way."

Conn's frown deepened, his darkly furious face reflecting momentary confusion. Then he caught Taw's meaning. "Oh, hell. You know I didn't mean that I didn't want her here."

"Mebbe. But she don't. An afore you go jumpin' down a body's throat, you'd best git yore facts straight. 'Cause there's somethin' 'bout Miss Elizabeth you don't know."

"Taw, no! You said you wouldn't—"

"I know, Missy. An' I kept quiet till now, mainly 'cause I didn't see no harm in it. But this thing's gettin' outta hand. 'Sides, Conn ort ta know." He leveled his faded old eyes on his partner in a stare that would have given a lesser man pause. "Miss Elizabeth ain't walkin' t' spite you, you danged fool. She's walkin' 'cause ridin' fer long in the wagon makes her sick."

Surprise brought Conn's head up sharply. "Sick? You get sick? That's what this is all about? That's why you're walking every time I turn around?"

At Elizabeth's nod his mouth thinned. "I see." He studied her for several moments, his eyes boring into her. Beneath the broad-brimmed hat, his expression was hard and unreadable.

Finally he turned back to Taw. "I'm going to ride ahead to the next town," he announced in a tight, hard-edged voice. "While I'm gone you're in charge. Get one of the drovers to drive the wagon so you can ride point. If I'm not back by sunset, go ahead and make camp as usual."

Taw nodded. "I'll do 'er."

Conn gave Elizabeth another long look, and without a word he wheeled his horse and headed down the narrow dirt road at a trot. Of late, for some strange reason, Pike had become attached to Elizabeth, and the big dog eyed her uncertainly; but after a brief hesitation he loped away after Conn.

Bewildered and hurting, Elizabeth stared at his broad back. She felt suddenly weak and trembly, as limp as an old dish towel that has been wrung out to dry. I should never have come, she thought. Never. Oh, God, he doesn't want me here.

Chapter 6

When they made camp that evening, Conn still had not returned. Taking advantage of his absence, Elizabeth lingered around the fire with Taw and Dr. Cavanaugh even after Millie and the children had gone to bed.

Taw had lifted the rocking chair down from the wagon for her, and as she tilted it back and forth over the uneven ground, she gazed at the fire and let her mind drift. She'd had plenty of time to think about her situation, and now that she'd come to a decision she felt much calmer.

As she'd trudged beside the wagon, fighting back tears, Hester's words of a few days before had come back to her. *"There's a shortage of marriageable women in the West. You'll have more proposals than you can shake a stick at. Just mark my words."*

The more she'd thought about it, the more she'd realized that marriage was the solution—the only solution. A shudder rippled through Elizabeth at the thought of a loveless marriage, but she staunchly pushed her repugnance aside. It was the best thing for all of them, and she would do it.

It won't be so bad, she told herself. There were many decent men in the world—nice, upstanding men who would be good husbands and providers. Why, there were probably some right here on the train. Of the two hundred and seventy-odd souls in their party, the majority were single men.

Unfortunately, so far the only one who had shown an interest in her was Garth Lathom.

A vivid picture of cold, dark eyes and a cruelly sensual mouth flashed in Elizabeth's mind. She could not put her finger on the exact reason she disliked the man. There was just something about him that made her uneasy.

She shivered again. No. Not even to escape the untenable situation she was in would she marry that man.

Elizabeth sighed and set the chair to rocking harder. There had to be someone else. Surely, with so many to choose from, there was a man she could respect and admire enough to build a life with. She would have a home of her own, security, companionship, and who knew, perhaps one day she might even grow to care deeply for him. She could be content with that. Love wasn't everything.

Seated on the ground, leaning back against the wheel of the cook wagon, Isaac began to play his harmonica. Elizabeth smiled as she recognized the tune as "Home Sweet Home." To her surprise, Taw drew a Jew's harp from his "possibles" bag and joined in. The twangy sounds, blending with the reedy notes of the harmonica, were oddly pleasing in a melancholy way.

Woodsmoke and the faint smell of cattle drifted on the breeze. At night the herd was corraled apart from the wagons, and in the distance Elizabeth could hear soft lowing and occasional whickers. The spring night held a lingering chill, and she wrapped her shawl closer about her. From farther around the circle came the murmur of voices, the occasional bang and clatter of cook pots. A woman's laughter rang out. A moment later a concertina, then a flute, took up the tune that Taw and Isaac were playing.

Smiling, Elizabeth leaned her head against the rocker's high back and gazed up at the stars, letting the music lull her. Save for the poignant strains, all was hush and repose as the fatigue of the day settled over the camp.

The peaceful mood was broken moments later by the approach of a horse and rider and the sentry's call.

"It's Conn," Taw murmured just moments before he rode into camp.

Elizabeth jumped to her feet and darted a look around, but it was already too late to escape.

Conn reined in his horse just beyond the circle of firelight and swung out of the saddle. Pike, his tongue lolling from one side of his mouth, circled the fire and lay down a few feet from Elizabeth. A soft whine and single thump of his tail served as a greeting.

Skirting the fire, Conn walked up to her and dumped a bulky object at her feet. "That's for you," he announced in a clipped voice.

"It's . . . it's a sidesaddle."

"That's right. I bought it in Milledgeville. Starting tomorrow, you'll ride."

She was touched. They would be in Milledgeville in a day or so, yet he had ridden ahead and back just for her. Elizabeth lowered her head. "That was very thoughtful of you, but—"

"Don't argue, Elizabeth. There are plenty of spare horses, and I know you can ride. I taught you myself when you were just a kid. You used to love it."

"Yes, but I haven't ridden in years."

"That doesn't matter. Once you learn you never forget. It'll be a lot easier on you. Actually, I should have thought to buy the darn thing before we started."

"But—"

"You're going to ride, and that's that."

She opened her mouth, then closed it, and with a nod she looked down at her clasped hands.

An uncomfortable silence fell between them, but neither moved. All around, the camp grew quiet and still as fires were banked for the night and the weary travelers took to their beds. Crickets began to chirp their night song, and an owl hooted in the distance. A stray tendril from the bun high at the back of Elizabeth's head stirred in the soft eddy of Conn's breath. He stared at it.

The faint smell of violets drifted to him on the night breeze. As he realized that it came from her, a sad smile of remembrance fought with his hurt and frustration. Elizabeth had loved violets since childhood. The scent suited her, he thought with an ache in his chest; it was sweet and gentle, not cloying like the perfume Millie preferred.

"Elizabeth." Her name came out like a caress, his deep voice soft and soothing and tinged with regret. He bent his knees and dipped his head, trying to catch her eye, but her gaze remained fixed on her clasped hands. "About what I said this afternoon . . . I didn't mean it the way it sounded." He waited, but she remained silent. "Of course I want you with us, little one. We all do. You must know that. It's just that I worry about you. That's all."

"There's no need."

Conn's hands curled into fists at his sides. He was getting damned tired of looking at the top of her head. He wanted to see her smile, to see the wariness and hurt banished from those soft gray eyes, but she wouldn't even look at him.

Finally she glanced up and gave a wan smile, but her gaze barely skittered over his face. "Thank you for the saddle, Conn," she said so dutifully that he wanted to shake her. "It was a very considerate thing to do. I . . . I'm sure I will enjoy riding. Now, if you'll excuse me, I'll say good night." She turned to leave, and Conn's patience snapped.

"Elizabeth!"

She jerked to a halt, startled by the harsh tone, but she didn't turn around. "Yes?"

Conn moved up close behind her. His hands settled on the rounded curves of her shoulders. "Elizabeth," he repeated more gently, then his voice went infinitely soft. "Beth."

The childhood diminutive of her name had just slipped out, but when he felt her draw in a sharp breath, he experienced a stab of satisfaction. He had been the only one ever to call her that. It had been something special just between the two of them, and he recalled that it had pleased her enormously. When had he stopped using the name?

"Why did I have to learn from Taw that riding in the wagon makes you ill? Why didn't you just come and tell me? Why have you been avoiding me lately? Dammit! What's happened to us, Beth?"

Elizabeth squeezed her eyes shut. *Us? Oh, Conn. There is no us. There hasn't been for years.*

"Y-you have so much to do, so much on your mind, I . . . I didn't want to be a bother."

"A bother! Dear God, Elizabeth, you could never be that."

Unconsciously his fingers began to massage her tense shoulders, their movement slow and caressing. A quiver of longing ran through Elizabeth, and she pressed her lips together and closed her eyes. Did he know what he was doing to her? No, of course he didn't. He would be horrified if he did. With every fiber in her being, she wanted his touch, yet she prayed he would stop before she gave herself away.

He leaned closer. She could feel the warmth of his body across her back, his breath feathering her ear. "I'm pleased that you came along with us," he murmured, and Elizabeth's heart soared, only to crash an instant later when he added, "If you hadn't, I doubt that I could have dragged Millie to Texas."

It was foolish to let his words hurt her, she told herself. He was Millie's, and all the longing in the world wouldn't make it otherwise. Besides, he thought of her as only a friend, and even if she could change that, she wouldn't.

Clutching her pride to her, she shrugged. "Oh, I'm sure you would have managed. Millie just needs a firm hand is all."

"Maybe."

He was quiet for a moment, his hands still moving hypnotically on her shoulders and upper arms above the knitted shawl that draped from the bend of her elbows. Elizabeth tried to steel herself against a response, but a delicious, bone-melting lethargy crept over her anyway. Her body felt heavy and warm, and her head began to loll forward.

"You still haven't told me why you've been avoiding me."

The question caught her off guard. She stiffened, her chin lifting. "Don't be silly," she replied too quickly, giving a nervous little laugh. "I haven't been avoiding you."

A wry smile twisted Conn's mouth. Elizabeth never could lie worth a damn. Still, he knew it would do no good to push. She was a private person, and in her own quiet way she was as stubborn as they came. If she'd made up her mind not to tell him, he could badger her till Judgment Day and still not get an answer.

He sighed. "All right, little one. If you say so." Exerting gentle but firm pressure, he turned her around. Her gaze fixed on his chest as though she found the sight utterly fascinating. Tenderly Conn studied the dear face, so closed off from him, and felt a profound sense of loss.

He grimaced and drew a deep breath against the tight ache lodged beneath his breastbone. He wanted to shake her until her teeth rattled, and at the same time he felt a powerful urge to hold her close until that terrible sadness left her eyes. Neither was a solution, and he knew it. All he could do was hope that whatever was bothering her would pass.

"You go get some sleep and I'll see you in the morning." His voice was a whisper, full of concern and sadness. He pressed a kiss to her forehead. "Good night. And remember, be prepared to ride."

"I will."

He walked away, and her head came up. Her eyes clung to his broad back as he disappeared into the gloom. Through tremulous lips she whispered, "Good night, my love."

Millie was asleep when Conn entered their wagon—or pretending to be. If she's feigning, she could've saved herself the trouble, he thought, peeling the buckskin shirt over his head and tossing it on top of a trunk. Tonight he was too tired to do anything about that particular ache even if she had been willing.

And Millie was anything but willing.

Since learning of the move to Texas she had flatly refused to make love with him. "If I must make that horrible trip, I certainly don't want to do it while carrying another child," had been her excuse before they'd left Charleston. Once they had gotten under way there had been the added complaint of too little privacy.

That sure hadn't stopped others, though. Conn scratched his furry chest, his stern face softening with the faintest of grins as he recalled the way the Polsons' wagon had been rocking when he'd made his night rounds. He sat down on the side of the bed and tugged off his knee-high moccasins. Of course, Caleb and Bonnie were newly married, two healthy young animals in the first throes of love and passion.

He started to rise but paused instead to look over his shoulder at his wife. Was that the problem? Had he and Millie simply outgrown that kind of youthful passion? No. Conn shook his head wryly. Hell, he and Millie had never shared those kinds of fiery feelings, not even in the beginning.

Why? he wondered. God knew, he'd loved her desperately then. Studying her doll-like beauty in the pale moon glow, he was saddened to realize how much that love had faded over the years. Mostly what he felt now was a gentle fondness and a sense of responsibility. Even the ache in his loins had more to do with months of celibacy than desire for this woman who had once meant the world to him.

Standing, Conn shucked off the buckskin pants, tossed them on top of the shirt, and slipped into bed. Millie made a little grunting noise and flounced over, turning her back to him.

With his arms folded beneath his head, Conn stared at the canvas top, glowing an eerie bluish white in the moonlight. Things would improve when they reached Riverbend, he told himself. They'd been apart too much, was all. Once they were settled in their new home and spending more time together, the old feelings would rekindle. He had to believe that.

Millie was not at all pleased the next morning when she learned of the new arrangements. "It's not fair," she complained as Conn lifted Elizabeth into the saddle. "She gets to ride and I'm stuck in a stuffy old carriage."

Conn's reminder, that she didn't know how to ride and had refused all his offers to teach her, made no impression. The sun was almost up, all the wagons were hitched, and everyone was waiting for the signal to move out, but that didn't concern Millie. She dogged Conn's footsteps like a worrisome terrier yapping at his heels. She pleaded, wheedled, and finally stamped her foot and demanded that he teach her as they traveled.

"How difficult can it be? You just sit there and the horse does all the work. Elizabeth won't mind walking a little longer. It will only be until we reach Milledgeville. Then we'll buy another sidesaddle and we can both ride."

Until that point Conn had spoken to her calmly, as though he were dealing with a child, but his patience abruptly ran out. He turned on her with his jaw thrust out and snarled through clenched teeth, "I said no! Now get back in that carriage. Now! Or so help me I'll haul you back there and stuff you in it myself!"

"You . . . you wouldn't dare!"

"Oh, I'd dare all right. The way I feel right now I'd even enjoy it. So get!"

"Oh! You . . . you . . . Ohhhh!" Millie spun away and stomped back to the carriage, curls bouncing and skirts swaying and flouncing so hard, they showed a froth of petticoats and an improper length of leg.

Watching her, Elizabeth caught her bottom lip between her teeth and worried at it. She had seen Millie in a temper many times, but she'd never seen her this angry before. Her cousin huffed and sputtered every step of the way to the carriage, and when she climbed inside she slammed the door so hard, several horses shied and the vehicle rocked for almost a minute.

Conn ignored her. He swung into the saddle with his face set and nudged his horse up beside Elizabeth's. "You ready?"

Elizabeth glanced back at the carriage, looked uncertainly at Conn's hard expression, and nodded. "I suppose."

"Good. It's been a long time since you've ridden, so until I'm satisfied that you haven't forgotten everything I taught you, I want you to stay by me. Understand?"

"Yes, of course. I understand."

Up until then Conn had looked as though he were expecting an argument, or spoiling for a fight, but at her quiet acquiescence his face softened a bit.

He twisted in the saddle and looked back at the line of wagons to see if all was in readiness, then gave the signal with his hat and called: "Wa-gons hoe-ooh!"

Amid curses and shouts and the crack of whips, the creaking procession began. Elizabeth and Conn cantered out ahead, pulling up to a sedate walk about two hundred yards or so in front of the train. For several minutes they rode in silence, each lost in his own troubling thoughts.

As her body adjusted to the undulating rhythm, Elizabeth cast a sidelong look at Conn. His profile seemed carved from stone, and just as unyielding. He's changed, she thought sadly. Grown harder. She could remember a time when he would have cut out his tongue rather than talk to Millie that way. A time when he had doted on her, petted her, would have given her the moon if only she'd asked.

Conn caught her appraisal and cocked one eyebrow. "What's the matter, little one? Something on your mind?"

"Don't, uh, don't you think you were a little hard on Millie?"

His faint smile disappeared, and he returned his gaze to the trail ahead. "As you said last night, Millie needs a firm hand sometimes."

"Yes, but—"

Conn looked at her again, and this time his eyes were filled with tenderness. "Don't worry, Beth. Millie and I still love each other."

Elizabeth's heart squeezed. As she met his steady gaze, her eyes grew moist and her chin wobbled. "Good," she quavered. "I'm glad."

It was true. She loved Conn with all her heart, but he was Millie's, and no amount of dreams or wishes would change that. And loving them both as she did, how could she want any less for them?

The emotion swirling in Elizabeth's eyes made Conn uncomfortable, and he looked away.

It was true, dammit. He hadn't lied to her. He did love Millie. Maybe not as he once had, but he did love her. She was his wife. The mother of his children. Of course he loved her.

Conn's jaw clenched.

The trouble was, he didn't like her much anymore.

Despite the rocky start, Elizabeth enjoyed herself tremendously. She had forgotten what a pleasure it was to ride. The animal Conn had assigned to her was a white-stockinged roan named Thistle, and she was a joy to ride, as dainty and light on her feet as her name implied. Riding the mare, Elizabeth felt an exhilarating sense of freedom she hadn't known in years.

Her third day in the saddle she was walking her mount between the lead wagon and Conn's position, when Ben rode up beside her.

"Mind some company?"

Half-asleep, her body undulating to the mare's lazy rhythm, she blinked at him slumberously and smiled. "Mmmm, I'd love some."

He grinned. "Keep dozing that way and you're going to

fall." He eyed the sidesaddle and frowned. "I never could figure out how you women could stick to those things, anyway."

A warm, lazy chuckle rippled from Elizabeth, and Ben's hazel eyes darkened. "It does take practice."

"I'll bet."

They exchanged small talk for a while, discussing the unusually long string of good weather they'd had since leaving Charleston, the progress they'd made, the towns they'd seen along the way.

The next one, Ben told her, would be Macon, Georgia, but they wouldn't get there for a day or so. Elizabeth wondered aloud if they would stop, but he didn't think so. Unless they were in need of supplies or repairs, Conn didn't like to tarry. Nor did he make camp close to a town if he could avoid it. Saloons had a way of drawing the men, which invariably led to sore heads and quick tempers the next day.

The conversation lapsed into companionable silence, and for a few moments the only sounds were the soothing clop-clops of the horses' hooves on the dirt track.

A fly buzzed around the mare's ears, and she tossed her head and blew. Ahead, a squirrel scampered across their path, a mockingbird in scolding pursuit. The gentle breeze, redolent with the scent of pine and flowers, lifted the loose ribbons of Elizabeth's sunbonnet, reminding her that they had worked loose. Absently she retied them, and the action drew Ben's gaze to the silky curve of her neck beneath the perky bow.

"I take it you're recovered from your dunking in the river," he said, breaking the silence.

Elizabeth suppressed a shudder. "Yes. I'm fine." Almost, she added silently. Her bruises were fading, and she had recovered her strength, but the fear was still with her. It shamed her to recall how, only the day before, she had abandoned Thistle to Conn's care and huddled in the back of the wagon, shivering and nearly sick with fright when they'd crossed a river. It had been only a small river, and they'd ferried across, but the sight of all that water had filled her with terror.

"In that case, I was wondering if you'd care to go for a walk this evening?"

She stared at him, her expression blank. "A . . . a walk?"

"Yes. Just around the camp. I would have asked you before now, but since you were walking so much every day I figured you'd be too tired. But now that you're riding . . ."

He let the words trail away meaningfully and waited, but Elizabeth was so stunned that she didn't notice. After a moment he raised one eyebrow. "Well, how about it? Would you like to?"

"I, uh . . ." Her first reaction was to decline tactfully, but then she thought of her vow. She swallowed hard. "Y-yes. I'd . . . like that very much."

A slow, satisfied smile curved Ben's mouth and crinkled the corners of his eyes. "Good. I'll be by after supper to get you. Now, though, I'd better get back to the herd." Dipping his head, he touched the brim of his hat with three fingers and rode away toward the back of the train.

Elizabeth gazed after him, thoroughly bemused. She could scarcely believe it. It didn't seem possible. But apparently it was. Unless she had misunderstood, it appeared that Ben Whitelaw was about to come courting.

Elizabeth had scarcely dried the last plate when Ben walked up to the Cavanaugh campfire, which made her wonder if he'd been watching from the shadows.

Conn looked up from the harness he was mending and nodded. "Evening, Ben. You looking for me?"

At the greeting Millie's head snapped up. At once her sulky expression vanished. "Conn Cavanaugh! Goodness, where are your manners? You really must excuse my husband, Mr. Whitelaw," she simpered, fluttering her hands prettily. "He spent too many years in the mountains, I'm afraid. Please, won't you sit down and join us? Jemma, get Mr. Whitelaw a cup of coffee. And a piece of that peach pie, too. I'm sure the poor man is simply famished."

"No, thank you, ma'am, I've already eaten. Anyway, I just stopped by to get Miss Stanton."

"Elizabeth?" Millie's face went blank. "Why, whatever for?"

Conn stopped working on the harness and watched the younger man, his eyes hooded and unreadable in the firelight.

Elizabeth snatched off her apron and pulled her best paisley shawl from the back of the cook wagon where she'd stashed it. Slinging the wrap around her shoulders, she stepped forward.

"Ah, there you are." Ben smiled. "Ready?"

"Yes. I . . . I'm ready, if you are."

Nervously Elizabeth smoothed her skirt and poked at a perfectly secure hairpin, acutely aware of the unnatural quiet that had fallen over the group around the fire.

They had everyone's attention. Joseph, Taw, the children, even Jemma and Isaac, had stopped what they were doing and were watching with unabashed interest.

"Ready for what? Elizabeth, what is going on?" Millie demanded.

"Miss Stanton has kindly accepted my invitation to go for a walk." Ben looked at Conn with unwavering directness. "Unless you have some objection. Perhaps I should have checked with you first, since she's part of your family."

Conn considered him, his face serious and still, as though carved from stone. "Elizabeth is a grown woman. She's free to do whatever she pleases. No, I have no objections, so long as you remember that she's under my protection."

Ben nodded. "I'll remember." He turned to Elizabeth, and Pike growled low in his throat, but at a word from Taw the dog hushed. "Shall we go?"

As the pair walked away Millie demanded under her breath, "Conn, for heaven's sake, why didn't you stop them?"

"As I said, she's a grown woman," he replied tonelessly,

his pensive gaze fixed on Elizabeth's back.

"Well, if you won't put a stop to this nonsense, I certainly will." With an angry swish of her skirt, Millie took a determined step after the strolling couple. Before she could take a second, Conn caught her by the arm and jerked her to a halt.

"You'll do nothing of the kind. Now sit down."

"Conn. That's my cousin out there."

"Yes. And she has a right to live her own life," he said in a grim voice. Then softer, but no less grim, "To find a little happiness for herself. Ben's a good man. If he's what Elizabeth wants, then we have no right to interfere."

"He's five years younger than her. That's . . . that's . . . why, it's obscene, that's what it is."

"It's unimportant. And none of your concern."

"It most certainly is. He can't be serious. What could he possibly see in a thirty-one-year-old spinster like Elizabeth? All she's going to do is make a fool of herself." Millie folded her arms beneath her bosom and set her mouth primly. The very idea. Ben simply couldn't be attracted to Elizabeth! Why . . . why it was ridiculous!

Beneath her skirt, Millie's slippered toe tapped the ground. "Well, I, for one, am not going to stand for it. When Elizabeth gets back I'm going to have a talk with her."

"No, you are not." Millie's eyes flashed at Conn, but his stony expression didn't alter one whit. "If I hear that you've said so much as one word to Elizabeth about this, so help me, I'll turn you over my knee and blister your bare butt."

"How dare you! You can't talk to me that way."

"The hell I can't."

"Ohhh!"

Millie felt as though she were going to explode. She huffed and sputtered for several seconds but couldn't seem to get a word out. Finally, with one last killing glare for her husband, she spun on her heel and stomped away.

* * *

A welter of emotions roiled within Conn as he watched Millie stalk away. Anger, sadness, disappointment, frustration, a strange kind of grief—they were all there, along with other, more complicated feelings he couldn't quite name. But uppermost was despair. For fading dreams, and fading love.

Disillusionment was a bitter pill that stuck in his craw.

Turning away from the sight of Millie's rigid back and angrily swishing skirts, he went back to the fire. He hunkered down and stared into the blaze, wondering how what had seemed so right all those years ago could turn out so wrong.

"Do you want to talk about it, son?"

The quietly voiced question brought Conn out of his reflections with a start. He looked up to find Joseph watching him kindly from the other side of the fire, his eyes full of concern and sympathy. They were alone. A bit surprised, Conn realized that he had been so lost in thought, he hadn't even noticed when the others had turned in.

For several taut moments father and son regarded one another across the flames. Conn was the first to look away. He picked up a poker and stirred the fire. Sparks shot up, crackling and popping. Conn stared at the dancing blaze and felt the burden weighing heavy on his heart.

"What happened to Millie and me, Dad?" His voice came out low, weighted with weary despondence. "When we married we were so in love. And so happy. We had such plans." He glanced up at his father, and his mouth flattened. "Now we're like two harnessed mules pulling in opposite directions."

"You and Millie have been apart a lot, son. It's going to take time for the two of you to adjust to each other."

Conn snorted. "Millie's not interested in adjusting." He looked off into the darkness, then turned his gaze back to Joseph. "It's strange. Sixteen years ago I thought her coquettishness and her headstrong ways were adorable and charming. I was even amused by her self-absorption. She was like a pretty, vivacious child. But now those are the very traits that irritate me the most about her. Now she just seems a willful, selfish, self-centered flirt."

"Perhaps that's because, in many ways, Millie still is a child," Joseph said. "And for that, I'm afraid we're to blame. You and I, Edward and Sarah, even Elizabeth, we've always petted and spoiled her. She's used to always having her own way. It's going to take time and a strong hand to change that."

"That's what I keep telling myself, but . . ."

"Son, I know things are difficult right now, but, for what it's worth, I think you're doing the right thing in taking her west. The right thing for both of you."

Conn stared into the fire. "I hope you're right, Dad," he said quietly. "God, I hope you're right." Because if he weren't the future didn't bear thinking about.

"I am. You'll see." Yawning, Joseph stood up and stretched. He started around the fire, then paused and put his hand on Conn's shoulder. "Just tell me one thing, son. You do still love her, don't you?"

Conn's hesitation lasted only a second. "Not in the same way, but yes, I love her."

"Good. As long as you have that, you can work out your problems." Joseph gave his shoulder a squeeze. "Good night, son."

"Night, Dad."

After his father had gone, Conn sat by the fire, staring pensively through the darkness at nothing. He thought about Millie and his confused feelings, about Riverbend and his hopes for the future. He thought about the past, and the things he'd do different if he had the chance.

And then he thought about Elizabeth, walking out with Ben Whitelaw.

They strolled with slow decorum, staying just inside the light from the circle of campfires that ringed the wagons, not touching. Ben walked with his hands in his trouser pockets,

Elizabeth with her arms crossed at her waist, the long, pointed ends of her fringed shawl dangling almost to the hem of her ankle-length skirt.

The cream-striped plum muslin with its dainty cream lace collar was one of her best dresses. She had stolen a few minutes to wash away the trail dust and change into it before helping Jemma prepare dinner.

Apparently Ben had done the same. His trousers and cotton shirt were spotlessly clean, and every now and then she caught a whiff of Hester's homemade lye soap.

Tonight he wasn't wearing his hat, and the soft breeze ruffled his longish brown hair attractively. She had left her bonnet behind also, and she felt the gentle tug of the wind on the cluster of soft curls cascading down the back of her neck.

The murmur of voices carried through the stillness of the spring night, punctuated now and then by a baby's cry, a trill of laughter, the sharp yip of a dog. From the woods down by the river came the monotonous croaking of a bullfrog. The pungent scents of pine and trampled grass, woodsmoke and fried pork, hung in the cool air.

Out of the corner of her eye, Elizabeth saw a dark shape slinking through the shadows beyond the firelight, and she smiled. Pike was keeping an eye on Ben.

As they approached the next campfire Elizabeth hugged her shawl closer and waved to the woman sitting there, staring at them with her mouth hanging open. "Good evening, Mrs. Haversom," she called politely. "It's a lovely night, isn't it?"

Elmira Haversom nodded. Recalling her manners, she snapped her mouth shut and went back to brushing her daughter's hair, wielding the brush with such vigor that the child cried out. Elmira and William were traveling to Texas with their six children, his parents, and her mother. They all pretended an interest elsewhere, but as Elizabeth and Ben strolled by, the entire family followed their progress with furtive glances.

They had aroused similar reactions at every campfire they'd passed. Some—less polite—had not even bothered to hide their surprise and had stared after them with unabashed interest. More than one of the looks sent their way, particularly by the mothers of marriage-age daughters, had been openly disapproving, even hostile.

"We seem to be attracting a lot of attention," Elizabeth ventured, sending Ben a sidelong glance.

"Mmm. So I noticed."

"I expect we'll be the main topic of conversation tomorrow."

"I guess so." He turned his head and looked at her. "Does that bother you?"

"No . . . yes . . ." She made a little gesture with her hand and smiled weakly. "I suppose I'm a bit self-conscious. That's all."

"Ignore them. They'll find something else to talk about soon."

They walked in silence for a few minutes, then Ben said quietly, "So tell me about yourself."

In response to his gentle probing Elizabeth told him about her life in Charleston, about her father's medical practice and how she'd assisted him, and how, after his death, Millie and Conn had insisted that she make her home with them.

She learned that he was from Virginia, the youngest of seven children, and Hester the oldest. He'd been just four when his sister had married Liam and moved to South Carolina. He hadn't seen her again until about five years ago, when he'd gotten itchy feet and left home to see some of the country. He'd been as far west as St. Louis and north to the Great Lakes.

Last winter he'd stopped by Liam and Hester's farm for another visit before returning home and discovered they were pulling up stakes and moving to Texas. He'd decided on the spot to go with them.

"Do you plan to farm?" Elizabeth asked.

"Maybe. Or I might raise cattle. There's no way to get beef to market, but I've heard there's money to be made in hides." He shrugged. "I might even do some trading, over in Mexico or Santa Fe. But first I'm going to help Hes and Liam build a cabin and get their place going."

Ben was an easy man to talk to. There was a relaxed, uncomplicated charm about him that quickly put Elizabeth at ease. Soon she forgot the age difference and the curious eyes following them. She even forgot her reason for accepting his invitation. She simply strolled along at his side, enjoying the conversation and companionship.

There was a steady, competent air about Ben that made him seem older than his twenty-six years. Experience, Elizabeth supposed—the result of all that roaming. She found herself wondering what had happened to him on those travels that had shaped him into the man he was.

By the time they had made one circuit of the wagons, many of the other travelers had retired. The Cavanaugh campsite was deserted when they passed by, the glowing coals covered with ashes, waiting to be stirred back to life before dawn when the sentries discharged their rifles, signaling the end of sleep.

"Thank you for the walk, Ben." Elizabeth said, coming to a stop beside her wagon. "I enjoyed it."

"Enough to do it again tomorrow evening?"

She smiled. "Yes. I'd like that."

He studied her, his handsome features serious. A respectable three feet separated them, but she could feel the intensity of those warm hazel eyes. Oh yes, she thought, suddenly nervous again. Ben had definitely come courting.

"I'll be by about the same time, then. Good night, Elizabeth."

Returning from his night rounds, Conn saw the couple stop by Elizabeth's wagon and halted in the shadows. Instinct told him that Ben was trustworthy. Still, it wouldn't hurt to make sure. He remained motionless, the strange tightness that had been squeezing his chest for the past hour intensifying as he watched the two talking quietly together.

It was odd, but he'd never thought of Elizabeth in connection with a man before. Had never questioned why she'd never married. She'd simply always been there in the background of his life, a familiar, cherished presence, and he'd taken it for granted that she always would be. That nothing would change.

God, Cavanaugh! And you were angry with Millie for being selfish. He shook his head, his mouth twisting in self-disgust.

Elizabeth would make a wonderful wife and mother.

The thought increased the tightness in his chest. He wondered at that for a moment, then pushed the matter aside, as he'd been doing all evening. If that was what she wanted, then by heaven, he'd see that no one stood in her way.

Glimpsing a movement in the shadows, Conn tensed. He relaxed an instant later when Pike lay down beside him. The dog whined, his yellow-eyed gaze fixed on the couple by the wagon.

"I know, boy, I know," Conn murmured as he watched Ben walk away. "It's tough to let go."

Chapter 7

"I tell you, you're making a fool of yourself."

"I'm very sorry you feel that way."

For an instant Millie blazed with anger at Elizabeth's calm reply, but with an effort she softened her expression. "Oh, dear heart, don't you see? I'm just worried that your reputation will suffer. Everyone is already talking. They're all positively scandalized." She paused and gave Elizabeth an ingenious look. "I mean, dearest, really. The man is much younger than you."

"I know that, Millie. But it doesn't seem to bother Ben, so I don't see why it should matter to anyone else."

"Does that mean you're going to keep seeing him?"

"Yes."

"Well." Millie's mouth drew up in a tight pucker. "Then there isn't anything left for me to say. If you end up with a broken heart, just don't say I didn't warn you," she couldn't resist adding as her parting salvo.

Elizabeth smiled sadly. She knew that Ben would never break her heart. Only Conn could do that.

She quickly discovered, however, that her cousin had been right about one thing: the women were talking about her.

Many thought the whole thing romantic and voiced the opinion that it was about time a fine woman like Elizabeth was wed, but Agatha and her cronies were openly critical. They tut-tutted over the age difference, denounced the relationship as scandalous, and speculated smugly on its early demise.

"Pay no attention to the old biddies," Hester advised as Elizabeth walked beside her, leading Thistle. "Agatha is just jealous that he picked you and not her precious Lisa. That brazen little hussy has been throwing herself at him shamelessly." She snorted. "I tell you, that girl is like a bitch in heat. Poor Ben can hardly turn around without practically falling over her."

At any other time Elizabeth would have blushed at Hester's blunt comment, but she was so preoccupied that she barely noticed. "You don't mind, then? About Ben and me, I mean?"

"That depends." Hester regarded her gravely. "A few years' difference in age don't mean diddly. It's feelings that matter. There's no one I'd rather have as a sister than you." Her gaze flickered toward the front of the train to Conn, then settled shrewdly on Elizabeth. "But only if you can give him the love he deserves," she added quietly.

In the middle of June, a little over a week after Ben began courting Elizabeth, Patrick Conlin, in an attempt to save the fifty-cents-a-head ferry fee on stock, tried to swim his mules across the wide Flint River and drowned.

Hardly had the last shovel full of dirt been spread on his grave than dissension flared over what to do about his widow and daughter.

Agatha and Karl and a few others insisted they be left at the next town.

"With no man to see to things, that dilapidated rig will fall apart before we reach the Mississippi," Agatha argued. "They'll be a burden on us all."

"That's right," someone else chimed in. "Besides, how's a lone woman and child going to work a farm?"

"Me an' my maw done it," Taw said, speaking up for the first time. " 'Sides, it don't strike me right t' jist abandon the poor woman."

Agatha sniffed. "If you ask me, that trash should have been kicked off the train long ago."

"No one's asking you, Mrs. Guetterman." Conn's voice cut like cold steel. His eyes glittered dangerously, daring her to say more. Agatha wisely refrained, though the effort obviously cost her. His hard gaze swept the others slowly. "As wagon master, the decision is mine to make, and I intend to abide by Mrs. Conlin's wishes. Is that clear?"

Averted gazes and the shuffle of feet were the only replies.

Margaret chose to stay with the train. "We don't rightly got nowheres else t' go," she told Conn listlessly. "Leastways, with land me an' Faith can grow enough food so we won't starve."

Conn accepted her decision without comment, but when he walked away Elizabeth hurried after him. "Conn, how will she manage, all alone in the wilderness?"

"We'll help her out all we can. If that isn't enough, we'll find something for her to do at Riverbend." His mouth set, and he raked a hand through his hair. Absently Elizabeth noted it need trimming again. "I'll be damned if I'll leave a helpless widow with a child to raise and another on the way to fend for herself."

Elizabeth watched him walk away, a sweet ache in her chest as her heart overflowed with pride and love for him. She wondered how she could ever stop caring when he kept doing things that only made her love him all the more.

As though the death had signaled the end of their good fortune, the slow drizzle that had begun during the funeral continued unabated, further dampening the spirits of the subdued travelers. The road quickly became a quagmire. They made such slow progress that Conn called a halt an hour before their usual quitting time.

The men rigged canvas shelters to cover the cook fires, but there was little dry wood to be found. Even when they managed to get a feeble fire going, the damp logs sputtered and popped, and blowing rain drenched food and people alike. They finally gave up, and everyone grabbed some jerky and hardtack and bowls of curds and whey and crawled into the wagons and tents.

The bad weather continued without letup, and illness and accidents abounded. In less than a week Dr. Cavanaugh and Elizabeth set three broken bones, treated a severe burn, stitched up seven cuts, reset a dislocated shoulder, strapped two sprained ankles and a wrenched knee, and treated countless cases of dysentery, croup, chilblains, and head colds.

Finally, after four days, the rain lessened to a fine mist that hung in the air like a gray veil. For once there were no new calamities or sickness to deal with, and Dr. Cavanaugh took advantage of the respite to go out with the hunting party.

Scarcely an hour later Elizabeth was summoned to Margaret Conlin's wagon. She found the woman in bed, moaning and writhing in pain, her bony hands clutching her swollen abdomen. Even in the dim light Elizabeth could see the beads of sweat on her face and the glazed, desperate look in her eyes.

Faith sat huddled in a corner, her pale eyes round with fear and fixed on her mother. Doing her best to reassure the child, Elizabeth quickly bundled her up and handed her out to one of the riders with instructions to take her to Hester.

A quick examination bore out Elizabeth's worse fear: the baby wasn't due for three months, but Margaret was in labor.

That the woman would almost certainly lose her baby was bad enough, but what filled Elizabeth with an icy feeling of dread was the possibility that she might lose her life as well. Margaret was pitifully thin and work worn, and her body bore evidence of the physical abuse she'd endured at the hands of her husband. Elizabeth doubted the poor woman had the strength or the will to survive the ordeal that most likely lay ahead of her.

When Conn was informed of Margaret's condition, he halted

the train. They had no sooner made camp in the marshy meadow than Jemma came bustling back to help. All day the two of them tended the tortured woman. Elizabeth did what she could, but the pains grew steadily more severe, and with each passing hour Margaret's strength dwindled.

The gloom of early evening had begun to settle over the camp when the hunters finally returned. Elizabeth was relieved to have Dr. Cavanaugh take over, but his efforts met with no more success than hers. Around nine that evening Margaret gave birth to a tiny, stillborn son, and ten minutes later she quietly passed away.

Exhausted and depressed, Elizabeth stepped from the wagon after helping Jemma prepare the body for burial to find the rain had stopped—temporarily, at least. Low-hanging clouds still scudded across the night sky, and the air was heavy with moisture and the smell of dank earth. Sighing, Elizabeth arched her back and trudged toward her own wagon, her shoes making squishing noises in the soggy ground. She wondered if anyone had told Faith yet that her mother had died. Poor little girl. What would happen to her now?

Elizabeth arrived at the Cavanaugh campfire to find a small crowd gathering there discussing what was to be done with Faith. Most of the married couples already had big families, and no one seemed anxious to take on another child, particularly not the scrawny, unappealing offspring of Patrick and Margaret Conlin.

When no one volunteered, Hester looked around at the reluctant faces and gave a resigned sigh. "Liam and me will take her if no one else wants her. We're a tight fit now with five of our own, but I guess one more won't matter much."

Liam nodded. "I ain't tickled about having another mouth to feed right now, but I'll not see the poor little mite go to no orphanage."

"Well . . ." Agatha pursed her lips and considered the matter. "I suppose I could take her on as a hired girl. She'd have to work for her keep. I won't have any slackers in my house," she declared with a self-righteous huff. "Of course, while I'm training her she won't earn any wages, but if she works hard and doesn't give me any sass, I'll see that she has a roof over her head."

"No!"

The sharp exclamation drew every eye in the crowd toward Elizabeth. She flashed them an anxious look and rushed on. "That won't be necessary. I'll take Faith."

The words had just tumbled out, but the moment they did she knew it was what she wanted.

"You!"

"But you're not even married!"

"Elizabeth, for heaven's sake, don't be ridiculous," Millie snapped. Her mouth twisted at the absurdity of the suggestion.

"You don't understand. I want to do this."

"Now, now, my dear, let's not be hasty." Speaking with his usual pious condescension and favoring the foot he'd put a bullet through, Harve Sillsby limped forward and took her hand. "I applaud your Christian charity, and I'm sure you mean well, but if you'll just give the matter a bit more thought, I'm sure you'll see that what you're suggesting just won't do."

"Harve's right," someone from the back of the group chimed in. "A spinster ain't got no business with a young'un."

Elizabeth withdrew her hand from Harve's. Her gaze moved slowly around the crowd, her soft gray eyes steady and unyielding. "Why not? I don't have much, I'll admit, but I can give her the love and attention she needs. Except for Hester and Liam, that's more than any of you are willing to do."

"Humph! What her kind needs is a hickory switch applied to her backside and someone who'll teach her the value of work. It doesn't pay to coddle shiftless riffraff."

"She's just a child, Agatha." Elizabeth's eyes rebuked silently, and Agatha's chins quivered with barely suppressed anger.

The mere thought of the frightened orphan at the mercy of the Guettermans made Elizabeth cringe. She'd seen how they treated their hired girl. The poor cowed creature worked from morning till night without a break and endured constant tongue-lashings and switchings from both Agatha and Lisa. She was only fifteen, but after two years of slaving for Agatha and Karl and their spoiled daughter, the girl looked fifty.

"Well, I won't have it," Millie put in. "You are not going to bring that filthy little urchin into my home, and that's all there is to it."

"That's enough, Millie. If Elizabeth wants the child, then she shall have her."

"Conn! You can't mean that. You can't want your own children to live under the same roof with the daughter of those low-class people."

"None of us can help who we're born to, Millie. And as far as I know, it's no sin to be poor. Now the matter is settled."

"Oh! I can't believe this." Millie turned on Elizabeth with her hands planted on her hips, eyes blazing. "See what you've done. Well, I hope you're satisfied. But just let me tell you something, cousin. If you do this, you can forget Ben Whitelaw. He won't want you with that brat hanging on your skirts."

Faith took the news of her mother's death with a stoicism that wrung Elizabeth's heart.

After her insistence on taking the child to raise, the task of breaking the news to her had fallen naturally to Elizabeth. Hester volunteered to go with her, but she refused her friend's offer. Elizabeth had noticed that Faith grew nervous when confronted by adults and for that reason felt it best that she tell her alone. But as Elizabeth knelt before the pathetic little girl, she yearned for Hester's comforting presence beside her.

"My maw's dead?" Faith stared at Elizabeth, her pale green eyes round and unblinking.

Elizabeth had found her huddled in a corner of the Grimeses'
wagon in a tiny wedge of space between two trunks, scrunched
up in a ball. According to Hester, she'd barely budged from
the spot since that morning. When Elizabeth had entered, the
child had gotten warily to her feet, and now she stood with
her back pressed to the canvas as though she could somehow
melt into it and make herself invisible.

"I'm sorry, sweetheart, but yes . . . she is."

Faith didn't move. She just stood there, staring back with
those big eyes. Finally Elizabeth saw the child's throat work,
and her own tightened painfully. After a moment Faith's chin
wobbled and her eyes filled.

"I'm so sorry." Elizabeth held out her hands, but the girl
made no move to take them.

A tear bulged over Faith's lower lid, hovered, then plopped
onto her cheek. Another quickly followed, and another.

"Oh, Faith." Unable to stand it a second longer, Elizabeth
lunged forward, intent on folding the child into her embrace,
but when she reached for her Faith cried out and recoiled,
throwing up her arms to shield her face and head.

Shocked, Elizabeth retreated at once. After a moment Faith
lowered her guard, but she kept a cautious watch.

For the next several moments Elizabeth could only kneel
there, helpless, and watch the child's silent grief. She didn't
cry aloud. Her face didn't crumple. She didn't even sniff. She
simply stood there in that cramped space and stared at Elizabeth as tears trickled down and dripped from her pointed
little chin.

Elizabeth had never witnessed anything so heartrending in
her life. Tears filled her own eyes, and she felt as though she
had an iron wedge stuck in her throat. Her chest hurt so she
could barely breathe. She ached to take the child in her arms
and rock her against her breast and croon words of comfort,
but Faith's reaction told her that her touch would not be
welcomed.

Finally, after an interminable time, the child swallowed hard, wiped her nose with her sleeve, and announced "I cain't drive the wagon."

Elizabeth blinked. "Wh-what?"

"I said I cain't drive no wagon. Cain't hitch the mules neither."

"Why, no, of course you can't." Elizabeth was still trying to puzzle out what was behind the statement when Faith blurted:

"Then how'm I gonna get to Texas? Maw said Miz Guetterman and them others would leave us behind if we didn't do for ourselves."

"Oh, sweetheart, no. You don't have to worry about driving your wagon. Mr. Cavanaugh will have one of the hands do it. Or perhaps he'll sell it for you in the next town."

The attempt at reassurance failed miserably. If anything, Faith grew more upset. "But if he sells the wagon, where'll I sleep? That's the onliest thing we got."

"Oh, Faith." The forlorn murmur was all Elizabeth could manage for a moment. Her heart felt as though it would crack wide open. That this child—that any child—had been dealt so many cruel blows by life that she expected nothing else was unspeakable.

As she looked at the girl, so scrawny and unappealing, with her greasy hair and her ragged clothes and her grime and tear-streaked cheeks, and her beautiful green eyes that seemed too big for the pinched little face they dominated, Elizabeth felt a fierce protectiveness surge up inside her. And there, kneeling on the rough plank floor of a wagon, in a soggy field somewhere in the middle of the Georgia wilderness, for the second time in her life, Elizabeth fell deeply, unreservedly, irrevocably, in love.

A wellspring of emotion bubbled up within, swelling her chest full to bursting. Instinctively she started to raise her hand to stroke the girl's cheek, but she caught herself in time.

She swallowed hard and had to clear her throat twice before she could speak, and then her voice came out weak and wobbly. "Faith, dear, you're not going to be left to fend for yourself. I want you to live with me."

Faith stared at her solemnly, a new wariness in her eyes. "How come?"

"Well, because you need someone to look after you, and because I have no children and I've always wanted to have a daughter. You're alone and so am I, mostly. So I thought we could keep each other company." She waited for a reaction, and when none was forthcoming she tipped her head to one side. "Do you think you'd like that?"

"I dunno."

"Well then . . ." Assuming a brisk air, Elizabeth stood up and shook out her skirt. "Why don't we try it for a while and see. We'll just go get a nightgown and a change of clothes from your wagon, then we'll go to mine and I'll show you where you'll be sleeping."

Faith didn't budge. "I ain't got no nightgown. I sleep in my shift."

"Oh, I see. Well, that's fine."

"An' these is the onliest clothes I got."

Elizabeth tried to hide her shock. Lord have mercy. If the child had only the clothes she stood up in, what did she do on washday? But then Elizabeth glanced at the soiled and tattered dress and realized that it had probably never known soap and water.

"Oh. Well we're all ready, then, aren't we?" she said brightly. She held out her hand to the girl, but Faith cringed back. Pretending not to notice, Elizabeth let her arm drop and started for the back of the wagon. "Come along, then. I haven't had anything to eat since morning, and Hester told me you haven't either. We'll go pilfer something form the cook wagon before we go to bed."

Elizabeth stopped by the back opening and looked around, but Faith still had not moved.

"Them others—they ain't gonna want me there."

"Oh, sweetheart, no! You mustn't think that. The Cavanaughs are wonderful people. They'll be delighted to have you join them. You'll see."

Much to Elizabeth's dismay, however, her assessment proved overly optimistic. Conn, Taw, and Joseph welcomed Faith into their circle warmly, but Millie pointedly ignored her. Ian watched her with suspicion from a safe distance, not quite sure what to make of this new child in their midst. Rachel took her cue from her mother and acted as though Faith were contaminated with the pox. Even Jemma and Isaac were faintly contemptuous of the poor white child.

As luck would have it, things could not have gotten off to a worse start. The next night, all during the first evening meal that Faith shared with the Cavanaughs, Millie flirted outrageously with one of the hands, a cocky young man named Yancy Pollard, who was either too stupid or too full of himself to exercise discretion.

Up until then Millie had favored all the men with her coy smiles and teasing comments, making of it a harmless game, which, if he sometimes found it annoying, Conn tolerated. But that night Millie turned the full force of her charm on Yancy, and suddenly there was nothing innocent or amusing about the flirtation. And the longer it went on, the tighter Conn's jaw set.

All those around the campfire, even the children, felt the tension building. Everyone grew quiet and concentrated on their meal until the only two talking were Millie and Yancy. The other hands finished eating as quickly as they could and left for safer ground. When they had all gone, Conn walked over and stood in front of Millie and the brash hired hand.

"It's getting late, Pollard," he announced in a flat voice. His eyes bored into the younger man, cold as steel.

"Conn!"

Yancy grinned. "Oh, that's okay, I'm not sleepy."

"Yes, you are."

"Conn! How dare—"

"Shut up, Millie." His gaze never left Yancy. "Mr. Pollard has better things to do than flirt with a married woman. Don't you, Mr. Pollard?"

At first Yancy's look taunted, but under Conn's steady regard his cocky grin began to fade around the edges. By the time he'd scrambled to his feet, it had collapsed.

"Sure thing, Mr. Cavanaugh." Twisting his hat round and round in his hand, he backed away. "Well, good night, everybody."

The instant he disappeared from sight, Millie jumped up, her face wild with outrage. "How could you be so rude!"

"I'll be a helluva lot ruder if you don't stop carrying on the way you did tonight. If you're trying to get back at me for bringing you west, you'd better find another way. Because I'm warning you, Millie, you're playing with fire. I won't have my wife acting like a bitch in heat."

Millie made a strangled sound and drew back her hand to slap him. Before she could complete the swing Faith jumped up and streaked away.

"Faith! No, come back!" Elizabeth cried, and took a step after her, but the darkness had already swallowed her up. "Oh, dear." Wringing her hands, Elizabeth looked around at the others. "We have to find her. She's upset. She may get lost in the dark, or . . . or hurt herself."

Conn had caught his wife's wrist before she could land the blow, but at Elizabeth's words he quickly released her, almost slinging her arm aside. "C'mon. Let's go." Motioning to the other two men, he started after Elizabeth, who was already hurrying away in the direction Faith had taken.

In the end it was Taw who found her. "Blamed if'n she weren't hidin' up a tree," the old mountain man said with a chuckle when he returned her to Elizabeth. To Elizabeth's surprise, Faith was holding on to Taw's horny old paw. It was the first time she'd ever seen the child voluntarily touch anyone.

When Taw lifted her up onto the tailgate, she scooted past Elizabeth as though she expected a blow and disappeared into the wagon without ever once making eye contact.

"Now don't you fret none, Missy," he said gently when he saw Elizabeth's worried look. "That little gal's like a wild thing what's been mistreated, but now that she's got you t' love 'er she'll be tame as a pup afore you know it."

"Oh, I hope you're right, Taw." Elizabeth cast a worried glance inside the wagon. Faith had already stripped down to her dingy chemise and was curled up on the bed. "I do so hope you're right."

Chapter 8

Millie paced beside the wagon, the anger that had become her constant companion simmering inside her. Never in her life had she felt so frustrated, so powerless. Nothing—absolutely nothing—was going her way!

And it was all Conn's fault, she told herself. Conn's and Elizabeth's.

Conn had turned just plain mean—always ordering her around, refusing to do what she wanted, siding with Elizabeth. Millie kicked a clump of grass, her small fists clenching. It wasn't fair!

She hated this endless trip. She hated being around these awful people. She hated having nothing interesting to do. Oh, what she wouldn't give for just one ball or garden party. Even one of Emiline Wilkins's dreary teas would be better than this.

Today was even more boring than usual because they'd had to make camp early. All because that stupid Harve Sillsby had not had sense enough to bring along a spare axle. And, of course, she thought irritably, as always, everyone expected Conn to see to the repairs. He and Harve and several of the other men had ridden ahead to Montgomery for a replacement.

Millie aimed another vicious kick at a clump of grass. No doubt they were all taking advantage of the opportunity. That very minute they were probably swilling down spirits in some low grog shop. Meanwhile she was stuck in the middle of nowhere with no one to talk to and absolutely nothing to do.

Her resentful gaze fell on Jemma, who was bent over the steaming washpot, stirring the clothes with a stick. All around the camp the other women were also busy, washing clothes, mending, sweeping out wagons, hauling bedding out to air in the sunshine.

Rachel emerged from the woods and meandered toward their wagons, looking as out of sorts as her mother felt. Hurrying over to her, Millie called, "Rachel, have you seen Elizabeth?"

Her daughter's sulky mouth twisted. "What do you want her for? You're with her all the time."

"Never you mind, young lady just tell me where she is."

"She's down at the creek. With Faith," Rachel tacked on in a sneering singsong.

Millie's jaw clenched, the resentment she felt mirroring Rachel's. "Oh, for heaven's sake!" Irritably she spun on her heel and stomped toward the creek. Elizabeth was always with that scruffy brat. Or else with Ben.

That was another thing. Ben hadn't been the least bit put off when Elizabeth took in that awful child. If anything, he seemed to admire her all the more. It had been almost two weeks, and he still came by every evening. Half the time they even took Faith with them on their strolls. It was infuriating!

The path to the creek was a narrow animal trail that wound through the woods. Splintered shafts of late afternoon sunlight angled through the tall pines and hardwoods, glittering with a universe of dancing, golden dust motes and creating patterns of mottled light and shadows among the bracken. Patches of tiny star-shaped blossoms grew in shady spots, and tender, verdant shoots pushed their way up through the layers of decaying leaves and pine needles that blanketed the forest floor. Someone had stepped on a pineapple weed at the side of the path, and its fruity scent blended with the sweet perfume of honeysuckle, the fecund aromas of leaf mold and rich, moist earth. High overhead a songbird trilled its jubilant notes.

Millie marched along the path, irritably slapping aside

branches and low-hanging vines, oblivious to it all. She was so caught up in her ire, she didn't see Ben until they came face to face around a curve and almost collided.

"Ben! Oh, my. I do declare, you nearly scared the wits out of me." Fluttering her hand against her breast, she smiled and batted her lashes, every vestige of anger gone from her face.

"Sorry, ma'am."

He stepped aside to let her pass, but Millie didn't budge. Now that she finally had him to herself, she wasn't about to let him rush off. "I see you've been fishing," she said, nodding toward the loaded stringer he carried.

"Yes, ma'am."

He had also bathed, she realized, though of course a lady wasn't supposed to notice, let alone mention, such things to a man. Still, it was impossible to miss the scent of lye soap that clung to his skin, or the way the water had darkened his hair to almost black, or the tracks left in the thick strands where he'd combed it away from his face with his fingers. A sultry smile began to form, and she edged closer.

"You know, Ben, I'm glad we bumped into each other this way. We really should get better acquainted."

"You mean because of Elizabeth?"

"Hardly." Millie gave a trill of laughter and flapped her hand, then let it come to rest against his chest. Ever so slowly, one fingernail raked against the coarse cotton shirt. She gave him a provocative look from beneath her lashes. "I mean, everyone knows you're not *really* serious about my cousin."

His hand covered hers, and Millie experienced a burst of triumphant elation, but when she looked up, the smile that had been forming on her lips collapsed.

Removing her hand from his chest, Ben stepped back. "If you'll excuse me, ma'am, I'd better get these fish to Hester before they spoil."

He was going to walk away and leave her. Just like that. The realization hit Millie like a slap in the face, and shock and outrage vied for supremacy. No man had ever rejected her. She certainly wasn't going to stand still for such shabby treatment from a homespun clod like Ben Whitelaw.

"Don't let me keep you." With a little nod of dismissal, she moved as though to walk around him, took one step, and pretended to trip.

"Oh!"

At the startled cry the fish hit the dirt path and Ben's arms shot out. He caught her in midstumble, and when he pulled her upright she stood within the circle of his embrace, leaning weakly against his chest. "Are you all right?"

"Yes," she said in a throaty voice. "I am now." She raised her head and looked at him, her eyes slumberous and sultry beneath half-lowered lids as her hands slid upward and encircled his neck. Her lips parted invitingly and lifted toward his. "Kiss me, Ben," she whispered. "Kiss me."

"There," Elizabeth announced, pulling the comb smoothly through Faith's wet hair. "All the tangles are out. Now that wasn't so bad, was it?"

"No, ma'am." The child's mumbled reply was almost lost in the folds of the towel wrapped around her. Standing with her back to Elizabeth, head lowered, bony shoulders hunched, she clutched the soft cloth in both hands beneath her chin.

When Elizabeth had moved Faith into her wagon two weeks ago, the first thing she'd wanted to do was clean her up, but she hadn't counted on the child's ingrained fear and distrust of adults. Conditioned to expect abuse—at the very least neglect—she had met all Elizabeth's overtures with suspicion, flinched at any sudden move, and resisted anything new or strange. It had taken a week to coax her into the slipper tub, and still another before she would allow Elizabeth to shampoo her hair, and only then if they did the deed in the creek. Elizabeth suspected the reason was that Faith felt she would be able to run if the experience proved painful.

The little girl's appalling condition had shocked Elizabeth the first time she'd seen her unclothed. She was so pitifully thin that her ribs resembled the tines on a hay rake. Each joint—shoulders, elbows, knees, wrists—protruded grotesquely from sticklike limbs. Worst of all, she had been covered with livid bruises and was so dirty and reeking such a stench that Elizabeth wondered if the poor thing had ever had a bath.

Elizabeth surveyed her handiwork with satisfaction. Faith was still thin, but the bruises had faded, and now that the layers of grime had been removed, her skin had a rosy glow. Her hair had appeared to be a lank, dull brown, but vigorous scrubbings had stripped away the grease and dirt and revealed a silky mass of rich auburn curls. Already a few strands were glinting with fire and coiling softly about her face as they dried in the sunlight.

"Oh, sweetheart, you're going to look beautiful. As soon as your hair dries I'll brush it into long curls for you."

"Really?" Faith looked back over her shoulder, her pale green eyes full of doubt as they searched Elizabeth's face.

Elizabeth laughed. "Yes, really. But first you'd better get dressed." Smiling, she watched the child look around, her brow puckering.

"Where're my clothes? I put 'um right there on that rock when I took 'um off." She scurried about the bank, getting anxious, and Elizabeth's heart clenched with pity as she realized the child was afraid she would be punished for losing her only set of clothing.

"Don't worry, Faith," she said gently. "Your things were dirty, so I put them to soak, there in the creek." She pointed to the water's edge, where the ragged garments, held down by a fist-size rock, waved beneath the surface. Actually they were so grimy and worn, they were not even suited for rags. Elizabeth had every intention of conveniently "forgetting" them.

Openmouthed, Faith stared down at the submerged clothing. "But what am I gonna wear?" she wailed.

"I made you some new things."

Faith's head came up, and she whirled around. Her eyes rounded in disbelief. "You did?"

"Well, they're not *new*, exactly. I cut down one of my dresses. And some underthings, too." She waved toward a large rock. "They're over there."

Faith stared, transfixed, at the pile of neatly folded clothing. She glanced at Elizabeth, then sidled over to take a closer look. Hesitantly she touched the green plaid gingham, trailed her fingers over the lace-trimmed petticoat, the embroidered ruffle edging the legs of the soft cotton pantalets.

Her eyes, filled with wonder, again sought her benefactor. "These are really for me?"

"Yes, darling, they are. Now why don't you put them on and let's see how they fit."

Faith didn't need a second urging. The towel hit the dirt with a plop. Hitching her bare buttocks against the rock, she pulled on the pantalets and cinched up the drawstring waist. She bent over to admire the new drawers, her pointed little chin jabbing her breastbone. Each vertebra stuck out along her spine like a white china knob. She looked up at Elizabeth with shining eyes. "Ain't they somethin'?"

Elizabeth's smile held a trace of sadness. Such joy over simple hand-me-downs. That they were, no doubt, the best garments the child had ever owned wrenched her heart.

"Here, let me help you with the rest."

Faith shot to her feet and held up her arms as Elizabeth dropped the cotton chemise over her head. Next came the petticoats, then the dress.

It was merely a sturdy gingham plaid of green, brown, and yellow, but as Elizabeth fastened the hidden hooks and eyes down the front placket, Faith ran her palms down over the bodice and skirt with something akin to reverence. "Ain't it pretty?"

"You look lovely, sweetheart, but we're not through yet."

From Hester Elizabeth had gotten a pair of her daughter's outgrown shoes and white cotton stockings. As she pulled them from the pocket of her apron, Faith's eyes grew round and her mouth dropped open.

Once she was fully dressed, Faith stared down at herself and touched the lace trim on the collar and cuffs with awe. Sticking out one shod foot, then the other, she turned them this way and that. She looked up, her chin quivering. "I ain't never had nothing so pretty before."

Blinking rapidly, Elizabeth swallowed the knot of emotion that threatened to choke her. She held out her hand, and as Faith took it Elizabeth smiled. At least they had made that much progress. "Come on. Let's go show Taw."

Hand in hand they walked downstream, Faith with her enthralled gaze on her new finery, Elizabeth staring straight ahead, her heart full to bursting. We're a fine pair, she thought with a wobbly smile. A spinster and a neglected little soul no one wanted. Savoring the feel of the small, warm palm against hers, she looked down at the top of Faith's shining hair. Maybe that's what makes it feel so right.

They found Taw where they'd left him, sitting on the creek bank fishing while he acted as their lookout.

"Well, now, would you lookee here," he said, slapping his knee when he saw them approaching. "I swan, girl, if'n you ain't 'bout the purtiest thing I seen in a month o' Sundays."

"Miss Elizabeth made me some new clothes," she said shyly, but her chest puffed with pride and she turned in a slow circle for Taw's inspection.

"Is that what it is? Well, 'pears t' me you look right spit-shined, too." Leaning closer, he screwed up his face and squinted at her. "Where'd all that red hair come from?"

Faith giggled and hid her face in Elizabeth's skirt, and the two adults looked at each other in astonishment. It was the first time either had heard the child laugh.

Elizabeth felt that what progress she had made with Faith was due largely to Taw. The old man had a way with children and wild creatures, and Faith was a bit of both. Over the past two weeks he had spent a lot of time with them, and a special bond had begun to form between the old trapper and the skittish girl.

Leaving her in Taw's care, Elizabeth headed back to the wagons to give Jemma a hand. As she followed the path through the woods, an amused smile played about her lips. Faith, exercising a touching, almost comic, fastidiousness, had settled on a rock in the sunshine to let her hair dry. As Elizabeth had walked away she'd looked back to see her arranging the full gingham skirt around her with the meticulous care one would give a coronation robe.

A gently determined gleam entered Elizabeth eyes. When Conn returned she would ask him if they could stop in Montgomery long enough to purchase some dress goods and stockings for Faith.

The sound of voices alerted her to the presence of others on the trail just ahead. Elizabeth recognized the voices at almost the same time the pair came into view, and the sight of her cousin standing so close to Ben caused her feet to falter. They halted altogether an instant later when Millie touched Ben's chest. As her words registered all Elizabeth could do was stand there as though turned to stone.

". . . knows you aren't *really* serious about my cousin."

Numbed, Elizabeth heard it all, watched it all: Ben's withdrawal, Millie's reaction, the artful charade that sent her pitching forward into his arms, the provocative invitation of twining arms and lips raised in sultry demand.

The strange, detached iciness that held Elizabeth did not crack even when Ben grasped Millie's wrists and put her from him.

"No." He said the word flatly, his gaze searing her with cold contempt.

Millie's eyes widened. "No? You can't mean that."

"Oh, I mean it all right. I don't dally with married women, Mrs. Cavanaugh. But even if I did, in your case, I wouldn't be interested. I admire and respect your husband too much to dishonor him that way. Besides," he added with deliberate insult, "I don't happen to find you attractive."

"Oh! You . . . you . . . Ohhhh!" Jerking free of his grasp, Millie whirled and took off down the trail in a huffy march that made her petticoats dance. When she had gone perhaps ten feet, Ben called her name. She halted and turned around, a smug smile on her face, but his next words wiped it away.

"You're mistaken, you know," he said quietly. "I'm very serious about Elizabeth."

This time Millie almost flew down the path.

Ben watched until she was out of sight. Then he picked up the stringer of fish, shook off the dirt, and ambled after her.

Still rooted to the spot, Elizabeth squeezed her eyes shut as the numbling iciness began to melt and pain consumed her.

Millie was in such a blind rage, she was unaware of the man, though he'd been watching her approach for a full minute before she slammed into him.

"Easy, there." Garth laughed and grasped her upper arms to steady them both.

"Mr. Lathom! I'm sorry, I was thinking about something else and didn't see you." Her bruised ego still smarting, she failed to notice that he didn't release her.

"Well, whatever it was, I suggest you forget it." Boldly he smoothed his thumb over the wedge of frown lines between her eyebrows. "It's a shame to mar such a pretty face with a scowl."

The compliment soothed Millie's ruffled feathers, and for the first time she gave him her full attention. Bit by bit her expression changed from fury to speculation as she noted his wolfish grin and the daring way he was looking at her breasts.

Preening, she returned the audacious look. "I agree, Mr. Lathom—"

"Please, call me Garth."

"Very well—Garth. But in order to take my mind off that awful ma— uh, off my problems, I would need a diversion." She looked at him from beneath her lashes, her smile coquettish, and lightly touched the back of his wrist with her fingertips. "Do you have any suggestions?"

The dark eyes glittered down at her with a dangerous sensual heat, and she felt a little thrill of fear and excitement race over her skin. A slow, rakish grin grew as he extended his arm. "Why don't we take a little walk in the woods?"

"Why, Garth Lathom. You know very well that wouldn't be proper," she scolded, giving his arm a playful rap.

"Maybe not. But I guarantee it will be a very . . . pleasurable diversion."

Millie considered him severely for a moment before allowing the corners of her mouth to curve upward. "Very well. But you must promise to be good."

"Oh, I'll be good. You can count on it, sweetheart."

Chapter 9

Turning down a lesser trail that bisected the path, Garth led Millie deeper into the woods where the honeysuckle vines grew thick, tumbling over bushes and twining sinuously about tree trunks, filling the air with their sweet scent.

Millie chattered happily and clung to his arm. Every now and then she let the side of her breast rub against him. She dismissed the little warning voice that told her she was playing with fire. She was fed up with being ignored and having her wishes pushed aside. Here was a man who appreciated her beauty, who wanted her company, a man who looked at her with a flattering hunger in his eyes. Garth might not be like those tame, refined gentlemen who had danced to her tune in Charleston, but she could handle him. After all, he was only a man.

Millie knew perfectly well he was going to try to kiss her. As they stepped into a small clearing she was debating whether or not she would let him when he snatched her into arms and covered her mouth with his.

At first Millie was too stunned to move. When at last she regained her wits and began to struggle, he simply ignored her puny efforts. Grinding his mouth cruelly against hers, he forced her lips apart and shoved his tongue deep into her mouth. Millie went rigid.

The kiss was hot and wet, a rough, rapacious ravishment that shocked her to her core. As it went on he widened his stance, gripped her buttocks, and lifted her against the bulge at his crotch. He thrust against her obscenely, groaning low in his throat with each jerk of his pelvis.

At last he released her mouth, and Millie gasped, then gasped again when his teeth nipped painfully along the side of her neck. "G-Garth! Stop this!" she demanded, shoving at his shoulders. "Stop at once!"

His low laugh rumbled against her skin. Her eyes widened at the sound. "Don't play the high-and-mighty lady with me," he growled. He thrust hard against her and laughed again at her whimper. "You want this, you hot little bitch. I've been watching you twitch your tail at me and every other man under sixty. You've been begging for it, and now I'm going to give it to you."

To Millie's shock, the words sent a jolt of excitement through her.

He dragged her to the ground and pinned her with his body. Capturing her wrists, he stretched her arms above her head and held them there with one hand while he worked open the tiny hooks down the front of her dress.

Millie bucked her hips and glared. Garth grinned.

"Let . . . me . . . *up!* If you don't, I swear I'll . . . I'll scream."

"Go ahead. No one can hear you. You'll be screaming with pleasure before I'm through, anyway."

He shoved the bodice aside and jerked down the thin chemise covering her breasts. His nostrils flared and his dark eyes burned as he studied the large brown nipples. He took one between his thumb and forefinger and pinched it, and Millie sucked in her breath. He tugged on the nub, then rolled it between his fingers and smiled with satisfaction as he watched her eyes glaze. "You like it rough, don't you, baby?"

"No," she insisted breathlessly, moving her head from side to side, but it was a lie and they both knew it. A new and thrilling, almost painful tension was coiling inside her, and the secret place between her thighs felt hot and swollen.

It couldn't be, she told herself. She didn't like sex. She had never liked sex. Conn had always been gentle and loving with her, but she had merely tolerated the act. Garth was crude, his touch harsh. But, oh, there was something so unbearably exciting about his rough handling.

Chuckling, Garth bent and took a nipple into his mouth. He nipped with his teeth and sucked strongly, drawing on her soft flesh with no hint of tenderness. The painful pleasure tugged all the way down to her feminine core. Millie arched her back, a keening wail issuing from her throat.

He released her wrists and took her mouth again. Her fingers dug into his shoulders as he cupped her breasts and squeezed, his tongue thrusting deep and fast, matching the pounding rhythm of his hips against hers.

Panting, he raised up on one elbow. His eyes were stormy, and his chest heaved. "That's the way I'm going to give it to you. Hot and hard and rough." He ground the words out between his teeth as he snatched at the buttons on his pants and shoved them down. "And you're going to love it, you little bitch. You're going to beg me for it."

Millie shivered, heat and a dizzying excitement shimmering through her. She was on fire. Frantic.

He jerked up her skirt, and she knew a moment of fear as she heard her pantalets rip. Then she felt him, hot and hard, prodding against her moist femininity. The next instant she cried out as he rammed into her, his swollen shaft impaling her.

She clutched at him wildly, bucking, her legs encircling his hips as he drove into her over and over, hard and fast and deep, his body slamming into hers. She was oblivious to the pinch of her stays and the hard ground scraping her back.

He grunted with every savage thrust. It was an animalistic mating, coarse and raw and rough. It was wonderful. Millie wanted to scream and claw and bite at the pleasure of it.

Panting and gasping, she clutched at him and strained to

meet each thrust, wanting more. More! Her eyes widened and she went rigid, her back arching like a drawn bow as a shrill cry tore from her throat.

Garth laughed and pumped harder. "That's it, bitch. Scream for me. Show me how much you love it."

Then his own climax seized him. He reared back, shuddering, the tendons in his arms and neck straining as his seed poured into her, and he shouted his pleasure, spewing out a stream of obscenities.

Groaning, he collapsed on her. Millie lay beneath him, spent and gasping for breath, her body still throbbing.

In only moments, however, sanity returned, and the enormity of what she had done took hold. *Oh, my God!* Catching him by surprise, she gave an outraged cry and shoved him off.

"What the hell!"

"You . . . you . . . filthy, rutting beast!" Millie jerked to a sitting position and snatched at her clothing. Crackling with ire, she fastened the front of her dress, her jaw clenched so tightly that she ground her teeth. "How dare you do this to me! Conn will kill you for this!"

Garth rested back on his elbows, an insolent smile tilting his mouth. "Oh, really? Who's going to tell him? You?" He chuckled and shook his head. "I don't think so. You don't want everyone to know that you've been screwing in the dirt with the hired help, now do you, Mrs. Cavanaugh?"

Millie glared, speechless with rage. It was true, damn him. She'd die if anyone were to find out. And they would if Conn exacted revenge.

"Besides, you enjoyed it too much," he continued cockily, and laughed when she scrambled to her feet, gasping and sputtering.

"You . . . *animal*! Don't you ever, *ever* touch me again!" she shrieked, backing away from him. "Just stay away from me! Do you hear? Stay away!" She whirled and took off down the path at a run, Garth's taunting laughter ringing in her ears.

"Just remember, sweetheart," he called after her. "There's more where that came from."

Oh, God. Oh, God. What had she done? Frantic with guilt and fear, she raced down the narrow trail as fast as her feet would carry her, heedless of the brambles and limbs that snatched at her clothing. If Conn ever found out . . . She gave a distressed little moan and put her hand over her mouth. It didn't bear thinking about.

The man was crude and vile. A disgusting beast. Why had she ever thought him attractive?

As she ran, vines and branches slapped at her and she stubbed her toe on an exposed tree root, but she didn't slow down until she approached the spot where the trail met the wider path.

At the sound of voices ahead, she stopped and ducked behind a spice bush at the side of the trail. Forcing slow, deep breaths, she pulled a handkerchief from her skirt pocket and dabbed at her perspiring face and neck. She became aware of the sticky wetness between her legs, and her mouth twisted in distaste. Almost at once her hand flew to her mouth. Above it, her eyes widened in horror. Dear Lord! What if she were with child?

"Oh, God. Oh, God. Oh, God," she whimpered against her palm. What could she do? Conn would kill her.

Her panicked thoughts skittered this way and that. Her heart thumped. She groaned and closed her eyes, but after a moment her lids lifted slowly. Unless . . .

Resolve firmed her mouth. Of course. She would simply seduce Conn tonight. If it turned out that she was with child, he would never know the difference. She hadn't let him touch her in months, so it shouldn't be too difficult to accomplish.

Her confidence restored, Millie slapped furiously at the twigs and dirt clinging to her dress and snatched leaves out of her hair. She should never have gone walking with Garth. Then none of this would have happened.

Of course, she wouldn't have gone with him in the first place if she hadn't been so upset, she told herself with a little sniff of vindication. If Conn and Elizabeth, and that awful Ben Whitelaw, hadn't made her so angry, she wouldn't have been driven to behave so rashly.

Giving her hair one last pat, Millie lifted her chin and started toward the camp at a more sedate pace, her mouth pinched self-righteously. It was all their fault.

She found Elizabeth at the cook wagon, rolling out pie crust. Millie was immediately reminded of her earlier pique. "There you are. I've been looking everywhere for you."

Elizabeth reacted to the caustic tone with a long, level look and a scathing, "How could you?"

Millie blinked, taken aback. "What?"

"How could you betray Conn that way?"

"B-betray . . ." She felt herself pale. Good Lord! Did Elizabeth know about her and Garth? How? "I . . . I haven't—"

"Don't lie. I saw you with Ben."

"*Ben? That's* what has you so upset?" Millie sagged with relief and gave a fluttery laugh. After what had happened, the encounter with Ben seemed a trifling matter. She smiled at Elizabeth sweetly, her expression indulgent and the tiniest bit amused. "Dearest, I assure you, you simply misunderstood what you saw."

"Charm won't work, Millie. Not this time. Don't you understand? I saw you kiss Ben."

"Oh, that." Airily she dismissed the accusation with a wave of her hand. "The whole thing was perfectly innocent. Ben saved me from taking a nasty fall, and I gave him a little peck to thank him. That's all."

"I was standing there, Millie. I saw you. You deliberately tripped, and when Ben caught you, you tried to seduce him."

"Oh, for heaven's sake! You sound like a jealous old maid."

Elizabeth simply looked at her, her gray eyes filled with censure and hurt and anger. "How could you, Millie?" she repeated. "How could you value Conn's love so little?"

The accusation hit home, and because it did, Millie's anger flared. "I don't have to take this from you. Just mind your own business!"

Shaking with the force of her feelings, Elizabeth worked the rolling pin back and forth over the flattened pie crust and watched her cousin stalk away. She marveled at Millie's bold self-assurance even as she longed, for the first time in her life, to slap her face.

Within an hour of the men's return the camp was abuzz over the rumors they had picked up in town. Besieged at every turn by questions and worried speculation, Conn called a meeting to discuss the matter.

"What's this Harve tells us about Austin still being in that Mexican pokey?" demanded Silas Winslow, a burly farmer from Maryland.

Before leaving Charleston, word had reached them that Stephen F. Austin had been arrested and imprisoned in Mexico. Austin was the most important, most respected man in the Mexican territory of Texas, and everyone had expected that the matter would be cleared up quickly and he would be set free.

The news that he had not been was cause for concern. Elizabeth, along with the others, looked to Conn for an answer.

"That's what we heard," Conn replied. "Word is, the Texans are none too happy about it. Or about the way the new Mexican president is running things. Seems General Santa Anna doesn't have much use for the constitution," Conn drawled. "He prefers to govern by decree."

"What!"

"He can't do that."

"We were promised—"

Everybody began to talk at once, their voices raised in anger. Conn waited to continue until the swell of protests died down. "According to what we heard, the settlers are uneasy over the political goings-on and they're keeping a close eye on the situation, but otherwise things are quiet. Even so, I realize that this may change things for some of you. So if anyone wants to turn back, go ahead. There'll be no hard feelings."

"What about you, Conn?" Liam asked. "You turning back?"

"No."

"Conn! Whatever can you be thinking?" Millie burst out.

Elizabeth's soft mouth twisted. Her cousin's strident voice held fear and pleading, but her eyes gleamed with jubilation.

"Of course we must go back," Millie stated with just the right amount of apprehension. "My goodness, if they're imprisoning innocent citizens, who knows what might happen next? Now, Conn, I must insist that you turn this train around and take us back to Charleston where we belong."

"We're going on, Millie."

"But what if things get worse? What if war breaks out?"

"Then I'll fight." His eyes glittered like blue diamonds in a face that looked carved from stone. "Most of what I've worked for the past seventeen years is tied up in that place. I'm not giving it up."

As little as a year ago Millie would have persisted, but the past months had taught her that when Conn used that tone there was no budging him, which made her all the angrier. Her nostrils flared, and her voice came out in a shaky rasp. "I will never forgive you for this, Conn Cavanaugh! Never!" She whirled and stomped away into the darkness.

Garth overtook her before she was halfway to the wagon. "Evening, ma'am," he said with exaggerated courtesy.

"What are you doing here? I told you to stay away from me."

"Me? Why, I'm just out for a stroll. It's such a nice night I thought I'd take a walk. Down by the creek," he added with a suggestive grin. "Care to join me?"

"Certainly not."

He shrugged. "Suit yourself. But if you change your mind, you know where I'll be."

She stood rigid and watched him saunter away, her chest heaving with each furious breath. Among the folds of her skirt, her hands knotted tighter. Odious man. Vile wretch. How dare he! She would never go near him again, she vowed. Never!

A short while later, her nerves atremble with anticipation, Millie stepped cautiously into the clearing.

A low chuckle reached out to her from the honeysuckle-scented darkness. "What kept you so long, sugar?"

She was given no chance to reply. Garth's rough hands hauled her close, and his mouth clamped over hers. Within seconds he had her backed against a tree, her dress and petticoats thrown up around her waist, her legs locked around his hips as he pumped into her.

His night rounds complete, Conn headed for his wagon, stifling a yawn. The meeting had gone on for more than an hour, with everyone asking questions and giving opinions or simply venting their feelings. He was bone-tired and had a hundred things on his mind and was in no mood for another squabble with Millie, but he knew it was inevitable. She had been far too angry tonight to simply let the matter drop.

Outside their wagon, he flexed his shoulders and looked up at the night sky, for a moment letting his cares drift away. But Conn was not one to run from trouble. With a sigh he rubbed his nape tiredly and stepped up onto the tailgate. He paused and braced himself for Millie's anger before ducking through the opening in the canvas. Inside, he straightened slowly and waited for her vitriolic attack to begin, but when his eyes adjusted to the darkness he stared, surprised.

Millie lay curled on her side in the bed, sound asleep.

After a restless night spent fretting over her cousin's faithlessness, Elizabeth arose the next morning with a heavy heart, no easier of mind than she had been the night before. She tried to put on a pleasant face for Faith's sake, but the child was not fooled. The eight-year-old had spent most of her life alert for trouble; she could sense tension and turmoil in others as keenly as an animal sensed an approaching storm.

While they dressed in the predawn by the light of a candle, Faith was quieter than usual. Several times she cast worried glances Elizabeth's way. Finally, eyes downcast, she mumbled, "You mad at me, Miz Elizabeth?"

"What? Oh, sweetheart, no!" Elizabeth had been tying back the child's hair with a ribbon, but she abandoned the task at once and grasped her shoulders, turning her around. The uncertainty and fear in Faith's green eyes flooded Elizabeth with remorse. "Of course I'm not angry with you, darling." She smiled tenderly and stroked a curl away from the girl's temple.

"Then you must still be angry with Miz Cavanaugh."

She shouldn't have been surprised. Very little escaped Faith. Elizabeth's smile flattened, grew tight. "Well, yes. I suppose I am."

"You don't love her anymore?"

The question, asked in a tremulous voice, twisted Elizabeth's heart, for behind it the child's fear was plain. If love could be given, it could be taken away.

"Oh, sweetheart." She cupped the thin little face with both hands and looked deep into wary eyes the color of spring leaves. "Just because you get angry with someone doesn't mean you stop loving them. I'm unhappy with my cousin right now, it's true. And it may be a while before I get over it. But, darling, anger doesn't last. Love does."

"You gonna forgive her for whatever she done, then?"

Elizabeth exhaled a deep sigh, and her smile grew sad. "Someday, perhaps."

But not yet. The offense was too serious, the pain it inflicted too severe. The disillusionment too shattering.

Perhaps if Millie had shown the least sign of remorse, or had admitted she'd done wrong and asked for forgiveness,

Elizabeth would have softened. But when Millie arrived at the cook wagon for breakfast, she acted as though the incident had never happened. With an insouciance that stunned and offended Elizabeth, she sailed up to her, bestowed a quick hug and a peck on the cheek, and said, "Good morning, dearest. Oh my, that ham looks good, Jemma. I do hope we eat soon. I declare, I'm positively famished this morning."

Elizabeth turned disbelieving eyes on her cousin, but Millie didn't notice. She flitted around the end of the wagon, chattering and getting in the way while she lifted lids and sniffed. Her mood was considerably brighter than it had been in weeks, and to Elizabeth that somehow made things worse.

Too angry to speak, she clenched her jaws and beat the bowl of cornbread batter with more vigor than necessary. Her silence and uncharacteristic aloofness from her cousin earned her a curious look from Jemma.

"Oh, Elizabeth, dearest, would you do me a favor and mend my pink silk petticoat? It's my very favorite, and I seem to have torn the hem. And you know how helpless I am with a needle. I know. Why don't you ride in the carriage with me today and you can do it while we talk. It'll be fun."

The hand holding the wooden spoon stilled. The cold tightness in Elizabeth's chest worsened as she stared at her cousin. "No, Millie, I will not do your mending, and I have no intention of riding with you. Today or any other day."

Millie's mouth fell open. "Why, Elizabeth, is something wrong?"

"Is something wrong? How can you even ask that, after what you did?"

"What I— Oh, that." She gave a little trill of laughter and flapped her hand. "Don't tell me you're still miffed over that silly business with Ben? I told you, it meant nothing."

"Nothing?" Elizabeth shook her head. "My Lord, Millie, don't you have any conscience at all? You don't seem to understand that you did a terrible thing."

Jemma looked up from slicing ham, her eyes bright with curiosity, cutting from one to the other.

"Oh, all right. Maybe I was a bit naughty. But heavens! I would have thought by now you would have forgiven me. You always do."

Elizabeth stared at her, her expression unyielding. "Not this time, Millie. And it may be a very long while before I do. Maybe not ever."

For the first time Millie looked stricken. "Elizabeth! You don't mean that!"

"I mean it." Turning away, she went back to stirring the cornbread batter.

"Elizabeth, please," Millie cried. "Don't be angry with me. I . . . I can't stand it."

Unmoved by the tremulous plea, Elizabeth lifted calm gray eyes. "I'm afraid you'll have to."

Elizabeth was not given time to dwell on her cousin's faithlessness. They had scarcely gotten under way when a fresh outbreak of sickness struck. The ailment, which produced high fever, chills, and nausea, brought low one after another of the travelers. During the morning trek both Dr. Cavanaugh and Elizabeth were kept hopping, going from one wagon to another treating those stricken.

At midday, Isaac succumbed.

That morning he had fetched water and firewood as usual and driven Millie's carriage without a word of complaint. No one noticed anything amiss until the nooning, when he refused to eat, and even then he had insisted he was fine. By the time they were ready to pull out again, however, he was shaking so hard that his teeth were chattering.

Elizabeth was about to ride back to the Newcomb wagon to tend Martha and her two sick children when she noticed that Isaac was having trouble climbing into the driver's seat of the carriage. Suspecting the problem, she hurried over to him and discovered that he was burning up with fever and so weak he could barely stand.

As Jemma hustled him off to bed, Millie stood by the carriage, her hands on her hips. "Just who is going to drive me now?" she demanded of Conn.

"I will. We should reach Montgomery in a couple of hours. We'll sell the carriage there."

"What! We'll do no such thing!"

Conn tipped his head back and exhaled a deep sigh. Elizabeth knew he was struggling for patience.

"Be reasonable for once, Millie. With so many sick I barely have enough drivers for the wagons as it is. Besides, I warned you before we left Charleston that we'd probably have to abandon the carriage before we reached Texas. The roads there are little more than dirt tracks."

He nodded toward the vehicle. "Now quit complaining and get in. I'll be back as soon as I get one of the men to take my horse back to the herd."

Millie watched him go with such fury in her eyes that Elizabeth had to turn away.

Unlooping Thistle's reins from the rear carriage wheel, she brought the mare alongside and used the hub to give herself a boost into the saddle. As she hooked her knee over the horn and adjusted her skirts, Millie, behind her, spat out furiously, "He will not sell my carriage! I'll drive it myself, if I have to!"

Elizabeth closed her eyes and ground her teeth, experiencing again the urge to slap her cousin silly. At any other time she would have gone to Millie and tried to cajole her out of her temper, but not now. Not after what she had done.

Since their confrontation that morning, they had treated each other coolly, scarcely speaking. Elizabeth wasn't sure she would ever forgive Millie, and at the moment she didn't care.

A whip cracked the air, and Thistle shied as the carriage shot forward without warning.

"Millie!" Elizabeth screamed the name as she fought to control the sidestepping mount, her horrified gaze fixed on

her cousin, perched in the driver's seat of the black vehicle, careering away at breakneck speed. "Millie, stop! Stop!"

Millie paid her no mind. Instead she cracked the whip over the heads of the frightened team again, urging them faster. They pulled out onto the road without slowing. Stunned into immobility, Elizabeth sat atop Thistle, not breathing, her eyes wide and fearful as she watched the carriage rumble away.

Down the straightaway it bounced over ruts and potholes, rocking and swaying drunkenly, wheels rumbling and clattering, trailing a boiling cloud of red dirt. The hooves of the matched grays struck the earth like thunder.

Ahead, the road curved. The team went into it stretched out at full gallop. Elizabeth's breath caught as the right wheels lifted off the ground, dropped, then lifted again. The carriage tipped slowly to the left as though drawn over by an invisible rope. Midway it balanced and hung there, careening around the arc of the road on two wheels.

Elizabeth heard shouts and the pounding of hooves. Conn raced past, leaning low in the saddle. Jolted out of her stupor, she dug her heel into Thistle's side and took off after him.

She'd gone no more than ten yards when the carriage lost its precarious balance.

"Mil-leeeee!"

The horses screamed. Stumbling and rearing, they fought the unexpected drag on the harness that threatened to flip them. Then the twisting carriage shafts snapped. The matched grays recovered and plunged on down the road at full gallop, dragging the broken shafts, their eyes rolling wildly.

The carriage crashed onto its side and rolled . . . and rolled. A horrendous noise like the wail of a thousand banshees filled the air: the snapping of struts, the screech of rending metal, the crack of hickory splintering, the awful concussion of a heavy object being slammed, over and over, against the unforgiving earth.

A wheel flew high. It hit the ground and bounced several

times before finally rolling drunkenly away. Brush popped. Dirt and dust boiled. Startled birds took flight.

At last, like a great, wounded beast, the carriage groaned to a stop and lay rocking on its side as though in mortal pain, the dust and debris settling around it. One wheel remained miraculously intact. It was still spinning with a soft hum when Conn reached Millie.

She had been thrown out of the driver's seat on the first revolution and lay on her back in the tall grass beside the road, unmoving. Conn galloped to within a few yards of her and flung himself from the saddle before his horse could stop. He hit the ground running.

As he dropped to his knees beside his wife, Elizabeth reined in Thistle behind him. "Millie. Oh, God, Millie." Sobbing brokenly, she kicked free of the stirrup, unhooked her knee from the horn, and pushed off the saddle. Her legs gave way beneath her when she hit the ground, and she fell to her knees. Scarcely noticing, she scrambled up and covered the few remaining feet in a stumbling run, her movements jerky and uncoordinated.

"Millie! Oh, Millie!" she cried as she dropped down beside her cousin, opposite Conn. Pike took up a position a few yards away, sinking down into the grass, head up, yellow eyes alert.

Millie lay still, her eyes closed. Scratches crisscrossed her face and neck, and one cheek was discolored and puffy. Beneath the abrasions her skin was deathly white. Blood trickled from one corner of her mouth.

Conn felt her neck for a pulse, then he bent and pressed his ear to her chest. He raised his head, his despairing gaze snaring Elizabeth's briefly before riveting on his wife again. "Millie? Millie, can you hear me?"

"C-Conn . . ."

The weak whisper caused him to suck in his breath, and as her eyes fluttered he reached for her. "Millie! Thank God!"

"No! Don't move her!" Elizabeth ordered. "We don't know

yet how badly she's injured. Or where."

Conn drew back, taking Millie's hand instead. Elizabeth took her other one and leaned close. She stroked the tangled hair away from her cousin's battered face. She stared into Millie's unfocused eyes and made her voice low and commanding. "Millie, I want you to listen to me. Can you tell me where you hurt?"

Millie coughed, and the blood trickling from her mouth flowed faster. "H-head . . . hur . . . hurts." She tried to swallow but coughed again and gasped for breath.

"Anywhere else? Do you hurt anywhere else, love?" Elizabeth probed, holding on to her self-control by a thread.

"N-no. . . . Don't . . . fe . . . feel . . . any . . ."

"Anything? You don't feel anything?"

Millie closed her eyes and gave an infinitesimal nod.

Elizabeth's worried gaze lifted to meet Conn's. "Go get your father. Quick."

His mouth flattened. "He isn't here. He rode out with the hunting party."

"They've only been gone a few minutes. Ride after them and bring him back. Conn, I don't have the skill or the knowledge to deal with this."

Others were arriving. Some had chased after them on foot, and some had driven their wagons. A few were mounted. As more people caught up, they gathered together at a respectable distance, watching quietly, hats doffed, faces solemn.

From the corner of her eye Elizabeth saw Faith dart behind a clump of tall weeds, ten yards or so away. She hovered there like a lost little wraith, peeping through the stalks, her big eyes wide with fright. It wasn't good for the child to be watching such a gruesome sight, but Elizabeth didn't have time to deal with her.

Conn glanced over his shoulder. "I'll send someone."

"No! You go."

"I'm not going to leave her," he ground out furiously.

"Conn, you must. You're the best tracker we have. You'll be sure to find them quickly." Her chin quivered, and she fought for control as her eyes filled with tears. "Please, Conn. Please! You have to hurry!"

He studied her face, his blue eyes glittering. The need to stay battled the need to go. His teeth grated together, his jaw bulged.

"All right," he snapped. "I'll be back as soon as I can."

Giving Millie's hand one last squeeze, he sprang up and ran for his horse.

Pike tensed and rose halfway. The dog glanced from Conn to Elizabeth and whined. "Go with him, boy," she urged.

The dog barked once and sped away. He caught up with Conn as he swung into the saddle and dug his heels into the horse's sides. Elizabeth watched him gallop away, more frightened than she ever been in her life.

"Miz Liz'beth! Miz Liz'beth!"

Looking around, Elizabeth saw Jemma running toward them, huffing and puffing, her skirt and petticoats hitched up almost to her knees. Hot on her heels came Hester.

"How's she doin', Miz Liz'beth?" Jemma came to a halt beside them and wrung her hands. "Oh, Lawdy, Lawdy. Look at that poor chile's face."

"Jemma," Elizabeth cautioned severely, shushing the black woman with a look. "Go get me some blankets and a canteen of water. Hurry, now."

"Yes 'm."

"Is there anything I can do, Elizabeth?" Hester asked as Jemma hiked up her skirt again and took off back the way they'd come.

"Yes. Would you mind seeing after Faith for me?" she said, nodding toward the clump of weeds.

"Mercy sakes! What is that child doing here? 'Course I'll mind her. Don't you worry none about Faith. I'll take her back to our wagon. You just see about Millie."

"E . . . liz . . . abeth."

The weak whisper captured her attention. Elizabeth squeezed her cousin's limp hand and fought back tears. "Ssh, Millie. Don't try to talk, dearest. Just rest. Conn's gone to get Dr. Cavanaugh. He'll be back soon."

"Ha . . . Have . . . to t-tell you."

"Millie, please—"

"Sor . . . ry. I'm . . . so . . . sorry."

"Sorry?" Elizabeth felt as though her heart would wrench from her breast. "Oh, dearest, don't. Please," she pleaded tearfully. "It doesn't matter. I probably overreacted. Lets just forget about it."

"N-no . . . not Ben."

"Not Ben? I don't understand? If you're not talking about Ben, then what . . . ?"

Millie tried to cough, but it came out a terrible gurgling sound that struck terror in Elizabeth's heart. A pinkish bubble swelled from one of Millie's nostrils, and more oozed from the corner of her mouth. Elizabeth tried to wipe them away with the hem of her dress, but that only seemed to make Millie more agitated.

"Didn't . . . mean to . . . b-but couldn't help . . . myself." She made the gurgling sound again and licked her lips. "Wi-with him . . . it was . . ." Her fingers squeezed Elizabeth's weakly. "Oh, God . . . it was so . . . ex-exciting. Ga . . . Garth . . . is . . ."

At the mention of Garth's name Elizabeth drew in a sharp breath. *Oh, my Lord! Millie, no.*

Bile rose in her throat, but she battled down her revulsion. "Shh. Shh. It doesn't matter. You just lie quiet and rest, dearest. Don't try to talk."

Instead of calming her, Elizabeth's gentle urging caused Millie to grow more frantic. She clutched feebly at Elizabeth's hand. "P-please. Prom . . . ise me you wo . . . won't tell Conn . . . what I . . . did. Pr . . . promise me."

"Yes, yes! Of course, I promise. Now, please, dearest, don't try to talk anymore. Rest." She smoothed her fingers over Millie's brow. "Just rest."

Jemma returned, and they tucked the blankets around Millie, for although it was warm she was shaking with cold. Elizabeth shushed her lovingly and crooned comforting words, but Millie mumbled on, her speech slurred and indecipherable.

Occasionally a horse stamped, a harness jingled, a dog yipped, but no one in the crowd of watching emigrants moved, not even the children. They murmured to one another in hushed tones, but every eye was on the tall grass where the two women were bent over Millie Cavanaugh's still form.

The pair kept a silent vigil, reassuring Millie as best they could with their soft words, their touch, their presence. Now and then their gazes met, then quickly skittered away, as though afraid of what they'd see in the other's eyes, of what could be seen in their own.

The wait seemed interminable. In reality, a scant twenty minutes after Conn had ridden away, he and his father came galloping into view.

One look at Dr. Cavanaugh's face after he examined Millie and Elizabeth knew. Deep down she had known all along, but she had not wanted to accept it. Not Millie. Not vibrant, vivacious Millie, her heart cried.

The look on Conn's face as he waited for his father's verdict nearly tore her apart. She would have given anything, done anything, to spare him this. If it had been possible, she would have gladly traded places with Millie for his sake.

Dr. Cavanaugh looked up, his blue eyes, so like his son's, full of sorrow and compassion as they met Conn's. He shook his head. "I'm sorry, son. There's nothing I can do."

Conn's head jerked back as though he'd received a blow to the jaw. His eyes glittered with furious intensity. "You mean she's . . . ?"

"I'm afraid so."

Shock, denial, anger, fear—all flashed across Conn's rugged face. His gaze snapped to his wife, and Elizabeth felt as though an iron fist were squeezing her heart at his anguished expression.

Millie had slipped into unconsciousness. Her shallow breathing barely lifted her chest, barely caused the pink bubble in her nostril to flutter. Conn picked up her hand and kissed her palm, then cradled it against his cheek. "Oh, Millie. Why did you have to do that?" he asked, his deep voice rough with despair. "Why?"

Jemma withdrew respectfully. Joseph, Elizabeth, and Conn knelt in the rough grass around Millie—the three who knew her best, who loved her most.

Tears flowed unchecked down Elizabeth's face. They blurred her vision and dripped from her chin, splashing, unnoticed, onto her and Millie's clasped hands. Across from her, Conn stroked his wife's temple over and over, still holding her other hand against his cheek.

Millie's chest rose, and the gurgling sound came again as the last breath softly sighed past her lips. Then she was gone.

Chapter 10

Shared grief and pain bound people together. That was what Elizabeth's mother had always told her, and she had believed it—until now.

As she dried the dishes she watched Conn disappear into the darkness outside the circle of campfires and felt the familiar ache in her chest.

Each of the Cavanaughs grieved separately, in his own way. Ian, who had always been painfully insecure, now sucked his thumb constantly and whined and cried over the least thing. Dr. Cavanaugh sought solace in his books and in long talks with Taw. Jemma and Isaac had ceased their good-natured bickering and went about their duties with a somberness that was disquieting. Much to Elizabeth's concern, Rachel gave no indication that she felt anything beyond mild regret over her mother's death. Mother and daughter had never been close; still, the girl's lack of reaction worried Elizabeth. The loss of a parent, no matter how strained and distant the relationship, should evoke some sorrow.

The one whose reaction disturbed Elizabeth the most, however, was Conn. He was inconsolable.

Mindful of his wife's nature, he had refused to leave Millie in a lonely grave in the middle of the countryside and had taken her body into Montgomery for burial. At the little cemetery adjacent to a white clapboard church, Elizabeth had stood next to him beside the open grave, her grief compounded by his suffering and her inability to ease it. She had wanted to put her arms around him, to offer comfort, to share his pain, but everything about him discouraged even the slightest overture. He had stood stiffly erect throughout the service, his face stony and withdrawn, unwilling or unable to share his agony with anyone.

In the two weeks since, he had gone about his duties stoically, but aside from issuing instructions or assigning tasks, he'd hardly spoken to a soul. Each night, as soon as he had eaten, he escaped into the darkness to brood alone.

Elizabeth knew that Taw and Joseph, Isaac and Jemma as well, were as concerned as she was. She ached for him, but all she could do, all any of them could do, was look after his children and give him their silent support.

The dishes done, Elizabeth spread the towel on the tailgate to dry and joined the others around the fire.

She knew Ben wouldn't be by. At her request he had suspended his courtship since Millie's death. He had not been happy about not seeing her, but he seemed to understand that she was still too bereaved even to consider her personal life just yet.

Elizabeth appreciated his thoughtfulness. She did so miss her beloved cousin. Her loss was a constant, dull ache in Elizabeth's heart, at times becoming so sharp and poignant that she could barely stand it. For all the pain Millie had caused, for all her faults, she had brought gaiety and sparkle into Elizabeth's otherwise quiet life, and they had shared a sisterly love that was deep and binding.

She had scarcely taken a seat in her rocking chair when Faith appeared at her elbow with the hairbrush Elizabeth had purchased for her in the little town of Cahawba, Alabama. It was part of a simple pewter vanity set of brush, comb, looking glass, and hairpin dish, but Faith could not have been prouder of it had it been made of pure gold.

Elizabeth still got misty-eyed whenever she recalled Faith's reaction at the mercantile store that day. As Elizabeth had made her selections and the owner had cut and stacked on the counter the dress goods and the cotton lawn for gowns and underthings, some serviceable woollen for a winter cape and bonnet, hair ribbons, several new pairs of stockings, and— wonder of wonder—a brand-new pair of shoes, the child's eyes had grown huge, first with disbelief, then with unadulterated joy. When, on a whim, Elizabeth had added the girl's vanity set to the top of the stack, Faith had started to cry. So had Elizabeth.

Though Taw had cautioned the child about climbing in and out of the wagon while it was moving, she still sneaked inside two or three times a day just to be sure the vanity set was still there, tucked lovingly away in the chest that Elizabeth had allotted for her things.

Every evening after dinner Faith brushed her hair over and over while she waited for Elizabeth and Jemma to finish the dishes. Then she would sidle up to have her hair braided for the night.

Smiling, Elizabeth took the brush and guided the child around to stand in front of her knees. She gave the shiny mass of curls one last brushing, divided the locks into three fat bundles, and began to weave them together. The braid was barely past Faith's neck when a group of women marched into their camp.

Keeping his place with a finger, Dr. Cavanaugh closed the book he was reading and rose politely. "Evening, ladies. Is there something I could do for you?"

Taw, sitting on a camp stool close to the fire, glanced up, gave a little snort when he recognized the women, and returned to his whittling.

"We've come to see Mr. Cavanaugh," Agatha informed him brusquely, folding her arms beneath her ponderous bosom.

Clearly the leader, she stood ramrod straight just a little ahead of the group, which consisted of Emma Watkins, Gertrude Posey, Betsy Sprague and Dot Sillsby. All were, Elizabeth noted a bit uneasily, Agatha's cronies.

"I'm afraid Conn isn't here at the moment."

"Where may we find him? We have an urgent matter to discuss."

Taw spit into the fire, making it sizzle. Without looking up, he offered, "You kin prob'ly find him down where the stock's corraled. That's where he goes mostly of an evenin'. But if'n I was you ladies, 'less'n it's all-fired necessary, I wouldn't bother him. Conn ain't in no mood fer talk."

Agatha sniffed and pursed her lips but otherwise disdained to acknowledge Taw or his comment. In her opinion the old trapper was of the same low class as the Conlins and therefore beneath her notice or unworthy of even the simplest courtesies.

"Taw is right. Perhaps it would be best if you postponed your visit until another time," Joseph suggested.

"I'm afraid this won't wait." Bidding them good night, Agatha nodded to Joseph, shot Elizabeth a persimmony look, and marched away, the contingent of straitlaced matrons trooping in formation at her heels.

"Hmm. Now what do you suppose that was all about?" Joseph mused, watching them.

"No good, if'n you ask me. That bunch is the worst troublemakers on the train." Handing the bear he'd been carving to Ian, Taw sheathed his knife and stood up. "Think I'll jist mosey on down t' the corral an' find out what they're up t'."

Standing with his shoulder propped against a tree that served as a post for the rope corral, Conn gazed across the backs of the milling animals. Picket guards ambled around the perimeter, one off to his right, the other on the opposite side of the flimsy enclosure. One was singing softly, a mellow tune that soothed nervous beasts and blended with the night sounds.

The cicadas set up a din, and a mother cow lowed for her calf. An owl glided by on silent wings in search of an unwary rodent. With each shift of the wind the smell of night-blooming jasmine competed with the pungent scents of animals and manure.

Conn absorbed it all without conscious thought as his troubled conscience grappled with the feelings that had been plaguing him for the past two weeks.

What should he have done differently? He had asked himself the same question over and over, but he still didn't have an answer.

For one thing, he should never have brought Millie west. But if he hadn't, if he'd stayed in Charleston as she'd wanted, he would have gone mad. It would have meant the end of their marriage.

Or had their marriage ended years ago and he just hadn't known it?

He drew a deep breath and released it slowly, looking up at the night sky. Dear Lord, he had loved her so much in the beginning. He had loved her still at the end. But it hadn't been enough.

As a young man he had foolishly thought that love was all that mattered, but it took more to build a strong marriage; he realized that now.

Deep inside it bothered him that he didn't feel more sorrow, more pain. He missed Millie; he supposed a part of him always would. And he was saddened that her life had been cut short so senselessly, but he felt anger, too. He grieved for his wife, but he grieved even more for dreams gone awry, for second chances lost.

Until Millie's death he hadn't realized just how much he had been counting on this change in their living-arrangement to allow them to start over, to rekindle their love and rebuild their flagging marriage. Now that hope, along with the dream of their building something strong and lasting together, was forever gone.

Conn's jaw clenched. Seventeen long years of toil and struggle and sacrifice, all for—

The stamp of feet and the murmur of female voices interrupted his thoughts, and he straightened away from the tree, frowning at the intrusion. Who the devil?

"Mr. Cavanaugh! Are you here, Mr. Cavanaugh?"

Recognizing Agatha Guetterman's imperious voice, Conn grimaced. He should have known; almost everyone else had the good sense to leave him alone. He was tempted not to answer and simply slip away into the darkness. He didn't want to talk to anyone, especially not Agatha, but he couldn't let her keep braying like that.

"Mrs. Guetterman, please lower your voice before you spook the stock," he commanded, stepping out of the shadows.

"Oh, there you are." Agatha changed course and herded her little band to where he stood. "We must talk to you, Mr. Cavanaugh."

His eyes narrowed at her tone. He planted his feet wide and folded his arms over his chest. "Oh? About what?"

"We want to know what you intend to do about Miss Stanton," she stated baldly.

"Do? I don't understand. What about Elizabeth?"

"Surely you realize that she can no longer travel with you? As for living with you once we reach Texas, why, that's simply out of the question."

"What the hell are you talking about? Elizabeth was my wife's cousin. She's also an old and dear friend of mine."

"Nevertheless, she is not your blood kin. It would be most improper for her to live with you, now that your wife is gone."

"Improper?" Conn growled the word through his teeth, but Agatha was either too insensitive or too stupid to perceive the warning.

"As good, God-fearing, Christian women, we consider it our duty to see to it that the standards of decency and morality are upheld," she informed him loftily.

"That's right," Betsy Sprague put in, emboldened by Agatha's fearlessness. "It's our bounden duty."

Immediately the others piped up, nodding vigorously and murmuring their agreement.

Something dangerous sprang to life in Conn's eyes. His nostrils flared and whitened. Leaning forward, he snarled, "Why, you self-righteous, sanctimonious, meddling old busybodies. You wouldn't know a decent woman if she bit you on the leg. Elizabeth Stanton has never done an immoral or improper thing in her life."

"Are you saying that she will remain with you? As part of your household?" Agatha demanded in an outraged voice.

"That's exactly what I'm saying. Now get the hell out of here. All of you. And don't come back to me again spouting that pious twaddle."

"Now see here!" Agatha said huffily.

Conn jutted his head forward until he was almost nose to nose with the woman. "I said get!"

Agatha leaned back, the whites of her eyes showing all around. She opened and closed her mouth several times, but nothing came out, and when Conn roared, *"Now!"* she and her cohorts nearly stumbled over one another to beat a hasty retreat.

Conn watched them scurry away, skirts swishing, jabbering and clucking like a bunch of wet hens. Fury boiled inside him.

"Well, now, if'n that don't beat all."

The comment drifted out of the darkness to his left, and Conn's head snapped around just in time to see Taw amble from the shadows. He looked at the old man and shook his head, his mouth twisted in a grimace. "I take it you heard all that?"

"Yep. Ever' last word."

"Damned pious, interfering old harridans."

"Well, leastways you twisted their tail feathers fer 'um right smart." Taw scratched his whiskered jaw and ruminated. "'Course, bad as I hate t' admit it, I s'pose they do got a point."

"What! Do you mean—"

"Now, now, afore you git yoreself all riled up, jist give a listen. *I* know that you an' the little missy wouldn't never do nothin' you hadn't orta, but the rest o' the world, well, they don't see it that'a way. The plain fact is, you an' her ain't no kin a'tall. She ain't no kin t' me ner Joseph neither, an' accordin' t' them what makes the rule 'bout sech, that means she cain't be a part of yore household. Now, me an' yore pa, we don't count fer much. But you're a healthy young widower an' she's a right purty, unattached female, an' with the both o' you under one roof, most folks is gonna think the worst."

Calmly, Taw took out his plug of tobacco and cut off a chew. "Tain't fair nor right, but that's the way humans is, an' there ain't no changin' it. If you're gonna start livin' amongst 'um agin, you gotta give a mind t' sech as that.

"Myself, I don't see it as much of a problem whilst we're travelin'. I think that's jist them old bitties tryin' t' flap up some dirt. Prob'ly nobody but Agatha an' her bunch'll squawk much. But onc't we git t' Riverbend, well now, then things is gonna git stickier'n a chicken in molasses."

Conn wanted to argue, but he knew Taw was right. Damn. He had enough on his mind without this foolishness.

"'Course, there's a simple way t' put ever'thin' right," Taw continued thoughtfully. He cut his eyes Conn's way and received a disgruntled look. Taking his time, he worked over the wad of tobacco, then shifted the lump into his cheek and spit. "You could marry up with Miss Elizabeth."

"What?" Conn couldn't believe what he was hearing. He looked at his old friend as though he'd taken leave of his senses. "For God's sake, man! I just buried my wife. How can you even suggest such a thing?"

Taw shrugged. "Seems sensible t' me. Fer the both o' you. Oh, I know, accordin' t' the way things is done back in Charleston an' the like, yore s'pose t' be in mournin' fer a year, but on the frontier a body cain't always afford t' foller customs.

You need a wife t' look after them young'uns o' yore'n, 'specially the boy. He ain't hardly more'n a babe. An' you need 'er now, son."

"Jemma can look after them. She's done most of the mothering up to now anyway."

"Huh. That ain't the same as havin' a ma. In case you ain't noticed, them two is gettin' plumb out o' hand. Rachel, why, she ain't got the least idee of female things, an' I ain't never seen a young'un what needed a ma's love worse'n Ian."

Unable to deny that, Conn shot the old man a resentful look. Taw ignored it.

"An' if'n yore countin' on Rachel t' be any hep with the boy, you'd best forget it. Pret' near afore you know it she'll be leavin' t' git married an' start her own family."

"Dammit, Taw—"

The old man held up his hands to fend off the explosion. "Now it won't do no good t' git riled at me. You know I'm right. You need a wife, an' the way things is now, Miss Elizabeth don't got no choice but t' marry up with somebody, whether she wants t' or not. Way I see it, might as well be you."

"Well, you can forget it! I'm not marrying Elizabeth! I'm not marrying anyone! And that's all there is to it."

Taw spat and shifted his wad to his other cheek. "Suit yoreself. Don't make me no never mind. It were jist a suggestion." He squinted at the night sky and hitched up his trousers. "Well sir, it's gettin' late. Reckon I'll turn in."

Conn watched him amble away, his big frame slightly stooped, the long mane a white beacon in the darkness. Crazy old coot, he thought. The whole idea was ridiculous.

The seed, however, had been sown. Over the next few days Conn found himself looking at Elizabeth in a different light, not as his lifelong friend, not as Millie's cousin, not as someone for whom he felt responsible, but as a woman.

He became aware of things about her that he'd never really

noticed before, not on any conscious level, at any rate. Little things, mostly, like the graceful way she moved, the sweetness of her smile, how small and slender her hands were and the expressive way she used them when she talked, that husky little catch in her voice when she laughed, and the elusive dimple that flashed at one corner of her mouth.

She wasn't merely pretty, as he'd always thought—she was beautiful. Stunningly so, he realized with a start one night as he studied her face across the campfire.

How had he missed that? Had he taken her presence in his life so for granted that he'd never really looked at her? She had told him once that beside Millie she always appeared pale. Was that it? She didn't have Millie's eye-catching sultry looks, it was true. Her features were more delicate, her fine-boned beauty classic and pure, the kind that would last throughout her life.

Taw had once commented that she looked like an angel. At the time Conn had been amused, but watching the flickering light play across her elegant face, he could see it clearly now.

There was an ethereal softness about Elizabeth that was breathtaking. It was there in the tender curve of her cheek and jaw, the soulful loveliness of big gray eyes framed by those incredibly long lashes. As he watched, firelight danced in her pale hair, making it shimmer and gleam like spun gold around her serene face.

It stunned him that he had been so blind. Even more incredible, now that he thought of it—why the devil had she never married? Surely there had been many men who had wanted to claim her for their own.

Had someone perhaps broken her heart?

Conn frowned. The thought of anyone hurting Elizabeth made him angry, but the possibility that she had loved some man, some nameless, faceless man whom he didn't even know, made him feel strangely like punching something. Hard.

Elizabeth was not only beautiful, she was the most maternal, nurturing woman he had ever known; there was no denying that. Nor the fact that she needed a husband. And God knew his children needed the love and the guiding hand of a good woman,

But he sure as hell didn't need or want a wife.

Furious with Taw for making the ridiculous suggestion and with himself for dwelling on it, Conn stood up so abruptly that he startled the others around the fire. Without bothering even to say good night, he stalked off to his bed.

Nevertheless, in the days that followed, whenever he saw Elizabeth with Ben something twisted painfully in his gut.

To his surprise and fury, Taw was not the only one who thought he should marry Elizabeth. A week later his father proposed the same thing, reiterating Taw's reasons and adding one of his own.

"Son, I know that right now the idea of marriage holds little appeal, but, believe me, the day will come when you'll want a wife. You'll need a helpmate and a companion and, well, to be blunt, a lover. Has it occurred to you that a woman, especially one like Elizabeth, won't be easy to come by in a land where the men outnumber the women by around thirty to one? Nor will she be single for long. If Ben Whitelaw doesn't talk her into marrying him soon, some other man will. You can count on it."

The statement did give Conn pause, but still he stubbornly resisted the idea of marriage. He suspected that Taw had enlisted his father's aid in trying to convince him otherwise. Despite his claim of indifference, it was obvious the old man had not given up. He constantly dropped hints and made subtle references to Elizabeth's beauty and her many virtues.

Though thoroughly annoyed, underneath, Conn could not help but be amused. Surely there had never been a less likely matchmaker?

Despite his intentions otherwise, Conn could not dismiss the matter from his mind completely. He told himself over and over that he couldn't possibly marry Elizabeth, yet he found himself thinking about her more and more. He watched her closely for some sign that she was uncomfortable or in any way embarrassed about remaining within his family group, now that Millie was gone, but Elizabeth seemed perfectly at ease and went about her routine with her usual quiet competence.

Conn finally decided that there was no problem at all, that Agatha simply liked to stir up trouble, and that Taw and his father had overreacted to her malicious meddling.

Then one evening as he was rubbing down his horse by the makeshift corral, Hester approached him.

Stroking the brush over the animal's back, Conn reined in his anger and impatience and listened as she added her own urgings to those of Taw and Joseph. Not a trace of emotion showed on his face. "So. You think I should marry her, too," he said disinterestedly when she was done.

At Hester's firm, "Yes, I do," he stopped brushing and looked at her over the sorrel's back, his eyes cool and hard. "I thought you and Elizabeth were friends?"

"We are."

"But you obviously don't think she should marry your brother."

Hester returned his gaze steadily. "There isn't anyone I'd rather have for a sister-in-law. If I thought she really loved Ben, I'd collar a preacher at the next town and get 'em hitched before you or any other man could come sniffing around her. But the fact is, she doesn't."

"Oh, I see. You don't want your brother to make a loveless marriage, but it's all right for me. Is that it?"

"It's not the same. There's plenty of deep feelings between you and Elizabeth. There always have been."

A thoughtful look entered Conn's eyes. He considered for a moment, then shook his head. "Well, I'm sorry, but the answer is still no. I'm not going to marry her, so you can save your breath." He went back to his task, running the brush over the sorrel's flank with long, rhythmic strokes.

Hester studied him, her eyes narrowed, her lips pursed. "You do know that Agatha is spreading her poison thick and fast, don't you?"

"What do you mean?"

"Well, she wasn't content to complain just to you. She's running around shootin' off her mouth to anybody that'll listen about how she thinks it's an outrage, and how the women of the train ought to band together and insist that Elizabeth separate her wagon from yours. She's even saying that Ben's stopped courtin' her 'cause he don't approve of the setup. Which is just plain foolishness. Ben's just biding his time till Elizabeth gets over her grief, like she asked him to."

"Surely no one is paying any mind to that vicious nonsense?"

"Not all of 'em, no. But some. Enough that I'm gettin' uneasy." Hester studied him, her eyes narrowed, her lips pursed. "And even level-headed ones like Doris Maybry and Martha Hilliard get to looking kinda funny whenever Agatha brings up her living with you in Texas."

Conn's head snapped up. "Oh, hell. Why in God's name is Agatha doing this?"

"You mean besides being a mean-spirited, holier-than-thou busybody?" Hester inquired with a wry grimace. "Well, if you ask me, I think Agatha is trying to get Elizabeth out of the way to give that daughter of hers a chance to snare you."

"*What?*" The hand gripping the brush stilled, and the other splayed flat across the horse's back. He stared at her, all trace of his steely control gone. "You can't be serious! That flighty girl who makes eyes at everything in breeches?"

"'Fraid so."

Conn cursed roundly. "Is everybody on this damned train trying to marry me off? Hellfire! Lisa's just a child. I'm old enough to be her father."

"You're also the most prosperous man in this whole company," Hester pointed out. "From the looks of your outfit and the talk we've been hearing about this plantation of yours, you just might be one of the most prosperous men in Texas. That makes you a prime catch, and Agatha wants the best for her precious Lisa." Hester paused and looked him up and down, grinning. "Besides, you're a fine figure of a man, Conn Cavanaugh."

He ignored the last. He didn't want to believe it—any of it—but Hester was an honest, common sense kind of woman, and he trusted her judgment.

"Oh, Lord," he groaned. "That explains why every time I turn around lately I practically stumble over that girl."

"Been stalking you, has she?" Hester said with a little chuckle.

"Last night she showed up down by the river while I was bathing," he admitted in utter disgust. "There I stood scrubbing my hide, bare-butt naked, when up she walked like she was out for a Sunday stroll."

Hester's chuckles became outright laughter, and Conn fixed her with one of his glittering stares, the kind that had frozen many a man in his tracks.

It had no effect on Hester. "Did she get a good look?"

"Dammit, it's not funny. I'd waited until long after the camp was asleep. I sure as hell didn't expect her to come sashaying down there at that time of night."

Hester laughed harder, and he scowled.

Damn the silly twit! His feet had slipped out from under him when he'd ducked down, and he'd nearly drowned himself in thigh-deep water. She had acted all flustered and surprised, but it had taken a sharply barked order from him to make her leave. Even then he'd had the uncomfortable feeling that she was standing in the bushes watching as he waded from the water and dressed.

"Well, I'm afraid you can expect that sort of thing for the rest of the trip, or at least until you remarry," Hester allowed.

"I suppose Elizabeth can expect to be treated like a pariah as long as she remains with me," he returned bitterly.

" 'Fraid so. The only way to stop the wagging tongues is for her to marry, or to separate her wagon from yours, and she's done refused to do that."

Conn's gaze sharpened. "You mean Elizabeth knows about all this?"

"Agatha and her cronies cornered her over a week ago and lit into her, but she sent them packing. I don't think they expected any resistance. Like most folks, they hadn't counted on that gentle strength of hers, or realized just how devoted she is to you and your family."

A warm burst of pleasure exploded in Conn's chest, easing the angry tension. His hard features softened. Yes, he thought, Elizabeth was loyal and devoted to those she loved. It both pleased and disturbed him to know that she meant to stand by him and care for his children, no matter the cost to herself.

He shook his head and scowled. "Damn, what a mess."

"Well, like I said, the best thing would be for you to marry her yourself." Hester held up her hand when he started to speak. "If you don't, someone else soon will. Probably Ben. Do you really want that?"

The answer was a resounding no, Conn discovered as he walked back to camp. It didn't make any sense, and he chided himself for the feeling, but the thought of Elizabeth marrying Ben—or any other man—didn't set well with him.

He supposed it was because she had always been a part of his life. If she married someone else, not only would that change, he might never see her again. Texas was vast, and Ben didn't strike him as a man ready to settle in one spot just yet. It was selfish of him, he knew, but after just having lost Millie, he couldn't bear the thought of losing Elizabeth as well.

Conn got little sleep that night. He tossed and turned and wrestled with the problem for hours. The awareness that his resolve was weakening exacerbated his already foul mood. Still, no matter how many times he went over the situation in his mind, it boiled down to two options: he could stand by and watch as some other man took Elizabeth out of his life—the very thought of which was intolerable—or he could marry her himself.

Out of curiosity, the next morning after breakfast Conn followed Elizabeth and Jemma when they went to the river.

More than a dozen women were already there when they arrived, some scrubbing out diapers or their monthly rags, some fetching water, and others, like Elizabeth and Jemma, rinsing out milk pails or empty crocks. They were talking among themselves, but the instant Elizabeth appeared on the bank they fell silent. She smiled tentatively and murmured, "Good morning," her soft gaze guarded as it swept over them.

From the cover of a sumac bush, Conn watched as some of the women's expressions grew uneasy and others, mostly Agatha's friends, grew distant.

Conn felt a sharp stab of annoyance. Damn stupid women! How could anyone with an ounce of sense doubt Elizabeth's virtue? He could barely restrain himself from storming out there and lighting into the silly females. All that held him back was the certainty that, beyond embarrassing Elizabeth, he would accomplish nothing—might, in fact, make matters worse.

He had already made his decision, and Elizabeth's cool reception at the river convinced him that what he was about to do was the right thing, not just for himself and the children, but for her as well.

Chapter 11

"I'd like to talk to you. In private."

The request surprised Elizabeth so, she almost dropped the plate she was carrying. She had expected Conn to go off by himself, as he did every evening after dinner. "Now? I was about to help with the dishes."

"Lawdy, child, don't worry none 'bout these dishes," Jemma scolded fondly. "You just go along with Mastah Conn. I'll have these dishes washed up in no time. An' Faith can dry them for me. Can't you, child?"

Faith nodded solemnly, her wary gaze darting between Elizabeth and the stern-faced man.

As he led her away Pike rose to follow, but a word from Conn stopped him. Elizabeth's heart thumped against her ribs like an Indian tom-tom. She had no idea why she was so nervous, but she was. Perhaps it was the grim look on his face. Or the way he'd been watching her all day.

The feel of his firm fingers gripping her elbow burned her skin like a branding iron through the bell sleeve of her calico dress. As though she were in the grip of a hard chill, a terrible quaking began deep inside her and spread outward. She was certain he could feel it.

Shamefully Elizabeth knew that her reaction was due to more than nerves. Even now, mere weeks after her cousin's passing, she responded to Conn's presence. Guilt besieged her, and she told herself over and over that it was wrong, but she

164

was helpless to control the warm flood of feelings. Dear Lord, she had loved him so long.

Without speaking he led her across the wide meadow, steadying her over the uneven ground, guiding her around bushes and other obstacles that she could barely see in the darkness. When they were perhaps fifty yards from camp he halted beneath a huge white oak tree. Its spreading branches seemed to enfold them in a private world of their own, and the intimacy of it set Elizabeth's heart to beating faster.

From among the thick branches overhead, the nasal *beent!* of a nighthawk sounded. Conn braced one arm against the massive trunk and looked up.

Small blotches of moonlight, filtering through the leaves, played over his craggy face and revealed the curve of his throat. Licking her dry lips, Elizabeth fixed her eyes on that brown column and waited, her pulses thrumming. Curling tendrils of hair stirred against her neck in the gentle breeze like a whispery caress. The long, leathery leaves of the oak rustled with a dry clatter.

"Wh-what did you want to talk to me about?" she asked when she could stand the silence no longer.

Conn looked at her, and even in the gloom she could see the determined glitter in his eyes. She could feel them boring into her. "First of all I want to know something. Are you in love with Ben?"

Surprise rendered her speechless, and for several seconds she merely stared at him, mouth open, eyes wide. Whatever she had expected, that was not it. "I . . . why do you want to know?"

"Just answer me, Elizabeth. It's important."

"I . . . I'm quite fond of him."

"That's not what I ask. Do you love him?"

"I . . . I . . ."

Elizabeth's heart sank like a stone tossed in a pond as the reason for his questions came to her. He *did* know about

Agatha's vicious talk. And he wanted to get her married off and out of his life.

She felt as though her chest were being squeezed by a giant fist. She wanted to cry. She wanted to curl into a ball and wail out her misery. Dear Lord, she wanted to die.

Taking a deep breath, she got a grip on her tattered emotions. But she wouldn't. She wouldn't. If this was what Conn wanted, she would make it easy for him, she vowed silently.

Folding her arms over her midriff as though to hold in the pain, Elizabeth fought down threatening tears and straightened her spine. "I think I could learn to love him."

"I take that to mean you don't now. Am I right?"

"Well . . . I . . ."

"Good. At least I don't have to feel guilty about that."

Elizabeth blinked.

"Beth, I know about the trouble that Agatha has stirred up," he said, confirming her suspicions.

"I see."

"I wish you had come to me and told me. I appreciate your loyalty, little one, but I can't allow you to sacrifice your reputation for my sake."

She did not reply. She couldn't. If she tried to speak, she would cry. Swallowing the ache in her throat, she waited.

"I've been giving the situation a lot of thought, and, well . . . I think the best solution . . . for both of us . . . is for us to get married."

The words hung in the air. She stared at him through the gloom of darkness, not quite believing she'd heard him right.

"You . . . you want to marry me?"

"I want to protect your good name," he said bluntly. "It's also been pointed out to me that my children need a mother to guide them, someone who can teach Rachel woman things and give Ian the attention he needs."

He could have no idea how much he was hurting her. She had loved Conn all of her life, had spun countless dreams around him, had imagined him asking her to marry him in a thousand different ways, but not like this. Never like this.

For the first time in her life, she wanted to strike him. She wanted to lash out, to shriek and rage and pummel his chest and inflict as much pain as he was causing her. But of course she wouldn't. He would be mystified. He didn't know of her feelings. She had taken great care to hide them from him and everyone else. To him she was simply his old friend.

Deep down, she knew in her heart that Conn would never deliberately hurt her. No doubt he thought he was being gallant.

"Conn, I know you love Rachel and Ian, but that's not a good enough reason to marry," she said in a voice that was not quite steady.

"It's as good as any."

Her dove gray eyes widened in astonishment. "How can you say that? What about love?"

"Love?" The word came out on a little ironic bark of laughter, and Elizabeth blinked. "I've had love. What I want now is some peace and contentment. I think we can give each other that."

So that was it. She would raise his children, run his household, provide undemanding companionship, and never cause a ripple in his life, never be a threat to the love he carried in his heart for Millie. How practical. How prosaic. How hurtful.

She turned away, but not before he glimpsed what was in her eyes. Swiftly he came to her, took her gently by her shoulders, and turned her to face him, his expression contrite as he gazed down into her unhappy face. "Aw, Beth, sweetheart, I'm sorry. I didn't mean to upset you. I know that sounded cold and unfeeling, but I didn't mean it that way. It's just that I thought . . . hell, I still think . . . that this is the best solution for both of us."

Solution? Elizabeth had to stifle the urge to laugh hysterically.

"You have no family left, little one," he continued not

unkindly. "And you can't fend for yourself, especially not where we're going. Since marriage seems to be your only option, you might as well marry me. It's the only way I can take care of you, and Millie would have expected me to do that."

The fist gripping Elizabeth's heart squeezed tighter. She stepped away from his touch and took three jerky steps, wrapping her arms tightly around her middle. Even the proposal, such as it was, sprang from his feelings for Millie, not for her.

Conn moved around to stand in front of her, his expression puzzled, a little hurt. Mutely, quivering with wounded pride, she stared at the fringe on his buckskin shirt.

Placing a finger beneath her chin, he tipped her head up to meet his eyes. "Do you find the thought of being married to me so distasteful, Elizabeth?" he asked softly, frowning at the look of despair on her face.

Distasteful! A hysterical sob rose in her throat, and she had to bite her lip hard to hold it in check. If he only knew. Marriage to Conn, to be able to share his life, to love him, to mother his children—it was all she had ever wanted or hoped for. It was more than she'd thought, for the past sixteen years, that she would ever have. But, dear Lord, she wanted it to be for love, not such cold, practical reasons.

Her bruised pride and aching heart demanded that she reject the offer. *Elizabeth, you fool. You don't have to settle for this. Other men want you. Other men have offered you love. Tell him "No, thank you" and walk away.* The words hovered on the tip of her tongue, but, to her shame, she could not quite bring herself to voice them. That was how weak she was where Conn was concerned.

She closed her eyes. "No. No, of course I don't."

"Well, that's a relief, anyway," he said with an attempt at lightness, and Elizabeth managed a wan smile. "We could have a good marriage, Beth. We're old friends who know each other well, so we won't be faced with any nasty surprises.

There is fondness and mutual respect to build on. The children know and like you, and I'm fairly certain that you like them."

"I love them both, but—"

"And . . ." He cupped her face in his palm and smiled tenderly. "You're a lovely, intelligent woman any man would be proud to have as his wife. I don't expect I'll find being married to you a hardship."

Was he talking about . . . ? Elizabeth's heart gave a little kick. He had not mentioned the intimate side of marriage, but then, that would hardly be proper.

Elizabeth blushed hotly, her body tingling at the thought of sleeping with Conn. How would it be, lying in his arms, holding him, making love with him? Oh, God, she had dreamed of it for so many years.

"So what is your answer, Elizabeth?" He looked at her steadily, his intense gaze oddly searching. "Will you marry me?"

"Conn, I . . . may I have some time to think it over? This . . . this is all so unexpected."

"That's only fair, I suppose. Just don't take too long. As soon as possible, I want to put an end to the gossip. And to Agatha's matchmaking attempts as well."

"Matchmaking?" Elizabeth flashed him a surprised look as he took her arm to lead her back to camp.

"Yes. It seems she and that daughter of hers have got it into their heads that Lisa would make me the perfect wife."

Elizabeth stumbled and would have fallen if Conn hadn't prevented it. Conn and Lisa Guetterman? Married? The idea was so abhorrent to Elizabeth that she shuddered.

Surely he wouldn't consider it? She looked at Conn out of the corner of her eye and felt a gnawing of unease in the pit of her stomach. Lisa *was* beautiful. And though he was grieving now, somehow she didn't think Conn was the sort of man to live alone forever.

That thought stayed with Elizabeth long after Conn had

left her at her wagon. Hours later, as she lay in her bed next to Faith, staring up at the canvas top, it gnawed at her, causing an unpleasant sensation in the region of her heart. She experienced an uncharacteristic, almost overwhelming urge to march to the Guetterman wagon, drag out that little hussy Lisa, and threaten to snatch her bald if she didn't stay away from Conn.

A weak smile curved Elizabeth's mouth as she pictured the scene. She could just imagine the talk that would spark. A tear trickled from the corner of one eye and streaked downward. Releasing a quavering sigh, she wiped away the trail of moisture and scrubbed at her eyes with her fingertips. Lying still so as not to awaken the sleeping child, she shed a flood of silent, scalding tears. They eased the ache in her heart somewhat, but they did not change anything.

She turned onto her side and sighed again as she pillowed her head on her hand. Her pride still smarted from Conn's insulting proposal. A part of her was tempted to refuse his offer.

So why don't you? she goaded herself mercilessly. She wasn't a desperate old maid who had to grab at his insensitive offer as though it might be her only chance. Ben was sure to propose soon.

The question was, would she accept him? Could she? Elizabeth's mouth twisted sadly. Probably not, she admitted with painful self-honesty. Any more than she could accept any of the other men who had asked for her hand over the years.

They had all been decent, good men, any of whom would probably have made her an excellent husband, but they had all shared one fatal flaw: they had not been Conn. Her heart simply could not accept anyone else, so she had remained unwed, not from lack of opportunity, but because she could not have Conn.

But she could have him now. She might never have his love, but she could share his life and his family.

Elizabeth blinked back another rush of tears. It wasn't what she wanted, but it was so much closer to her dreams than she had ever thought to come.

Her pride pulled her one way, her heart another, but in the end her heart won. She knew full well she could be letting herself in for even more heartache and pain, but she had no choice. Conn was too virile, too masculine a man, to live without a woman for long. If she did not marry him, he would eventually find someone else to warm his bed and care for his children, and, dear God, she could not go through that again.

Elizabeth gave him her answer the next morning, and that evening, in a stubbled meadow beside their camp outside Natchez, they were married.

"There's no sense in putting it off," he'd told her when she expressed concern over the haste. "Besides, we won't have many more chances. There are only two more towns between here and the border. Once we cross the Sabine River we'll be in Texas, and only a priest can marry us there. There aren't many east of San Antonio, and we can't wait months for a wandering padre to show up."

The brief ceremony bore not the slightest resemblance to the wedding of Elizabeth's long-ago, girlish dreams.

Wearing her best pale blue tissue silk gown, her legs shaking so they threatened to give way beneath her, she stood beside Conn before the Reverend Mr. Haig, the singularly unprepossessing minister he had fetched from Natchez, barely hearing the words of the ceremony.

All around them, decked out in their best finery, stood every last soul on the train. After their initial shock on hearing of the marriage plans, nearly everyone accepted the necessity, given the circumstances, for dispensing with the usual period of mourning. With but a few exceptions, they were smiling. Some of the women even sniffed and dabbed at their eyes and noses with handkerchiefs or the hems of their good aprons.

All the children watched with awe, their solemn faces scrubbed and shiny, the girls with their hair tied with ribbons, the boys with their cowlicks slicked down with tonic or lard.

Conn took her icy hand in his, and Elizabeth jumped. As the words of the ceremony flowed over her, she peeked up at him, seeking reassurance, encouragement, hope; but Conn was staring straight ahead, his face set and serious.

Sliding her gaze along his strong jaw, Elizabeth noticed a tiny nick in the freshly shaved skin, and she wondered if perhaps he, too, was nervous. The thought was heartening somehow.

In honor of the occasion, Conn had dressed in his finest black frock coat and blue satin, shawl-collared waistcoat that matched his eyes. A black silk cravat created lavish folds at his throat, and against the white linen shirt and stock his skin resembled polished bronze.

His ebony hair curled under over his ears and nape, barely touching the wide coat collar, and she realized that Isaac had trimmed it. His clothes smelled of the cedar chips scattered in all the trunks. He smelled of soap and starch and bay rum hair tonic, and to her loving eyes he looked so impossibly handsome, so beautifully masculine, that she melted inside.

Reverend Haig cleared his throat and looked at her pointedly. "And now, if you will repeat after me: 'I, Elizabeth . . .'"

As though in a trance, her insides a quivering mass, she turned and looked up into those beloved blue eyes. "I, Elizabeth Louise Stanton, take you, Conn Ramsey Cavanaugh, to be my lawful wedded husband . . ."

A numbing sensation of unreality enveloped Elizabeth as there, at long last, in the grassy field beside their camp, her voice quavering with emotion, she pledged her troth and repeated the solemn vows that forevermore bound her to the man she had loved for a lifetime.

Then it was Conn's turn.

Elizabeth's heart boomed, and her throat tightened. He held her icy hand, his vivid eyes never wavering from hers, and in his strong, sure voice spoke the same profoundly moving words. Over their joined hands their gazes met in silent acknowledgment of the unbreakable bond they were forging.

Elizabeth, her heart overflowing with love and hope, strove for composure, but despite her best effort a wall of tears banked up against her lower lashes, blurring his face. As Reverend Haig declared, "By the power vested in me, I now pronounce you man and wife," one slipped over and trickled down her cheek.

At once, tender concern softened Conn's serious expression. Leaning close, he cupped her cheek with his callused hand and brushed away the crystalline drop with his thumb. "Don't cry, little one," he whispered. "I'll do my best to make you happy. I swear it."

"I know," she replied with a wavery smile.

Without warning, as they regarded each other in the last rosy glow of the setting sun, something sparked between them and held them spellbound. Oblivious to the watching crowd, oblivious to Reverend Haig's pompous presence, they stood absolutely still. Their gazes caught and locked, glittering blue to the softest tear-washed dove gray. For endless seconds they simply looked at each other while feelings churned and awareness grew, and all around them people watched in breathless silence.

"You may now kiss the bride, sir," Reverend Haig intoned.

Both Elizabeth and Conn started and looked at him, their eyes wide with a combination of surprise and uncertainty.

Again their gazes met, searched, softened.

The hand cupping her face slid around her neck, fingers tightening as they tunneled into the cascade of curls at her nape. Conn's other arm slipped around her waist and drew her nearer. Then, slowly, his head lowered.

Elizabeth's whole body began to quake. Her heart filled

with such sweet pressure, she thought surely it would burst. His head drew near and his sculptured lips parted, and Elizabeth's eyes drifted shut as though weighted with lead. She felt his breath feather over her skin. Then, for the first time, their lips met.

The kiss was brief—a mere brush of flesh upon flesh, a mingle of warm breaths, a tentative taste—yet it was devastating, a soft, stunningly sensual caress that made her pulses pound and her knees go weak and surpassed every dream she'd ever had.

Elizabeth almost shattered with delight. Her body went weak and warm, melting against him until only his hard arm supported her. If it had been possible to die of joy, she would have in that moment.

The kiss ended, and for an instant Conn looked at her, his eyes curious and searching.

Before either could speak, the spell was broken by the murmur that went up all around them. Tucking her hand into the crook of his arm, he turned with her to accept well wishes and hearty congratulations as everyone surged around them.

The men shook Conn's hand and thumped his back, and he watched with a cynical twist to his mouth as Elizabeth received hugs and busses on the cheeks from the women.

All, it seemed, was forgiven.

Inevitably the men began to claim their right to kiss the bride. Amid much good-natured pushing and jockeying for position, they lined up, all the while taunting Conn. He stood to one side, arms folded over his chest, an amused twist to his hard mouth.

Taw was the first in line, his eyes atwinkle with mischief and joy, and Elizabeth laughed as his lips puckered at her from the midst of the bushy white beard. She obliged, but the whiskers tickled, and he slapped his knee and guffawed when she scratched at her upper lip.

For the most part Elizabeth suffered it all with good grace, her cheeks a becoming pink as she was soundly smacked, bussed, and pecked by young and old alike. Only Garth's attention seemed to disturb her, causing Conn to frown briefly and wonder what had caused the reaction. The idle speculation slipped from his mind a moment later when he noted that Ben was conspicuously absent from the line of men.

Conn frowned, wondering how Ben had taken the news. Probably not well. *He* wouldn't have, in Whitelaw's shoes. He'd offered to tell him for her, but Elizabeth had insisted it was something she had to do herself. Now he wished he had not listened to her.

Because of Millie's recent passing, Conn had not wanted a fuss made over the wedding, but matters had quickly gotten out of hand. After months of hardship and monotonous travel, everyone was eager for some gaiety, and a wedding, no matter the reason for it, was always a cause for celebration. The women had spent all afternoon cooking, and when Conn and Elizabeth were ushered inside the circle of wagons, a feast awaited, the likes of which none of them had tasted since leaving Charleston. No sooner had they eaten than the squawk of a fiddle tuning up sounded, and an area was cleared for dancing.

Conn did not have the heart to deny them their pleasure, especially after his father pointed out that this was Elizabeth's first marriage and she deserved to celebrate it with a bit of gaiety. For her sake, he put aside his misgivings, and as the musicians launched into a ragged but spirited rendition of a popular waltz, he took Elizabeth into his arms.

Her face aglow, she smiled up at him as they twirled and glided in time to the music.

"Well, we did it," he said with grim satisfaction.

"Yes," Elizabeth agreed softly. Her gaze went to her left hand, resting against his broad shoulder, and the gold band that encircled her finger. It gleamed dully in the flickering light from the fires. *Elizabeth Cavanaugh. Mrs. Conn Cavanaugh.*

Her heart swelled with joy, and a tiny smile tilted the corners of her mouth. She could scarcely believe it.

She looked up at Conn again and waited for him to say more, but an odd constraint overtook them, and he stared silently over her head, his expression pensive and remote. An uneasy feeling gripped Elizabeth. As other couples joined them she wondered if Conn already regretted marrying her.

When the waltz ended Dr. Cavanaugh claimed the next dance, and Taw the one after that, swinging her around to an exuberant Virginia reel with a spryness that belied his age.

The band, an incongruous mix of fiddle, flute, concertina, harmonica, banjo, and Jew's harp, played one rousing tune after another, making up in volume and enthusiasm for what they lacked in talent. No one seemed to mind; they were having too good a time, clapping and dancing and simply taking advantage of the rare opportunity to relax and visit.

Elizabeth quickly lost sight of Conn, but between the hired hands and the other men on the train, she danced almost every dance, sitting one out only now and then to catch her breath or whenever she spotted Garth approaching. This was her wedding celebration, and she was determined to enjoy it to the fullest. Dancing helped take her mind off of Conn's strange mood . . . and the night that was to come.

From the sidelines Conn watched her thoughtfully. She was so tiny, so delicately made, not exactly the kind of woman a wise man would pick for a helpmate on the frontier. Yet he didn't regret marrying her. Though he had never once imagined that he'd end up wed to Elizabeth, it seemed right somehow. He wasn't sure just why.

Probably because you're so comfortable with her, he told himself, watching her tip her head to one side and smile at something Asa Strack had said, never missing a step as he galloped her around in circles. The old windbag could talk the horns off a billy goat and would drive a saint crazy with his incessant chatter, but Elizabeth's attention never wavered.

For all her delicate appearance, there was a quiet strength about Elizabeth, a tranquillity that soothed a man's soul and lifted his spirit. She had a way of listening—really listening—those soft gray eyes filled with understanding and fastened on a person as though what he was saying were the most important thing in the world.

Even as a child she'd been a restful little thing. With a smile Conn recalled the way she had followed him around, hanging on his every word and gazing up at him with those big adoring eyes. As a callow youth he had accepted her hero worship as his due, but looking back, he realized how precious a gift it had been. He would have given everything he had if, just once, Millie had looked at him that way.

Millie. The thought of her brought the familiar rush of grief and anger, but Conn gritted his teeth and pushed it aside. It was pointless to hanker for what could no longer be, what—if he were honest—had never really been. Millie, underneath the petulance and willfulness, had been a good woman, but she had never possessed Elizabeth's warm, generous nature. It had taken him years to realized that it simply had not been in her to bestow unconditional love and devotion.

Angry with himself for letting thoughts of Millie intrude, tonight of all nights, he focused on his bride with renewed determination.

As Elizabeth swayed and curtsied and twirled in the arms of one man after another, she laughed and her eyes sparkled like diamonds in the firelight. Exertion and the warmth of the summer night had put a flush on her face and stolen her breath, and damp ringlets clung to her nape and temples. The sight brought a surprising rush of heat to Conn's loins.

Shifting his position, he cursed himself roundly. Dammit! What kind of man was he? Millie had only been gone a few weeks. He had no business lusting after Elizabeth, even if she was his wife. That wasn't why he'd married her. After months of celibacy the reaction was not surprising. But hellfire! *Elizabeth* of all people!

He had deliberately refrained from thinking about the in-

timate side of this marriage. He didn't know whether that
was because of the guilt he felt over Millie's death and this
hasty remarriage, or because he hadn't wanted to accept that
he was physically attracted to Elizabeth.

What he did know was that if he didn't get control of his
wayward desire before they turned in for the night, she'd
probably run from him screaming.

Several jugs were unearthed and passed among the men on
the sly, and as the evening wore on the level of gaiety and
laughter increased.

When the band struck up yet another lively tune, Elizabeth
laughingly begged off in favor of a breath of fresh air and a
cooling drink.

"This has turned into quite a bash, hasn't it," Hester commented when she joined her on the sidelines. "I'm glad, for
your sake. A wedding should be a happy time."

Elizabeth smiled gratefully. "Thank you, Hes."

"I just hope Conn isn't upset about it. You don't think he
is, do you?"

"I haven't seen him for the past hour, so I couldn't say."
Scanning the crowd, Elizabeth waved her ivory-and-lace fan
in front of her face and dabbed a handkerchief over her neck
and the upper curves of her bosom, bared by the off-the-
shoulder gown. "Have you seen him lately?" she asked with
a casualness she was far from feeling. After the first dance,
Conn had claimed her for two more, cutting in front of the
other men with flattering forcefulness, but he had still seemed
withdrawn and somber.

"He's probably over there tipping a jug with the others."

Elizabeth searched for Conn among the group of men on
the opposite side of the camp, but he was not there. She started
to look away when another man in the group caught her
attention.

She bit her lip, her heart squeezing with compassion as she
watched Ben hoist the crockery jug onto his shoulder and take
a long swig.

He was hurting, and it was her fault. Her only excuse was she hadn't dreamed that his feelings for her had developed to such an extent.

If she lived to be a hundred, Elizabeth knew she would never forget the look that had come over Ben's face that very morning when she'd told him she was going to marry Conn. It had reflected exactly the anguish and pain she had felt all those years ago on learning that Conn was to wed her cousin. Elizabeth would not have wished that agony on anyone. Especially not Ben.

The torment in his voice had twisted her heart.

"Marry Conn?" He had shaken his head as though dazed from a blow, his eyes a little wild. "You can't be serious."

"We . . . we're going to be married this evening."

"Why? Why are you doing this? Is it because of that damned talk Agatha started?"

"Partly, but—"

"Surely you knew that I was going to ask you to marry me soon?" He flung the words at her, more accusation than question, and all Elizabeth could do was wring her hands, too miserable to speak. "I was just biding my time—at first to let you get used to the idea. Later I waited to let you get over your cousin's death, but I was going to ask you."

"I . . . I'm sorry."

"Sorry!" He stared at her. Muttering a curse, he turned away but just as quickly spun back. "Do you have any idea how hard it was for me to hold back?" he demanded. "I wanted you the first moment I saw you, and these past weeks have just made me want you more. But, fool that I am, I was trying not to rush you." He gave a disgusted snort. "Hell, I never even kissed you."

"I know," she said softly, her face filled with sympathy. "But—"

"It's not too late for us, Elizabeth." Gripping her elbows, he looked into her eyes, a desperate plea in his own. "We can go to Conn and explain, tell him that—"

"Ben, I can't. It's not just the gossip. Conn really needs me. To . . . to look after his children and run his home."

"That's why he's marrying you? To have a mother for his children and a housekeeper? Dammit, Elizabeth, you don't have to settle for that. I need you, too. And I can offer you love."

"Ben!"

His expression softened. "You didn't know?" At the dazed shake of her head, his mouth twisted. "You're probably the only one who didn't."

Stricken, she stared at him. "Oh, Ben," she whispered in a small, aching voice. "Ben."

His hands tightened on her arms. "Elizabeth, don't say no. We can—"

"Ben, don't!" She placed four fingers across his lips, stopping the desperate flow. Her heart ached for him, but she had to tell him the truth. He deserved nothing less.

She gazed up at him, her wide gray eyes awash with sorrow and silently beseeching. "You don't understand," she said in a gentle voice. "It's true that for Conn this is a practical and convenient arrangement, but I'm marrying him because I love him. I always have."

He went perfectly still. Only his blazing eyes betrayed his emotions. The muscle along his jaw twitched. His throat worked as he swallowed hard. Finally his chest swelled with a ragged breath.

His hands fell away from her arms, and he stepped back. "I see," he said flatly. "Does he know?"

Elizabeth shook her head unhappily.

"So tell me, would you have married me if I had asked you sooner? Even loving another man?"

"I . . . oh, Ben, please try to see it from my side. I had no hope of ever having Conn, and I wanted a husband and family of my own. Is that so wrong?" Her eyes fixed on him with desperate entreaty, but he turned away and stared at the Mississippi countryside, his back rigid.

The crushing weight of despair and defeat settled over Elizabeth, but still she struggled for words to make him understand. "I had no idea your feelings for me went so deep. I thought that you merely wanted a wife. Truly, Ben, I never meant to hurt you."

"I know." He looked at her over his shoulder, and his mouth twisted in an ironic half smile. "The funny part is, I do understand. You see, even if I'd known how you felt about Conn, I would have married you anyway."

Those words, uttered so despondently, had torn at Elizabeth's heart and made her sad beyond measure. Even now, hours later, just remembering them brought tears to her eyes. She, of all people, knew well the helplessness of a love so deep and unrequited. It saddened her even more to realize that, had she not already given her heart to Conn, she could have fallen in love with Ben.

She was attracted to him far more than she had ever been to any man, other than Conn. Perhaps if she had married him, love might have taken root in her heart and eventually choked out the hopeless feelings that had dominated her life for so long.

But it was too late for that now.

Across the way, Ben handed the jug to another man and swiped the back of his hand across his mouth. Over it, as though he had divined her thoughts, he looked straight at Elizabeth. From that distance she could not make out his eyes in the dim light of the fires, but she felt them boring into her.

Her heart gave a little thump when he started for her. With long, determined strides, he strode through the dancing couples as though they did not exist, his eyes never wavering from Elizabeth's face. Several of the dancers slowed their steps or stopped altogether to watch him, and along the sidelines near

Elizabeth the chatter faded away into expectant silence. Little by little the hush spread around the circle until the only sound was the music, which seemed suddenly loud.

Ben halted in front of Elizabeth, his gaze locked on her face. The smell of corn liquor drifted to her across the few feet separating them. His lips curved upward in a hard smile that held the bitter defiance of defeat. In his hazel eyes swirled a painful longing, but mixed with it was a reckless glitter that she never seen there before.

He swept her a gallant bow. "Mrs. Cavanaugh. I believe this is our dance."

Leaning back with his elbows hooked over the rim of a wheel, one knee bent and the heel of his boot braced against the hub, Conn listened to his father, Taw, and Liam rehash the rumors they'd heard that day in Natchez.

The closer to the border they came the more news they picked up at each town. If only half the stories out of Texas were true, the situation still wasn't good.

"When I was getting my mules reshod the smithy told me he'd heard Santa Anna'd done dissolved the republican Congress," Liam said, shaking his head.

"Yep, heerd that, too. An' accordin' t' the feller down t' the livery, they're sayin' he's dismissed all the cabinet ministers but one, an' got rid o' all the local o-ficials an' *ayunta . . . ayunta . . .* Oh, shoot fire! Whatever that Mex word is fer mayors. Done it all by dee-cree," Taw added, expectorating a prodigious stream of tobacco juice to punctuate his disgust.

Joseph looked at his son. "How do you think the Texans will react to all this?"

Conn shrugged. "I imagine they'll take a wait-and-see attitude for now. Maybe call a few meetings and draw up petitions, but—"

A low growl from Pike halted him. Becoming aware of a change in the atmosphere, he looked around for its cause. He had positioned himself so that he could keep an eye on Elizabeth, and when he spotted Ben approaching her, his eyes narrowed.

"Uh-oh. Cain't say I like the looks o' that," Taw muttered, following the direction of his gaze. Pike rose, showing his teeth, his growl deepening.

"Take it easy, boy." Abruptly Conn pushed away from the wagon wheel. Falling silent, the big dog followed.

He reached Elizabeth as Ben completed his bow and requested a dance. Slipping his arm around Elizabeth's waist, Conn fixed the younger man with a commanding look. Something hard and frightening glittered in his blue eyes. "Sorry, Whitelaw. But this one is already spoken for."

The double meaning was not lost on Ben, or anyone within earshot. For several seconds the two men stared at each other in stony silence. The air around them crackled with barely restrained male aggression.

Slowly Ben's hard smile returned, and he reached for Elizabeth. "In that case, since I missed out earlier, I think I'll claim my kiss from the bride."

Chapter 12

Ben's look dared Conn to object. Boldly he grasped Elizabeth's hands and tugged.

Hard fingers bit into her flesh as Conn's hand tightened on her waist. His eyes narrowed dangerously on the younger man.

All around them was absolute silence. Even the band stopped playing.

Pale with distress, Elizabeth looked up at Conn's hard face, then at Ben's. "Please . . . you mustn't—"

Conn flicked her a glance, his nostrils flaring at her stricken look. "All right, Whitelaw," he said at last. His tone was casual, even pleasant, but his expression remained harsh. "I suppose you're entitled. This once."

Ben's mouth curved into a thin smile of victory that radiated cold anger. Tugging her hands, he pulled her to him, and she obediently lifted her head for his kiss.

Elizabeth expected a chaste peck on the lips or forehead, like those she had received from the other men, but Ben had something else entirely in mind, and her eyes widened as she read his intent.

Sliding one arm around her waist, he brought her close and pressed her tight against him. With his other hand he cupped her jaw. Her heart pumped wildly as his gaze roamed her upturned face. Gradually his expression softened, and anger gave way to abject hunger and longing, and a pain so great that Elizabeth nearly cried out at the sight of it.

His gaze seemed to burn into her, and she felt the hand at her jaw tremble. "Be happy, Elizabeth," he whispered. His head began a slow descent, and heavy eyelids closed drowsily over his smoldering eyes. "Now kiss me good-bye," he urged against her lips. "Give me something to remember."

His hold on her waist tightened, and as their lips touched his other arm encircled her back, folding her even more into his embrace and locking her to the hard warmth of his body. Elizabeth stiffened reflexively, stunned by the intimate contact, but she was powerless to move; though not as big as Conn, Ben possessed a surprising steely strength.

He kissed her with all the passion and heat at his command, his tongue delving over and over into the moist warmth of her mouth. Taking his time about it, he hungrily savored the taste and feel of her.

The sharp bite of corn liquor flavored his tongue and its fumes filled Elizabeth's head, making her dizzy. Had he been anyone else, she might have been repulsed, but she was merely heartsick knowing that she was the reason he had imbibed so heavily.

The astonishing intimacy of it left her dazed. She had been kissed before—soft entreaties bestowed by the men who had sought her hand—but never like this. It struck her as ironic, and a bit sad, that she should receive her first passionate kiss on her wedding day, from a man other than her husband.

A response of any kind was beyond Elizabeth. Every nerve ending in her body tingled with the awareness that Conn was standing mere feet away, watching.

At last Ben lifted his mouth, and she gasped for breath. She hung in his arms like a rag doll as he looked straight into Conn's narrowed eyes. "Any complaints?" he asked with such deliberate provocation that several gasps sounded around them.

Conn took a step forward and gently removed Elizabeth from Ben's embrace. Placing an arm around her, he tucked her securely against his side. "A few," he said smoothly. "But given the situation, I'm willing to let them slide. This one time. If it happens again, I won't be so understanding. You can count on it."

They exchanged a long, steady look, while those around them held their breath. After a moment Ben nodded. "Fair enough. All I ask is that you treat her well and take good care of her."

"You have my word on it," Conn replied solemnly.

Ben nodded again, and after one last, yearning look at Elizabeth, he turned and walked away, his back straight, his features set in an expressionless mask as he shouldered his way through the crowd and disappeared into the darkness.

Releasing Elizabeth, Conn swept his gaze over the silent spectators. "Time to call it a night, folks. Elizabeth and I appreciated the party, but it's time we all turned in. Tomorrow's going to be a hard day."

"Conn's right," someone called out. "Tomorrow we cross the Mississippi!"

Released from the thrall in which they'd been held, the clusters of people began to stir and drift apart.

Partly out of habit, and partly to escape her jangling nerves, Elizabeth rushed over to the tables to help the other women clean up, but she had barely picked up a bowl when Hester removed it from her hands.

"Here, now, give me that. What do you think you're doing?"

"I'm going to help—"

"Nonsense. Not tonight, you aren't. The rest of us can take care of these piddlin' dishes."

"Hester's right. You just run along, Elizabeth," Doris Maybry concurred. "You don't want to keep your husband waiting, now, do you? Not tonight of all nights."

Elizabeth turned scarlet, but several of the other women bustling about chimed in their agreement, and amid giggles and sly looks they shooed her on her way.

Two steps away Elizabeth spun back and grasped Hester's hands. Biting her lower lip, she searched her friend's face. "Hester . . . I . . . I'm so sorry about Ben. I never meant—"

"Now, don't you worry none about Ben." Hester squeezed Elizabeth's hands hard. "He'll get over it. You'll see. That baby brother of mine is a tough one."

"I know, but if I hadn't encouraged him—"

"He'd 've still fallen in love with you," Hester insisted. "Feelings aren't something a body can control. They have a way of just sneaking up on you whether you want 'em to or not. You know that. Besides, at the time, things were different." She gave Elizabeth's hand another encouraging squeeze, though her smile was a trifle forlorn. "It just wasn't meant to be, is all. That's something Ben is just gonna have to accept."

Hester's understanding touched Elizabeth, and she knew a moment of fierce regret. If things had worked out differently, they could have been sisters. They looked at each other wistfully, the knowledge there in their eyes for each to see.

Overcome with emotion, Elizabeth surged forward and hugged her friend. "Oh, Hes, I wish—"

"I know. I know," the older woman crooned, returning the embrace. "Me too. But leastways we'll always be friends. Nothing can change that."

Both women were misty-eyed when they parted. "Here now, enough of this foolishness," Hester declared, and with a bracing smile she turned Elizabeth around and gave her a little shove. "Run along with you, now. Else that husband of yours is liable to come and drag you away."

Shakily, unable to look at him directly, Elizabeth walked to where Conn stood waiting.

"Ready?" he inquired.

An attempt at a smile resulted merely in a nervous wavering of her lips. Giving up the effort, Elizabeth settled for a nod, and he fell in step beside her.

Her legs felt like wooden stumps, and she was amazed that they continued to work. The cook fires rimming the camp had long since been banked, and as they left the torch-lit area behind, darkness quickly swallowed them up.

The warm night air flowed against their skin like a lover's breath, caressing arousing. It carried with it the pungent scent of pine and the sweet perfume of crushed clover. Overhead, a half-moon hung like a broken disc in the dark, star-sprinkled sky, bathing everything in its faint glow.

They walked in silence, not touching, each lost in thought. Their feet moved with a slow cadence that marked the sluggardly passing of time and built anticipation to a fever pitch. The rustle of grass underfoot and the swish of Elizabeth's silk skirt mingled with the night sounds—the croaking chorus of frogs down by the stream, the distant low of a cow, the whir of the cicadas.

All Elizabeth could hear was the thunder of her heart, reverberating in her ears.

Excitement pounded through her veins. If it was tinged with fear, that was only normal, she told herself. For it was merely fear of the unknown, not Conn. Never Conn.

She had dreamed of this night for most of her life, wondered about it, yearned for it, and now, at long last, it was here. Her heart gave a little thump, and she shivered as a tingle raced over her skin, leaving goose bumps in its wake. Arms crossed over her midriff, she hugged her happiness to her and gazed up at the velvet sky, savoring the sweet anticipation. Soon—very soon—in Conn's arms she would learn what it was to truly be a woman . . . a wife. Conn's wife.

Turning his head slightly, Conn looked down at Elizabeth from the corner of his eye. He always thought of her as small—tiny, even—but with a start he realized that the top of her head came level with his shoulder, making her taller than most women, several inches taller than Millie had been. It was her wand slenderness that created the illusion, he supposed. That, and the ethereal quality of her beauty.

The dim moon glow bleached her golden hair to a shimmering silver. A few wispy ringlets, dislodged by the evening of energetic dancing, floated flirtatiously about her face. The rest, caught up high at the back of her head and adorned with a circlet of wild flowers, cascaded down her back in a froth of loose curls that reached well below her shoulder blades.

Eyeing the shining mass, Conn wondered how long it was, how it would look unbound and spread out on a pillow. The only time he could recall seeing it completely loose had been when he'd pulled her from the river, and he'd been too terrified then to notice. He had only a vague memory of it hanging about her hips when he'd rocked her in his arms afterward in the wagon.

She strolled along beside him with such innocent calm, he wondered if she even knew about the intimacies married couples shared. An intriguing hint of a smile hovered about her lips, and with her face lifted to the sky the moonlight caught her drowsy, half-closed eyes, making them sparkle like stardust.

She was so soft, so feminine. The subtle scent of violets, warmed by her skin and enhanced by her own womanly fragrance, wafted to him, making his nostrils twitch and firing his body.

He needed a woman desperately, and though he tried to control his wayward thoughts, the image of him running his mouth over her, searching out that tempting scent all along her creamy skin, rose to tempt him even more.

He had every right to bed her, he told himself, scowling into the darkness. She was his now. His wife.

His wife.

Pain seared his heart like the stab of a hot knife. Grimacing, Conn cursed silently. No matter how great his need, he couldn't do it. He couldn't make love to Elizabeth. It was too soon. He needed time—time to get over Millie, time to let go of the past, time to sort through the last sixteen years and try to make some sense of them.

Regardless of the vows he'd made before Reverend Haig, Conn knew that if he made love to Elizabeth now, it would seem like a betrayal. It didn't matter that his marriage to Millie had been less than fulfilling, or that their love had faded to a pitiful, pale thing. He still thought of her as his wife.

His throat tightened. She was no longer his wife, of course; in his mind he could accept that. But they'd been married for sixteen years, and he'd taken it for granted they always would be.

Conn gritted his teeth against a rush of anger and grief. If there was one thing he should have learned, it was that things had a way of going awry. Life changed, and we had no choice but to take a different path. The future he had planned with Millie was lost to him forever. She was lost to him forever. For them there would be no second chance. But until his heart accepted that, he couldn't be a husband to Elizabeth.

He wanted her. But that was part of the problem, he thought as his gaze skimmed over her elegant profile. This unexpected physical attraction to Elizabeth made him feel worse. How could he want another woman? Especially this woman?

It seemed strange to think of Elizabeth in those terms; he wasn't comfortable with it.

As long as he was being honest, he might as well admit, too, that he felt guilty about pressuring her into this marriage. Because that was exactly what he'd done. Oh, he'd made it seem that he was insisting for "her sake," to save her reputation and provide her with a home. But he'd known that by mentioning the children he was making it impossible for her to refuse. She would no more turn her back on Millie's children than she would bay at the moon. Loyalty was as much a part of Elizabeth's makeup as her gray eyes.

But the real reason he'd rushed her into marriage was just plain selfishness: he didn't want to lose her, too.

Of course he didn't expect passion from this marriage. Experience had taught him that gently bred females were repelled by a man's needs. Certainly Millie had found no pleasure in the physical side of marriage, and he didn't expect things to be any different with Elizabeth. She was a refined, genteel lady right down to her fingertips.

No, Elizabeth was hardly the earthy type. She was a soothing woman—a gentle, quiet, giving woman.

Which, he told himself, was exactly what he needed. They might not have romance and passion, but they would have a good life together. With Elizabeth there would be no false expectations to end in disillusionment. Moreover, her tender heart and generous nature would make her an excellent mother and a pleasant companion. She would bring order and peace to his life with that sweet serenity of hers.

Forcing her into this marriage might have been a selfish thing to do, but it wasn't a mistake. He would do his damnedest to make her life happy, and she would be good for the children, for him as well. He had no doubts about that. Deep down he was even sure that this was what Millie would have wanted, for if there was one person in the world whom she had truly loved, it was her cousin.

By silent, mutual consent, they drew to a halt beside Elizabeth's wagon. She hesitated and peeked up at him, a shy smile wavering on her lips.

"Elizabeth," Conn began, but his voice trailed away. He wasn't sure what to say. Or even if he should say anything. How the hell could he tell her that he did not expect her to sleep with him? That she was safe, for now at any rate, from what Millie had so disdainfully called his "carnal cravings"? She would probably be offended by the mere mention of such things.

"Yes?"

Elizabeth looked up at him with those wide, soulful eyes, and the desire he had thought conquered came surging back, hot and pulsing. His brain and his heart might tell him that it was wrong to want Elizabeth, but his starved body wasn't listening. They gazed at one another in silence. Around them a heady tension crackled in the air like heat lightning.

Without intending to, without being aware of doing it, Conn gripped her upper arms. His fingers flexed around the soft flesh as he stared at her trusting, upturned face. Intent and hungry, his gaze roamed over her features one by one, touching briefly on the graceful winged brows, the delicate nose, the exquisite curves of high cheekbones, the elegant line of her jaw. Finally he focused on that soft mouth, pink and slightly parted, quivering ever so slightly, and his eyes darkened.

"Elizabeth." This time her name sighed from his lips, a zephyr of sound, a whisper of longing.

A low, raw groan came from his throat when the tip of her tongue darted out and swept over her lips. He felt a tremor ripple through her. Whether the reaction was prompted by fear or longing, he didn't know, and he was beyond caring. His fingers tightened on her arms. With his burning gaze fixed on her mouth, his head tilted to one side and began a slow descent.

Elizabeth's eyelids lowered slowly.

The moist warmth of his breath eddied across her skin, and his lips hovered a mere hair's breadth from hers when a loud cough sounded within the wagon.

Conn straightened with a jerk, his head snapping around toward the opening in the canvas.

"Oh!" Elizabeth jumped, and her hand flew to her bosom. Surprise widened her eyes, and when Conn's gaze sliced back to her, she met his hard stare with an apologetic grimace. "It's Faith. Oh, dear . . ." She looked anxiously from the wagon to Conn, her lower lip caught between her teeth. "I . . . I guess she got tired and went to bed. She didn't know . . . that is . . . I should have . . . I'll just move her to—"

"That's all right, Elizabeth." He stopped her with a hand

on her arm when she would have stepped up onto the tailgate. "Let her sleep."

Finding the child still occupying Elizabeth's wagon confirmed what Conn had suspected. Had she been expecting a traditional wedding night, she would have made arrangements for Faith to sleep elsewhere.

He looked at Elizabeth curiously, wondering if keeping the child with her was her way of telling him she wanted no part of the physical side of marriage. It was exactly the kind of thing Millie would have done in her place.

The thought nettled him. Unreasonably so, he told himself, considering his own reluctance to consummate the marriage. Hell, what did he expect?

Elizabeth looked surprised. "Oh. Well, if that's what you want . . ."

Assuming he intended for them to sleep in one of his wagons, she waited uncertainly, expecting him to take her arm and lead the way. But he didn't move.

For several moments Conn studied her, his strong face set and unreadable. Finally he cupped his hand around the side of her face. Glittering blue eyes followed the absent brush of his thumb back and forth across her chin, as though testing the hint of a cleft there. Elizabeth's heart thundered. Head tipped back, she waited, the trembling expectancy growing to a tormenting, delicious agony.

A sharp constriction squeezed her chest and stopped her breath altogether as he leaned toward her. Her eyes fluttered closed in anticipation. But it was her forehead, not her parted lips, that felt the touch of his mouth.

"Good night, Elizabeth."

Good night? Her eyes opened slowly, and shock rendered her speechless. In a daze, she stood as though frozen and watched him walk away. For several seconds after he had disappeared from sight, her wide, disbelieving eyes stared into the darkness that had swallowed him up. At first she was too numb to take it in or to feel anything, but gradually she understood, and with the understanding came pain.

He didn't want her.

She squeezed her eyes shut. Her lips folded together in a straight line as her balled fist pressed against her midriff. Oh, God. Conn didn't want her.

The hurt was excruciating. It permeated every cell in her body. It pressed in on her, crushing her until her chest felt as though it would cave in, and her knees threatened to buckle.

A sob rose, but she clamped her hand over her mouth to hold it in. Another followed, then another, and her shoulders began to jerk. Tears seeped from between her lashes and streamed down her face. Blindly Elizabeth groped behind her, and when her fingers closed around a spoke, she turned and leaned against the wheel for support, laying her forearm over the rim and burying her face in the bend of her elbow.

She wanted to wail and moan and unloose her grief, but the fear of being heard wouldn't allow it. She struggled to contain the anguished sounds, only sharp little gulps, muffled against her arm, escaping her. They hurt her throat and caused her entire body to convulse.

She wept as though her heart would break, the wrenching cries all the more painful for their silence. Tears flowed from her eyes in unending torrents, making her face and forearm slick. Loose tendrils of hair clung to the wet skin and got in her eyes and mouth, but she didn't care or even notice. Her misery was soul deep. Fathomless.

The convulsive sobs went on and on until her chest ached and her throat was raw. At last, wrung dry, her weeping gradually subsided to sniffles, then to choppy sighs.

Elizabeth lifted her face from the bend of her elbow, turned her head, and rested her drenched cheek against her forearm. Except for an occasional shuddering sigh, she stood still and stared into the darkness through spiked lashes. Her eyes burned, and her heart felt like a lead weight in her chest.

Conn didn't even find her attractive enough to bed. She closed her eyes and let the thought sink in, fighting back a renewed freshet of tears. She repeated the words over and over in her mind, imprinting them on her consciousness in an act of deliberate flagellation. It was time to face the truth. But, oh, God, it hurt so.

It was her own fault. She should have known from his blunt proposal not to expect anything. Conn had probably intended all along for the marriage to be one of convenience, but, as usual, she had responded like the lovelorn fool she was.

Would she never learn?

Elizabeth straightened away from the wheel and wiped her eyes with the backs of her hands. Sadly she knew the answer was probably no. It hurt her pride to admit it, but even had she known the kind of marriage he was proposing, she would still have accepted. Loving him as she did left her with no choice; any kind of life with Conn was preferable to one without him.

At four the next morning as they were getting dressed by the light of a candle, Faith darted several apprehensive glances at Elizabeth's red-rimmed eyes, but she asked no questions. The child's way of dealing with anything unpleasant or scary, Elizabeth had already realized, was to run away from it or pretend it didn't exist. Elizabeth didn't doubt that Faith knew full well what had caused the damage. She had probably seen her mother's eyes tear-ravaged more times than she could count.

In many ways Faith was doing better, but she was still painfully shy and withdrawn. She was touchingly appreciative of everything Elizabeth did for her and seemed to regard her with something akin to worship. Wherever Elizabeth went the child was never far from her side, always hovering like a little ghost in the background, much the same as Pike. Even so, Faith did not completely trust anyone, and she darted away like a skittish colt at the least sign of trouble or dissension. She almost never talked, except to answer when spoken to. Elizabeth worried about the child's reticence, but for once she was grateful for her silence.

Rachel, however, was not the least bit hesitant about broaching the subject. The girl was the first person Elizabeth encountered when she and Faith arrived at the cook fire. The instant Rachel spotted Elizabeth's wan face, her eyes narrowed.

"So, you've been crying." She smiled with malicious satisfaction. "Good! I hope you bawl your eyes out every night. Serves you right."

"Rachel!" The unprovoked attack so stunned Elizabeth, her jaw dropped. She stared at the girl in shock as Faith sidled away and Pike growled from beneath a nearby wagon.

"You thought you were so smart, getting Daddy to marry you. But it didn't work, did it? He doesn't want you."

"Rachel, please! Keep your voice down."

"Why should I? Everybody in camp already knows he didn't share your bed last night. I heard the other ladies talking about it when I visited the woods a few minutes ago."

Elizabeth's face paled even more. She felt sick. Traveling together as they were, with almost no privacy, it was impossible to keep anything a secret from the other members of the train. She had known that before long everyone would be talking about her and Conn, but she hadn't expected to face the humiliation quite so soon.

"I see," she managed shakily. "You shouldn't listen to gossip, Rachel. What . . . what happens between your father and me is no one else's business."

"Nothing happened between you and Daddy," she sneered. "And nothing is going to, because he doesn't care anything about you. So don't think you can take my mother's place, because you can't. Daddy loved her. He'll always love her. You're nothing but a skinny old maid. He only married you so he'd have someone to look after Ian. And because he felt sorry for you."

With that parting shot, she whirled and stalked off, leaving Elizabeth standing there, shattered and aching.

"Don't you pay that child no mind, Miz Liz'beth."

Elizabeth jumped at the sound of Jemma's voice, her gaze darting to where she stood at the back of the cook wagon. The wiry little black woman was watching her pityingly, and Elizabeth realized she had heard every word.

"She's just jealous, is all. And a mite confused."

"Jealous?" Struggling to regain her composure, Elizabeth pulled her tattered pride about her and walked to the wagon. She dipped her hands into the bowl of water that Jemma had set out, then scooped up a bit of soft soap and worked up a lather. "Why should she be jealous of me? As she said, Conn doesn't care for me that way."

"Humph! Mebbe. Mebbe not. We'll just have to wait an' see 'bout that. All I know is she pitched a hissy fit when her daddy told her he was gonna marry you."

"You mean Conn knew how she felt beforehand?" At Jemma's nod, Elizabeth's brow puckered. "I'm amazed that he didn't call the wedding off."

"I reckon he knows she'll come 'round. She's just worried that now her daddy's got hisself a new wife, we'll all be forgetting her mama. That's all."

"I suppose." Elizabeth dried her hands and dug down into the cornmeal barrel for eggs, pulling out enough to fill a bowl. She set them on the tailgate and gathered the other ingredients she needed. "It's strange, though. Rachel and Millie were never close. She's shown very little grief over her mother's passing."

"Mebbe that's the problem."

Elizabeth stopped pouring milk into the mixing bowl and looked at the bustling little woman, her expression arrested. There were times when Jemma's keen insight truly amazed her.

It was possible that Rachel felt guilty because she was not overcome with grief over her mother's death. Sadly, Millie's passing had not had a profound effect on Rachel's life. In truth, it had hardly created a ripple.

Her inability to mourn was understandable; Millie had not taken an active interest in either of her children. That they stayed out of her way and presented a proper appearance those times when the occasion warranted their presence was all she required of them. Jemma had been more of a mother to Rachel and Ian than Millie ever had.

Perhaps, though, sensing that there should have been more, Rachel felt guilty and therefore doubly compelled to guard her mother's memory.

That would account for her sudden animosity, Elizabeth mused as she mixed the first batch of cornbread batter. Over the years she had kept her distance from Conn's children, it was true, but until recently, when Rachel had begun to appear resentful of her closeness to Millie, their relationship had always been amicable.

Or maybe she was just grasping at straws because she already had more problems than she could handle.

"Morning."

Elizabeth had been so deep in thought, she hadn't noticed Conn's arrival, and at the sound of his voice she nearly dropped the crockery bowl. Looking up, she found him standing beside the back wheel, a cup of coffee in his hand. Taking a sip, he looked at her over the rim of the tin cup.

She quickly lowered her gaze to the batter she was mixing. The humiliation of the night before was still fresh. Nor did she want him to notice her eyes. It would be embarrassing for both of them if he realized she'd been crying. He obviously wanted their relationship to continue unchanged, and she had no intention of making him uncomfortable with her unwanted feelings. She tried to ignore the banging of her heart. "Good morning."

Conn swallowed the scalding coffee and watched her, anger rising inside him. There she stood, calmly going about her work exactly as she did every morning. She acted as though that ceremony the previous evening had not even taken place. Dammit! They were married. Things should be at least a little different between them. Couldn't she smile at him? Maybe offer him a peck on the cheek? Do something to indicate she was aware of their changed situation?

"I told the men not to saddle your horse today," he said, watching her. "We'll start crossing the Mississippi at first light. We'll ferry, of course, but I figured you'd want to ride inside the wagon anyway."

Elizabeth started, and the hand holding the spoon paused briefly, then resumed stirring with even greater vigor. With all that had happened in the past twenty-four hours, she had forgotten about the monstrous river that awaited them.

Color bloomed in Elizabeth's cheeks at the subtle reference to her problem. It embarrassed her to be so terrified of something everyone else seemed to take in stride, but try as she might, she couldn't conquer the fear. At every crossing she huddled in the back of her wagon like a ninny, with her hand clamped over her mouth and her eyes squeezed shut, shaking as if she had the ague.

The last time, Faith had wrapped her skinny arms around Elizabeth's shoulders and murmured soothing words of comfort and encouragement to her during the entire crossing, as though she were the adult and Elizabeth the child. Elizabeth had been both touched and mortified.

"Thank you," she said, and without looking up she poured the batter into an enormous iron skillet.

From the corner of her eye she saw Conn's mouth tighten. He watched her for a moment longer, but as the first of the men arrived with their milk pails, he took a last swallow of coffee, slung the dregs out of the cup, and walked away.

At breakfast it quickly became apparent that the gossip about her and Conn had already reached every ear. The hired hands ducked their heads and mumbled self-conscious thanks

as she served their plates, and during the meal not one of them
would meet her eye. The whole time Taw glowered at Conn
and muttered under his breath, while Joseph, his brow furrowed with concern, looked back and forth between his son
and Elizabeth. Garth smirked.

Watching, Rachel gloated, the malicious glee in her eyes
and her smug smile stinging Elizabeth's pride like salt in a
raw wound.

Conn appeared oblivious to it all, and of her.

Only Ian's shy overtures eased the dull ache in Elizabeth's
heart. Since waking, he had practically become her shadow,
sticking closer to her even than Faith, though he never uttered
a word. When he hadn't dogged her steps he'd sat on Taw's
knee, diligently sucking his thumb, and over the balled little
fist those big blue eyes, so like his father's, had solemnly
tracked her every move.

Instead of taking his usual place between his grandfather
and Conn, when they'd all gathered around the campfire to
eat, Ian had squirmed in between her and Faith, forcing the
girl to scoot farther down the log they were using as a bench.
Typically, Faith had made the shift without a protest.

Throughout the meal he sat as close to Elizabeth as he could,
his sturdy little body pressed against her side. He still didn't
speak, but he peeked up at her often, and every now and then
she felt his pudgy hand stroke her arm, as though reassuring
himself that she was still there.

By the time everyone finished eating, all the hands had
drifted away and only the family remained, enjoying a last
cup of coffee. When Jemma lifted the kettle from the fire to
heat up the dishwater, Elizabeth started to rise, too, but Ian
chose that moment to break his silence.

The ever-present thumb made a pop as he pulled it from
his mouth. "Did you an' my papa really get married?" he asked
in his piping little voice, peering up at her cautiously.

Elizabeth sat back down on the log. "Yes, we did."

"An' er you gonna live with us forever an' ever?"

The innocent words and the vulnerable look revealed a world of fear and wrung Elizabeth's tender heart. She put down her plate and ruffled his black hair. He looks so much like his father, she thought, smiling into the dark-fringed blue eyes staring at her so hopefully. "Yes, Ian," she reassured him softly. "I'm going to live with you from now on."

"Faith, too?"

"Uh-huh. Faith, too. Would you like that?"

He looked at Faith, thought about it for a moment, and nodded. "Are you her new mama?"

"Well, sort of."

"You gonna be my new mama, too?"

"Oh, Ian—"

"She's not your mama," Rachel snapped.

Elizabeth looked up to find the girl standing on the other side of the fire, glaring her dislike.

Faith eased farther down the log, twisting one long curl round and round her finger.

"Is too!" Ian insisted, turning on his sister in a rare display of aggression. "Grampa said so."

"Just because Papa married her doesn't mean—"

"That's enough, Rachel." Conn's stern voice cut across his daughter's. "Elizabeth is your stepmother now, so you may as well accept it."

"I won't! I don't care what you say, she'll never be *my* mother!" she shrilled, glaring at Elizabeth. "I hate—"

"Rachel!" Conn thundered. "That will be enough."

"I don't see why you had to go and marry her. She's—"

"I explained all that to you, Rachel. I know you miss your mother. We all do. But I am married to Elizabeth now, and as my wife she deserves your respect. Now I want you to apologize to her at once."

"Conn, no, please—"

"Yes," Conn insisted, cutting off Elizabeth's protest. "I

won't have her behaving this way toward you."

An uncomfortable silence fell. Faith eased off the log and slipped away into the shadows. Sucking his thumb once again, Ian buried his face against Elizabeth's arm and began to whimper.

After a tense moment, Rachel muttered a surly, "I'm sorry," not quite meeting Elizabeth's eyes.

"That's all right, dear, I understand," she replied, but the statement merely earned her a narrow-eyed look of intense dislike.

Chapter 13

The first morning of their marriage seemed to set the tone for the days that followed. Conn treated Elizabeth with a respectful deference; he was cordial, solicitous of her comfort and needs, and often thoughtful, but he remained distant. He spent little time with her, and then only in the company of the others. He never sought her out, never asked her to ride beside her, never directly engaged her in conversation.

To Elizabeth's growing sorrow, it seemed more and more that in getting married, they had somehow forfeited their friendship. She wondered if Conn wasn't already regretting the marriage. It was obvious that he didn't find her attractive, and early in the trip he had expressed doubts about her ability to cope with the rigors of travel and the frontier.

Not that she blamed him. She couldn't even cross a stream without quaking in her boots. Whenever she thought of the spectacle she'd made of herself when they'd crossed the Mississippi, the morning after their marriage, she burned with shame.

At the first sight of that mighty river she had panicked. The prospect of crossing it on one of the flimsy river crafts moored to the docks at Natchez had brought on a bout of hysteria so mind numbing that she shuddered to recall it.

She remembered staring at the water and shaking her head. "No. No, I won't. I won't do it."

"There now, Missy," Taw had consoled her. "Don't go

gittin' yoreself all het up. Jist climb on in the back with them young'uns an' we'll be on t'other side afore you kin—Here now! What're you doin'?" He stood up and hauled back on the reins as Elizabeth swung one leg over the side of the wagon. "Whoa, mules! Whoa, I say!"

By the time the wagon came to a full stop Elizabeth had both feet on the ground and was backing away, her terrified gaze fastened on the rushing river.

"Now, Missy, you git back here—"

"No! I'm not going."

Taw looked around and spotted Conn astride his horse down by the dock, talking to the boatman. The three wagons and teams in line ahead of Elizabeth's were already loaded and secured, and lines were being cast off. Waving both arms, Taw bellowed, "Conn! Conn, git up here quick!"

One glance Taw's way and Conn broke off his conversation and spurred his mount in their direction.

"It's the little missy," Taw called out as he cantered up the incline. "Took one look at that river and bolted outta this wagon like it were a'fire. Says she ain't gonna cross."

Conn frowned, his concerned gaze fixing on Elizabeth's white face. Without taking his eyes from her, he swung down from the saddle and ground-hitched his horse. "Elizabeth, sweetheart, take it easy. Come on, now. There's nothing to be afraid of." He held out his hand and walked toward her slowly.

Elizabeth backed away, shaking her head. She stared at the water as though it were a serpent about to strike her.

"I'm not going to let anything happen to you, Elizabeth. I promise. Now come on. Let me take you back to the wagon."

"No. No, I can't. You can't make me!"

"All right. All right. Just take it easy, sweetheart. Take it easy. Everything's going to be fine." Cautiously Conn stalked her, coaxing in a soft, soothing voice. His eyes never wavered from her face as he edged closer. Pike stood to one side, looking worriedly from Conn to Elizabeth, a shrill whine issuing from his throat.

Elizabeth took another step backward and bumped into a stump beside the road. She let out a little cry and flailed her arms for balance, and at that instant Conn sprang.

"No! Let me go! Let me go! Nooo!"

She resisted with all her might, struggling and twisting in his arms, yelling every breath.

Conn tried to subdue her without inflicting pain, but finally he gave up. Bending, he rammed his shoulder into her midsection, and her breath *whooshed* out. He clamped an arm around the backs of her knees and straightened with her dangling, head down, over his shoulder. She hung there dazed, choking and gasping, as he strode back toward the river.

Taw had the tailgate lowered by the time Conn reached the wagon. In one fluid motion he hitched himself up onto the platform and rose to his feet. "Let's get moving."

"Nooo! Nooo! Let me out of here! Oh, please!"

Ignoring her, and the goggled-eye children huddled together in the rocking chair, Conn tossed her onto her bed. She landed on her back with a loud "Ummph," her billowing skirt and petticoats falling in a frothy pile about her thighs. Before she could spring off the bed, Conn came down on top of her.

"Be quiet, Elizabeth. Dammit, calm down. You're scaring the children." He glanced over his shoulder at Faith and Ian, who had begun to bawl. "You kids get down on the floor and stay there until we get to the other side. Now!" he barked.

Her eyes wide with fright, Faith scrambled to obey the rough command, pulling Ian down with her.

"Oh, please! Please! Let me up." Elizabeth struggled mindlessly, but Conn lay between her legs, his big frame pinning her to the mattress.

Arching her neck, she tipped her head back and started to scream, but he clamped his palm over her mouth. She tasted the salty tang of his skin and inhaled its sharp, masculine scent, but she scarcely noticed. The wagon rocked as it rolled forward. Over the top of his hand, her eyes widened, and she whimpered against his palm.

"Take it easy, sweetheart," he crooned in a softer voice. "I'll be right here with you. I'll take care of you. Trust me, little one."

Elizabeth barely heard him. Hooves clattered and iron wheels rumbled over the wooden dock. Then the whole rig bumped and lurched as it rolled onto the flatboat. Elizabeth moaned.

Ian's wailing cries went on unabated, despite Faith's frantic efforts to comfort him. From outside came shouts and curses, the frightened braying of mules, the slap of water against the side of the vessel. The dank, muddy stench of the river made Elizabeth's nostrils flare. She shivered, remembering the taste of murky water filling her mouth, her nose.

Beneath her back, the bed began to bob and roll. She jerked and made a strangled sound against Conn's palm as she realized they had cast off and were moving out into the current.

"It's all right, sweetheart," he murmured. "You're safe."

She twisted and squirmed and tried to get free, but Conn pressed her deeper into the mattress and held her there, spread-eagle beneath him, her breasts flattened against his broad chest, her thighs cradling his narrow hips and the hard bulge there, which pressed against that secret part of her.

Elizabeth made the entire trip across the river in that ignominious position, too terrified to be embarrassed. It wasn't until the wagon rolled onto the opposite bank and the mind-numbing fear began to recede that she became aware of the shocking, intimate alignment of their bodies.

The instant the wagon stopped, Faith, with Ian in tow, scooted out the back. Outside, Taw grumbled something to the mules, and the wagon rocked as he jumped to the ground.

Elizabeth grew still, except for the trembling deep in the

pit of her stomach, which had nothing to do with fear and everything to do with the awesome male body stretched atop hers. She looked into Conn's eyes as he braced up on his elbows, her gaze cautious and uncertain.

He returned the look. Slowly he lifted his hand from her mouth. He winced at the marks his fingers had put on her cheeks and stroked them gently with the backs of his knuckles.

The silence grew thick and heavy. His eyes glittered down at her in the dim interior of the wagon. She could feel the heavy thudding of his heart against her breast. Or was that her own? As though her senses had suddenly awakened, she became acutely aware of every hard line of his body, pressing against her, of the heat that seemed to fuse them together, of the heady masculine scent that surrounded her, and most of all, of his hips locked so tightly with hers and the yearning ache the contact created in her lower body.

Self-conscious under that penetrating stare, she shifted, and Conn groaned. Elizabeth sucked in her breath, her eyes growing wide as she felt that hard ridge of flesh stir against her.

"Elizabeth." He uttered her name in a low, raw voice that wasn't much more than a whisper. His eyes darkened and the lids lowered halfway, as though they'd suddenly grown heavy. "Elizabeth," he repeated, and her heart kicked against her ribs as his head descended.

"Conn? If the little missy's all right, you'd best git out here," Taw called from just outside the wagon. "Looks like that danged fool Sillsby's havin' trouble controllin' his stock."

Conn stiffened and leaped to his feet. "Be right there."

Stunned, Elizabeth lay unmoving. She felt confused and bereft and suddenly cold from the loss of his warmth. Raking a hand through his hair, Conn looked at her over his shoulder, and a flush replaced the chill as Elizabeth realized that her dress and petticoats, even her chemise, were still hiked up around her hips. She bolted upright and jerked down her clothing, her face burning.

"Are you going to be all right?"

She looked up and found him watching her, but his expression held only concern. Her mortification deepened, and so did her flush when she realized the passion she'd thought she saw in his eyes had been merely her imagination. She lowered her head and nodded. "I—I'm fine. I'm . . ." She stared at her fingers and the tiny pleats they were making in the skirt of her calico gown. "I'm sorry to be so much trouble."

He exhaled a beleaguered sigh. "Don't worry about it. Your fear is understandable, after what you went through. Besides, you're my wife now. It's my job to look after you."

Elizabeth knew he had meant the dutiful statement to be reassuring, but it had made her feel worse.

The memory of the episode tormented her. It had been bad enough that everyone was gossiping about her and Conn without her making a utter spectacle of herself. If Conn was having second thoughts, who could blame him? She couldn't cope with a simple river crossing. How could she cope with Indians and wild animals and God only knew what else?

Elizabeth had never considered herself pioneer stock, and the more she thought of what being Conn's wife entailed, the more inadequate she felt. Though she had not been pampered and spoiled like Millie, she had led a quiet, sheltered life in a modest home. What did she know about being mistress of a plantation? She had never run a big house. She knew nothing of overseeing servants or looking after their needs. For that matter she knew nothing of farm living; her entire life had been spent in Charleston.

She knew even less about raising children.

Even so, it was through the children that Elizabeth found a measure of comfort and happiness—at least, with Ian and Faith.

With Ian she had been lucky. Since the wedding he had become her devoted slave. He was a bright, affectionate child, as starved for a mother's love as she was to give it, and she doted on him.

Elizabeth loved it in the evenings when he climbed into her lap and snuggled close, and when she tucked him into bed and he clamped his chubby arms around her neck and gave her a wet, smacking kiss, she never failed to get a lump in her throat. She even found bathing him to be a delight. Amid the squeals and giggles and splashing, she usually ended up as wet as Ian, but it was worth it. When he clambered from the slipper tub for her to dry him, his sturdy little body all warm and rosy and smelling of soap and his wonderful little-boy smell, his blue eyes gleeful, she knew a poignant joy beyond measure.

Ian needed constant reassurance, however. Most of the time he clung to her like a limpet, trailing along with her as she moved about the campsite each morning and evening, one grubby little hand clutching her skirt, the other curled into a fist above the thumb stuck firmly in his mouth. He had even insisted upon sleeping in Elizabeth's wagon with her and Faith, and before long his clothes had been transferred there also.

With Faith things were not quite so easy. Despite her touching gratitude and quiet worship of Elizabeth, in many ways the girl remained skittish and withdrawn. At the least sign of discord or anger, no matter at whom it was directed, she almost always took flight, often disappearing for long stretches at a time. At first Elizabeth worried and fretted, and her instinct was to go after the girl, but Taw counseled otherwise.

"Now, now Missy, they's a time t' cluck over yore chicks and they's a time t' let 'um be. That little gal's jist protectin' herself the onliest way she knows how. She'll be back when she thinks it's safe."

"But, Taw, it is safe. No one's going to hurt her anymore."

"But she don't know that yet. In time, I 'spect she'll learn t' trust us, but you gotta remember, she didn't git that'a way over night. Jist be patient an' don't crowd her, an' she'll come around."

Deep down Elizabeth knew he was right, but she still worried. To ease her mind Taw made her a promise that if Faith was ever gone for more than an hour, or after dark, he would fetch her back himself.

In other ways Faith was an absolute joy. Though woefully ignorant and uneducated, the child was bright and inquisitive and quick to learn.

Which was a blessing, for Faith had a lot to learn.

It both surprised and saddened Elizabeth to realize that there was much about her life and habits, which were really quite ordinary, that were new and strange to the deprived child. Things that Elizabeth took for granted, that were so much a part of her training that she never gave them a thought, were foreign to Faith—like bathing regularly and washing her hands before meals, like saying "Excuse me" and "Please" and "Thank you," like saying grace at mealtime and her prayers at night, like keeping her abode and person tidy. The poor child lacked the most basic of manners, such as knowing to cover her mouth when she sneezed or yawned, not to belch or scratch herself in public.

To Faith, Elizabeth's modest belongings were riches beyond imagining. At first she could scarcely credit that she was allowed to sit in the oak rocking chair or actually sleep in the big carved mahogany bed with its goose feather mattress and clean sheets, or that she could have all she wanted to eat and didn't have to gobble her food before someone snatched it away.

Whenever Elizabeth did fancy work, such as embroidery or tatting or knitting, Faith observed each movement with fascinated awe. The times Elizabeth played the dulcimer and sang, or merely hummed while she worked, the little girl stared in wide-eyed amazement. With a child's wonder she noted the wealth of dresses and feminine underthings, the bonnets and gloves, and fine linen handkerchiefs, all lace-trimmed and neatly pressed, the horde of fluffy patchwork quilts and soft bed linens—and most amazing of all, the lacy bags of sachet in the trunks that kept everything smelling as sweet as spring flowers.

For the most part Faith adapted readily to the changes, but some things were just too strange, and she viewed them with suspicion, even downright resistance. One of those was Elizabeth's suggestion, made one evening as they sat around the fire, that she learn to read and write.

"What for?" Faith asked with just a touch of wary belligerence.

"For many reasons," Elizabeth replied patiently. "The ability to read and write is a skill that will help you get along in life. If you can read, you can learn anything you want. And no one can cheat you. And it's enjoyable. Everyone needs to know how to read."

"Taw don't know how, and he's done just fine."

"Shoot, young'un, don't go pointin' t' me. Why, I'm jist a broken-down ole trapper without much t' show fer all them years in the cold. Conn, now, with his learnin', had the good sense t' put aside the money he made over the years, but a ignorant ole cuss like me, I'd winter up in St. Louis an' live high. By spring ever' year, what I hadn't spent, the river rats and flimflammers'd done took. 'Sides, if'n I'da had me the chanct t' learn t' read, I'da shore took it." He squirted a stream of tobacco juice into the fire and gave the child a pointed look. "And you'd better, too."

"I don't wanna." Faith's thin face set with that look that said she would run if pushed.

Elizabeth let the matter drop. She had quickly learned that Faith could not be ordered or cajoled into doing anything once she bowed her neck, but she could be enticed.

Which had been exactly how she'd gotten her to take her first bath. Faith had been aghast when Elizabeth filled the tub and explained what she wanted her to do.

"You mean wash all over? Sit down *in* all that water?"

"Yes, dearest, that's right."

"Without . . . without a stitch on?" The child had stopped to dart a quick look around the cramped interior of the wagon before lowering her voice to a whisper. "Buck *nekked*?"

At Elizabeth's nod she had set her jaw and flatly refused. Instead of arguing, Elizabeth had proceeded to use the bath herself. She made such a show over enjoying herself—that night and every night afterward for almost a week—that she finally lured Faith into trying it. Ever since, she'd had a hard time keeping the child *out* of the tub.

So Elizabeth did not mention the matter of lessons again. Instead, in the evenings, after Faith's hair had been braided and Ian had been cuddled and tucked into bed, she set a candle on a box beside her chair, pulled out a book, and read . . . silently.

At first Faith ignored her. By the third night, however, Elizabeth could sense the child's covert scrutiny and her curiosity about Elizabeth's absorption. On the fourth night, when she judged the time was right, fifteen minutes or so after she'd begun reading, Elizabeth gasped.

Faith gave her a sharp look. Her gaze sought Taw, but the old man merely shrugged. A minute later Elizabeth placed her hand to her throat and whispered, "Oh, my."

The child sidled over and bellied up to the rocker arm. "What's wrong?"

"What? Oh! Oh, nothing. It's just that this story I'm reading is so exciting." Without pause Elizabeth's gaze went back to the print.

Faith peered over her arm and frowned. "Just looks like chicken scratches to me."

"Oh, no, dear, it's much more than that. You see each of these marks? They're letters. Each letter stands for a certain sound. When you know their sounds and you put them together, they form words. It's really not difficult."

Elizabeth pretended to go back to the story. After a moment a bony finger poked the page. "What's that one?"

That's the letter *b*." She demonstrated the sound the letter stood for, and at once Faith wanted to know another, and Elizabeth complied. "This one's an *f*. That's the first letter in your name. See, I'll show you."

Leaning over, she picked up a twig and scratched in the dirt the letters *FAITH*. "There. That's how you spell 'Faith.'"

The child stared and pursed her lips. She looked back at the book and pointed. "What's that say?"

"That? Well . . ." Elizabeth paused and tipped her head to one side. "Would you like to hear the story?"

Faith nodded, and Elizabeth scooted over and made room for her in the rocker. When the child was tucked under her arm, she turned back to the front of the book. "This story is titled *The Spy,* and it was written by a man named James Fenimore Cooper."

As Elizabeth began to read the tale, everyone around the fire went back to what they were doing: Taw and Joseph to their nightly game of checkers, Conn to poring over a map, Rachel, who refused to ask Elizabeth for help, to trying without much success to mend a pair of stockings. Isaac and Jemma sat off to one side, bickering quietly, as always.

As the story began to unfold, Elizabeth could feel the excitement mount in Faith's thin frame. Around the fire all grew quiet and still as the other activities gradually stopped. By the time Elizabeth halted, Taw, Rachel, Isaac, and Jemma were all sitting forward, watching her, tense and enthralled. Leaning back against a wagon wheel, Dr. Cavanaugh pulled on his lower lip and studied her. Even Conn looked up from his maps.

"Well, I think that's enough for tonight," Elizabeth said, snapping the book closed.

A chorus of grumbles backed up Faith's, "But you cain't stop now. We gotta know what happened next!"

"It's getting late, sweetheart. Besides, my voice is tired. A person can only read aloud so long, you know."

"Will you read some more tomorrow night?"

"I might. If my throat is up to it." Taking the child's hand to lead her toward their wagon, she added, "Of course, when a person reads silently she can keep going as long as she wishes."

Faith tipped her head up and gave Elizabeth a long look but said nothing.

For the next four nights, while Elizabeth read from Mr. Cooper's book, those around the fire hung on every word, even Rachel, though she pretended she was not even listening. When Elizabeth reached the end, Taw slapped his knee and whooped:

"By dingies! That thar' were some tale! I tell ya, Missy. I shore wouldn't mind hearin' me anuther."

Jemma and Isaac nodded in vigorous agreement, and Faith gazed at her hopefully.

"That's a splendid idea, my dear," Dr. Cavanaugh encouraged, looking at her with a shrewd smile. "I know just the one. Somewhere in my wagon I believe I have a copy of *Ivanhoe*."

The next evening Elizabeth began to read aloud the romantic tale, revealing to her listeners an ancient time shrouded in mystery and pomp and circumstance. As the story of knights of old and their fair ladies began to unfold, a hush fell and the expressions of those around the fire grew rapt.

Afterward Faith was quiet as they walked to their wagon. A while later her voice, small and uncertain, floated through the darkness as she lay beside Elizabeth in the big mahogany bed.

"Miz Elizabeth?"

"Yes, Faith?"

"I . . . I reckon I changed my mind 'bout learnin' to read an' write."

All Elizabeth's maternal instincts, so long held in check, came rushing to the fore in response to Ian's and Faith's obvious need of her. At the same time, in their innocent adoration, she found a degree of solace for her bruised heart.

With Rachel it was a different story. No matter what Elizabeth said or did, the girl continued to meet all overtures of friendship with sullen hostility.

"Just be patient," Hester counseled when Elizabeth sought her advice. "Give her time and she'll come around."

Leading Thistle, Elizabeth walked with her friend beside the line of creaking wagons, a faraway look on her face. "I hope you're right. I don't seem to have much choice, since I don't know what else to do."

"Conn'll come to his senses one of these days, too," Hester said kindly.

A wan smile served as Elizabeth's reply.

Like everyone else, Hester had known the hurtful truth about her marriage since the first morning. A few, like Agatha and her daughter, were openly contemptuous and spiteful, and Garth, with his leering looks and malicious smile, took every opportunity to make snide innuendos.

The man was clever, though. He always worded his comments so that they could be construed as perfectly innocent, especially if repeated. For that reason, and because she was embarrassed even to broach the subject of their marriage, Elizabeth didn't report him to Conn.

Most of the women had the good manners to pretend they knew nothing, but they were ill at ease and nervous in her presence. Elizabeth was aware of the whispers and titters and surreptitious looks that followed her everywhere. All she could do was hold her head up and ignore them. At times she wondered if Conn had any idea of the humiliation he was causing her.

"It's not uncommon, you know, for a man to fall in love with his wife *after* they're married," Hester persisted.

"I suppose." Elizabeth glanced at her friend, warmed by her concern, her smile sad. "But for that to happen, a man has to at least notice his wife once in a while. Most of the time Conn doesn't even know that I'm around." She looked up at the sky and widened her eyes against the foolish urge to cry. Lightly she slapped the loose ends of Thistle's reins against her palm. "Sometimes I wonder if he even knows I exist."

Dammit! You've got to stop thinking about her every waking moment. Even as the admonishing thought crossed Conn's mind, his gaze sought Elizabeth across the campfire.

She sat in her rocker with Faith perched on her knees, brushing the child's hair. When finished, she gathered the thick mane in her hands and began to plait it into a single braid. Ian, dressed in his nightshirt and diligently sucking his thumb, leaned against the arm of the rocker and watched the procedure with interest.

Conn wondered if Elizabeth brushed out her own hair and braided it every night before retiring. Immediately his body tightened in response to the mental image the thought conjured up, and he cursed beneath his breath.

The muttered words drew a raised brow from his father and a shrewd look from Taw. The old man's gaze flicked to Elizabeth, then back, and his beard twitched in what Conn suspected was a grin.

Dammit, he had to stop this foolishness. But he found himself staring at Elizabeth's raised arms, watching the way the blue calico pulled taut beneath them, emphasizing her full breasts and tiny waist. The hunger deep inside gnawed at him.

When Elizabeth finished with Faith she gave her a hug and kiss and set her on her feet. With a playful pat on her skinny little rump, she sent her scampering toward the wagon they shared to fetch the slate Faith used to practice her letters. No sooner had the girl vacated Elizabeth's lap than Ian climbed onto it.

Conn watched his son cuddle close, his small body curling

against her. Elizabeth's arms enfolded him. One hand tenderly stroked his baby-fine hair away from his face. With the tip of her toe she set the rocker in motion. Sighing his contentment, Ian wriggled closer and snuggled his cheek against her breast. In only seconds his heavy eyelids began to droop.

The sight created a restive flutter in Conn's stomach, and he cursed himself for a fool. Jesus! He couldn't be jealous of his own son. Ian was little more than a baby!

Elizabeth gazed down at the sleeping child, her face, in that moment, so soft and serenely lovely that it took Conn's breath away. She looks like a madonna, he thought. A beautiful, golden-haired madonna.

It struck him forcefully then that in all the years they had been married he'd never once seen Millie hold either of their children that way. Nor had he ever seen her look at them in that loving manner.

Immediately he was awash with feelings of disloyalty and guilt. Millie had loved Rachel and Ian, he told himself. In her own way. She simply hadn't been the maternal type. Elizabeth was. So what?

But he found the sight of Elizabeth nurturing his child strangely exciting, erotic even.

As Ian drifted into a deep sleep, his mouth stopped its sucking action and went slack. Slowly his wet thumb slipped out, and the chubby hand came to rest atop Elizabeth's breast.

Conn stared at that lax hand and felt his loins tighten. He swallowed hard. Jesus.

A tender smile curved Elizabeth's mouth, and she lowered her head and kissed Ian's baby-smooth brow.

The simple, loving gesture sent fire streaking through Conn, and with a smothered groan he lunged to his feet. Elizabeth looked up, startled.

"Gotta make rounds," he muttered curtly, and strode away.

Conn spent the next two hours berating himself for lusting after Elizabeth like a randy adolescent and swore it would not happen again.

Keeping the vow, however, proved an impossible task.

With each passing day the attraction he felt for her seemed to grow. He dreamed about her at night, and during the day he found himself thinking about her more than was wise. He tried to banish the feelings by recalling the towheaded child who had followed him about, or the shy, skinny adolescent who had been all eyes and elbows, but it was no use. Those images had been replaced by new memories. Countless times, Conn relived those moments in her wagon, remembering her softness, the sweet scent of violets and woman that emanated from her, the delicious feel of her soft body beneath him.

He found himself tempted beyond measure almost daily. It seemed to Conn that suddenly everything about Elizabeth was subtly seductive. The mere sight of her quietly mending his shirt by the light of the campfire, or tucking his sleeping son into bed, or simply arching her back after a long day's trek aroused him beyond anything he'd ever known. Her soft smiles made his heart leap, and her lightest touch tied his insides into knots. Reminding himself that this was his oldest and dearest friend, and that Elizabeth would be repulsed if she knew, had not the slightest effect on his desire.

He tried to keep his distance, but his efforts met with little success.

Twice, while making his night rounds, he ran into her as she returned from looking in on a patient. Each time he walked her back to her wagon, neither saying much to break the strained silence, his senses were tormented by her nearness.

One afternoon he came upon her at the creek close to their camp, wading in the shallows with Ian and Faith, the back of her skirt pulled through her legs and tucked into the front of her waistband. She was giggling and squealing right along with the children as they splashed and cavorted. Conn stood mesmerized, unable to look away from those pale, shapely legs or the look of joyous abandon on her face.

That night his sleep was disturbed by erotic dreams of long

golden hair twining about his naked body, of soft, sweet-scented ivory skin and pink-tipped breasts, of long legs with shapely calves and trim ankles wrapped around his hips, tender hands caressing him, touching him intimately, and wide gray eyes burning with desire and love, for him.

He awoke with a start, hours before the sentries' signal, drenched in sweat, his heart pounding.

In early August the train reached Alexandria, Louisiana, in weather so hot and humid they could scarcely breathe. They made camp a couple of miles west of town in a clearing surrounded by towering sweet gums and sycamores. Not a leaf stirred in the still air, and heat lightning flickered eerily in the distance.

Few campfires were lit that night. Most folks chose to make do with a cold supper of ham and leftover cornbread, washed down with buttermilk. The oppressive heat made babies and children cranky and sapped their parents of energy and patience. By early evening everyone had retired and the camp was dark.

Conn had gotten into the habit when making his nightly rounds of stopping at Elizabeth's wagon last and checking on her and the children before turning in. That night when he tapped on the tailgate and received no response, he assumed she was asleep, but a quick check inside revealed that the Rachel and Ian were there, but Elizabeth's side of the bed was empty.

He frowned, a vague uneasiness gripping him. A search around the wagon turned up no sign of her. He went to his father's wagon and tapped on the side. "It's me, Conn. Wake up, I need to talk to you a minute."

"I'm awake. It's too hot to sleep." Almost at once Joseph appeared in the canvas opening, dressed in only his cotton summer underdrawers. "Something wrong?"

"Elizabeth's not in her wagon. Do you know if anyone is

sick enough to need her tonight?"

"No, not a soul. Everyone's amazingly hale and hearty at the moment. Where do you suppose she is?"

"I don't know. But I'm not comfortable being this near Alexandria. The closer you get to the border, the rougher these towns are. There were some real hard cases hanging around when we rode through earlier." He didn't add that some of the shadier-looking characters had watched Elizabeth like wolves eyeing a lamb.

"What's goin' on?" Taw appeared at Conn's side out of the darkness. In inclement weather he slept in Dr. Cavanaugh's wagon, but because of the heat he had spread his bedroll beneath a sycamore a few yards away.

"I was just about to wake you," Conn said. "Elizabeth is missing. I want you to help me look for her."

"What! Well, what in thunderation're we standin' 'round jawin' fer? Let's go."

"Wait. I'll help, too." Dr. Cavanaugh ducked inside his wagon but was back only seconds later, pulling on his trousers.

They fanned out in three directions. Dr. Cavanaugh took the immediate camp and the road back to Alexandria, and Taw went west. Conn headed generally southwest toward the little creek, moving silently through the woods in a zigzag pattern.

He told himself he was worrying over nothing. In all likelihood there was a simple explanation for Elizabeth's absence. She had probably just gone out to answer nature's call rather than use the chamber pot in her wagon, in which case she would be mortified if he came upon her. Still, he could not shake the uneasy feeling in his gut.

Fifty feet or so from the creek a sound alerted him. Conn froze, listening. It came again—a splash that stood out from the gentle murmur of the stream. He crouched and moved forward through the woods, a silent, dark shape darting from tree to tree. At the water's edge he flattened himself against a bald cypress and peered cautiously around the trunk.

A few feet away, in water that reached to midthigh, stood Elizabeth . . . stark naked.

Conn's first reaction was relief, so great it almost buckled his knees. His second was shock.

He stood as though turned to stone, staring. She faced away from him, turned slightly in one-quarter profile. Conn's heart rate soared. He clenched his teeth. Look, away, you ass. Don't stand here ogling like a farm boy in a bawdy house, he told himself angrily. But he didn't. He couldn't.

Instead his gaze roamed over her, tracing the elegant line of her back, the way it curved inward to her tiny waist, the delightfully rounded derriere, and those beautiful long legs. She turned a bit more toward him, and his throat went dry as his gaze homed in on a full, uptilted breast in profile.

She looked like a goddess, standing there in the water. Her white body, tinted a pale, iridescent blue by the moonlight, stood out from the dark night shadows.

Bending, she scooped up water in her cupped palms and splashed it over her neck and chest. Fire shot through Conn's loins as the liquid flowed down her breasts and streamed from her nipples, returning to the creek with a tiny trickling sound.

An ominous splash farther up stream jolted him out of the sensual haze and sent a shaft of fear through him. He exploded in fury, stepped out from behind the tree, and splashed into the water.

Elizabeth gave a little shriek, but he reached her in three long strides, and before she could move he plucked her from the water and headed for the bank.

"Conn, no! Oh, please—"

"Shut up, Elizabeth!"

"But—"

On dry land he set her on her feet none too gently. "You stupid little fool!" Grasping her shoulders, he gave her a shake that sent the pile of loose curls atop her head tumbling about her shoulders and back. "What the devil do you think you're doing out here all alone in the middle of the night?"

Elizabeth moaned and tried to cover herself with her arms. "Conn, please!"

Her agonized tone penetrated his rage, and he finally noticed her mortification, her frantic, futile attempts to protect her modesty. With an impatient growl he snatched her cotton wrapper off of a nearby bush and thrust it at her. "Here, put this on. And then, by God, I want an answer."

She accepted the garment gratefully and fumbled into it. "I . . . I . . . it's so hot. I was just trying to cool off. That's all. I, uh . . . I thought everyone was asleep." She overlapped the front edges of the wrapper and held it closed with both hands. Warily she glanced up at Conn but couldn't quite meet his eyes.

"Cool off! Dammit, woman, don't you know there are alligators in these rivers?"

"*Alligators!*" Elizabeth scuttled closer to Conn and shot a terrified look at the shiny surface of the creek. "I—I didn't know." Despite the heat, she began to tremble.

Conn grasped her shoulders again and held her at arm's length. "Even if there weren't, it's still dangerous for you to be out here alone at night. Don't you know that?"

"D-dangerous?"

She stared up at him, those innocent gray eyes wide with bewilderment, and he knew she hadn't the least idea what he was talking about.

His mouth compressed into a straight line, and he closed his eyes for a moment, struggling for patience. As his eyelids lifted he noticed that the thin wrapper had become soaked wherever it touched her skin. It clung in dark splotches to her breasts, her abdomen, her thighs. Through the wet, almost transparent cloth he could see the pink areolas of her nipples, the tiny nub at each center, the indentation that marked her navel, and the shadowy triangle below it.

The desire that simmered just below the surface rose to mingle with fury and frustration. Conn's jaw clenched. His nostrils flared as his breathing became heavy and rough. The hands cupping her shoulders flexed. Finally, with a low growl, he hauled her into his arms. He took her mouth roughly, hungrily, kissing her with all the pent-up passion that had been building for weeks.

Shock slammed through Elizabeth. Too stunned to think, or even react, she stood docilely within his embrace, consumed by the twin sensations of sizzling fire and shivering ecstasy.

His mouth rocked against hers as though he would devour her. One hand slid down her spine and cupped her buttocks, his long fingers kneading the firm flesh as he pressed her hips tightly against his.

Jolted from her stupor by the bold caress, Elizabeth gasped, and Conn thrust his tongue into her mouth to plunder its sweetness with slow, sure strokes.

Unbearable pleasure shuddered through Elizabeth. Her heart raced and her blood began to pound through her veins. Her chest grew so tight, she could barely breathe. Mortification and shock quickly gave way as the love and longing of a lifetime surged to the surface. For years she had daydreamed endlessly of Conn holding her like this, kissing her like this. Those dreams faded into nothingness beside reality. This was a thousand times more potent, a shattering delight that robbed her of strength and set her soul afire.

Her hands climbed to his shoulders, and she clung to him, helpless to deny her heart. Her lips flowered eagerly beneath the onslaught, and she pressed closer, kissing him back. Despite inexperience, she responded to him with an instinct as old as Eve.

Her innocent kisses nearly drove Conn over the edge. His arms tightened around her, molding her to him as the kiss became hotter, more urgent. The hand splayed across her bottom pressed her against his aroused body with a slow, undulating rhythm. He lost all sense of time and place and purpose. In that moment all that existed in the world was Elizabeth. All that mattered was losing himself in the sweet warmth of her body. Now.

With his mouth still fastened on hers, he bent one knee to lower her to the ground, but before he could a rustle sounded in the woods nearby. He broke off the kiss abruptly, his head snapping up. Elizabeth hung in his arms, dazed.

"Missy? Missy, you out here?"

Conn grasped Elizabeth's shoulders and moved back until they were again at arm's length. They looked at each other in silence, as hearts pounded and chests heaved. Studying her stunned expression, so clearly revealed by the moonlight, he felt his stomach knot. He'd been right all along; she *was* revolted by his passion.

Disappointment and an odd hurt pierced him, and he reacted with defensive anger that made his voice harsh. "For God's sake, cover yourself," he snapped. "He'll be here any second."

Confused, Elizabeth looked down and gave a little cry. During the embrace she had released the robe, and it gaped open from neck to hem. Making distressed little sounds, she frantically snatched the edges together and overlapped them, holding them against her body with both hands.

Scarcely had she completed the action than Conn scooped her up in his arms. Elizabeth let out a shriek and made another frantic grab at her wrapper. Ignoring her struggle, he headed back to camp with long, angry strides. On the way he called out to Taw that he'd found her, but otherwise he didn't say a word until they reached her wagon. There he set her on her feet, snapped out a curt, "Go to bed, Elizabeth," and marched away before she could find her voice.

Chapter 14

 "Dad and I are going into Natchitoches to see what news we can pick up from Texas. You coming?"

At the terse question, Taw looked up from the harness he was oiling and met Conn's flinty stare. Yessiree, somethin' was shore 'nuff ailing the boy, he thought sagely. And it didn't take a whole lotta smarts to figure out that somethin' was a purty little blond-haired angel with gray eyes.

Taw fought back a grin. Conn had been tight-lipped and out of sorts ever since the wedding, but for the past four days, since the night he'd found her splashing in the creek, he'd been touchy as a grizzly with a bad tooth.

Yessiree, things was heatin' up right smart, betwixt them two. 'Bout time, too.

"Shore thing. I'd like to hear what ole Santee Annie's up t'. Jist let me put this tack away." Taw hove to his feet and squirted a stream of tobacco juice at a bee buzzing around a clump of clover. "Whilst I do that, I'd 'preciate it if'n you'd carry the little missy's rockin' chair back t' her wagon fer me. Don't look like she'll be needin' it none tonight, and she'll most likely be asleep by the time we git back."

They'd made camp that afternoon a half mile out of town and had an early dinner. Immediately afterward, as she'd done each of the past three evenings, Elizabeth had excused herself and returned to her wagon.

"I'll send Isaac."

"Cain't. He stepped in a hole an' twisted his ankle. Yore pa's got him soakin' it. Say's he'll have t' stay off that foot fer a day er so."

Pretending not to notice Conn's scowl, Taw took his time gathering up the rags and the tin of neat's-foot oil he'd used to lubricate the harnesses and tack. "I'll be ready t' go by the time you get back," he said guilelessly.

Conn hesitated, then made an aggravated sound. From the corner of his eye, Taw saw him snatch up the rocker and stalk away. The old man grinned. Sometimes a body jist needed a nudge in the right direction.

With every step that took him nearer Elizabeth's wagon, Conn's mood worsened. Dammit! Why was it that the harder he tried to stay away from her, the more fate seemed to throw them together? he wondered furiously. Well, he'd just put the damned rocker in her wagon and leave. It wouldn't take but a second. If Elizabeth didn't like it, that was too bad.

Since the night he'd kissed her, she'd made her feelings more than clear. If he got within so much as ten feet of her, she scurried away like a frightened rabbit. Hell, she wouldn't even look him in the eye anymore. "Probably thinks you're going to ravish her on the spot," he muttered under his breath.

Because that was precisely what he wanted to do, Conn had kept his distance.

The knowledge that he'd brought the situation on himself did not help his mood. What in heaven's name had he been thinking of, shackling himself to another prim, passionless woman? Hell, after sixteen years, you'd think he'd know better.

He should have bedded Elizabeth on their wedding night and been done with it. Waiting wasn't going to change the past or bring Millie back. The problem was, despite his frustration and growing anger, he didn't relish the thought of initiating an unwilling wife. Conn's mouth firmed into a grim line. Hell, the last thing he wanted was to hurt or frighten Elizabeth.

But by heaven, when they reached Riverbend they were going to sort out their relationship. He'd be damned if he'd spend the rest of his life living like a monk.

He reached Elizabeth's wagon and opened his mouth to call out to her, but the words died on his tongue when he rounded the back corner. He halted in his tracks and stared.

Elizabeth sat on the edge of the tailgate drying her freshly washed hair in the sunshine. Humming softly, her head tilted to one side, she ran her fingers over and over through the thick mane, shaking it gently. The pale tresses cascaded about her shoulders and back like a shimmering waterfall. In the slanting rays from the setting sun, each strand glittered like gold.

She picked up the brush from her lap and pulled it through her hair with long, smooth strokes. Conn's fingers tightened around the arms of the rocking chair until his knuckles turned white. He wanted to plunge his hands into that fragrant silk, bury his face in it, inhale its sweet scent, feel it slide against his skin.

She wore a voluminous white night robe with deep lace ruffles about the neck, hem, and elbow-length sleeves. With every stroke of the brush the cobwebbed flounce fell back, exposing the tender undersides of her arms and causing her unfettered breasts to sway beneath the cotton cloth.

Her legs swung back and forth in time to the tune she was humming, and Conn caught a glimpse of bare pink toes peeking out from beneath the bottom edge of the garment.

Elizabeth tipped her head to the other side and jumped when she caught sight of him. The brush halted in midstroke. Her legs stopped swinging. "Conn." She said his name in a breathy whisper of surprise.

Conn surfaced slowly, irritated to find that he was having trouble breathing. As a result his words came out harsher than he intended. "I brought your chair back." He set the rocker on the tailgate with a thump that made her flinch and fixed her with a hard look.

"I'm going into town. Natchitoches is the last U.S. settlement before we cross the border, and I want to find out if
there's any more news from Texas."

"Oh. I . . . I see."

Her uneasy tone and the self-conscious way she clutched her
night robe together and smoothed the heavy fall of hair away
from her face rankled. She crossed her feet one atop the other
and drew them up, her bare toes curling beneath the ruffled
hem of the robe. Conn gritted his teeth. Dammit! He was her
husband. There was nothing improper about him seeing her
in her night clothes. Or out of them, for that matter.

Giggles and splashes sounded inside the wagon. Through
the opening in the canvas he saw that Ian was in the slipper
tub. Kneeling beside it, dressed only in her chemise, Faith
was blowing soap bubbles with the lather she'd worked up
between her cupped palms, much to his son's delight.

Their innocent enjoyment warmed his heart and eased the
churning in his gut. Until recently he'd never heard Ian giggle
like that. Faith either. Elizabeth is good for them, he thought,
a reluctant smile tugging at his mouth.

It faded when he looked back at Elizabeth. She ducked her
head quickly, but not before he saw the unhappiness in her
eyes.

"Is there anything you or the kids need from town?" he
asked in a tight voice.

Looking up, she smiled faintly, her golden hair shimmering
about her shoulders as she shook her head. The movement sent
its sweet scent floating to him. "No, I don't think so. But
thank you anyway."

Conn gave her a long, piercing look. Finally, teeth clenched,
he muttered a taut, "Very well," and stalked away.

The air in Ackerman's Grog Shop was close and stuffy,
smelling unpleasantly of unwashed male bodies, open spit-
toons, and rotgut whiskey. All the shutters and doors stood

open, but the August night was warm and humid, and only the faintest of breezes stirred the thick pines around the settlement. Mosquitoes, moths, and other night-flying insects buzzed and fluttered freely through the openings and around the guttering tallow candles.

The puncheon floor of the log building was mottled with stains of countless spilled drinks, the near and not-so-near misses of expectorating customers, and a few splotches of what appeared to be dried blood.

The murmur of voices created a steady hum that was punctuated by the clink of glass, the dry riffle of cards, the click and clatter of poker chips, and an occasional bark of rough laughter. At the bar men in frock coats rubbed elbows with buckskin-clad frontiersmen and backwoods farmers in baggy homespun. The only woman in the room was a buxom soiled dove with frowsy yellow hair, wearing a low-cut red satin dress trimmed with scraggly black marabou feathers.

The room contained only four tables. A scar-faced man with a sinister look about him sat alone at the far one with his back to the corner, nursing a bottle of whiskey. Games of poker and reddog were in progress at two others. Conn, Joseph, Taw, and a riverboat captain by the name of Phineas McSweeny occupied the fourth.

"Yes sir, on my last trip up the Brazos I heard they still got Austin locked up in that ancient rock pile them Mexicans call the Prison of the Inquisition. Rumor has it he's kept in solitary for weeks at a time."

"What are the charges against him?" Conn asked, watching the red-haired captain swill down another shot of rye. The more the man drank, the more expansive he became, and Conn had kept his glass full for the past hour.

"Charges!" McSweeny gave a snorting laugh. "What charges?"

"Are you saying that a man, even one of Stephen F. Austin's stature, can just be thrown in jail at Santa Anna's whim?"

Joseph demanded. "Without even a trial?"

"That's about it. Since he assumed power, Santa Anna has handpicked every official in the country, including the Congress, and one by one they've legalized all his acts, after the fact." The bottle clinked against McSweeny's glass as he poured himself another drink of whiskey with an unsteady hand.

"What's the general sentiment among the settlers?" Conn probed.

"Well, there's a small faction that's agitating for war and independence, but Sam Houston and other leaders are against it, and most folks are backing them. Even Austin himself, in his letters from prison, is urging caution. They all still have hopes of Texas being granted statehood and Mexico returning to the republican government they had when Austin brought in the first Anglo settlers. Me, I don't think so. Santa Anna's all but abolished the constitution. But for now everybody's just biding time and waiting to see what happens next."

"I see. So the situation—"

A hand cupped the back of Conn's neck. He stiffened and looked up into the painted face of the yellow-haired woman. Her lips curved into a sultry smile. Before he could object, she plopped herself down on his lap and cuddled close.

"Come on, sugar," she coaxed. "You're not gonna talk politics all evening, are ya? I can think of better things a big strapping man like you could be doing."

Conn eyed her with tolerant amusement, his hard mouth twitching. "Is that right?"

She ran her tongue along the edge of her teeth and gave him a heavy-lidded look. "Uh-hmmm. And I promise it'll be a lot more fun than chewing the fat with these fellas." Wiggling her bottom against him, she scraped a fingernail lightly along his jaw and pressed closer. The move afforded him an unobstructed view of her voluptuous breasts, which strained over the top of the low-cut gown like overripe melons.

McSweeny gave a lascivious chuckle. Joseph cleared his

throat and swirled the whiskey in his glass. Taw glowered.

"Git along with you, woman," the old man snarled. "Conn ain't got no use fer the likes o' you."

The woman was coarse and unkempt and reeked of cheap cologne. Normally Conn would not have given her a second look, but the provocative way her bottom nestled against him, coupled with months of celibacy and frustration, produced the normal male reaction.

The blond woman grinned and rotated her hips again. "From the feel of things, I'd say you got a powerful use for me, don't you, sugar? And Lord knows, I do for you. It ain't every day a man like you comes into this place." Her voice dropped to a seductive murmur. "I got me a big ole feather bed in the back room. So whadda you say, sugar. How 'bout you and me go bounce around on it for a while? Dorie'll give you a ride like you never had before."

Conn looked into the woman's come-hither eyes. His hand rested on her thigh, and unconsciously his fingers flexed around the plump flesh. He needed a woman. Desperately. His body ached from months of denial.

Temptation tugged at him. His eyes scanned the woman's brassy hair, the coarse skin caked with powder, the fleshy, overblown charms. Unbidden, a memory rose to taunt him— of creamy skin and slender curves, of innocent gray eyes, and of sweet-smelling long golden hair shining in the sunlight.

"C'mon, sugar." Dorie smiled enticingly and slipped one finger in between the buttons on Conn's shirt. "Let's you and me go have some fun. You know you want to."

Taw's beefy hand thumped the table. Chuckling, Conn looked up at the sound, but he immediately sobered when he spotted Ben. The younger man stood just inside the door, leaning against the crude log wall. His arms crossed over his chest, he watched Conn coldly.

Their gazes clashed and locked, each hard and filled with challenge. For several seconds they stared at each other across the dimly lit tavern, two dominant males locked in silent battle.

Annoyance rippled through Conn. Man to man, he liked and respected Ben. He was aware, and he suspected Ben was also, that under different circumstances they would have been friends. But Conn's marriage to Elizabeth had made that impossible.

Ben's cold watchfulness held a silent censure that pricked Conn's conscience and roused his anger. Dammit, he didn't need a watchdog. He had no intention of easing his frustration with the woman. Why the hell should he, when he had a wife waiting for him at the wagon? He and Elizabeth were legally married, and he had every right to expect her to share his bed.

In his anger and frustration, Conn forgot that he, not Elizabeth, had made the decision to delay the physical side of their marriage, and his ire grew.

All right, so they hadn't married by choice. But she must have known when she accepted him that a man had needs, that there was more to marriage than just cooking a man's meals and looking after his children.

His jaw hardened. Well, if she hadn't, she was damn well about to find out. Without a word he sprang to his feet, dumping the blowsy blonde from his lap.

"Hey! Wh—Owwww!" she howled as her plump backside hit the floor. "Why, you sorry piss-poor jackass! What's the matter? Think you're too good for Dorie, do you? Well, you ain't," she screeched at his retreating back. "You hear me? You ain't nothing but a—"

Ignoring the woman's shrieked curses and the ribald comments and guffaws of the other patrons, Conn shouldered his way through the crowd and strode purposefully out into the Louisiana night.

The bed creaked as Elizabeth turned onto her back. Raising her head, she peered through the darkness to see if her restless shifting had disturbed Faith, but the child slept on peacefully beside her. On a pallet next to the bed, Ian lay sprawled in the innocent abandon of the very young, his soft baby snores a pleasant buzz in the darkness.

Elizabeth rested her head back on the pillow and sighed. Sleep wouldn't come, no matter how much she willed it.

She stared up at the pale canvas. Her mind drifted back once again to Conn, and the closed expression on his face when he'd left for Natchitoches. Before he had merely been distant, but for the past three days, ever since he'd found her cooling off in that creek outside of Alexandria, he been coldly furious.

She could feel her face heat up. Whenever she thought of the way she had responded to his kiss that night, she nearly died of shame. She felt so foolish. The kiss had been nothing more than an expression of anger. If she hadn't been so inexperienced and so blinded by love, she would have realized that. Instead she had just infuriated him all the more. She was so humiliated, she hadn't been able to face Conn since.

Suddenly the wagon rocked as someone stepped up onto the tailgate. Clutching the thin cover to her breasts, Elizabeth bolted upright in the bed. The shadowy form of a man appeared in the opening of the canvas, and her heart began to pound.

"Who . . . who is it? Who's there?"

"It's me."

"Conn?"

"He didn't reply. She heard his fumbling search for the tin of matches she kept on the small table beside the bed. Then came a scrape, and the smell of sulfur hung heavy in the air as the flame flared. Still without speaking, Conn lit the candle on the table.

"Is something wro—Conn! What are you doing?" Elizabeth's eyes widened as he bent and scooped up his sleeping son from the pallet on the floor.

"I'm moving the children in with Rachel."

"With Rachel? But . . . why?"

Ignoring her, Conn hefted Ian's limp form up onto his shoulder and reached across Elizabeth to nudge Faith.

"Faith. Wake up, Faith."

"Conn, what are y—"

He shook the little girl again, harder this time, and she blinked at him sleepily. Sitting up, she knuckled her eyes and yawned and looked around, befuddled.

"Get your shoes on, Faith, and come with me."

The child came awake at that, and she glanced uncertainly at Elizabeth. "Do I have to?"

"It's all right, honey. You do as Conn says," Elizabeth told her with a soft smile.

Faith caught her bottom lip between her teeth, but she nodded and scooted off the bed, pulling herself along by her heels. When she'd stuffed her bare feet into her shoes, Conn put a hand on her shoulder and ushered her to the rear of the wagon.

They were about to step out when he swung back to face Elizabeth. "As soon as I get them settled I'll be back." He gave her a long, steady look that made her heart boom crazily. "For the rest of the trip I'll be sleeping here."

With his son draped over his shoulder, he ducked through the canvas opening behind Faith. Elizabeth sat with her eyes wide, the sheet still clutched to her breasts in both hands, and stared after him, barely able to draw breath into her constricted lungs. Conn was going to sleep with her. Tonight she would truly become his wife.

Elizabeth closed her eyes and pressed her lips together, hugging the thought to her. Her heart pounded so hard, her chest shook with each heavy thud.

Earlier when he had left he'd been so stern and aloof. What had happened to bring about this change? Not that he was noticeably softer, she admitted wryly, but at least he was no longer ignoring her.

She gasped. Dear Lord! This was to be her true wedding night!

In a fit of panic she whipped back the sheet and scrambled from the bed, only to stand there turning in circles, her hands flapping like the wings of a trapped bird. Surely there was something she should be doing? She had to get ready!

She scurried to the front of the wagon and peered into her mother's gilt-framed looking glass. A few wispy curls had worked out of the loose night braid that hung to her waist, and she pushed them back into place with shaking fingers. She pinched her cheeks and smoothed each golden brown eyebrow with the tip of her little finger.

Thank heaven she was wearing her best nightgown, she thought, eyeing the white dimity garment in the looking glass. A row of ten tiny pink satin bows, marching from the top of the high neck to her waist, held the voluminous gown closed. With quick, jerky movements Elizabeth retied every one and fluffed the full sleeves and the deep ruffle edging the lace yoke.

Her anxious gaze fell on the rumpled bed. She rushed back and hurriedly straightened the sheets and plumped the pillows. When done she looked around franticly, but there was nothing left to do.

Gnawing the pad of her forefinger, she eyed the immaculate bed, and the quivering in her belly tripled. Her bare toes curled against the rough planks of the wagon bed. She had loved Conn for so long, had dreamed of being his wife, but now she was afraid. Dear Lord, what if she disappointed him? She wouldn't be able to bear it.

A short while later Conn stepped back into the wagon and stood for a moment just inside the canvas opening, studying Elizabeth, trying to gauge her reaction. She sat propped up against the walnut headboard with her hands folded primly atop the covering sheet, which was tucked up under her armpits. She watched him, her soft gray eyes glazed and dilated.

Had fear put that feverish look in her eyes? Conn sighed and stepped forward. At least she had left the candle burning. He'd half expected to find her cringing in the dark.

Her eyes followed him as he moved to the edge of the bed and sat down. The awkwardness between them was palpable.

Without a word he bent over and pulled off his moccasins. His body still ached with desire, but the strange anger that had carried him that far had faded, and he was no longer sure he was doing the right thing. But he had committed himself. Turning back now would only make it harder the next time.

He felt her eyes on his back as he unbuttoned his shirt and tugged it free of his trousers. Instead of shrugging it off, he sat motionless and stared straight ahead at the clever storage pockets Elizabeth had stitched to the inside of the canvas top.

"You're my wife, Elizabeth," he said with a defensive edge to his voice.

"I know," she whispered, and he turned his head sharply to look at her over his shoulder.

"Do you? And do you know that a man has the right to expect . . . certain things from his wife?"

"Yes. Of course I do. I'm a doctor's daughter, remember." She gave him a look of gentle rebuke. "I'm not a child anymore, Conn."

His gaze roamed over her face and down the shapely form beneath the sheet. "No. No, you're not, are you?"

Turning sideways, he brought one bent knee up on the bed. He saw her eyes widen and color bloom in her cheeks. A hint of exasperation firmed his lips when he glanced down at the strip of bared chest between the gaping chambray and the wrinkled shirttails that hung about his hips. Elizabeth had probably never been that close to a partially dressed man before in her life. Not one who didn't need her medical skills, at any rate. She might not be a child, but neither was she experienced.

"Elizabeth . . ." He looked into those soft gray eyes watching him with such intensity and felt a pang, but he refused to let it sway him. "I'm going to make love to you," he stated with deliberate bluntness.

Her blush deepened and her gaze dropped to her hands for

an instant, but she looked up quickly with a shy smile. "I know."

His black brows arched. The reaction was not at all what he'd expected. "The idea doesn't frighten you? Or repel you?"

"Of course not. Oh, Conn, I could never be frightened of you. And I can't imagine that anything you could do would repel me."

For several seconds he studied her, his narrowed gaze probing those guileless gray eyes. She really means it, he thought in amazement. He well remembered Millie's reaction on their wedding night, and he'd come prepared for tears, even hysterics—at the very best, stoic submission. But Elizabeth was welcoming him with all the warmth and sweetness of her generous nature.

The tightness in his chest eased, and an overwhelming tenderness filled him. The affection he'd always felt for her swelled his heart and brought an ache to his throat. Elizabeth. Sweet, gentle Elizabeth. She had been his good and constant friend all of her life. How could he have thought for a moment that she would be cold? She had been tender and openhearted even as a child, and now she was a giving woman, a nurturing woman; it simply wasn't in her to hold back once committed to someone.

Conn's rugged face softened. He reached out and caressed her cheek with the tips of his fingers. "You're amazing, Elizabeth Cavanaugh."

A tremulous smile touched her mouth, and her eyes grew liquid. "Not really," she denied in a breathless voice.

But she was, he realized with something close to wonder. He had known her always, but he was only now beginning to appreciate just how special she truly was.

As he studied that dear face, an uprush of emotion created a sweet pressure in his chest—soft, lush, undefined feelings that mingled with his desire for her and intensified it.

Smiling, he moved closer and reached for the curling end

of her braided hair. The heavy plait trailed over her shoulder and breast and hung to her waist like a golden rope, as thick as a man's wrist. He tugged loose the satin ribbon that secured it, his smile growing as he watched her expression turn bewildered.

"Conn, what are you—"

"Shh. I want to see your hair down. The way it was earlier."

He quickly untwined the thick sections of hair and combed his fingers through them. "Lean forward," he instructed huskily. Lowering her gaze to her hands, twisted together in her lap, she complied, and he spread the luxuriant mane about her shoulders. When done, he angled back to look at her, and his breath caught.

Elizabeth sat with her eyes lowered demurely, the impossibly long lashes creating dark crescents against her creamy skin. A delicate pink stained her cheeks, and her soft mouth quivered every so slightly. All that glorious hair hung about her like a pale silk cape. Catching the light of the dancing candle flame, it shimmered like flowing, molten gold.

Slowly Elizabeth's eyelids lifted. She gazed at him, her soft gray eyes wide and vulnerable and filled with uncertainty, and Conn felt his heart turn over.

Mesmerized, he reached out and ran his fingers over her hair, all the way down to the curling tips that lay on the mattress about her hips. With a sigh he gathered bunches in both hands and rubbed it between his fingers, testing its silky texture, its thickness. Bringing his hands together, he buried his face in the shining mass, inhaling the intoxicating scent deep into his lungs.

At last he raised his head and released the golden strands. He watched them slither from his grasp and tumble to the mattress. He was fascinated by the contrast between the pale soft silk and his callused brown skin.

Again his gaze captured hers, blue flame to softest gray. "I've wanted to do that for weeks," he said in a rough whisper, barely noticing her stunned look.

He leaned closer, helplessly drawn by her alluring, fragile beauty. Tenderly he framed her face between his palms, his long blunt fingers threading into the golden strands at her temple. "Oh, Elizabeth." Her name was a sigh on his lips, breathy and full of wonder. His thumbs brushed the hollows beneath her cheekbones as he gazed into her wide, luminous eyes. "My sweet Beth. Little one, you're so beautiful you take my breath away."

With utmost tenderness, Conn kissed her forehead, and when her eyes fluttered shut, he pressed his lips to first one satiny lid, then the other. He felt her shivering reaction and smiled, the small movement pleasing him immeasurably.

Stringing tiny kisses across her temple, he sought her ear. He nibbled her lobe and rubbed his parted lips over the delicate shell, filling it with his warm breath. Elizabeth moaned and swayed against him. Reaching out for support, she slid her hands beneath the parted shirt and grasped his waist.

The feel of those small, soft hands against his flesh drew a low groan from Conn, and his mouth found hers. He kissed her with exquisite gentleness and care, his lips rocking, rubbing, nipping, his body shaking with barely restrained hunger. Elizabeth kept her mouth closed, and the sweetness of her inexperience touched something deep inside him, that transcended passion and need. In that moment he would have sooner cut out his heart than do anything to frighten her.

A tremor shook the big hands that cupped her face. With exquisite delicacy, he traced the seam of her mouth with his tongue, slowly, back and forth. His control was rewarded when he felt her lips quiver, then part in hesitant invitation.

The tip of his tongue stole past her lips and touched hers, and she gasped. Her hands tightened on his waist, the slender fingers digging into his hard flesh with an urgency that sent his heart soaring.

With innocent eagerness, Elizabeth followed her instincts

and pressed closer, her mouth open and seeking. A hard shudder rippled through her. Her breathing became rapid and erratic, and from her throat came desperate little sounds that sent fire streaking through Conn.

He wrapped his arms around her, molding her pliant body to him as the kiss grew hot and heavy and urgent. With their mouths still joined he eased her down on the bed and stretched out beside her, pulling her close. He kissed her until they were both breathless and panting, and even then their lips parted with agonizing slowness.

Drawing back, he rested on his elbow and looked down, transfixed, into gray eyes that were feverish and cloudy with desire . . . for him.

"Wh-why did you stop?"

The artless question caused his mouth to tilt in a sensuous half smile. "I haven't stopped, sweetheart." He raised his hand and tugged on the end of the pink ribbon securing the top of her gown. The tiny bow came undone, and the lacy edges of the high collar fell open. She sucked in her breath and held it, and his smile grew. His hand moved down to the next bow. "I just paused to catch my breath is all."

The second bow collapsed, and Conn bent to brush a kiss across her mouth as his fingers went to work on the third. "And to look at you." The fourth bow came open, and the fifth, and the edges of the dimity garment spread wider, exposing the rounded inner curves of her breast, the silken valley in between. The faint scent of violets, mingled with her entrancing women smell, rose from her warm flesh. "But first we have to get rid of this gown."

Bow six went the way of the others, and heat washed up from Elizabeth's soles all the way to her hairline at the look of feverish anticipation in Conn's eyes as they followed his fingers' progress.

He chuckled and ran his forefinger over her rose-tinted flesh, from a point between her breasts to the pulse throbbing in her throat. "Are you nervous, Beth?"

"I . . . a little."

"There's no reason to be. We're friends, remember. And we'll still be friends tomorrow." He brushed his thumb over her lower lip, his eyes growing dark and heavy-lidded as he watched it tremble. "Friends . . . and much more," he whispered, picking up her hand and bringing it to his chest.

Elizabeth shivered as her palm made contact with the wedge of black curls, and a feeling of fierce satisfaction slammed through Conn as he watched her pupils expand.

Her other hand lifted of its own accord, and slender fingers threaded through the silky pelt as though they had a mind of their own. When they touched his warm flesh a shock of pleasure pulled a moan from both of them.

Enthralled, Elizabeth explored his shoulders and chest shyly, her small, pale hands grazing over tanned skin and hard muscle. His hair was damp, and he smelled of castile soap and clean male. Realizing that he had taken the time to bathe before coming to her, she felt foolishly pleased.

She wanted to press her face against his chest, to bury her nose in those raven black curls and fill her lungs with his heady scent, to taste his skin; but she lacked the nerve.

The small hands moved across Conn's chest, creating havoc with his breathing, and as he watched the avid fascination growing on her face, he quickly dealt with the remaining bows.

He spread the edges of her gown wide and went utterly still. "Oh, God, Beth."

The hoarsely whispered words captured Elizabeth's attention, and her hands stopped their restless exploration. She felt as though she were melting inside as she watched Conn's beloved, harshly handsome face grow flushed and rigid with desire.

Slowly, reverently, he lifted a handful of her hair and arranged it over her body. When done, he stared down at her full, pink-tipped breasts, softly visible through the fine strands that covered them like a misty veil of gold. She could almost feel the scorching touch of that burning blue gaze on her skin.

The fire in his eyes flared hotter as he ran his brown hand beneath the fall of hair and cupped one breast. His long, callused fingers flexed around the creamy mound, and Elizabeth made a little whimpering sound of pleasure. He looked up and met her gaze, a hard smile of male satisfaction curving his mouth.

As their lips met in feverish passion he rolled half over her, his hand, beneath the silky veil of hair, curved possessively around her breast, his palm rotating against the swollen nipple. His crooked knee insinuated itself between her legs and pressed against that private part of her that was suddenly moist and aching.

Writhing beneath him, Elizabeth clutched his shoulders and cried out at the tension building inside her, so sweet and hot it was almost pain. Years of longing surged to the surface, and she wrapped her arms around him beneath the shirt, her hands moving restlessly, fingers digging into the hard, flat muscles that spanned his broad back.

"Easy, sweetheart. Easy," Conn soothed, feeling his control slipping perilously. He was stunned and delighted by her response, but her innocent movements were pushing him over the edge. He wanted to draw it out, to give her that shattering pleasure which he was only now suspecting she was capable of experiencing. Stroking the hair at her temple, he gazed down at her, entranced by the sight of that lovely, gentle face flushed with passion, the feel of her going wild beneath him. Lord, where had all that quiet fire come from?

"It's all right, Beth," he crooned, stringing kisses along her arched neck. "Take it easy, sweetheart."

Elizabeth was too caught up in the spiraling need to heed his words. And she had waited years already.

She clutched him, her hands frantic, her expression rapt. For so long she had yearned to touch him, and now she reveled in the freedom, her fingers exploring his ears, his shoulders, the hollow at the base of his throat, threading through the mat of hair on his chest, finding the tiny nubs buried there.

"Conn, I . . . I . . . Oh, Conn . . ."

The incoherent cry sent a shudder through Conn's big body. With a helpless groan, he took her nipple into the warmth of his mouth, and Elizabeth gasped, her back arching as the slow, sweet suction seemed to tug at the core of her femininity.

Her high, keening wail snapped the last of Conn's control. He rose to his knees and with swift, desperate movements stripped the gown from her, pausing only a moment as it fluttered soundlessly to the floor of the wagon to gaze at her nude beauty, before stripping away his remaining clothing.

Elizabeth's soft gasp of delight as his warm body covered hers was the sweetest sound Conn had ever heard. Gently he nudged her legs apart and moved into position between her thighs. Braced above her, he looked into her slumberous eyes, stunned anew by her ardency, the rapturous expression on her face. His hesitation lasted only a moment, then he lowered his head and took her sweet mouth in a searing kiss as he entered her.

He sank into her slowly, the muscles in his arms quivering under the strain of holding back. As he met that fragile barrier, he felt her stiffen, and he paused. Then, steeling himself, he thrust deeper, catching her cry of pain with his mouth. When completely seated within her he forced himself to hold still while her body accommodated itself to his possession. He held her gently, murmuring soothing words in her ear through his clenched teeth. Her body sheathed him so tightly and felt so warm and good around his yearning flesh that he thought he would die from the pleasure of it.

Finally, sensing a subtle relaxation, he rocked his hips against her. She reacted with a breathless little murmur and a spontaneous movement that sent a flash of fire through him, and with a low groan he began the slow, undulating rhythm that their bodies craved.

"Oh, Beth . . . sweetheart . . . ah, yes, love. Yes!"

Elizabeth felt her body tightening, reaching. She was awash with sensations so exquisite, she didn't think she could bear them a second longer, and yet they grew stronger and stronger. Instinctively matching Conn's thrusting movements, she clung to him, frightened, expectant, exhilarated. Her breathing grew rapid. Her hands clutched him in anticipation.

"Wrap your legs around me, Beth," Conn whispered, running his hands down her thighs and lifting them. "Hold on tight to me, sweetheart. Hold on."

Elizabeth obeyed, and an instant later she cried out as a paroxysm of delight seized her and the world seemed to explode around them.

"Yes, love. Oh, God, yes!" Conn stiffened, his body arching above her. He threw his head back, his teeth clenched, and as shudder after shudder rippled through his powerful frame a hoarse cry tore from his throat.

They collapsed, exhausted, sated, their bodies slick with perspiration, boneless.

Gradually Elizabeth's breathing quieted. She became aware of Conn's delicious weight upon her, the warmth of his skin, melded to hers, their mingled scents, and most of all—the incredible, beautiful intimacy they had shared . . . still shared.

Her heart squeezed with emotions so intense they were painful, and the smile that curved her mouth came from the depths of her soul. She ran her hands over her husband's sweat-slick back and gazed at the canvas overhead, tears of joy trickling from the corners of her eyes. *Conn. Oh, my darling, Conn.*

Chapter 15

The next morning Elizabeth awoke to the sentries' signal and was disappointed to find herself alone.

"What did you expect?" she chided herself as she slid out of bed and lit the candle. "That Conn would be so smitten he would forget his duties and linger in bed like a besotted bridegroom?" After tying her hair back with a ribbon, she hefted the china pitcher and poured water into the matching washbowl. She splashed her face, then grimaced at her reflection in the looking glass as she patted her skin dry with a towel. "Don't be silly, Elizabeth."

Over and over, while she laced her stays tight over a clean chemise and pulled on her petticoats and dress, she reminded herself that Conn had married her for practical reasons. He had been honest about that, and she had no right to expect more. Only a fool would think that one night of lovemaking had changed anything.

Still, as she braided her hair and wound it into a coronet atop her head, she couldn't resist stealing wistful glances at the bed, and the dented pillow next to her own.

The look in Jemma's eyes when she reached the cook wagon told her that the black woman knew everything. Holding her head high and pretending her face wasn't flaming, Elizabeth wished her good morning as usual and reached for the mixing bowl and wooden spoon. No doubt by now half the people on the train knew that Conn had slept with her.

Her suspicion was confirmed moments later when Ian accosted her. He latched onto her skirt as she was mixing batter and looked up at her with his lower lip stuck out.

"I woked up in the wagon with Rachel," he announced accusingly. "So did Faith."

She glanced up and smiled at Faith, who hovered right behind the boy, looking worried and uncertain. "I know, sweetheart. Your papa carried you there."

"But we don't want to sleep with Rachel. We want to sleep in your wagon."

"Rachel, she don't want us there, neither. Leastways not me," Faith added.

"Please, Lith'beth," Ian whined. "Can't we sleep with you? Can't we, huh? Can't we?"

"Now hush up whining, child," Jemma ordered before Elizabeth could reply. "What I done told you 'bout that, huh? And Miz Faith, child, don't you worry none 'bout Miz Rachel. Her papa, he'll take care o' her."

Ian's baby face took on a sullen droop. He cut his eyes around resentfully at the housekeeper, but when he looked back at Elizabeth his expression grew thoughtful. "What's pri . . . pribacy?"

"Pribacy?"

"Jemma says mamas and papas is 'spose to sleep together, an' that's why my papa's sleepin' in your bed now, 'stead of Faith. She says we have to sleep in the wagon with Rachel so's you can have pribacy."

Elizabeth felt her face burn. She glanced at Jemma, but the little woman was hunched over the fire, suddenly busy. "Ian, dearest, I . . ."

"What's it mean?"

She looked down at the child in dismay. She knew she had to answer him; Ian was nothing if not tenacious. "Well, in this case privacy means that your papa and I wa . . . uh . . . need to be alone together."

"Oh." He studied her, his rosy little mouth pursed, and after a moment he nodded. "Well, if you an' my papa sleep together, then you'll *really* be my mama, won'tcha. So I guess it's all right."

With the simplicity of his childish logic he had cut right to the heart of the matter, and for him it was settled.

Rachel was not so understanding or accepting.

"Just because he's sharing your bed doesn't mean he cares about you," she snarled at Elizabeth the moment she caught her alone. The girl stood with her hands clenched at her sides, her young body rigid with fury. "When it comes to . . . to . . . that, men are just rutting animals. I heard Mama tell Mrs. Henderson so. So any woman would do," she sneered.

Elizabeth's white face told Rachel that the thrust had struck home, and with a smirk and an arrogant toss of her head, she sauntered away, leaving Elizabeth staring after her, horrified and deeply hurt.

She could well imagine her cousin making such a statement, but that Rachel had heard it and taken it to heart distressed her. It wasn't strictly so. Elizabeth knew that love was not necessary to a man's pleasure. But she also knew that when love was present in a marriage, the physical act was so much more than a mindless coupling. Her father had adored her mother and had never looked at another woman, and she was certain that Conn had been faithful to Millie.

But in her own case there was too much truth in Rachel's hurtful words to dismiss them completely. Conn was fond of her and would honor and protect her as his wife, but she was painfully aware that he did not love her.

When she thought of the night they had just shared and the way she had responded to his slightest touch, she cringed inside. Her actions had been an outpouring of her love for him, as instinctive as breathing, but not, she realized, particularly wise. If she wasn't careful, she would reveal what was in her heart and embarrass them both.

Elizabeth vowed to work harder at hiding her feelings. She would not make Conn feel uncomfortable or guilty by wearing her heart on her sleeve.

The decision sounded so sensible, so simple, but the moment Conn appeared her pulse began to pound at triple time.

When he stepped into the firelight she was slicing cornbread in the heavy skillet she had just retrieved from the coals. Out of the corner of her eye she saw Conn pour himself a cup of coffee. That morning he wore trousers of brown osnaburg and a tan linen shirt. As he reached for the coffeepot suspended over the fire, she watched the cloth strain across his broad back and shoulders, and her hands stilled. She stared at the coarse linen, the play of muscles underneath, recalling vividly how that firm flesh had felt beneath her hands, how sleek and warm his skin was to touch.

He headed her way, and with a start she went back to slicing cornbread, fixing her gaze firmly on the iron skillet.

"Morning," he said softly. He watched her over the rim of the tin cup.

Elizabeth returned the greeting, flashing him a weak smile, and sawed the knife through the bread. Her stomach fluttered. The smell of coffee drifted to her, along with a hint of shaving soap and his exciting musky scent. She had awakened with that smell on her skin, she recalled, fighting a blush.

Conn put his cup down on the tailgate. One of his hands settled on the side of her waist and the other tipped up her chin. He looked at her searchingly, his eyes warm and intent. "Are you all right?" he asked in an intimate tone that sent a little thrill shivering through her.

"I . . . I'm fine."

The night before, when they had recovered from the tempestuous lovemaking, he had asked the same question, and she had given the same answer. Those had been the only words that had passed between them, for he had immediately pinched out the candle and silently pulled her back into his embrace, tucking her close against his side with her head cradled on his shoulder.

Elizabeth had wanted to say more. She had longed for them to talk about what they were feeling, perhaps discuss the future, but the unfamiliar constraint had come back, and shyness held her silent. So she had snuggled close and given herself up to the blissful feeling of lying naked in the arms of the man she loved, and before long, sated and content, they had fallen asleep.

"Good."

He leaned down and brushed her mouth with a soft kiss, and Elizabeth felt the bottom drop out of her stomach. When he raised his head his gaze roamed over her face, surprise glittering in his eyes, along with something darker, more intense, that made her skin tingle. "I never want you to be sorry that you married me. This family needs you, Elizabeth," he said in a husky murmur. "I need you."

Elizabeth's heart boomed like a kettledrum. He didn't love her, but surely need was the next thing to it. And in time, who knew . . . maybe . . .

She shied away from completing the thought, chastising herself for giving in to such wishful dreaming, but it lingered in the back of her mind all the same, a tiny kernel of hope to which her foolish heart clung.

The hand beneath her chin slid upward and curved around her cheek. Conn's gaze dropped to her mouth, and something kindled in his eyes. "Elizabeth . . . I—"

He looked up sharply, his words halting at the approach of the hired hands. A moment later they tramped into the firelight with the pails of fresh milk, and to Elizabeth's disappointment, Conn gave her an apologetic look and moved away.

After that she had no chance to talk to him for the rest of the day. During the morning trek there was a problem with one of the wagons, and when they stopped to noon Conn gobbled down his cold food and hurried off to see to it. Elizabeth didn't catch sight of him again until dinner, and then they were surrounded by other people.

He had barely finished eating when he was summoned to break up an altercation that had erupted over Lisa Guetterman. The silly girl had been playing with the affections of both men involved, and when one young swain caught the other kissing her, he took offense.

The excitable man who brought the news seemed certain that the two would kill one another if Conn didn't do something quickly. Elizabeth watched her husband stride away with his jaw set and an icy look in his eyes, and she knew that Lisa and her beaus were soon going to wish they'd never met.

After she'd put Faith and Ian to bed, Elizabeth lingered around the fire with the others, but after a while, when Conn did not return, she gave up and retired.

With Pike ambling along after them, she walked beside Taw, who carried her rocking chair back to the wagon for her, barely hearing the old man's comments. All day she'd thought of little else but Conn and the incredible night she had spent in his arms, and as evening had approached her excitement had grown steadily at the thought of being alone with him again. Now she wondered if Conn had had second thoughts about sleeping in her wagon. Or if he even remembered that he'd intended to.

Conn's heart gave a little leap and picked up speed when he saw the faint glow of candlelight seeping from the back of the wagon. He had expected to find it in darkness.

He glanced with satisfaction at the shadowed rigs to the front and rear of Elizabeth's. Her position, tucked in among the freight wagons, afforded the maximum of privacy from the other occupied rigs.

Conn had stopped by the creek for a quick wash just moments before, and he wore only his trousers and moccasins. The linen shirt he carried slung over one shoulder. He stepped lightly up onto the tailgate, moving with care, just in case Elizabeth was asleep. The wagon barely rocked beneath his lithe movements. Silently he ducked through the opening and came to an abrupt halt just inside.

Pleasure moved through him as he watched Elizabeth. She stood at the other end of the wagon, her head tilted to one side, brushing her hair before the looking glass. The thigh-length tresses swayed and bounced about the stroking brush, glittering in the soft light.

God, she was beautiful. And desirable. It took his breath away just to look at her. He was still amazed that it had taken him so long to notice. All those years, he had looked at her and seen only a familiar friend. But now . . . now he was seeing her from a different perspective. Now he was seeing her as a woman. His woman. His wife. Conn smiled, the thought pleasing him.

The nightgown was the same one she'd worn the previous evening. Well, for a while, anyway, Conn corrected, his hard mouth twitching.

The modest garment was high-necked and long-sleeved and delectably feminine, but with each tiny movement the flowing folds of sheer dimity allowed enticing glimpses of the peach-tinted flesh beneath. As Conn's gaze tracked the veiled curves of one long, slender leg, he felt a hot surge of desire.

He shook his head. After the shattering fulfillment they'd shared the night before, he had expected his ardor to cool, but it hadn't. All day he had thought of her—her flushed face, the desperate little sounds she'd made, the feel of those soft hands on his skin. Conn snorted. Faded, hell. He'd spent almost the entire day in an embarrassing state of arousal.

Damn, he'd enjoyed making love to her. It had been the most fulfilling experience of his life. Her innocent eagerness had nearly driven him wild.

She had surprised him with all that flaming passion. He still had difficulty relating soft, sweet, serene Elizabeth Stanton with that woman who'd caught fire in his arms. He could hardly believe it, after all the years of Millie's coldness, to suddenly find himself with a loving, sensual wife. He shook his head. Elizabeth, of all people. Who would have thought it?

Guilt niggled at him, interrupting his pleasant musings, and his smile faded. How, he wondered, could he feel such delight so soon after losing Millie? And why had he never experienced this kind of fulfillment with her?

With nimble fingers Elizabeth began to work her hair into a braid, and Conn took a step toward her. The movement caught her attention, and she whirled, her face lighting. "Conn!"

He cocked one eyebrow. "Why do you look surprised to see me? I told you last night I'd be sleeping here."

"I thought that, uh, well, that maybe you'd forgotten. Or changed your mind."

He gave her a long look. "Were you hoping I would?"

"No! Of course not. I . . ." She started to reach out, then stopped and lowered her eyes. "No."

"I hope you mean that, because I warn you—want me or not—I'm here to stay," he said in a hard voice. "There'll be no polite pretense of a marriage between us, Elizabeth. No separate beds, either." The thought that she might reject him—now, after the night they'd shared—made him feel violent. He had put up with Millie's excuses and rebuffs and long-suffering martyrdom for years, but no more . . . not from Elizabeth.

She looked up, and though there was a touching vulnerability about her, her eyes were direct and honest. "I mean it. I want you here."

Conn almost sagged with relief. Tossing his shirt onto a trunk, he stepped forward and pulled her into his arms. She nestled against his chest with a willingness that warmed him, and as her arms circled his back the angry tension eased. He rested his cheek against the top of her head and sighed, a feeling of deep contentment seeping into his bones.

"Why did you think I wasn't coming back?"

"You stayed away all day," she mumbled against his chest. "Then, this evening when you didn't return, I just supposed . . ."

The words trailed away, and he felt her shrug. Beneath the soft diffidence, Conn was almost certain her voice had carried a note of accusation. A puzzled frown tugged at his black brows. Could she possibly be hurt because he hadn't spent time with her?

His arms tensed around her. "Elizabeth. I'm sorry I couldn't be with you today," he said, testing her reaction.

Elizabeth pulled out of his embrace and moved back to the looking glass. Gathering up her hair, she divided it into three thick sections and with quick, jerky movements began to braid. "That's all right. I understand."

Frowning, Conn watched her agitated movements. Why, she *was* upset. The thought that she might want his company had not occurred to him until now. "I didn't have a choice. One problem after another cropped up today that required my attention. I couldn't get away."

She glanced at him and sighed, a look of forlorn acceptance in her eyes. "I know."

Conn moved closer and cupped her face between his palms. "Elizabeth, I'm sorry. This isn't much of a honeymoon, is it?" he asked softly. Elizabeth bit her lower lip and stared at the mat of hair on his chest, and he shook his head. "Sweetheart, believe me. I wish we could have spent the whole day together, just the two of us."

"Really?" Again her gaze sought his, and the raw hope he saw in her eyes made him catch his breath. Her unfeigned eagerness for his company filled him with a pleasurable warmth and made him feel ten feet tall, exactly as it had all those years ago when they'd been kids.

Only now, he could fully appreciate exactly how precious a gift was Elizabeth's friendship. She gave of herself wholly, bestowing her allegiance, her affection, without condition or reservation. Now that she was his wife, his mate, she was bringing that same steadfast devotion to their marriage.

"Yes, really," he said tenderly. "I want this marriage to be a happy one, Elizabeth, for both of us. That's important to me," he stressed in a husky voice. "*You're* important to me."

He lowered his head and kissed her, and because Elizabeth wanted to believe him, needed to believe him, she melted into his embrace and let her doubts slip away.

Hard arms wrapped around her and pulled her against his bare chest. His warmth, his male scent, enveloped her, and her hands trembled against his flesh, her fingers twined in the mat of dark hair. His lips were hot and soft on hers, exquisitely arousing, and Elizabeth moaned beneath the tender assault.

When he raised his head she blushed. She wasn't used to Conn kissing her or touching her so intimately, and though she loved it, she was terrified of giving herself away.

A teasing glint entered his eyes, and he touched her warm cheek with one finger but made no comment.

To hide her embarrassment Elizabeth turned away and picked up one of the petticoats that lay spread across the top of a trunk. She started to fold it, but Conn reached out and took the garment from her. Her eyes widened as he carelessly tossed it aside. "What are you doing?"

"I'm going to make love to my wife." He snagged her hand and towed her to the bed. Sitting down on the edge, he pulled her onto his lap and smiled at her startled expression.

"Conn! What—"

"Shh. I want your hair down when we make love," he said huskily as he released the braid. "I like to feel it sliding over my skin."

The flickering light danced across the hard angles and planes of his face, and Elizabeth's heart began to thud when she saw his intent look, the heavy-lidded eyes that were fixed on her with blatant desire. Her body grew warm, and a trembling started deep inside her. It was a fantasy come true, one she'd had countless times over the years, seeing that hunger and heat in Conn . . . for her.

His glittering eyes locked with hers. "I want you, Beth," he said in a velvety murmur. "I want you desperately. Over and over." Reaching out, he slowly untied the row of bows. "For hours."

So excited she could barely breathe, Elizabeth sat docilely and allowed him to strip her. When he eased her onto the bed and stood to remove the remainder of his clothes, she lay watching him shamelessly, fascinated by his male beauty, the lithe perfection of his hard, fit body, enthralled by the fierce passion in his dark expression.

With a hard smile, Conn stretched out beside her and gathered her to him, and Elizabeth gave a helpless little moan as he pulled her into his heat. He kissed her temple, her cheek, her arching neck. "You, my sweet Beth, are like an addiction," he growled in her ear. "One taste, and I can't get enough."

Some time later the candle had become a stub, the flame guttering in a puddle of melted wax, but Elizabeth could not sleep. Feeling sated and smug and filled with soaring hope, she lay with her head cradled on Conn's broad shoulder, smiling into the shadows.

The hours of passion had been delicious. Conn might not love her, but he desired her. She didn't know how that had come about, but she accepted her good fortune gratefully. Feminine instinct told her that desire that strong might—just might—eventually lead to love. If they could make the transition from friends to lovers, surely anything was possible.

It could happen, she told herself, daring for the first time to hope. But even if it didn't, she already had so much more than she had expected. Tomorrow, the day after, and for all the days to come, she had a family with whom she would share whatever life brought. She had a husband. She had Conn.

Elizabeth started to shift positions but changed her mind when she felt a sharp tug on her scalp. Her hair lay all around them, entangling them together in a golden web. Conn had spread one swath across his body. The pale strands caught in the black curls on his chest and lay fanned out on his belly, in sharp contrast with his dark skin.

Elizabeth sighed. Unbound, it was a nuisance, but if Conn liked it that way, she would put up with it.

She had thought him asleep, but suddenly he shifted her head from his shoulder to the pillow and raised up beside her, propping his elbow and resting his chin in his palm. He looked down at her, contentment in his eyes, his harsh features softened by a lazy half smile.

With great daring, she reached up and touched his mouth with her forefinger. He stroked it with the tip of his tongue, and she felt a tingle shoot down her arm. "What are you thinking?" she asked in a voice as soft as a sigh.

Conn nibbled the pad of her finger, then he grasped her hand and held it against his jaw. Beard stubble rasped against her palm. "I'm thinking," he said quietly, "that a marriage between friends is the best kind."

Elizabeth didn't know what that meant. She didn't even know if it was good or bad. She wasn't sure if he was trying to tell her that friendship was all they would ever have, or that it provided the best basis for love.

She thought about the comment a lot during the days that followed, while she looked after the children and worked alongside Jemma, while she helped Dr. Cavanaugh patch up cuts, bruises, and sprains and tend those struck low by the latest outbreak of fever and dysentery. She puzzled over the remark during the long, somnolent hours in the saddle as they plodded along, during companionable evenings around the fire with the family, and in the quiet aftermath of passion, lying in

Conn's arms in the warm darkness.

Vacillating between despair and hopefulness, she examined the statement from every angle, while doing whatever needed doing and coping with the hardships that grew increasingly severe as they inched their way slowly westward.

The last week in August the fifty-two wagons crossed the Sabine and rumbled into Texas. That night the emigrants celebrated their arrival in their new homeland with an impromptu dance.

Loud, lively music echoed through the wilderness, along with hand clapping and foot stomping and hoots and hollers. The night was hot, the shouts and laughter and whistles of the celebrants unrestrained and raucous, the food plain, but Elizabeth couldn't remember ever having such a good time. She whirled in Conn's arms until her feet ached, her head spun, and her face glowed with happiness, a circumstance that did not escape Hester's notice.

"Well, now, you're sure having a high old time tonight," she drawled, eyeing the becoming color in Elizabeth's cheeks.

Elizabeth laughed and fanned herself, her eyes on Conn, who was leading Elmira Haversom's sixty-year-old mother through a reel. "Of course I am. This is a celebration after all."

"Huh. If you ask me, it ain't arriving in Texas that's put that twinkle in your eye but crawling between the sheets at night with that delicious hunk of man." Undeterred by Elizabeth's reproving look or heightened color, Hester poked her friend in the ribs and went on audaciously, "Married life plumb agrees with you, my girl."

"Hester! Hush now!" Elizabeth scolded, but her voice lacked heat, and she couldn't control the smile that played about her lips.

No matter how outrageous her teasing comments, Elizabeth could not get angry with Hester. Through everything she had been a true and loyal friend, and no one had been happier for her than Hester when her marriage had become a real one. After nearly four months Elizabeth was heartily sick of constant travel and anxious to reach Riverbend, but the one thing she dreaded about coming to the end of their journey was parting from her dear friend.

"Liam tells me that Conn's a sight easier to get along with nowadays, too," Hester went on undaunted, sliding Elizabeth a devilish look. "Now why do you suppose that is?"

"Hes! You're terrible!"

"Mebbe so. But I know a satisfied man when I see one."

A dreamy softness settled over Elizabeth's face. She hoped with all her heart that Hester was right. Occasionally Conn was moody and withdrawn, and she suspected that he felt a lingering grief and guilt over Millie, but for the most part he seemed content.

He was gentle and affectionate, and she was aware that he was making an effort to spend more time with her. He sat beside her in the evening, retired when she did or soon after, and now, whenever she had the time to ride Thistle, he kept her by his side unless other duties called. And—though she cautioned herself against false hopes—dear heaven, there were times when he looked at her with such warmth, her toes curled inside her slippers.

Of course she still had to contend with Rachel's snippiness, and she hadn't made as much progress with Faith as she would have liked, but she had Ian's devotion, and her life with Conn held promise. For now she would be happy with that.

Several jugs of corn liquor were consumed, and as the evening wore on the gaiety increased. It was late when Conn finally called a halt, but despite little sleep, pounding heads, and queasy stomachs, the train rolled out at dawn, as always.

Texas proved to be a wondrous place. Elizabeth and many of the others had been surprised to find the rolling hills of the eastern portion covered with lush forest, so dense in places it was impenetrable. Elizabeth doubted even a small child could squeeze through. Towering pine, oak, elm, sweet gum, black gum, walnut, pecan, cedar, sassafras, and dogwood trees, and many others she didn't recognize, crowded right up to the edge of the road, at times meeting overhead, enclosing them in a leafy tunnel that blocked out the sun.

The forest was so unbroken, sometimes they found no clearing big enough to accommodate the wagons, and they had to camp strung out along the road. Those nights Conn posted extra guards to protect the cattle against predators—human and animal—for several times they caught sight of lurking Indians, and from the dark forest came the hair-raising screams of a panther.

On the fifth day of traveling through Texas they arrived at Nacogdoches. There, for the first time since leaving Charleston, they experienced the sadness of parting when Tobias and Minerva Potts and their brood of ten split off from the train to head for their land, an eight-hundred-acre plot fifteen miles northwest of the settlement.

The Pottses' departure for their new home created excitement among the emigrants, and that night in camp almost everyone was fired up and impatient to reach their own land. There was some uneasy talk from a few, but they'd all come too far, and with their destinations so close no one was willing to turn back. With few exceptions no one had a place to return to or the means to make the trip in any case.

Almost daily the size of the train shrank as all along the way wagons separated from the main body and men and families struck out on their own when they drew near their grants. By late September when they reached the ferry crossing at Washington, a primitive town of ten or so log structures on the Brazos River, only five other wagons remained with the Cavanaughs' twenty, and there they all parted company.

The Grimeses' place lay seven miles northwest of town on a little creek that fed into the Brazos, while Riverbend's twenty-four thousand acres of rich farmland ran along the river's west bank, nine miles south.

When it came time to go their separate ways, Hester and Elizabeth clung to each other and cried and promised to visit often. As the Grimeses' lone rig headed one way and the Cavanaugh caravan another, the two women hung out of their respective wagons and waved until each was lost from the other's sight.

"Cheer up, little one. You'll see her again," Conn said gently, reining in his horse beside her. "Probably sooner than you think. There's a lot of visiting done in these parts."

After one last look behind her, Elizabeth straightened around on the plank seat and wiped her eyes with the back of her hand. "Oh, don't mind me," she said with a sniff. "I'm fine."

"You sure? Look, why don't I saddle another horse for you. You don't have to ride in the wagon just because your horse has a sore foot."

"No, no. I'm fine. Really. Don't worry about me. I'm . . . I'm just being silly."

"No, you ain't, Missy," Taw put in. "Shoot, sayin' good-byes is always sad. But don't you worry none. You'll perk right up onc't we git to Riverbend."

Elizabeth swiped her eyes again and gave him a determined smile. "I'm sure you're right. How much farther is it?"

Conn watched her struggle to conquer her feelings and felt a pang. Elizabeth's tears disturbed him. Until then he hadn't given much thought to how isolated they would be. He'd spent so much of the past seventeen years in the mountains with only Taw for company that he'd grown used to being away from other people. He even preferred it. But it was different for women. They liked to get together and talk about female things and cluck over children and fashions, and swap gossip and recipes and God knew what else. They seemed to need it.

"Won't be long now," Taw told her. "Should make it by noon or there 'bouts."

"Oh, wonderful! I can hardly wait. Does it look like this?" she asked, sweeping her hand toward the rolling, tree-dotted land around them. "Can you see the river from the house?"

Taw launched into a colorful description of the plantation. Riding beside the wagon, Conn watched Elizabeth.

He had uprooted her from the only life she'd ever known, trekked her over a thousand miles under primitive conditions, and married her for convenience and his own selfish reasons. Now he was taking her to a kind of life she'd never known, in a place where the only company she would have for months on end, other than the slaves and an overseer she detested, would be two old men, three children who weren't even her own, and himself.

He had turned a deaf ear to Millie's constant complaints, telling himself that she would adjust and eventually come to love the plantation and the life as much as he did. He knew now that she would have hated it.

Would Elizabeth?

With each passing mile his worry grew apace with excitement. They were almost there. After seventeen long years, they were almost there.

On a whim, that morning Conn had put Elizabeth's wagon in the lead, and the line of lumbering vehicles, with its trailing herd of livestock, snaked across grassy meadows and around sloping hills topped with stands of enormous oaks, some so ancient their massive branches spanned a hundred feet or more.

Horace Munson, the man from whom Conn had purchased his property, had come to Texas with Stephen F. Austin in 1822, and the rutted path they were taking had been laid down by the comings and goings of those at the plantation during the past twelve years. It followed the Brazos, though taking a more direct route, coming close to the wide, looping river in places and losing sight of it altogether in others.

Around noon they began to pass cultivated fields bordered with rail fences. In most, the tattered remnants of cotton bolls still clung to the plants like tiny white flags. Elizabeth sat high in her seat and twisted her neck this way and that, trying to take it all in, and behind him Conn could hear the excited chatter of the children. Even the hired hands were talking animatedly now that the end of the long trip was at hand.

Finally they turned in between the stone gateposts marking the entrance and started up the half-mile-long drive. Trees lined either side, not the ordered, stately rows of planted sentinels like those that guarded the drives of plantations in the Deep South, but two twenty-foot-wide strips of natural woods that had been left standing when the fields had been cleared, tough old hickory trees, mighty oaks, persimmon, plum, and pecan trees, their branches loaded with ripening nuts, growing wild like the land that had spawned them.

Toward the end the drive curved, and the house came into view. Conn drew rein, and so did Taw. He gazed at the two-story brick structure for a moment, then drew a deep breath and turned to Elizabeth. "Well, this is it. This is Riverbend."

Chapter 16

🖤 Riverbend. How she loved it—every tree, every blade of grass, every last clod of rich Texas dirt.

Pausing to arch her back and wipe the sweat from her brow with her forearm, Elizabeth let her attention wander from the score or so of black women tending the boiling cauldrons as she gazed with pleasure at her surroundings.

Oh, yes, she loved it all—the white brick house with its shady galleries all round on both levels, the wide lawn and massive magnolias and oaks that dotted it, the beds of daylilies and azaleas and boxwoods with forsythia bushes cascading at each corner.

The house was set majestically at the end of the drive on a slight rise, more than a half mile from the river. To Elizabeth's delight, the east galleries afforded a view of the wide waters of the Brazos, and the landing where the boats tied up.

A covered walkway led from the back of the house to the kitchen. Beyond that, among the thinned-out trees, were the domestic buildings—the little spring house that kept things icy cold, straddling the stream bubbling out of a rock formation; the smokehouse that smelled of hickory and spicy meat; the elegant carriage house with its row of dormer windows and twin weather vanes on the roof, which as yet housed only the wagons remaining from their journey.

It's almost a self-contained community, she thought with pride, surveying the blacksmith shop and the massive barn and stock pens. In between, the sturdy sugarcane press stood in the center of a large rutted circle formed by the team of mules that powered it, the depth of the track mute testimony to years of use.

From down by the river came the distant rumble and screech of the cotton gin, where the hands were readying the last of the crop for market. A thin cloud of chaff from the operation hung in the air, its musty smell mingling with the scents of wood smoke and boiling fat. Thanks to Mr. Munson, most of the cotton had already been picked and baled and sent to market, but the second and third pickings had yielded enough almost to fill the storage sheds by the landing yet again.

Their arrival two months before had been followed the very next day by that of the side-wheeler *YellowStone*. Elizabeth smiled, remembering the excitement that erupted when the blast of the whistle preceded the riverboat around the bend. When it had headed back downstream two days later with their first cotton crop, Mr. Munson had been on board.

Personally Elizabeth did not understand how he could bear to leave Riverbend. She didn't think she ever could. A feeling of immense satisfaction filled her as her gaze swept beyond the buildings to the fields spreading out as far as the eye could see. Yes, she could well understand Conn's determination to have this place. She was a city girl, born and bred, and she had a lot yet to learn about being mistress, but from the moment she had set eyes on Riverbend she had experienced a sense of homecoming.

The only thing lacking that would make her happiness complete was Conn's love, she thought wistfully.

"Miz Liz'beth. I thinks this be 'bout ready to dip up," called the large black woman named Pearlie, drawing Elizabeth's attention back to the soap-making operation. "Come see what you think."

"Yes, this is perfect for soft soap," Elizabeth agreed, stirring the jellylike mixture in the cauldron. "There should be enough here to fill the crocks. We'll keep the other kettles boiling to make into soapcakes."

As she straightened, a continuous shrieking cry drew her attention to the pallet spread beneath a nearby cottonwood tree. There the wizened old woman, Zena, with the help of several older children, tended five babies, ranging from an infant to a strapping toddler, who was sitting in the middle of the blanket, flailing his arms and wailing piteously.

Faith was there also, down on her knees before the little boy and trying to distract him by making faces. Lately she had developed into a little mother hen. She doted on Ian and could not stand to see any child in distress.

As always, wherever you found Faith, you found Ian. Ignoring the squalling baby, the four-year-old sat squatted on his haunches a few yards away, absorbed in the fascinating pastime of rolling pill bugs with a twig.

"Is there something wrong with that child?" Elizabeth asked, glancing around at the women. "He's been crying for hours."

A young woman feeding wood into one of the fires looked at Elizabeth fearfully. "Oh, no, ma'am, Miz Liz'beth, he's fine. I'll go tell Zena to make him hush up, so's he won't bother you no more."

"Wait! Dulcie, is that your child?"

The young woman tugged nervously on the red kerchief tied about her hair. Her eyes grew round, and she began to tremble as though in the grips of a chill. "Yes'm."

"Is he sick? Or hurt in some way?"

Dulcie looked around at the other women for help, but they averted their eyes and concentrated on their tasks. The young mother twisted her hands together and shifted from one foot to the other. "No, ma'am. He's not sick, 'zackly. He's got a carbuncle, is all. But I can take him back to the quarters where you won't hear all that racket," she went on in a rush, and took another step toward the child.

"You'll do nothing of the kind. Bring the baby to me, Dulcie, and let me look at him," Elizabeth commanded, not unkindly, but Dulcie looked as though she had ordered the child flogged with a bullwhip.

"Oh, please, Miz Liz'beth—"

"Bring me the baby, Dulcie," Elizabeth insisted, and the young woman reluctantly obeyed. Faith trailed after her, her thin face puckered with sympathy and worry.

The child's shrieks and restless flailing did not diminish even when his mother took him in her arms. When Elizabeth removed the rag tied around his head, they increased. It took all her control not to gasp at the sight of the angry purple lump on the baby's crown. "Land sakes, Dulcie! Why haven't you brought this child to Dr. Cavanaugh before now? This needs lancing. No wonder he's crying so."

"But Zena says we can't 'cause it be too close to his brain. She say it'll kill him if'n we do. 'Sides, Mistah Lathom, he have my hide, I bother any you folks."

"It is in a bad spot, but nevertheless it must be lanced. There, there, sweetheart. I know it hurts," she crooned when the child's screams rose to a piercing level. Taking the distressed baby and bouncing him on her hip, she swept Dulcie and the other women with a stern look. "In the future, whenever any of you need medical attention you're to come to me or Dr. Cavanaugh. You hear? Don't worry about Mr. Lathom. I'll speak to him myself. Now, Dulcie, you run up to the house and ask Isaac for my bag. Dr. Cavanaugh is out somewhere with Conn, and this can't wait, so I'll have to do it myself."

"You ain't gonna hurt him, are you, Miss Elizabeth?" Faith asked, shifting from one foot to the other.

"Aren't going to hurt him," Elizabeth corrected automatically. "Maybe—a little. But sometimes, dear, you have to hurt someone in order to help them. He'll feel much better when I'm done. I promise."

Dulcie obeyed with obvious reluctance, but when she and Zena held the screaming toddler still, Elizabeth performed the unpleasant task with a steady competence that left the women gawking with surprise and admiration. Before she finished smearing salve on the sore and bandaging it, the exhausted babe was sound asleep.

That evening, as the family relaxed in the parlor after dinner, Elizabeth told Conn about the incident.

"Dulcie was terrified. So were the other women. I could see it in their eyes."

"Why would they be afraid of you?"

"Not me. They're afraid of Garth. Of what he'll do if they come to me with their troubles. Conn, I think he's been mistreating them."

Conn expelled a long-suffering sigh. "Elizabeth, aren't you letting your dislike of the man color your judgment?"

"Conn, I tell you—"

"Did any of the women say they'd been mistreated?"

"Well . . . no. But—"

"Then you haven't a shred of proof that Garth has done anything wrong. Have you?"

"No," she admitted reluctantly, avoiding the smirking look Rachel sent her way. The girl took perverse delight in the slightest disagreement between Elizabeth and Conn.

Faith sat on the settee, holding a skein of silk embroidery thread looped over her wrists while Elizabeth wound it into a ball, her gaze going from one person to another.

"Well, if'n I was you, I'd give a listen to the little missy. I don't trust that Garth fella as fer as I can spit."

Elizabeth sent Taw a grateful smile. Bless him. As always, he wasn't in the least reluctant to buck Conn.

"I'm inclined to agree," Joseph said. "I don't know . . . there's just something about Garth that makes me uneasy."

"Look, personally, I don't cotton to the man, either," Conn admitted. "But that's not a good enough reason to accuse him of something. Besides, Munson trusted him."

In Elizabeth's opinion he shouldn't have. After going over the books, she strongly suspected that Garth had been robbing Horace Munson blind. For the first six years after Mr. Munson cleared and built Riverbend, the plantation had prospered, but for the last six years, since Garth became overseer, things had gone the other way. Riverbend was vast, with fertile land, abundant water, and a large work force. Other than mismanagement or outright theft, there was no excuse for such a drastic decline in productivity and profit.

Of course, she didn't dare mention her suspicions to Conn. Not only did she have no proof, she was certain he wouldn't approve of her going over the books, even though she had kept them for her father routinely. Conn had a disconcerting tendency to cosset her. Despite all she'd done on the trip from Charleston, he persisted in thinking of her as fragile. He expected her to run the house and look after the children, but he did not want her to be burdened with any of the worry or responsibility of the day-to-day running of the plantation.

"By the way, son, have you told Elizabeth about the invitation we received?" Joseph asked.

"No. To tell you the truth, it slipped my mind." Conn smiled at Elizabeth, clearly glad of the change in subject. "Jared Groce is having a New Year's celebration at his place. While we were down at the cotton gin one of his boys came poling upriver on a raft with an invitation for us. Seems this is an annual event and everybody from miles around will be there. Including the Grimes family," he added with a dry look.

"Hester will be there? Oh, how wonderful! I'll have to start planning right away. We'll take some food, of course. And a gift for our host. And if I hurry, I may have time to make new dresses for the girls and myself."

"Don't bother making one for me. I'm not going."

The statement, delivered in a flat, uninterested voice, drew every eye to Rachel. "What do you mean?" Conn demanded of his daughter. "Of course you're going. We all are."

"Not me. I don't want to go to any dumb old party."

"Rachel, dearest, you can't stay here alone."

"Don't you tell me what I can do," she flared at Elizabeth. "I don't have to take orders from you. I'll stay if I want to."

Rachel jumped to her feet and started for the door, but her father stopped her before she'd taken three steps.

"Rachel! Get back here!"

She whirled, her face mutinous, but when he repeated the command she flounced back and threw herself onto her chair.

Tensing, Faith scooted forward on the cushions, but Elizabeth put a restraining hand on her knee and gave her a reassuring look. Panic swirled in the leaf green eyes, but she stilled, perching on the edge of the settee like a bird about to take flight.

"You, young lady, will do as you're told, which means you're going to that party, like it or not. Now, you apologize to Elizabeth at once."

"But Papa!"

"Conn, I don't think—"

"Stay out of this, Elizabeth," he snapped, never taking his eyes from his daughter's petulant face. "I will not tolerate rudeness from a child of mine."

Elizabeth recoiled as though she'd been slapped. She barely heard Conn's next sharp words to Rachel or the girl's ungraciously muttered, "I'm sorry."

Conn emerged from the dressing room and paused, his attention arrested. Wearing only the blue brocaded robe, belted loosely about his waist, he propped a shoulder against the doorjamb and watched his wife.

She sat at her dressing table, her head tilted to one side, methodically brushing her hair. He never tired of watching her perform the evening ritual. There was something so sensual about the simple act, so intimate.

He drew a deep breath and let it out slowly. Was it wrong to feel as he did? Perhaps. He simply didn't know. Certainly guilt and regret still plagued him, but there was no denying that with Elizabeth he had at last found the happiness that had eluded him with Millie.

His gaze trailed over the shimmering cascade of hair that hung below her hips, and the familiar tenderness filled him, softening his stern mouth. Her passion still staggered him. He felt like a man who had just emerged from a long bitter winter into the lush warmth of spring.

Who'd have thought that Elizabeth, so calm and serene on the outside, possessed such an ardent nature? One of his greatest pleasures was to stoke those quiet fires into a blazing inferno, to watch that lovely, serene face grow flush with desire as she went wild in his arms. For these past months he'd reveled in her passion, wallowed in it, indulging his desires to the limit. Conn's mouth slanted in a derisive half smile. Hell, by now he ought to be sated, but he wasn't.

He pushed away from the door and crossed the room to stand behind her. When his hands settled on her shoulders, she jumped and stiffened.

"What's the matter, honey?" he ask, smiling crookedly as he rotated his thumbs over her shoulder blades. "You're as tense as a fiddle string. Don't tell me you're still shy?"

Her somber gaze met his in the looking glass, and his teasing look faded into a frown. His voice deepened with concern. "What is it, Elizabeth? What's wrong?"

"I guess I'm just confused."

His frown deepened. "About what?"

"I don't know what you expect from me. You said you wanted me to be a mother to your children, yet whenever I open my mouth you tell me not to interfere."

"Oh, hell, Elizabeth. Are you still fretting over that scene with Rachel? She was being disrespectful to you and behaving like a rude, obnoxious brat, and I put a stop to it, that's all. It's over. Settled."

Elizabeth rose and faced him, her arms folded over her midriff. "Conn, you can't *make* Rachel accept me. Forcing the issue is just going to make things worse."

"So what am I supposed to do? I won't have her treating you that way. I don't understand what's ailing that girl, anyway. Lately she's either bawling her eyes out or flying off the handle about something."

"Fifteen is a difficult age for a girl, Conn. Especially for one who's just lost her mother. I believe Rachel thinks I'm trying to take Millie's place. You and I know that I could never do that, and she will too eventually. But we must give her time to figure it out on her own." She stepped close and put her hand on his chest. Her soft gray eyes beseeched him. "Let me work this out with Rachel myself, Conn. Please."

Conn cupped his hand around the back of his neck and sighed. "All right. It's sure you can't do any worse than I've been doing," he said wearily. "From now on, when Rachel throws one of her conniptions I'll let you handle her."

"Good." A sad smile wavered around Elizabeth's lips. "After all, that's why you married me."

Conn frowned. The statement irritated him. Yet he couldn't deny it. Feeling unsettled and somehow at fault, he watched Elizabeth walk to the bed and slip beneath the covers. Thoughtfully, he blew out the candles and followed.

In the darkness he reached for her, and as always Elizabeth came willingly into his arms, her sweet, soft body pliant against him. For the first time he took her powerfully, a little roughly, driven by a compulsive need he didn't understand.

Later, as Elizabeth slept at his side, Conn lay staring at the darkened ceiling, trying to puzzle out the disquieting feelings that plagued him.

The next morning Elizabeth tapped on Rachel's door, then opened it partway and stuck her head inside. "Rachel? May I come in? I'd like to talk to you."

The girl sat on the window seat with her knees drawn up

close to her chest, her arms locked around them. She shot Elizabeth a resentful glare but shrugged. "I can't stop you. If I say no, you'll probably tell Papa and get me in trouble."

Ignoring the remark, Elizabeth sat down on the end of the fainting couch and met Rachel's glower with equanimity, her expression pleasantly composed. "Now then. Tell me why you don't want to go to the Groces' party."

I just don't, that's all."

"Come now, Rachel, you'll have to do better than that. There must be a reason."

Rachel shot her a belligerent glare and burrowed her chin deeper between her updrawn knees.

"Don't you like to dance? Most girls your age do."

"I don't know how."

"Someone here could teach you. It isn't difficult."

"What for? Nobody's going to ask me to dance anyway. No one ever even notices me."

Elizabeth raised one brow, getting an inkling of the problem. "They would," she said gently, "if we did something about your appearance."

That earned her a sharp look. "What do you mean?"

I mean it's time you started dressing in more fashionable clothes. After all, you're a young lady now, not a child."

For a moment interest flared in Rachel's face, but she quickly brought it under control. "It wouldn't make any difference. I'd still be plain old Rachel."

Elizabeth rose and walked to the window. Taking Rachel's chin, she turned her face this way and that. "Well, you're wrong. With the right hairstyle and a pretty dress, you'd be every bit a beautiful as your mother was. Blue, I think, to go with your lovely eyes. Yes, that would be perfect."

Rachel's eyes widened, then narrowed suspiciously. "You . . . you thought my mama was beautiful?"

"Of course I did. I have since we were girls." Elizabeth

stroked the dark hair at Rachel's temple and gave her a long, steady look. "I also loved her very much," she added quietly.

Chewing her lip, Rachel studied her uncertainly, and after a moment Elizabeth tugged her pigtail. "Now then, what do you say? Are you going to accept my offer?"

Rachel plucked at a bump on the nubby window seat cushion and stared at it. "Are you sure you can spare the time?"

"Of course. I know I've been busy lately, but most of the big chores are done now, so . . ." She stopped, studying the girl's sulky expression. "Spare the time from what, Rachel? What made you ask that?"

She shrugged elaborately and kept her eyes on the cushion. "Well, you're always so busy looking after Faith and Ian, I just figured . . ." Her voice trailed away and she shrugged again, affecting a bored look.

Why, she was jealous! Elizabeth was so stunned, for a moment she could only stare. That possibility had never even occurred to her.

Warmth filled her, and the girl's touching insecurity tugged at her heartstrings. Tears stung her eyes, but she blinked them back and picked up Rachel's hand, giving it a squeeze. "Rachel dear, I've devoted a lot of time to Faith because she's had such a terrible life, and Ian requires a lot of attention because he's so young. But that doesn't mean that I don't care about you. No matter how busy I am, I'll always have time for all of you, Rachel."

Rachel's mouth twisted and she transferred her gaze out the window, but Elizabeth ignored the disinterested pose and gave her hand a little tug.

"I tell you what. Since all three of us need new gowns for the party, we'll just have to work together. It's time I taught you girls how to sew, anyway."

Rachel rolled her eyes and groaned, but she allowed herself to be pulled from the window seat.

* * *

December came on with a cold "blue norther," bringing freezing rain and sleet that turned the roads and fields into seas of mud and made outside work impossible.

Confined to the house, Taw and Joseph passed the time playing checkers before the fire. Ian divided his time between watching them, pestering the girls, and wheedling treats out of Jemma and Isaac in the kitchen. Conn spent most days in his office going over the accounts, a chore that he detested, but which Elizabeth suspected he tackled simply to avoid the hubbub of feminine activity taking place in the parlor.

For days the floor was strewn with material and tissue patterns from Mr. Godey's book. While unpacking, Elizabeth had been astounded to discover that her cousin had brought with her almost a wagonload of dress goods. The extravagance, though typical of her self-absorbed cousin, had appalled Elizabeth at first, but it was proving to be a blessing.

Faith, though awkward, was eager to learn to sew and thrilled at being included in so grown-up an undertaking. She made each tiny stitch with painstaking concentration, and every few minutes she thrust whatever piece she was working on under Elizabeth's nose with a "How does that look? Am I doing it right?" or a "Did I really do good, Miss Elizabeth?"

Winning Rachel over proved not quite so easy. Despite her initial capitulation, she balked frequently, her moods swinging back and forth like the pendulum on the grandfather clock in the hall. At times she stubbornly resisted Elizabeth's every suggestion or instruction—about her hair, the style of dress that best suited her, the color, the proper way to sew it. But for all her foot-stamping temper tantrums and tears, Rachel was no match for Elizabeth's gentle determination.

"I hate my hair this way. I hate it!"

"Fine, then we'll try something else."

"It's too long. It won't curl."

"I'll cut it for you."

"*Taw* is going to teach me to dance? You must be kidding!"

"Not at all. He's a superb dancer. You'll see."

"I tell you I can't make these stitches straight."

"Yes, you can, dear. Just keep trying."

"Why are we doing this? It's hopeless!"

Elizabeth merely looked at her and smiled.

The wide central hallway of Bernardo, Jared Groce's plantation south of Washington, rang with fiddle music and laughter and the shuffle and thud of dancing feet. A giant Yule log still burned in the parlor fireplace, and wreaths of holly and evergreen boughs adorned the house from top to bottom. Their sharp, resinous scents mingled with the smell of candles and spiced wine and a heady blend of perfumes and hair tonic.

Standing to one side, Elizabeth watched with pride and pleasure as her stepdaughter whirled by in the arms of a young swain, her cornflower blue skirts billowing, her young face alight with laughter.

Up on the landing, under the watchful eye of Jemma and several other women, Ian and Faith and the other children who were too young to attend the party peered down through the banisters, their faces bright with excitement.

Lifting the fine crystal goblet, Elizabeth took a sip of syllabub. Beneath her ankle-length gown, her foot tapped the polished wood floor in time to the music. The dainty slipper was of the same soft rose satin as her gown, the ribbons that tied it about her white stocking-covered ankle the same rich claret velvet that trimmed the off-the-shoulder neckline, the lace inset in the bodice, and the cuffs on the full, leg-o'-mutton sleeves.

"My, my, that girl sure has blossomed since we parted company three months ago," Hester remarked. "She's got half the young men over sixteen falling over their own feet just trying to claim a dance. There's a stampede every time a new set starts."

"Not quite all of them." Elizabeth gave her friend a dry

smile and looked pointedly at the Grimeses' eighteen-year-old son, standing alone on the opposite side of the hall, his face stiff with studied indifference. "I noticed your Johnny hasn't gone near her."

"Humph! He's just got his nose out of joint is all. He ignored her all the way from Charleston, and now all of a sudden she's the belle of the ball, and he's feeling like a fool. And the fact that she's paying him no more mind that a June bug isn't helping his pride much neither."

"The funny thing is, I think he's the one she most wanted to impress."

"Shoot, I know that. The way those two have been working so hard at ignoring each other, anybody with eyes can figure out what's ailing 'em."

"Young love." Shaking her head, Elizabeth sighed. "Lord, it can be so painful."

"Yep," Hester agreed. She looked at Elizabeth, her gaze narrowing shrewdly. "But then, so can love at any age. Speaking of which, how're things working out between you and Conn?"

Elizabeth took another sip of syllabub and looked through the wide parlor doorway. A clutch of men stood in the front corner of the room, deep in discussion. As though drawn by a magnet, her gaze went to Conn's broad-shouldered form. Unconsciously her face grew soft with love as she took in the handsome picture he made in his black frock coat and blue vest, his ebony hair gleaming in the light from dozens of candles.

For an instant Elizabeth considered evading the question, but this was Hester, her friend, and she deserved better. Besides, she was the only person in the world in whom she could confide. "Oh, they're about the same, I guess. We get along well. He's affectionate and considerate, and he treats me with respect."

"All of which means he hasn't told you that he loves you."

"No. No, he hasn't," Elizabeth admitted quietly. She lifted her chin. If her smile wavered a bit, it was brave and determined. "But then, I knew when I married him that I might never hear those words."

"It could happen yet. It takes some men a while to see what's right before their eyes."

"Maybe. But if it doesn't, I'll survive. I'm Conn's wife, after all. I have a lovely home, three fine children, and Taw and Dr. Cavanaugh. It would be selfish and poor of me not to appreciate all that."

"True," Hester agreed, but they both knew that underneath the bright words, she still yearned . . . would always yearn.

Hester slipped her arm through Elizabeth's and started for the parlor. "C'mon. Let's go join our menfolk, and find out what Mr. Houston's saying that they all find so dad-blame interesting."

As they approached the group of men, Elizabeth's attention switched to the man standing beside Conn. The celebrated former governor of Tennessee and her husband were of a same height, though Sam Houston was of a heavier build. To Elizabeth he seemed a tall, powerfully muscled, battle-scarred warrior, part woodsman and part buccaneer. After meeting the man she was no longer surprised that he was now a prominent figure in Texas, despite the mysterious scandal surrounding his short marriage and divorce and his abrupt resignation from the governorship, or the stories of his heavy drinking afterward.

Sam Houston was a flamboyant, magnetic man, the direct opposite of Conn with his quiet forcefulness, yet, strangely, the two had taken to one another immediately. Both were strong men, in character as well as physically. And they're both natural leaders, Elizabeth thought with pride as her gaze shifted between her husband and the rugged Houston. The kind of men who commanded respect and inspired trust, and though opposites in personality, she supposed that each recognized in the other a kindred soul.

"Evening, Mrs. Cavanaugh, Mrs. Grimes. Won't you lovely ladies join us? We'd be honored, I assure you," Mr. Houston said gallantly at their approach.

"Why, thank you, sir. I hope we're not interrupting anything important."

"My, no. As usual, we were merely discussing the political situation. And of course Mr. Austin's incarceration. The poor man has been imprisoned for almost a year now. Much of the time, we hear, in solitary confinement."

"Yeah, and what for?" a disgruntled member of the group grumbled. "Just for delivering a petition drawn up by a peaceful assembly and pushing for statehood for Texas. Didn't get a trial or anything."

"Is there no recourse at all?" Elizabeth asked. "Surely something can be done to help the poor man."

"I assure you, my dear, we're doing all we can. As soon as word of Mr. Austin's arrest reached Texas, two attorneys rode to Mexico to try to secure his release. So far, however, their efforts have met with little success, I'm afraid." Sam Houston cleared his throat and took another sip of spiced wine. "What troubles me is the state of his health. Stephen Austin was never a robust man, and his tireless work for the good of Texas these past twelve years has taken a heavy toll."

The old-timers all around murmured their agreement and nodded their heads in concern.

"What I want to know," Hester said in her usual forthright manner, "is how the dickens things got to this sorry state? It couldn't have been this way to start, or nobody would've come here."

"You're sure right about that," declared Jasper Simpson. "When I brought my family here back in twenty-four, Mexico was a democracy . . . well, of a sort, anyway. Fact is, that was the only reason I was willing to leave the States and settle in Mexican territory. Things went along real fine for about five years, then ole Bustamante seized power. That's when our troubles started."

"I'll say," John White agreed. "Why, the first thing we knew, he was abolishing the constitution and moving in garrisons and closing the border to any more Anglos. We were supposed to be exempt from customs duties for ten years, but Bustamante sent in officials to collect them anyway. When William Travis and Patrick Jack spoke out against it they were arrested, and most of the ports were closed. Some folks over in Liberty even had their land confiscated."

A fresh chorus of grumbles went around the small circle.

"When Santa Anna waged a revolution against Bustamante he swore to restore the constitution," Jasper continued, "and we all thought he was going to be a savior. Huh! The man's a tyrant, if you ask me."

George Willowby, a leader among the peace faction, joined the group in time to catch Jasper's comment. "Now, Jasper," he argued, "Santa Anna has been a disappointment, I'll grant you that. But those of us with cooler heads still have hopes of resolving our problems with him."

"Resolve? Ha! I don't know what else we can do. We assembled peacefully, drew up a petition stating our grievances and requests, and pledged loyalty to the Mexican Confederation and the constitution. Then, when we presented it to Santa Anna through our most respected citizen, the arrogant little bastard threw him in the pokey."

"Yes, indeed," Sam Houston ruminated. "It does make you wonder how far the populace is willing to let the little tyrant push us before we stand up and fight."

"Surely, sir, you're not advocating war?" George demanded with the beginnings of outrage.

"No, Willowby, I'm not. At least, not yet. Our men are not yet trained, organized, or provisioned for battle. It would be disaster to push for rebellion at this time."

"Oh, my." Elizabeth's face paled, and her eyes grew round.

"Mr. Houston . . . are . . . are you saying there *will* be war?"

Sam was instantly contrite. "No, no, my dear. Please don't upset yourself. I'm sure it will never come to that." As Conn's arm went around her waist, Mr. Houston took her hand in his and patted it solicitously. "Forgive me for letting my clumsy tongue run away with me. I was merely indulging in a bit of verbal saber rattling. You just put this nasty business right out of that pretty head. It was vulgar of us to even bring it up on an occasion like this. After all, this is a party." He cocked his ear and smiled. "Listen. I do believe they're tuning up for a reel."

Sam quickly set his glass of wine on a nearby table and swept Elizabeth a low bow. "You would do me a great honor, Mrs. Cavanaugh, if you'll allow me this dance."

Giving him a wavering smile, Elizabeth put her hand on his arm and allowed him to lead her into the central hall.

For the next several hours she danced and laughed and visited with neighbors and friends, many of whom she had not seen since the wagon train. They enjoyed a late night repast, choosing from venison, wild turkey with prune dressing, roasted quail, fried catfish, rabbit, candied yams, corn fritters, cabbage, turnips, peas, beans, potatoes, melons, stewed apples, pears in rum sauce, and all manner of cakes and pies. Elizabeth exchanged recipes and gossip with the women, instructed Gladys Pinder in how to make a plaster for her child's chronic croup, and learned from Grandma Mitchell how to make a cool summer sunbonnet from river rushes. But no matter how busy she stayed or how hard she tried, she could not forget the disturbing conversation.

"Sam's right," Conn told her impatiently when she peppered him with questions during their ride home. "Forget it. Put it out of your mind. The chance of us going to war with the Mexican government is so unlikely it's not worth thinking about."

Elizabeth stopped asking questions, but the fear would not

go away. Later, as she lay beside him in the darkness listening to his even breathing, her thoughts tormented her. What would they do if they had to leave Riverbend? Would all Conn had worked for be lost? It wasn't fair! It wasn't right! They both loved this place so.

Then an even worse thought occurred to her, and her heart contracted with pain. Oh, God. What if something happened to Conn? She wouldn't be able to bear it!

No. No, she wouldn't think that way. She couldn't lose him. Not now. God wouldn't be so cruel. Conn had said that war was unlikely. She had to believe that. She had to.

Chapter 17

![icon] "Have you heard about the ruckus in Anahuac? There was shots fired, and two men got thrown in jail!"

The sight of the Grimeses' wagon barreling up the drive less than a month after the social at Bernardo had surprised everyone in the Cavanaugh household and brought them hurrying out onto the front veranda, but Liam's excited announcement, shouted out before he brought the mules to a complete stop, stunned them even more. Elizabeth pressed her palm flat against her pounding heart and steadied herself against one of the pillars with her other hand. Conn, Taw, and Joseph hurried down the steps.

"What happened?" Conn demanded, holding the bridle strap of the lead mule while Liam jumped down from the driver's seat.

Johnny Grimes and his younger brother, seventeen-year-old Daniel, tied their horses to the back of the wagon and helped their mother and sister alight, while the two younger Grimes males, thirteen-year-old Luke and five-year-old Jeremy, scrambled out on their own. The whole family had come, except for Ben.

"Santa Anna sent customs officials to Anahuac and Velasco to collect import taxes," Liam explained gravely.

Conn spit out a low curse. "Dammit, he agreed we would be exempt from customs for three more years."

"Yeah, well, when a couple of the merchants in Anahuac

complained about the high fees and started agitatin' others, there was a squabble and some shootin', and the pair was arrested and locked up in the garrison there. Both are big men in them parts, too."

"When did this happen?"

"Just a few days ago. Me'n Hes was in San Felipe when we heard the news. Lots of folks is plenty stirred up about it."

On the porch, Elizabeth and Hester exchanged a hug and a worried look. The older woman's mouth flattened and turned down at the corners as she noted Elizabeth's pallor. Swinging around, she glared at the men, hands on her hips.

"You gonna stand out there in the cold all day jawin'? If you just got to chew this thing to death, leastways come inside where it's warm." Not waiting for a reply, she looped her arm through Elizabeth's. "C'mon, hon. While they're cussing and discussing you can show me this house of yours. Whoowie! It's sure something."

As they headed for the door, nine-year-old Annabelle held out her hand in a tentative overture to Faith. Elizabeth caught her breath, expecting the wary child to scurry away, but after a brief hesitation she cautiously accepted the offer, and the two girls disappeared inside, hand in hand, with Ian scampering at their heels.

Scowling blackly at Rachel, who stood to one side shivering, waiting for him to notice her, Johnny snapped, "You'd better go in before you catch your death."

Rachel reacted as though she'd been stung, and with a toss of her saucy side curls, she picked up her lavender wool skirt and sailed past him with her chin in the air.

All day the talk centered around the incident at Anahuac. They worried at it from every angle, speculating on what the feeling would be among the settlers, whether or not any action would be taken on the men's behalf, how the Mexican government would react if there were.

They were all anxious to learn what was going on, and over

dinner Conn announced his intention to leave for the coast the next morning. "I've got to pick up a load of goods in Velasco anyway—things I arranged to have shipped before we left Charleston. The schooner should be arriving any day now. On my way, I'll swing by Anahuac and see what I can learn."

"Well, I'm goin' with you," Taw declared.

"Think I'll tag along, too," Liam chimed in.

That night, after their guests were bedded down and the house was quiet, Conn made slow, sweet love to Elizabeth. She clung to him with all her might, tears in her eyes, the dread of parting squeezing her heart. It had been over a year since she had been apart from Conn for even a day.

"Shh. Easy sweetheart, easy." He chuckled when she made a desperate little sound and arched frantically beneath him. "This has to last until I get back."

He held her hips in his big hands and stroked into her with a lazy, undulating rhythm that was exquisite torture, and all the while his deep voice murmured in her ear—erotic things, exciting things, beautiful things—things that made her heart pound and her blood run hot and her body tauten and tremble. He told her how good it felt to be inside her, how beautiful she was, how wild she made him feel. The words, whispered in that deep voice, were raw and shocking . . . and wonderful. He told her how much he wanted her, how much he needed her, how much he would miss her.

But he never told her the one thing she longed to hear.

The next morning on the front veranda, in full view of the others, Conn took her into his arms and kissed her good-bye, so long and hard and thoroughly that Elizabeth felt as though she were melting. When he released her his eyes glinted as he stroked her cheek and murmured, "I'll be back in a week or two. Three at most."

Elizabeth could only nod and press her lips together to keep them from trembling.

"If you need anything, just tell Dad. And be sure to keep the pistols I gave you loaded."

"I will. I promise," she said in a quavering whisper.

He took a step away, then swung back and kissed her again, hard, but a moment later, as he and Liam rode down the drive ahead of the wagon Taw was driving, she knew that he had already dismissed her from his mind. Even Pike, trotting ahead of the men, appeared anxious to be off.

Huddled in her thick wool shawl, Elizabeth watched until he was out of sight. Her skirt whipped around her legs, the wool cloth flapping and popping in the icy January wind. Snatched from their moorings, curling tendrils of hair danced wildly about her face, getting in her eyes, sticking to the corners of her mouth, but she barely noticed. Hester stood beside her, and inside, the house was full of guests and family; still Elizabeth felt woefully alone.

Three days later, when Hester and her brood started for home, Elizabeth's loneliness deepened.

"I wish you'd change your mind and stay a little longer," she said, standing with her friend beside the wagon. Despite Rachel and Johnny's constant squabbling and her own melancholia, she had enjoyed the visit. She and Hester had talked for hours, and the company of the lively family had helped her keep her mind off Conn and how much she missed him.

"We'd better be getting on home. We told Ben we'd be back today, and he'll worry if we're not."

A wave of sadness washed over Elizabeth at the mention of Ben. She had not seen him since they'd parted company with the Grimes family in late September. He had skipped the social at Bernardo and had declined to come on the visit to Riverbend. Elizabeth feared that she was the reason, and it pained her that he was still hurting. "Give him my best, won't you."

"You know I will." Hester hugged Elizabeth again, then addressed her eldest son. "Well, Johnny. I guess we'd best be getting on."

"Yes, Maw."

Johnny put one foot on the wheel hub to climb into the wagon, but he suddenly stopped. His mouth set, he strode back around the end of the wagon, took the veranda steps in one leap, and, to the utter astonishment of everyone watching, snatched Rachel into his arms and kissed her senseless.

Ending the kiss as abruptly as he had begun it, he grasped her upper arms and held her away from him, his young face stern and remarkably fierce. "We're both too young to get married, so we'll have to wait a few years. But from now on you belong to me. Understand?"

Standing as docile as a lamb within his grasp, her face flushed, Rachel smiled up at him dreamily. "Yes, Johnny."

"No more flirting with other men."

"No, Johnny."

"If Aaron or Frank or any of that bunch come calling, you're to tell them you're spoken for. You hear?"

"Yes, Johnny. Whatever you say."

He narrowed his eyes and stared at her suspiciously, not quite trusting this new submissiveness, but she met his scrutiny with an adoring look and a beguiling smile that made Elizabeth catch her breath, so sharply did it remind her of Millie.

At this vision of soft, feminine acquiescence, the fierceness went out of Johnny. "Good." He still strove for a commanding tone, but the word came out husky and selfconscious, his voice lacking even a shred of its former heat. As they stared into each other's eyes, Johnny's face softened, and he bent his head and kissed her once again, gently this time.

Mouths agape, Elizabeth and Hester stared at the couple, exchanged a disbelieving look, and burst out laughing. "Shoulda known all that bickerin' would lead to this," Hester whooped. "Where there's that much heat, a fire's sure to flare."

Giggles and taunts from the others finally broke the couple

apart. Johnny glowered at his siblings, but it took a sharp word from Hester to quiet them. "All right, son, tell the girl good-bye and let's get going," she said, climbing into the wagon.

Johnny obeyed reluctantly, his lovesick gaze clinging to Rachel's even as he got into the wagon and clucked the team into motion.

For the remainder of the day Elizabeth felt weighted down with loneliness. She missed Conn and Taw terribly, and without the boisterous Grimes family, the big house seemed empty. Rachel spent most of her time in her room in a dreamy, lovesick haze, and Ian and Faith were still absorbed in playing the games they'd learned from Annabelle and her brothers.

Around noon a rider arrived with a summons for Dr. Cavanaugh, requesting his services in San Felipe, where an outbreak of influenza had reached near epidemic proportions. He was reluctant to leave Elizabeth with no man in the house, but she insisted that he go.

Scarcely an hour after he left, Dulcie tapped on the back door.

"Isaac said you wanted to see me, Dulcie," Elizabeth said. "Is something wrong?"

The young woman shifted to one foot, then the other, and tugged at the red kerchief covering her hair. Her eyes darted this way and that. She was shaking much harder than the temperature warranted, and Elizabeth had the feeling she was terrified.

"C-can you . . . can you come to the quarters, Miz Liz'beth?" she finally managed to stammer. "You . . . you said to come to you if we needed doctorin', an' my brother, Ebon . . . oh, Lawdy, Miz Liz'beth, he's in a bad way."

Elizabeth knew he must be for Dulcie even to be there. It had been two months since she'd told them to bring their medical problems to Dr. Cavanaugh or herself, but in all those weeks none of them had sought help, though she'd seen signs of minor injuries and ailments.

"Of course. Wait here, Dulcie, and I'll be right with you."

Isaac insisted on going with her to carry the heavy doctor's bag. Elizabeth suspected that he was uneasy about her going anywhere alone, now that all the men were gone, and had appointed himself her watchdog.

She expected to find Ebon down with a fever or an injury of some kind. She was not prepared for the sight that greeted her when she stepped into the dimly lit cabin.

"Oh, my Lord!" Elizabeth looked down in horror at the prostrate man as one of the women in the crowded room held a candle aloft over him. Ebon's back was a bloody mess. Deep lacerations crisscrossed his dark skin from shoulders to waist, each oozing blood, the narrow ribbons of flesh in between swollen and angry. Ebon was a giant of a man, his massive frame thick with muscles, but he lay as weak as a newborn kitten, sprawled on his stomach, moaning, barely conscious.

Elizabeth stared at the marks that could only have been made by the lash of a whip, and a rage like nothing she'd ever known boiled up inside her. "Who did this to him?" she demanded, her soft voice shaking with fury. The question met only silence, and Elizabeth's gaze raked the frightened faces around her. "Answer me! I want to know who did this?"

Ebon stirred, and his eyes blinked open. Spotting Elizabeth, he groaned louder. "Oh, Lawdy . . . Dulcie," he gasped. "Girl . . . what you gone an' done? I . . . told you . . . not to fetch Miz Cav'naugh."

"But I had to, Ebon!" Dulcie cried, falling on her knees beside the bed. "You need doctorin' bad! I couldn't just let you die!"

"Garth . . . he kill us for sure when . . . when he find out."

Elizabeth had her answer. "You did exactly right, Dulcie," she said briskly, and shifted the distraught girl out of the way. "Zena, bring me a bowl of warm water and some clean rags."

Rolling up her sleeves, Elizabeth sat down on the bed beside the injured man. Taking the pan of water from Zena, she placed it on her lap and wrung out the rag. As gently as possible, she began to clean Ebon's wounds, grimacing when her careful ministrations caused him to jerk and moan. Within minutes the water in the pan was red and had to be changed.

"Why did Garth do this?" she asked Dulcie as she worked.

"Well, when Mistah Garth ordered Lottie to go to his house, Ebon got mad. Ebon an' Lottie be sweethearts. He's just been waitin' for a chance to ask Mastah Cav'naugh if he can marry up with her. Lottie, she didn't wanna go, and when Mistah Garth started to drag her off, Ebon tried to stop him. That's when Mistah Garth whupped him."

Elizabeth stopped working and stared at Dulcie. "Are you telling me that Garth . . . *forces* himself on you women?"

"Yes'm. Lately he's been takin' his pleasure on L'teese over yonder, but now that she's gonna have his baby, he's taken to usin' others."

Following the direction of Dulcie's nod, Elizabeth saw a girl of no more than thirteen huddled in the corner, her swollen belly obvious beneath the coarse homespun dress.

"Where is Lottie now?"

"At Mistah Garth's, I 'spect. He was haulin' her off when we carried Ebon in here."

Gritting her teeth, Elizabeth set the pan of water on the floor and took a jar of ointment from her bag. "Isaac, go back to the house and get the pistols Conn left with me," she ordered tightly as she began to smear the smelly yellow salve over Ebon's lacerated back.

"*Pistols!*" Isaac squawked. His eyes grew round as dinner plates. "What you gonna do with pistols?"

"Never mind, just do as I say. On your way back stop by the barn and bring me a bullwhip as well."

"Oh, Lawdy, Lawdy, Miz Elizabeth, you ain't—"

"Just go, Isaac."

He went—reluctantly—wringing his hands and grumbling

under his breath. Fifteen minutes later, as Elizabeth finished
tending to Ebon's wounds, he returned with the bullwhip
looped over his shoulder and a pistol in each hand.

"This powder will ease his pain," Elizabeth said, handing
Dulcie several small folded papers. "Give him one in a cup of
warm milk every few hours."

She snapped her bag closed and took the pistols from Isaac.

"What you gonna do, Miz Liz'beth?" Isaac inquired worriedly. "You not careful, you gonna shoot somebody."

"I will if he gives me any trouble." Ignoring Isaac's gasp,
she slipped the guns into her apron pockets and turned to the
others. "Don't worry about Garth. I promise he won't be
hurting any of you, ever again."

The statement created a stir, and when Elizabeth swept
from the cabin with the bullwhip in her hand, everyone inside
rushed to follow her. Even Ebon, with the help of two other
men, staggered along in her wake, and more people joined
them as she marched through the quarters.

When she reached the overseer's cottage, tucked among the
trees between the quarters and the big house, she stopped a
few feet from the porch. Except for Isaac, her curious audience
pulled up about twenty feet behind her in the shelter of the
trees.

Concealing the whip in the folds of her skirt, Elizabeth
called to Garth and waited.

"Mr. Lathom, I said come out here at once," she called
again when he didn't respond. A moment later Garth stepped
outside, buttoning his shirt, a loathsome grin on his face.

"Well, well. This is a surprise. What can I do for you, Mrs.
Cavanaugh?"

"For a start, you can send that poor girl out."

"Girl? I'm afraid I don't know what you're talking about."

She shot him a disgusted look. "Lottie? Lottie, if you're in
there, come out. This is Mrs. Cavanaugh speaking."

Almost at once the door creaked open a few inches, and

Garth swung around scowling. "Dammit, girl, I told you to stay put! Now get back in—"

The whip cracked the air just inches from Garth's face. He yelped and jumped back, cursing.

"You be quiet, Mr. Lathom," Elizabeth ordered. "And stay put. Come on out, Lottie, No one's going to hurt you."

Garth gave Elizabeth an incredulous look, but other than a fierce scowl he made no move to stop the frightened woman, who sidled past him clutching her torn clothing to her body.

Eyes downcast, Lottie hurried toward Elizabeth. She'd taken only a few steps when Ebon called her name. Lottie's head jerked up. "Ebon? Oh, Lawd, Ebon," she cried as he stumbled from the cover of the trees. She rushed to his side, lending her support to keep him upright.

"Ah, now I see," Garth drawled, his eyes cold as he watched the reunion. "They came whining to you, did they?" His gaze swept menacingly over the group of people that crept forward out of the woods and aligned themselves behind Elizabeth. "I'll deal with the lot of you tomorrow, don't think I won't."

"You won't be having dealings with anyone on Riverbend tomorrow, Mr. Lathom, because you'll be gone. You're dismissed, sir, as of this moment. I want you off this property immediately."

Hooking his thumbs in the waistband of his trousers, Garth chuckled nastily. "Well now, that's too bad, ma'am. 'Cause I'm not going. I don't take orders from women."

"You'll take orders from this one."

"And if I don't? What're you going to do?" he sneered. "Beat me with that whip?"

"No, Mr. Lathom." Elizabeth tossed the whip aside, brought a gun from her apron pocket, and leveled it on his chest. "I'm going to shoot you."

"Is that suppose to scare me? You've only got one shot there, lady, and you probably don't even know how to use that thing."

"I assure you, I do. Quite well, in fact. But even if I miss with the first shot, I still have this." She brought the other pistol out of her pocket and pointed it at his crotch.

"Isaac," she called, not taking her eyes from Garth. "Take two of the women and go inside and pack Mr. Lathom's things."

Garth's face turned ugly. "I'm warning you, lady. Your husband isn't going to like this."

"Maybe not. But when I tell him what you've done, he's going to like that even less."

A week passed, then two, with no word from Conn. By the middle of February Elizabeth was beginning to get concerned. Then one afternoon Liam arrived with a note from Conn.

She wanted to read it right away, but good manners demanded she see to her guest first. "So, what did you find in Anahuac?" she remembered to ask once they were snug before the fire.

"Not much. Things are quiet there. The two men are still in jail. Looks like it'll be June before they have their trial day, just like Conn predicted. There's a lot of mumbling and such amongst the men in town, but nobody's making any moves.

"Soon as we saw the way things was an' that nothing was gonna happen anytime soon, we moseyed on down to Velasco. Been waitin' there ever since for that danged ship. Conn an' Taw are still there, but I had to get on back to start plantin'."

When she offered to have Isaac take his horse to the barn, he replied, "Thank you all the same, Elizabeth, but I can't stay. I got to be gettin' back to Hes and them young'uns."

She couldn't get him to change his mind, but he put up only token resistance to her suggestion that he have a hot meal before leaving. As Jemma plied him with food, Elizabeth sat with him at the dining table and read Conn's note with growing dismay.

"Something wrong?" Liam asked, helping himself to another pork chop.

"Conn wants me to have Garth start plowing. He says if he's not home within a week, to go ahead and start planting corn and cotton."

"Yep. That's the thing to do all right. Down here, it's best to make one plantin' in late February and another a month or so later."

"But I can't." Elizabeth looked at Liam helplessly. "You see, I . . . I dismissed Garth."

Thunderstruck, Liam listened as Elizabeth explained what had happened. When she'd finished he shook his head and chuckled. "Run him off at gunpoint, did ya. I'd've liked to see that. Never did take to Lathom. Reminded me of a snake." He chuckled again and looked at her with a new respect. "Who'd' a thought it, a little thing like you?"

"What am I going to do, Liam? There's no one to direct the hands, and I certainly don't know anything about farming."

Liam sobered and mulled over her predicament. "Well," he drawled thoughtfully after a minute. "I suppose I could ask Ben if he'd come give you a hand. Me and my boys can work my place fine without him." When her eyes lit up with hope, he hastened to add, "Now I ain't promising he'll do it, you understand."

"But you will ask him for me?"

Liam sighed and rubbed his jaw. From his expression she knew he didn't relish the task. "I'll ask."

"I'm just doing this for you," Ben stated when he arrived the next afternoon. Still sitting astride his horse, he looked down at her, his expression closed, and Elizabeth knew that being there was costing him a lot.

"I know, Ben," she said softly. "And I appreciate it. Really, I do."

"I'll do what I can until Conn returns, but when he does, I'm leaving."

"I understand." She gestured toward the house. "Won't you come inside?"

"No, thanks. I'll stay in the overseer's cottage. If you'll point the way, I'll go get settled in."

The brusque conversation set the tone for their relationship. Ben came to the house every evening at quitting time, reported on the day's progress, and laid out his plans for the next, but he never stayed for dinner or to visit. Mostly she saw him from a distance, astride his horse in the fields directing Ebon and the others, or around the barn and stock pens. He was polite but remote, and Elizabeth knew he was avoiding her.

Daily, through the trees that surrounded the house and lined the drive, she could see the progress. The rich black soil toppled in waves before the plow blades, burying the winter stubble and leaving neat furrows and windrows in its wake. By the end of the month the weather had turned mild, and the fertile smells of newly turned earth and sunshine filled the air.

Dr. Cavanaugh returned from San Felipe a few days after Ben began work. Though he was a bit startled over the turn of events, he assured Elizabeth that she had done the right thing. Since Joseph knew no more about farming than did she, they persuaded Ben to remain at Riverbend.

The time dragged for Elizabeth, but she did her best to stay busy. When she wasn't directing household chores or sewing or seeing after Ian, she instructed Faith in her studies.

Faith was a bright child. Already she was reading and writing remarkably well, and her grammar had improved immensely. She had a fair grasp of geography and adored history, which, Elizabeth suspected, was due to her love of historical novels. Reading a few chapters of a story each night had become a family ritual, and Elizabeth was thankful for Dr. Cavanaugh's supply of books. Her own had long ago been exhausted. Not that it really mattered. Faith could happily have listened to *Ivanhoe* night after night.

The one subject with which Faith had difficulty, and there-fore detested, was arithmetic. Addition and subtraction she could understand, but when Elizabeth tried to explain mul-tiplication and division she might as well have spoken in a foreign language. Faith's response was always the same—a blank look, followed by tearful frustration.

"I just can't do it, Miss Elizabeth," she wailed. "I *can't!*"

"Oh, dearest—"

"What can't she do? Is something wrong?"

Startled, Elizabeth and Faith looked around and saw Rachel standing in the dining room doorway. She looked from one to the other, her eyebrows raised in inquiry.

"Oh, hello, Rachel. No, nothing is wrong. Faith is simply having a bit of trouble understanding division. That's all."

"Really? I can't imagine why. I always thought it was easy. Even kind of fun."

Her mouth drooping, Faith ducked her head. At once Rachel hurried forward into the room and put her hand on the child's slumped shoulder. "Gracious, Faith, there's no need to cry. You just need to learn the rules. That's all. Then it's simple."

A speculative gleam entered Elizabeth's eyes as she studied Rachel's expression. Why, she was genuinely sorry to have upset the child.

"Perhaps you could teach her?"

Rachel shot Elizabeth a startled look. So did Faith.

"Me.?"

"Yes. Why not? Faith is smart, but I don't seem to have the knack of explaining it so that she can understand. Since you enjoy arithmetic, I'm sure you would do much better."

"Well . . ."

"You would be doing both of us a tremendous favor, Rachel," Elizabeth wheedled shamelessly. "Wouldn't she, Faith?"

"Well . . . I reckon, but . . .", Faith ducked her head again. "Rachel don't want to teach me," she mumbled, lapsing into her former atrocious grammar, as she always did whenever she felt threatened.

"Don't be silly. Why, it will be fun," Rachel said briskly, and pulled up a chair at Faith's other side. "Here, let me show you. First you . . .",

Smiling, Elizabeth leaned back in her chair and watched their heads bend together over the slate, one black as coal, the other the color of autumn leaves. Why hadn't she thought of this sooner? Since the three of them had worked together to make dresses for the party at Bernardo, Rachel become more tolerant of Faith, but there was still a stiffness between them. Elizabeth had been searching for a way to overcome it, and now here it was. This was the perfect way to bring the two girls closer.

Rachel had changed a lot in the past two months. The aloofness and anger was gone. No longer did she lash out or sulk or nurse grievances, real or imagined. She was softer now, more open to others, more giving. Happier. Elizabeth knew that the credit for that belonged mostly to Johnny Grimes. Watching Rachel laugh and tug playfully on one of Faith's curls, Elizabeth smiled wistfully. What an amazing difference knowing you were loved made.

Conn had been gone a little over five weeks when, from an upstairs bedroom, through the still bare branches of the trees, Elizabeth spotted the wagon and rider coming down the road. Out on their left flank, nosing through the plowed field, trotted a big brute of a dog.

"It's Conn! It's Conn!" she cried as she tore down the curving stairway. At the commotion, Isaac came hurrying from the back of the house and Joseph appeared in the doorway of the study, an indulgent smile on his face as she dashed by.

Elizabeth didn't even see them. She raced down the central hallway, out the door, and down the veranda steps, her skirt and petticoats lifted almost to her knees and billowing out behind her. She was a quarter of the way down the drive before she saw the wagon and rider coming from the other direction.

Pike barked and broke into a run. Spotting her, Conn put his horse into a gallop. He reined in yards short and hit the ground running.

"Conn! Oh, Conn!" Elizabeth cried as she launched herself into his arms.

He caught her high against his chest and whirled her around, both of them laughing and breathless. "God, little one, it's so damned good to be home."

Then the dizzying spins slowed and stopped. Conn loosened his hold, letting her slide down his body until their faces were level and their gazes met and held. His rugged features softened as he took in her flushed face, the sparkle in her eyes, and the joy she made no effort to hide. His own eyes darkened and grew heavy-lidded. "Elizabeth," he whispered. "My sweet, sweet Beth."

Her arms encircled his neck, and she buried her fingers in his hair, clasping him to her as their lips met in a long, burning kiss. She hung in his arms, her feet still not touching the ground, and kissed him with all the love in her heart, seeking to banish the hunger and loneliness of the past weeks. She clasped him tightly, reveling in his nearness, the feel of him, the smell of him, the wonderful taste of him.

Lips rocked. Breaths mingled. Tongues mated. They stood in the mottled shade cast by the bare trees. Around them bees buzzed, and high overhead a songbird trilled, a squirrel chattered. In the distance the field hands were singing a low spiritual. From down the drive came the rumble of wheels and the jingle of traces, the slow clop of shod hooves, announcing Taw's approach in the wagon. Still the embrace went on as hearts pounded and hands stroked and bodies yearned. They might have been the only living creatures in the world, so complete was their absorption.

"Whoa, mules. Whoa." The clopping halted a few feet

away. "Either you two gotta come up fer air or git outta the way. I'm too old and too tired t' sit here all day."

The kiss ended reluctantly. Letting Elizabeth slide down until her feet touched the ground, Conn gave his partner a dry look. "Don't pay any attention to him, sweetheart. He's just jealous."

"Dad-burned right, I am!"

Laughing, Elizabeth hurried over to the wagon, climbed up on the wheel, and gave the old man a hug. "Oh, Taw, I missed you, too. I'm glad you're home." Her gaze swept back to Conn, and her voice softened. "I'm glad you're both home."

Conn lifted her down and drew her against his side. Leading his horse, their arms looped around one another, they walked up the drive beside the wagon. Pike trotted ahead, stopping now and then to sniff, reacquainting himself with his surroundings.

"Garth's gotten a lot done," he said in a pleased voice, gazing around. "Good job, too, from the looks of those fields."

Elizabeth stumbled. Garth! Oh, Lord. In her excitement she'd forgotten all about Garth. And Ben.

Conn's arm tightened around her and he sent her a teasing glance, but his attention quickly reverted to the fields surrounding the house.

"Uh . . . Conn. There's something I have to tell you. It's, well . . . Garth isn't the one who's been doing all this. He, uh . . . he isn't here anymore."

"Hmmm. I see." His head snapped around. "What?" He frowned, his eyes boring into her. "What did you say?"

Elizabeth almost flinched beneath that fierce look. Instead she lifted her chin and said calmly, "I dismissed Garth."

Chapter 18

Conn halted and released her. "You did *what*?"

With a murmured, "Whoa, mules," Taw brought the wagon to a halt a few yards beyond where they stood and looked back, listening unabashedly.

Elizabeth laced her fingers together and glanced at him for support. "I had no choice, Conn. He was—"

"You *dismissed* my overseer?" he shouted as though she hadn't even spoken. "Just like that? The minute my back was turned? Hell, Elizabeth, I knew you didn't like Garth, but it never occurred to me that you would do something like this!"

She sucked in her breath. "You think I fired him because I don't like him? You really think I would do such a thing?"

"All I know is he's gone."

Elizabeth went very still, her delicate shoulders erect. Anger she had expected, at least initially, and she'd been prepared to deal with it, but his insulting opinion of her character cut deep.

It wasn't in her nature to argue, to flare back with angry words of her own. Though she didn't back up, or even move, she withdrew from him, erecting a mental barrier between them against further hurt. "Whether you believe it or not, my personal feelings about Mr. Lathom had nothing to do with my decision."

Her remote calm only made him angrier. "Dammit, woman, do you have any idea how hard an overseer is to come by here?

Men come to Texas because the land is cheap. Here they can have a place of their own, be their own boss. They don't have to work for someone else."

"I'm sorry. I did what I felt I had to do."

Frustrated, Conn raked his fingers through his hair. "God spare me from an interfering woman," he muttered. "Hell, she had her faults, but even Millie wouldn't have dared to pull a stunt like this."

Elizabeth's face whitened. That was the cruelest cut of all. She stared at him bleakly, her eyes full of hurt. "I'm not Millie," she said without inflection.

That had been the crux of their problem all along, she thought. Or rather, her problem. Foolishly she had been waiting, praying that Conn would come to love her—really love her—but now she realized she possessed a major flaw that would always prevent that from happening: she wasn't Millie.

Conn grimaced and reached out to her, but he let his hand drop to his side when Elizabeth backed up a step. "Sweetheart, I'm sorry. I didn't mean—"

His words halted abruptly, his attention caught by a movement at the far end of the field bordering the drive. Narrowing with a dangerous glitter, his eyes locked on the man astride the big sorrel horse, directing a crew of workers. "Who the hell is that?" Conn's eyes snapped back to Elizabeth. "If you got rid of Garth, then just who's responsible for all this?" he demanded, sweeping his hand toward the cultivated fields.

"Ben. He was good enough to help out until you returned."

"Ben? You got rid of my overseer and brought Ben Whitelaw here?" he said in a low, savage voice that made her flinch.

"Yes. When Liam suggested—" Elizabeth gasped, her face growing even whiter as she took in his pinched nostrils, the black fury in his face. "What are you accusing . . . ? Oh, God, you don't really think . . . ?" She couldn't continue, couldn't voice the vile suspicion she knew he harbored.

"Dammit, Elizabeth, come back here!" he roared when she turned and walked away.

She ignored him. She wasn't going to stand there and let him rip her heart to shreds; she couldn't bear it.

The angry shout brought Pike doubling back, tense and watchful, hackles raised.

She'd made it only a few yards when he caught her arm and spun her around. "Don't walk away from me! Dammit, I want to know what's going on here!"

Pike growled, then whined, looking from one to the other.

"Do you?" She tilted her chin, her face a pale mask. "Then I suggest you talk to Ben. And your father. When you've finished with them you might want to have a word with Isaac. Or Ebon or Dulcie or Lottie or any number of the others. Maybe you'll listen to them without jumping to conclusions."

Her words were cool, but pain clouded her eyes. The sight touched Conn, even through his anger, and when she tugged against his hold he let her go. Feeling savage, he watched her walk away.

"You know, up till now I always figured you fer a purty smart fella. But danged if'n I ain't wonderin' whether you got the sense God gave a lop-eared mule."

"Butt out, Taw," Conn growled. He swung into the saddle and put his horse into a trot. Cutting through the trees bordering the drive, he headed for the mounted man at the far end of the field.

Torn, Pike gazed after Elizabeth, his yellow eyes mournful, but after a moment he gave a low *woof* and loped after Conn.

That evening when Conn slipped quietly into their bedroom, Elizabeth was asleep. He sighed heavily, remorse hitting him anew as he stood beside the bed and studied her. Her face was pale, and the delicate skin around her eyes appeared bruised, the lids puffy. The end of her nose was pink and raw, and her cheeks bore the tracks of countless tears.

Even so she looked incredibly lovely, lying there curled on her side, one hand cupped beneath her cheek. Her long lashes lay against her white skin like dark fans. In her sleep she drew in a little shuddering breath, the exhausted remnant of spent emotion. Conn smiled with tender regret, his gaze skimming the prim nightgown and the thick braid that draped over her shoulder.

When he'd returned from the fields he hadn't been surprised to hear that Elizabeth wasn't feeling well and wouldn't be down for dinner. Hell, after all he'd learned he didn't blame her for avoiding him.

He had hurt her. Badly.

God, how could he have said those things to her? He'd regretted the words almost the instant they'd come out of his mouth. Not for a minute had he thought she'd betrayed him with Ben. Theirs might not be a love match, but Elizabeth was nothing if not loyal.

Still, he couldn't deny that what he felt was jealousy. Ben was in love with Elizabeth, and Conn didn't like the idea of his being there with her, no matter how innocent the situation.

He had to hand it to Whitelaw, though; the man had not backed down an inch when he'd lit into him. Didn't waste any time setting him straight, either.

Damn that Lathom! Conn thought furiously, remembering the condition of Ebon's back and all the things he and Lottie and the others had told him. Elizabeth had done the right thing. If he'd been there, he would have done the same, only he would have flattened the man, then given him the boot.

Conn's eyes softened on Elizabeth, and his hard mouth twitched. She'd popped a whip in Lathom's face and run him off at gunpoint. His sweet, doe-eyed, gentle wife. He shook his head. Amazing.

When they married he'd been certain that he knew all there was to know about Elizabeth, but she continually surprised him. He thought about the way she'd come tearing down the drive to meet him, her dress hiked up to her knees, her hair streaming out behind her, that lovely face alight, and his heart swelled with an exquisite ache. In all the years of their marriage, Millie had never once been that happy to see him.

Dear God, how could he have compared Elizabeth unfavorably with anyone? Especially Millie?

Conn unbuttoned his shirt and shrugged out of it, draping it over the back of a chair before sitting down to tug off his boots. He owed her an apology, he acknowledged, removing his trousers and underwear and tossing both atop the shirt.

He blew out the candles and eased into bed, being careful not to disturb her. Bracing up on one elbow, he studied his wife in the soft moonlight, his expression tender. Her skin was silky smooth, her pink lips slightly parted in slumber and very inviting. With a grimace, he resisted the urge to kiss her and instead brushed a lock of pale hair off her face.

It struck him there in the quiet stillness of the night that Elizabeth was the most utterly feminine woman he had ever known. Soft. Nurturing. Without an ounce of guile or coyness. It shamed him to admit it, but there had been a time when he wouldn't have noticed or cared. Now, however, he found those subtle virtues infinitely more attractive and arousing than sultry beauty or coquettish charms.

And beneath Elizabeth's tranquil surface were secret depths that fascinated him more each day.

He had missed her these past weeks, far more than he had anticipated. Just looking at her made his body tighten with desire, and for a moment he debated on waking her. He would apologize, then make love to her until neither of them could move.

He ran a callused finger over the elegant curve of her cheek and smiled when she made a sleepy sound and shifted away from the feathery touch. No, he'd let her sleep, he decided reluctantly. He brushed her forehead with a kiss and settled beneath the covers. He would set things right between them in the morning.

But the next day began for Conn before daylight when he was awakened by the urgent clanging of the yard bell and shouts of "Fire! Fire! Come quick!"

The fire turned out to be in Zena's cabin. No one was hurt, but Conn and every man on the place had to work like madmen to keep the blaze from spreading to the other cabins. By the time they extinguished it, the sun was well up. Not taking time for breakfast, Conn grabbed some biscuits and sausage from the kitchen and ate them on the way to the fields.

At quitting time he returned home to learn that Elizabeth had gone to midwife a neighbor woman about twenty miles away. She didn't return for two days, and then she was so exhausted she slept the clock around. Before she awoke, Conn and a crew of men left for a remote section of the plantation to cut trees and split rails and stack them to cure for fencing.

Finally, midafternoon on the fourth day after his return, Conn rode into the yard behind the house. He was tired and hungry, and he needed a bath. He was also anxious to put things right with Elizabeth, but those weren't the reasons he'd returned home instead of going to check on the workers in the fields. He wouldn't lie to himself. He was there because he couldn't stay away a minute longer. The admission brought a wry smile to his mouth as he dismounted and handed his horse to the stable boy. Turning up the collar of his coat against the blustery March wind, he headed for the house, anticipation building in his chest.

Elizabeth stood bent over the loom set up in the wide back hall, busily instructing Lottie on the finer points of weaving, and didn't hear him enter the house. He leaned back against the door and watched her, his expression softening.

He hadn't expected this attraction, this deep yearning to see her. Touch her. Be near her all the time. He had expected their long friendship to make for a comfortable marriage.

The union *had* brought him contentment and happiness, there was no denying that. But comfort? Hell, since he married

Elizabeth he'd been anything but comfortable. He was thirty-seven years old, but she made him feel about eighteen, eager and hot and lusty and able to take on the world. He felt foolish admitting it, but he was becoming obsessed with his wife. A woman he'd known all of his life, for heaven's sake!

Foolish or not, it excited him to know that beneath that serene exterior there was a fiery passion that could burn a man right to his soul—and that it was all for him.

Still, it wasn't enough. Making love with Elizabeth was the most fantastic experience he'd ever known. The satisfaction he'd found in her arms exceeded every dream he'd ever had. Yet he sensed that there was a part of herself that she was holding back. Despite all the years that bound them in friendship, and despite the new physical intimacy between them, there were times when she retreated from him behind those gentle smiles. And the longer they were married, the more it bothered him. Dammit, he wanted it all. Everything she had to give.

At Elizabeth's instructions, Lottie stopped weaving to change color thread, and into the silence he said, "Hello. Remember me?"

Elizabeth gasped and spun around, a shuttle in her hand. "Conn!" She closed her eyes and sagged against the sturdy loom. "You scared me half to death."

"Sorry." He looked around. "Where is everyone?"

"Your father went to town to check on a patient and Rachel went with him, and Taw has taken Ian and Faith fishing."

Conn crossed the hall and stopped in front of Elizabeth. Absently, her gaze fixed on his face, she handed the shuttle to Lottie, who was watching the two of them with interest. "Continue as you were, please, Lottie."

"Yes'm," she replied with a sly smile, and slipped the shuttle through the warp.

In silence Conn's gaze roamed Elizabeth's face. His big hand curved around the side of her neck, his thumb sliding beneath her chin, tipping it up.

"Conn," Elizabeth cautioned in a whisper, cutting her eyes toward Lottie, but he ignored her. Tunneled into the fall of golden curls at her nape, his fingers tightened as he lowered his mouth to hers.

The kiss was soft and hot and hungry, his lips rocking over hers with a slow, sweet passion. Beneath his hand Conn felt the quiver that ran through Elizabeth, felt the throbbing beat of her pulse that so exactly matched his own. Somewhere in the background the loom's batten thumped in rhythmic counterpoint.

When the kiss ended their lips clung, parting slowly. He raised his head, his vivid blue eyes intent and filled with male satisfaction as he studied her dazed expression. He rubbed his thumb back and forth across her chin and smiled when her lips trembled. "I've missed you," he whispered.

"I've missed you, too," Elizabeth managed in a breathless little voice.

He bent to kiss her again but stopped and drew back, a rueful smile kicking up one corner of his mouth as he glanced down at his soiled and sweat-stained shirt. "Much as I hate to, I'd better stop and get cleaned up. I'm as filthy as a pig and probably smell worse." He touched her cheek with his forefinger and winked. "I'll be right back."

He released her and strode down the hall, calling over his shoulder, "Lottie, go find Isaac and tell him I need a bath."

Lottie scurried away, and Elizabeth leaned back against the loom, her heart beating crazily. With trembling fingers, she touched her lips. The last time they had spoken he'd been angry, but there had been nothing angry about that kiss.

Over the past few days her own pain had faded to a dull ache, but even that was pushed aside as hope burgeoned inside her, thrusting up within her breast with the fragile insistence of a flower unfolding.

Surely, *surely*, he couldn't kiss her that way unless he was beginning to love her. Just a little.

A short time later Conn returned, bringing with him the fresh scents of castile soap and starch. Elizabeth sat in the front parlor sewing a shirt for Taw, and when she looked up to greet him, her throat went dry. Wearing gray wool trousers but no coat, he strolled in still buttoning the cuffs of the full-sleeved white shirt. As yet he had neglected to fasten the front, and the garment gaped open to his waist. His hair was wet, the raven strands hanging in soft curls across his forehead. Tiny beads of moisture still clung to the mat of·hair that covered his chest and arrowed downward to swirl around his navel and disappear beneath the waistband of his trousers. He looked big and bold and impossibly virile.

With an effort, Elizabeth dragged her gaze away from his body and found that he was watching her intently. She squirmed and fluttered a hand toward the dining room. "You, uh, didn't come home for lunch. Are you hungry?"

"Yes. I'm starving." His unwavering gaze bored into her.

"Would you like some chicken? We had some left over."

"No."

"Then why don't I have Jemma fry you some ham?" She stood and started for the door. "It won't take but a few minutes."

"No. Not ham."

"Oh." Elizabeth stopped and blinked at his flat refusal, then brightened. "I know, how about soup? There's always a pot of that simmering out in the kitchen."

"No."

"Then what do you want?" she asked with faint exasperation.

Conn moved toward her with that slow, sexy, loose-limbed saunter, and Elizabeth's heart began to thump as she watched his eyes grow heavy-lidded and hot. He stopped in front of her and smiled. "I want you."

Elizabeth felt as though she were melting. She could only gaze at him weakly, her eyes soft with emotion. The effect on him was startling and instantaneous, and her heart gave a little skip as she watched his face grow taut, his pupils expand.

"Conn!" she gasped in surprise when he scooped her up in his arms and strode from the room. "Conn, the servants!"

"To hell with them," he growled, sweeping past a goggling Isaac and taking the stairs two at a time. "We're going to bed."

"Oh, Conn." His name sighed from her lips with aching tenderness, and she laid her cheek against his shoulder.

Much later they lay in the jumbled bed, luxuriating in the quiet aftermath. Even with their passion spent they were loath to move, and Conn snuggled his face into the warm curve of her neck, keeping her beneath him, their intimate embrace unbroken.

Relishing the heavy contentment of her body, Elizabeth gazed dreamily at the ceiling and stroked his damp back. Outside, the March afternoon had turned gray, and fat drops of rain began to splatter the window panes. The blustering wind moaned around the eaves, and the bare branches of a sheltering oak scraped against the shingles with a screech. In the shadowy room Elizabeth felt warm and secure, wrapped in Conn's arms.

She loved the feel of his skin, so warm against hers, the heavy weight of him crushing her into the mattress. During those long, lonely years when all she'd had were her dreams, this was how she had imagined it would be between them— a storm of passion, then this lovely, quiet closeness, a blending of souls. In that moment she almost felt loved.

Conn nuzzled her neck, inhaling the sweet fragrance of her skin, her hair. "Beth?" he murmured as he mouthed her earlobe.

"Hmmmm?"

"About the other day . . . the things I said . . . I was wrong. I'm sorry."

Her hands stopped their absent rotation, then started up

again. "That's all right. You had a right to be upset."

"No. No, I didn't. I should have listened to you instead of flying off the handle. Everyone told me what happened. You did exactly the right thing, and I'm proud of you. My only excuse is that I was tired and out of sorts. Forgive me?"

"Of course." Her voice held a smile, and her arms tightened around his back. Still, she could not help but wonder if the exquisite loving they had just shared had simply been an apology. As quickly as the thought came, she pushed it away. Even if it were true, it wouldn't matter, she admitted to herself with a touch of sadness; she would always forgive Conn any-thing—everything—so deep and abiding was her love for him.

Chapter 19

 That first spring and summer at Riverbend they truly put down roots, sinking them deep into the rich new land, making it home. Their lives settled into a comfortable pattern, defined by the mundane necessities of daily living and the demands of the changing seasons.

As Conn toiled in the fields and tended the stock, Elizabeth saw to the household: training servants, teaching Jemma and the kitchen helpers her mother's recipes, directing the spinning and weaving and sewing as well as the cleaning and laundry. The huge vegetable garden and orchards next to the house required constant attention, and the produce that wasn't eaten immediately had to be preserved. In addition, Elizabeth taught the children their school lessons, did her best to instill in them morals and manners, gave them religious instructions, and helped Dr. Cavanaugh care for the sick.

There were times of pleasure and quiet contentment as well that Elizabeth treasured: evenings with the family on the veranda after dinner; lying in Conn's arms in the sweet warm darkness, flush with the afterglow of lovemaking, listening to him talk of his plans; poignant moments of discovery with the children, like the time a butterfly lit on Ian's nose or the time Faith found a baby bird that had fallen out of the nest. There were also occasional visits to and from neighbors and trips into San Felipe or Washington.

Taw, at last, had his rocking chair on the porch. He spent

many hours there with the two younger children, spinning tales that kept them enthralled and whittling toys and figures. The friendship between him and Dr. Cavanaugh deepened, and the two spent hours playing cutthroat games of checkers.

That spring and summer Johnny Grimes became a frequent visitor. He courted Rachel with a maturity and patience that seemed odd in one so young, but his serious nature was the perfect counterbalance for her burgeoning effervescence and impulsiveness. Rachel bloomed in response to his attention like a rosebud opening to the warmth of the sun.

There was a sense of purpose, of continuity, to the placid flow of rural life that Elizabeth loved. Being close to the land, witnessing the constant renewal of nature, living off its bounty, was immensely satisfying.

Now and then rumors and tales of Santa Anna's oppressive regime reached them, rippling the peaceful tenor of their lives like a stone dropped into a tranquil pond. Grievances mounted, and the possibility of conflict seemed ever more likely. It hovered over the peaceful countryside like a specter.

In April they heard the disquieting news that Santa Anna had turned his force on Zacatecas, a Mexican state that, like Texas, supported the constitution. The people had objected when Santa Anna moved to replace the state militia with his own troops, and he responded by brutally crushing the Zacatecan forces. Worse, disdaining to take prisoners, he permitted his troops to rape and plunder the state capital.

On the heels of that atrocity, when a political squabble between state officials in Coahuila occurred, Santa Anna sent his brother-in-law and chief military officer, General Martin Perfecto de Cos, to break up the local government and render it obedient to the president.

Since Texas was officially part of the state of Coahuila, the move stripped the settlers of what little political voice they had and put them at the direct mercy of Santa Anna. It also placed General Cos and his large army poised right across the

Rio Grande from Anglo Texas. All during May and most of
June, as Conn and the other planters and farmers tended their
crops, a state of uneasy watchfulness reigned.

At the end of the third week in June, Conn had some
business to attend to in San Felipe, and Elizabeth went along
with him. When they rode into town they found a crowd of
men gathered before the alcalde's office, to the rear of the
Whiteside Hotel, a story-and-a-half log structure with a huge
stick-and-mud chimney at each end.

Conn dismounted and hitched their horses to the rail before
the hotel. As he lifted Elizabeth from the saddle someone hailed
him, and they turned to see Liam disengage from the crowd
of men and hurry toward them.

"Conn! Elizabeth! Good to see you." The two men shook
hands, and when they were done Liam tipped his hat to Elizabeth. "Afternoon, Elizabeth. Hes is shore gonna be sorry she
missed seein' you."

"You mean she's not here?" Elizabeth asked, disappointed.

"Naw, I just came in 'cause today was supposed to be trial
day for them two merchants, and I wanted to find out what
was gonna happen, now that we ain't got nobody to hold
court."

"Is that what that's all about?" Conn asked, nodding toward
the crowd. The street was jammed with men, and more were
coming into town in a steady trickle.

"Yep. They've been gatherin' since morning. Tempers are
runnin' high, and there's been a lot of talk about what should
be done to help those two in jail." Liam tipped his head toward
the group. "Why don't you mosey on down and listen?"

"Maybe later. First I have to see my lawyer about some
business."

Conn left Elizabeth at Dinsmore's store while he went to
consult with Mr. Hosea League over a letter he wanted drafted
to his agent in Charleston.

They were running low on flour on Riverbend, and Elizabeth

had hoped to purchase some, but according to Mr. Dinsmore there was none to be had in the whole state. "What little comes in by clipper ship to Galveston gets snapped up before it leaves the docks," he told her. "This far inland, we hardly ever see the stuff."

Elizabeth thanked him, and after purchasing new corset stays, a jug of castor oil, and a sack of horehound candy for the children, she browsed through the store's meager stock while she waited for Conn.

When he returned for her and they walked back to the alcalde's office, the crowd was even larger. A man on the porch, whom Conn recognized as a young firebrand lawyer by the name of William Barret Travis—"Buck" to his friends—was haranguing the assemblage.

"Well, what are we going to do about it?" he shouted. "Just let those men rot? I tell you it's an outrage. Are we going to stand for this kind of tyranny?"

The collective roar of "No!" went up, and the grumbling and shouts grew louder.

Spotting Liam's battered leather hat, Conn looped his arm around Elizabeth's waist and began to elbow his way through the press of men. They had barely reached their friend when a rider came galloping down the center of the dirt street, sending people scattering.

"Hey, look at those saddlebags!" someone shouted. "It's a Mexican courier! I bet he's heading for the garrison!"

"Grab him! Grab him! Let's have a look at those messages!"

The cry spread through the crowd like wildfire, and almost as one the men surged toward the rider. Pushing and shoving, they buffeted Elizabeth in their haste. She cried out and stumbled, and would have fallen if Conn hadn't managed to hook his arm around her waist and haul her against his side.

The soldier's horse pulled up and reared as the crowd surrounded him. Several pairs of hands pulled the man from the saddle, while others tore the courier bags from the horse's back.

The bags somehow ended up in Buck Travis's hands, and shouts of "Whadda they say, Buck?" and "Read 'um!" went up all around as he pulled the three sealed packets from the bags and ripped them open. Standing among the shouting men, Travis quickly read the dispatches, his face growing first grave, then wild with rage. When finished, he raised his hands and called for silence. As the voices faded he clenched his jaws and stared at the messages as though they were viperous snakes about to strike.

"Men, there are three dispatches here. One is for the alcalde from General Cos," he shouted. "It says that all civil government in the state of Coahuila has been suspended and Cos is in complete charge."

That set off a chorus of protests, but Travis held up his hands for silence. "Another one is from Cos to the commander at Anahuac, informing him that a contingent of troops is on the way to bolster his garrison."

More protests, louder and more prolonged, and again Travis signaled for quiet. When it returned he went on, his voice turning harsher.

"And the third is from another Mexican general to the Anahuac commander." Travis paused dramatically, his furious stare sweeping the crowd. "It says that when Santa Anna has finished grinding the Zacatecan people under his heel, he will personally lead his troops on a punitive sweep across Texas to discipline the upstart Anglos!"

The outraged roar that erupted was deafening. The men shouted and cursed and shook their fists, and for a few moments pandemonium ruled.

Then Travis jumped up onto an overturned barrel and shouted, "I say we march on the Anahuac garrison and throw Captain Tenorio and his troops out before Cos's men get here!"

Shouts of approval and encouragement followed instantly all around, and Travis whipped off his hat and brandished it in the air. "C'mon, men! Who'll go with me to Anahuac?"

Shaking with fright, Elizabeth clung to Conn as the bold young man leaped from the barrel and strode away down the dusty street leading a throng of shouting, gesturing men. She looked up at Conn and saw that his face was grave as he watched the procession.

"Whaddaya think, Conn? You gonna join up with Travis?" Liam asked.

Appalled, Elizabeth's gaze snapped to their friend. Liam was almost crackling with excitement, and she knew that he was only waiting for Conn to say the word and he would be marching off to Anahuac, without a thought for Hester and the children.

Fearfully she switched her attention back to her husband. His gaze remained fixed on the fired-up group of men.

"What I think," he said in a low, measured voice, "is this is a harebrained act of folly, and I don't want any part in it."

Weak with relief, Elizabeth sagged against him and closed her eyes.

"Conn!" Liam looked scandalized. "You don't think we should fight for our rights?"

"Of course I do. But if we're going to take military action against Mexico, first we need to form some sort of government to take charge. And we need a military commander with a cool head who thinks things through and has some kind of strategy. Not go off half-cocked, stirring up more trouble. Everybody's egging Travis on now because they're angry, but give them a week and they'll be calling him a fool."

Liam disagreed, but within two weeks Conn was proved right.

When word of the dispatches spread, public sentiment swung solidly behind the war faction. After a few hurried public meetings, at which approval was given to Travis's plan, he and a small band of twenty-five volunteers marched off to Anahuac. They arrived there by the end of the month, deployed their lone cannon in front of the garrison, and fired one shot.

The next morning General Tenorio and his forty-four men surrendered and promised to leave Texas. Buck Travis returned triumphant to San Felipe, only to discover that most of the people of Texas were now denouncing him for a rash, irresponsible idiot. Prominent men wrote letters of apology, and a peace commission was formed to travel to Saltillo in the hope of mollifying General Cos.

For weeks afterward the incident, and what would come of it, was all anyone talked about. Would Cos accept the apologies? Would the peace commission be able to reason with him? If not, what action would he take?

The men found the subject endlessly fascinating, but not so Elizabeth. She could not bear to think of anything disrupting the life they had. Though not completely happy, she was content—more content than she had been in years.

The children were happy and thriving. Faith was coming out of her shell, and she and Rachel were on much better terms. Ian had stopped clinging to Elizabeth's skirts and showed every sign of developing into a normal, rough-and-tumble little scamp. Even Elizabeth and Rachel were getting along.

Joseph and Taw were the father she had lost and the grandfather she'd never known. This was her family. Riverbend was home. Here she belonged. Even if Conn never grew to love her as she wished, she would still find joy in that.

But somehow, the threat of war hanging over them made Elizabeth more anxious than ever to gain Conn's love. She continually cautioned herself not to expect too much from Conn. He seemed perfectly satisfied with their relationship just as it was, and she had to face the strong possibility that there would never be more. But hope, once it flamed, could not easily be extinguished.

Conn might not love her, but Elizabeth knew that he desired her. Incredibly, that desire seemed to be growing day by day. Over and over she told herself that a need that strong could eventually lead to love. As long as there was passion between them, there was hope.

All through the torpid, tension-riddled days of summer Elizabeth clung to that hope. But as August passed and the first anniversary of their wedding came and went with no declaration from Conn, it became harder and harder to do.

Foolishly, Elizabeth realized later, she had looked forward to that day with the expectancy of a child awaiting Christmas, certain in her heart that the occasion would prompt the words she so longed to hear.

She had worked for weeks in secret, making Conn a new gray satin waistcoat and embroidering it in silver and blue. When their anniversary arrived the cooks worked all day preparing quail and partridge in currant jelly, smoked trout, roasted corn, black-eyed peas, turnip greens, and fresh-baked cornbread. And to top it all off, under her supervision they'd baked a beautiful pyramid cake and elaborately decorated it with swags of icing and candied violets and mint leaves.

She had dressed in her best gown and waited, her heart aflutter with excitement and anticipation, but when Conn at last came in from the fields and saw the feast, his expression held only bewilderment. When prompted by the good wishes of the rest of the family, he'd tried to pretend otherwise, but she knew he had forgotten.

It was understandable, she told herself. The cotton picking had begun, and he'd been working from daylight until dark. In addition, the political situation was constantly on his mind, as it was on everyone's. Elizabeth hid her disappointment behind a smile and pretended it didn't matter. But she put the waistcoat away to give to Conn at Christmas, and that night when she went into his arms there was an ache in her heart.

Early in September Abel Harper, the new overseer Conn had hired through an agent in the States, arrived by riverboat.

He was a young man without much experience, and Conn wasn't overly impressed with him, but he needed someone to do the job and couldn't afford to be choosy.

Barely a week after Harper began work, they had a surprise visitor.

Company was always welcome at Riverbend. Hospitality was extended freely and graciously to all who came, and they were particularly honored to have as a guest such an illustrious man. Elizabeth genuinely like him as well, and she extended every courtesy. Deep down, however, she was troubled by the visit. For whenever the men talked of war, the man whose name was mentioned most often, the one most looked to for leadership, was Sam Houston.

The first half hour or so of Sam's visit was purely social. They talked genially of the weather, and Sam inquired about the operation of the plantation. He even professed a desire to have a look at the gin before he left. Still, Elizabeth waited tensely for him to get to the point of his visit. Not for an instant did she believe he'd ridden all that way to talk about the cotton crop and the price it was bringing.

When eventually the discussion turned to politics, she was torn between relief and dread.

"I suppose you've heard the latest news from San Felipe," Sam said casually.

"No. We've been too busy getting the cotton picked to go to town or do any visiting. I'm also ginning my neighbors' crops."

It was getting on to sunset, but even then the distant rumble and screech of the cotton gin could be heard from where they sat on the veranda. At that moment there were five wagons full of cotton belonging to various neighbors lined up awaiting their turn down by the gin, and more came in every day. At that rate they would be operating into November again this year.

"Then you haven't heard that Stephen Austin is back in San Felipe?"

They all sat forward on their chairs at the announcement. Elizabeth had been braced for something terrible, and her heart gave a little flip at the unexpected good news. "Oh, that's wonderful!"

"Danged if it ain't!" Taw crowed, slapping his knee.

"My, yes. That's the best news we've heard in over a year," Joseph agreed.

Conn's surprised look faded, his expression growing skeptical. "You mean after more than a year and a half in prison they just turned him loose? Why?"

"Purely a quirk of Mexican politics, my friend," Sam replied with a chuckle. "Seems he was released under a general amnesty in July and given a passport to take a ship to New Orleans. He crossed the Sabine the first of the month and rode back into San Felipe a week or so ago."

Sam took another sip of mint tea, his face sobering. "But I'm afraid he's much changed by his ordeal. For one thing, his health is completely broken. He's terribly frail and looks old far beyond his forty-two years. But the biggest change is he has become a bitter, disillusioned man.

"All these years, ever since he brought in the first settlers in twenty-two, Stephen Austin has been completely loyal to the Mexican government. Even from his jail cell, in the beginning he wrote letters urging everyone to stay calm and keep the peace. But during his long incarceration Stephen had ample opportunity to witness firsthand Santa Anna's underhanded and willful undermining of the constitution, and his trust in the man is completely destroyed. Stephen is now publicly denouncing Santa Anna as a base, unprincipled monster. A call has gone out for another convention to be held next month. I expect he'll urge everyone to prepare to fight. He seems to think that soon we'll have no choice."

Elizabeth's heart sank. What had begun as such joyous news was turning into a disaster. She twisted her hands together and looked at Conn. If war broke out, he would be part of it.

"And what do you think?" Conn asked.

"Well, naturally, I hope it doesn't come to that, but frankly, things don't look good. General Cos is in no mood to forgive Travis's little foray down in Anahuac. He is insisting that all the participants be arrested and turned over to him." Sam snorted. "Not even William Travis's worse critics are willing to do that. It's one thing to call him and his cohorts fools, and quite another to turn fellow Texans over to a Mexican firing squad.

"The peace commission brought back word from Cos that we are expected to submit, unconditionally, to any changes in the law made by the supreme government—meaning Santa Anna. No consultation or colonist assemblies will be permitted or recognized. To insure compliance, Cos intends to bring in garrisons and disarm all Anglos."

"What! Why, he cain't do that," Taw squawked. "No Texan's gonna give up his freedoms. An' he shore won't give up his gun. How would we defend ourselves against the Indians? Humph! I'd like t' see some tin soldier try t' take my Hawkin."

"Precisely," Sam agreed. "Nevertheless, General Cos plans to try, and he's going to make San Antonio his headquarters. According to the good general, we can either submit or fight. The matter is of supreme indifference to him." Sam paused to sip his tea and let that soak in. Then, quietly, he added, "Cos also made the statement that it was 'time to break up the Anglo settlements in Texas.'"

In silence, the four men exchanged a long, somber look.

"Which brings me to the reason for this visit," Sam continued after a moment. "As I said, I hope we can settle our difficulties peaceably, but if war becomes unavoidable, at the first sound of the trumpet I intend to offer my services to lead the volunteers, and I've come to ask you, Conn, if you would serve as my scout. I've heard about your exploits as a trapper and Indian fighter. Believe me, a man of your experience would be invaluable to the Texas army."

"Scout, huh? You want me to check out troop movements and keep you informed, is that it?"

"That, and report on numbers, how well they're provisioned and armed, how much artillery power they have. As you've probably surmised, we're going to be severely outnumbered. If we're to be victorious, we'll need every advantage we can get." He waited a moment, watching Conn's face as he mulled over the request before asking, "So what do you say? Will you do it?"

No! Elizabeth wanted to shout. Soldiering was bad enough, but scouting was even more dangerous. Conn would be on his own, at close quarters with the enemy. She held her breath and waited for his reply. Her hands curled into fists, the nails cutting tiny half-moons in her palms.

Conn nodded, and she felt sick. "All right. You've got yourself a scout."

"Good man. I knew I could count on you." Sam's expression turned commiserating when he noticed Elizabeth's pallor. Reaching across the small space between their chairs, he patted her hand. "Now, then, Mrs. Cavanaugh, don't look so worried. We're not at war yet. More than likely it won't come to that."

Sam stayed for two more days. He rode with Conn around the plantation and visited with the farmers who brought their cotton in to be ginned. Elizabeth knew that most of the talk was about the convention that was to be held the following month and speculation over the outcome.

In the evenings during dinner Sam entertained them all with fascinating tales about his years among the Cherokee Indians and his political career in Tennessee. Not once did he mention his marriage or refer to his ex-wife in any way, and neither did they.

Sam was courtly and a bit flamboyant, but he possessed profound notions of patriotism and honor that exactly matched Conn's, and the friendship and trust that had begun at their first meeting all those months ago deepened during his stay.

There were several people with whom Sam wanted to confer before the convention, and on the third day he took his leave. They were all waiting on the veranda for the stable boy to bring his horse around when a rider came pounding up the drive, waving his hat and shouting.

"War! We're at war! Call to arms!"

Elizabeth felt as though all the blood had suddenly drained from her body. She stood rooted to the spot, her crossed hands pressed over her clubbing heart as the men hurried down the veranda steps.

"What's happened? Who sent out the call?" Sam demanded, catching hold of the lathered horse's bridle. "Speak up, man!"

"Mr. Houston! I didn't know you were here. Stephen F. Austin himself sent out the call to arms, sir. We got word from some Mexican farmers sympathetic to our cause that General Cos has crossed the Rio Grande with a large army and is heading for San Antonio."

"Do you have a paper signed by Austin?"

"Yessir, right here." The man handed an oiled-skin packet to Sam, and he withdrew a single piece of paper.

"Hmmm. It's from Stephen all right. He says, 'Citizens of Texas. War is our only recourse. No halfway measures, but war in full. We must defend our rights, ourselves, and our country by force of arms.' "

The second the courier whirled his horse and took off back down the drive, the men snapped into action. Everyone in and around the house was sent scurrying as preparations got under way. Powder and shot were readied, dried meat and hardtack were wrapped in oilcloth and packed in saddlebags, guns were oiled and checked, bedrolls were fashioned, knifes sharpened.

"As soon as you're ready I want you to ride hard for the southwest border country." Sam swung into the saddle, then looked down at Conn. "If you push, you should be able to intercept Cos's troops before he reaches Goliad. I need facts and figures, Conn, and I need them fast."

"I'll do my best, Sam."

The general nodded and started to leave, then stopped. "Oh, and Conn . . . Be careful. The Comanches have been raiding all along the frontier down that way. When they get wind of the troubles you can bet they'll take advantage of the situation."

Conn nodded. "I'll keep my eyes open, don't worry."

Within the hour Conn and his father were provisioned and ready to leave.

During the frantic preparations there had been little time to talk, and Conn had been distracted and remote, his mind already on the task that lay ahead of him. Now it was too late. Elizabeth stood on the veranda and watched him kiss the children good-bye, her chest aching with emotion and all the things that needed to be said.

Then it was her turn. He stood before her, so big and rugged-looking and so very dear, she felt as though her heart would break. "Don't fret, little one," he murmured, taking her into his arms. "I'll be back before you even know I'm gone."

"Oh, Conn," she quavered, and then her aching throat seemed to close up, making speech impossible. She gazed up at him, her chin wobbling, the tears she could no longer control spilling over. "Be careful," she finally choked out. "And come back to us."

"I will. You can count on it."

He kissed her long and hard, and Elizabeth clung to him, her whole body trembling. The embrace ended all too soon, and she was left standing alone and bereft as he loped down the stairs and swung into the saddle.

"Look after them, Taw. And keep an eye on Harper."

"I'll do er," the old man replied.

Conn nodded, and with a last look at Elizabeth and a wave he rode away.

Long after he had disappeared from sight she stood on the veranda staring down the drive, her face streaming with tears, acutely aware that she might never see him again . . . and that he had left without saying one word of love.

Chapter 20

Rolling the stem of grass between his lips, Conn squinted against the glare of the sun and studied the long column of Mexican soldiers. Except for his eyes, he didn't move.

He lay flat, a little short of the crest where he could just see over the ridge. His buckskins, seasoned by rain and sun and sweat, smelled stale, but their neutral color blended into the parched earth. Down a draw to his rear, he'd left his horse hidden among a dark clump of cedars. Pike lay beneath a saltbush a dozen or so yards off to his right.

The slightly rolling terrain of the mesquite and chaparral land south of Goliad had the dry, faded look that spoke of a hard summer just past. Even now the day was still and hot for October. Sweat trickled down Conn's lean cheeks and down his body under the buckskins. The hair at his nape and across his forehead stuck to his skin in wet ringlets. Five more caissons went rolling by, boiling up dust. Conn added them to his mental tally.

Another half hour passed before he spotted the end of the column. Scooting backward on his belly, he eased down the slope. At the bottom he hunkered low and ran along the shallow draw, head up, his Hawkin in his hand. Pike moved out ahead of him at a slinking trot. Ears pricked, the dog darted a few yards, stopped, listened, and darted again. Conn did the same.

According to his calculations, General Cos had twelve to

fourteen hundred men and six cannon—four nine-pounders and two five-inch Howitzers. He'd reach San Antonio within the week if the weather held, Conn thought, when up ahead Pike suddenly stiffened.

Jesus! Conn dropped to the ground and lay perfectly still. The only cover was the sparse grass and a few scattered rocks. Ahead, the dog flattened out beneath a creosote bush.

A moment later Conn heard the movement off to his right. There were seven of them. Comanches—he was almost certain of it. They were riding slow in a loose bunch, parallel to the column of Mexican soldiers. And he was in the middle.

Damn. Two years away from the mountains had made him careless. He'd known they were in the area. Only that morning he'd come across a burned-out homestead. The Mexican troops were raising a cloud of dust that could be spotted for miles. He should have figured the Indians would come for a look-see.

Seven. If they spotted him, he wouldn't have a chance. He couldn't risk a shot with the Mexicans so near. He might take out one with his knife—two, at most—before they got him.

Conn didn't so much as blink. With no shelter, only absolute immobility and the concealing neutral color of his clothing kept him from being seen.

They didn't talk. He heard the dry rustle of the coarse grass, the occasional clack of a hoof on stone.

They rode past. Twenty yards ahead of where he lay they crossed the draw, and Conn caught his breath. Not more than ten yards beyond them, around a slight bend, was his horse. If the animal moved or made a sound, they'd find him. Then they'd come looking for him. A man alone, Anglo or Mexican, was too tempting a target for the Comanches to pass up.

A sharp stone dug into his thigh, and pea gravel gouged his cheek. An ant stung him on the wrist. Conn hugged the ground, not moving. From the cover of the ridge, the Indians watched the column for several minutes before they rode back down, recrossed the draw, and took up their stalking pursuit again.

Within minutes they were out of sight. Conn didn't move for almost a half hour. Then he rose cautiously, looked around, and sprinted for his horse.

That night he made a cold camp. After the close call he wasn't taking any chances. At first light he'd head for Cibolo Creek and his rendezvous with Sam. He bit off a chunk of venison jerky and chewed absently. After that, unless Sam had other plans for him, he'd join the Texans marching on San Antonio. Given what he'd learned, they were going to need every man they could get to beat General Cos.

What he'd like to do was go home, he admitted ruefully. To Riverbend. To Elizabeth.

God, he missed her. He'd been gone a little under a month, but it felt like years. He was surprised and disturbed by the pull that one small woman had on him.

During their marriage, he'd spent months at a time separated from Millie. Actually they'd been apart more than they'd been together. Yet he'd never, not even in the beginning, felt this gut-wrenching longing and loneliness. And he had loved Millie. This desperate yearning for Elizabeth just didn't seem right, somehow.

He'd married her for practical reasons. But he hadn't reckoned on the passion that flared so hotly between them, the need. He hadn't reckoned on Elizabeth.

Elizabeth. A reluctant smile softened Conn's hard face, and he sighed. With her gentle graces and valiant spirit she had wound herself around his heart. He wondered what she was doing. If she was all right.

Of course she was, he told himself. Taw was there with her.

Conn grinned, remembering the old man's ire and disappointment at being left behind. He'd been all fired up to join the volunteers gathering at Gonzales.

Taw had slowed down a lot in the last year or so. His rheumatism had been bothering him lately, and he was seventy-five if he was a day. Maybe older. Conn had been worried about how he could tactfully talk him out of joining up when his father had solved the problem by announcing his intention to join the militia and offer his services as a doctor. Taw had grumbled and sulked when Conn had ask him to stay at Riverbend and look after Elizabeth and the children, but as much as the old war-horse wanted to be in on the excitement, he hadn't been willing to leave Elizabeth unprotected.

Conn grimaced, realizing that his thoughts had returned once more to his wife. She was becoming an obsession. Finishing his jerky, he rolled in his blanket and ground sheet. It was time to stop thinking about her and get some sleep. He had a lot of miles to cover the next day.

As always, he slept with his pistol in his hand. His saddle, with the Hawkin propped against it, lay within reach, and his horse was picketed only a few feet away.

Nearby, Pike crept under a patch of sage brush on his belly and lowered his dark muzzle to his paws, his yellow gaze fixed on Conn.

Conn closed his eyes and willed sleep to come, but in his mind he saw a procession of alluring images—Elizabeth cuddling Ian close, brushing Faith's hair, patiently teaching Rachel to sew . . . watching him as he rode away, her mouth trembling and her lovely gray eyes flooded with tears.

Dodging bands of hostile Indians and Mexican patrols, it took Conn ten days to reach Cibolo Creek, and when he arrived there was no sign of Sam Houston. Conn made camp and settled down to wait.

Midmorning of the next day Sam arrived riding a dainty yellow Spanish stallion, so small the big man's long legs nearly touched the ground. Conn grinned at the sight he made, but Houston did not appear in the least discomfited.

"Sorry about the delay. My horse went lame on me, and I had to walk nearly forty miles before I found a farmhouse where I could pick up a new mount." He swung out of the saddle, slapped the delicate horse on the rump, and grimaced wryly. "This was the best I could do." Sam led the little horse over where Conn's big bay was grazing. "So, tell me. What did you learn?" he asked as he drove a picket stake into the ground.

Conn quickly gave him a rundown of the number of troops and supplies, the amount of heavy artillery, the size and type, and the discipline and physical condition of the soldiers. "I figure Cos made San Antonio a week ago, if he didn't delay too long at Goliad. He left a small detachment there to guard a stash of powder and shot and keep his supply line open."

Over a noon repast of cold jerky and hardtack the two men discussed the situation and possible strategy. Conn also reported on the unusually large number of Indians he'd seen, how far south along the frontier the Comanches were roaming, and the many homesteads that had been raided and plundered. "The owners must have gotten word that Cos was on the march because they had already lit out. Except for one family." Conn paused a beat, looked at Sam, and added quietly, "I buried them."

Sam said nothing.

Midafternoon, after they'd finished eating and Sam and his mount had rested, they saddled up and moved out, following the creek for half a mile or so to the ford.

Pike started growling a hundred yards before they reached the crossing. Sam and Conn drew out their long guns and approached with caution, but at the ford they met up with a group of about five hundred Texas volunteers who had just crossed and were setting up camp.

There were several familiar faces in the crowd—Liam and his two oldest sons, Johnny and Daniel, and other neighbors from the Brazos River area, lawyers, doctors, blacksmiths, and shopkeepers from Washington and San Felipe. They all waved and called to Conn, but it was Sam Houston who created a stir. He was recognized at once, and the men came rushing to greet him, cheering and shouting.

"It's Sam Houston!"

"Sam! Sam! You come to help us whip ole Cos?"

"Hey, Sam! Where'd you get that horse?"

"Yeah! You ortta git off and carry him awhile."

Sam smiled good-naturedly as he and Conn reined in their mounts. "Where're you men coming from?"

"Gonzales!" several shouted.

One buckskin-clad militiaman stepped forward, grinning. "Couple of weeks ago Colonel Ugartechea, over at San Antonio, sent Captain Castañeda and a detachment of two hundred or so dragoons to take away our cannon. There was only 'bout a hundred and sixty of us then. The rest of these fellas joined us later. Well, sir, we put that cannon on an oxcart and marched out to meet them Mex soldiers. They took one look at our flag and stopped cold."

The man gestured to the small brass cannon hitched to two longhorn steers, and both Conn and Sam threw back their heads and laughed. The cannon was festooned with a large white flag on which was painted in black a cannon and the words *COME AND TAKE IT*.

The artillery piece itself was so small, it was practically worthless, but Conn fully understood the men's stubborn refusal to surrender the piece.

"We told ole Castañeda there was only one way he'd get our gun, and that was one shot at a time. When he just kept insisting that we turn it over, we opened fire. Well, sir, those dragoons went hightailing it out of there like the devil hisself was after 'um. Now we're on our way to San Antonio to run General Cos back across the Rio Grande where he belongs."

The laughter that followed had barely died down when the group was holloed from down the trail, and a contingent of a half dozen or so men came riding up.

They rode to within a few feet of the group of men and stopped. The one in the lead, a dark-haired man of medium height, stood up in his stirrups, brandished his long rifle high over head, and shouted, "Can you fellas use a few more good fighting men?"

The question, as intended, set off a boisterous round of shouts and whistles. A slow grin climbed Conn's face. As the noise died down, he pushed back his wide-brimmed hat, leaned forward, and propped his forearm on the saddlehorn. "Well, would you lookie here. If it isn't Jim Bowie. Man, I thought you were alligator bait long ago."

"Well, I'll be—Conn Cavanaugh! I sure as hell didn't expect to see you here. What're you doing in Texas?"

"I've been here a little over a year now. Bought the Munson plantation over on the Brazos."

"Riverbend?" Jim Bowie whistled softly. "That's a helluva place." He shook his head and grinned. "So you've given up trapping and brawling to be a gentleman planter, have you? Who would've thought it."

Conn's mouth twitched. He'd met Jim Bowie ten years before in New Orleans, on his way back to Charleston from the mountains. Conn had been set upon by three river rats outside a dockside tavern when Bowie appeared out of nowhere and joined forces with him. They'd fought back to back, in a sharp, quick skirmish that had sent the scurvy lot running. After a couple of victory drinks and an all-night poker game, Conn and Jim had left the tavern the next morning the best of friends.

Unless you counted Indian fights, Conn hadn't been in a brawl since, but he doubted that the same could be said of Jim. "Are you a Texan now, or did you just come to lend a hand?" Conn asked.

"Shoot, I've been here since twenty-eight. San Antonio is my home now. When the call to arms came, I was over in

Nacogdoches on business, so I rode across the Sabine and rounded up a few of my Louisiana friends to help out." Jim looked around at his companions. "Isn't that right, men?"

Immediately the men raised their long guns and shouted agreement. One even let loose with a shrill "Yip, yip, yip!" that made the horses sidestep.

Conn grinned again. It was clear that Jim Bowie and the Louisianans were spoiling for a fight.

"You and your men are a most welcome addition to our ranks, sir," came a voice from the crowd.

Looking around, Conn saw a thin, scholarly-looking man work his way to the front of men on foot.

"Stephen!" Jim Bowie jumped from his horse and embraced the man, giving his back a vigorous thumping. "I heard you were back, my friend, but I didn't expect to see you here."

Watching the greeting, Conn realized that he was seeing Stephen F. Austin for the first time. Sam had been right, he thought. The man looked terrible. He was thin to the point of emaciation, and he had the sickly pallor of one who hadn't been out in the sun for a long time. His face was lined and his body slightly stooped, and he looked fifteen years older than the forty-two years Conn knew him to be.

"And you, Sam, have you come to join us?" Austin asked when the greeting was over. "If so, I'd like to turn the command of these men over to you. The good Lord knows I'm no military man."

"I'm afraid I must decline, Stephen. I'm on my way to the convention in San Felipe. I'm only here to round up delegates so that we may form a quorum."

Surprised, Conn gave Sam a sharp look and had to suppress a grin. Why, the wily old war-horse was killing two birds with one stone.

The volunteers, not being regular army, did not feel constrained to a chain of command, and they did not want to release the delegates. Nor did the men want to go. After a heated debate Houston and Austin managed to persuade them to release all delegates who were not staff officers. Unfortunately the stipulation meant that not only Austin, but Travis and William Wharton, who was the elected president of the convention, could not be present at the consultation. When that was pointed out to the men, they merely shrugged and said the meeting would simply have to get along without them.

Before the delegates left, Sam gave the troops a short, impassioned talk, stressing the need for concerted action among the colonists and telling them that the first order of business at the convention would be to decide if they were fighting for their rights as Mexican citizens under the constitution or for independence.

"Are you coming with me, Conn?" Sam asked as he prepared to ride east.

Conn was tempted. His yearning for Elizabeth was an ache that never left him. He wanted to see her, see the children, and his father, and Taw. He wanted to see Riverbend.

Shifting in the saddle, he looked around at the motley collection of buckskin-and-homespun-clad men. Side by side were coonskin caps, wide-brimmed sombreros, slouchy felts, tall top hats, and military-style caps. Some sported boots, but most wore moccasins or run-down shoes, and more than a few were sockless. Bedrolls consisted of everything from "store-bought" blankets to homemade patchwork quilts, to bright counterpanes of every color and shaggy buffalo robes.

They were untrained and undisciplined and unprepared, an army made up, down to the last man, of independent, individualistic, self-reliant pioneers who had never taken orders from anyone. They were not soldiers in any sense of the word. But each carried an American-made long rifle that he used with deadly efficiency. For the most part, these were men born and bred to the frontier, and Conn was quite certain that they were the deadliest fighting force ever brought together on that or any other continent.

They were the only hope for Texas. They were his only hope of holding on to Riverbend and all he'd worked for.

With a sigh, Conn tamped down his longing and turned back to the big man on the small horse.

"No, Sam. I think I'll go to San Antonio."

Two weeks later the volunteers reached the San Antonio River at old mission San José, eight miles below the town of San Antonio. Austin halted the main body and sent two companies of men, those of Colonel Fannin and Colonel Coleman, out to reconnoiter, under the command of Jim Bowie.

Bowie's prowess as a fighting man was well known, and Austin had made him a staff officer immediately upon his arrival at Cibolo Creek, giving him the rank of colonel. Conn, because of his experience as a trapper and tracker, was afforded the same honor. He was in neither Fannin's nor Coleman's company, but because of their friendship Bowie requested that he be included in the group of ninety men.

Moving carefully down the road, the small band scouted ahead. Trotting out in front, his nose up, Pike sniffed the air. They'd gone only a few miles when the dog stopped and growled. An instant later a party of Mexican soldiers rode out of the woods toward them.

"Take cover, men!" Bowie shouted.

The men fanned out, but before they could carry out the order the soldiers stopped and fired from long range. Their musket balls thudded into the earth far short of the mark.

Surprised, the Texans looked at one another. Bowie flashed Conn a grin and shouted, "Let's return the compliment, men!"

The long rifles cracked and kicked up dirt at the heels of the retreating soldiers.

After that the road remained clear. They stole to within two miles of town, checked things out, and discovered that Cos had split his forces. One division was quartered in the Alamo, east of the San Antonio River, and the other was entrenched in the center of town to the west in two plazas, occupying the stone buildings that enclosed them. Both divisions had artillery. All appeared quiet, and Bowie decided against further action until the rest of the troops caught up.

"We'll make camp here and wait for them," he said.

Conn looked around, assessed the position, and silently approved. The spot Jim had chosen was at a wide bend in the river, about a quarter of a mile above Mission Concepción. The river was low, and the steep bank would provide excellent cover if the need arose. On the west side of the river a bluff and thick timber protected their backs. Conn's opinion of Jim Bowie rose another notch.

They set up camp and waited for Austin to bring up the rest of the volunteers. At sunset Conn started laying out his bedroll. He had no sooner spread his ground sheet than a dull boom sounded in the distance.

"What the hell?"

Startled, the men looked around just as a cannon ball shrieked overhead and buried itself in the soft earth fifty feet or so beyond the camp. Everyone dove for cover as the distant boom sounded again. With an unholy hiss five more cannon balls, fired from a gun mounted in a church tower two miles away, whizzed over, one after another. Then, all grew still.

No one moved for ten minutes, but as darkness fell Bowie, Conn, and several others stood up.

"No fires tonight, men," Bowie called, and a ripple of laughter spread through the darkness.

Austin and the rest of the troops did not arrive as expected. Though concerned, Bowie posted guards and ordered the men to get some rest.

At dawn the next morning, Conn and the others came awake to musket fire and a countryside encased in heavy fog. Pike rose and stood stiff-legged, hackles up, growling. No sooner had the men rolled from their beds and grabbed their guns than two of their pickets came stumbling into camp through the mist.

"They came . . . out of nowhere," one gasped.

"You hurt?" Conn asked, assisting the man down onto a log.

"No . . . but I . . . th-think Willie is. They just shot off . . . my . . . powder horn."

Conn hurried over to the other man, who lay on the ground writhing in pain. For an instant Conn was sure he was gut shot, but closer examination revealed that the man's injury was nothing more than a painfully bruised stomach, suffered when a musket ball struck his Bowie knife, which he carried in front, tucked under the waistband of his breeches. The force of the striking ball had broken the knife neatly in two.

"We've got to get to cover!" someone yelled through the fog. "The Mexicans are crossing the river down by the mission!"

Conn assisted the injured man down the riverbank, then leaped back up onto the plain and raced to help drive the horses out of range. Pike tore along at his side, a dark form cutting through the gray cloud.

The dense fog masked the movement and strength of the Mexicans, but through the eerie mist came the clop of shod hooves and the unmistakable rumble of caissons. Ghostlike, muted calls in Spanish and the clink and thud of running infantry floated closer.

"To the river, men! To the river." The command, repeated in several different voices, rang through the swirling murk.

Running behind a group of horses, Conn gave the one in the rear a slap on the rump and hied them out of range. Pike raced on after the bunch and added a sharp nip for good measure before swinging back.

A musket popped somewhere off to Conn's left. Hawken in hand, he crouched low and made for the river.

The Texans poured over the rim of the bank like swarming locusts. "Spread out, men! Spread out!" Bowie shouted. "Fannin's company to the right, Coleman's to the left!"

Footsteps pounded along the dry outer edges of the riverbed as the men took up positions along both sides of the wide bend in the river and drew up close under the five-foot-high bank. Except for an occasional murmur, all was quiet along the line of Texans.

Conn hunkered beside Bowie at the apex of the bend. Pike flattened out on the ground a few feet behind them.

"Well, well. Lookie there," Bowie murmured when the fog began to lift.

Conn eased up and peered over the lip of the bank. The Mexicans had moved up onto the open plain fronting the camp. At dead center, just out of rifle range, sat a cannon, flanked by several companies of infantry. Down by the mission, where they'd crossed the river, two more companies waited. "I suppose they're there to cut off a retreat," Conn observed dryly.

Jim gave a snorting chuckle. "Retreat, hell."

"Way I figure, we're outnumbered about"—Conn's gaze swept the field—"four to one, I'd say. How about you?"

"Thereabouts," Bowie concurred with a complete lack of concern.

The Mexican officer to the rear of the cannon barked out an order, and the gunner brought up a lighted torch. Conn and Jim ducked back below the bank.

"Keep under cover, boys, and reserve your fire. We haven't a man to spare," Bowie admonished in his calm voice.

The cannon boomed, and grape and canister ripped through the pecan trees overhanging the bank at their backs, sending a shower of ripe nuts down on them. Conn picked up two, cracked them together in one hand, and plucked out the sweet meat. Catching Bowie's amused look, he swallowed a mouthful and grinned. "I'm hungry. I didn't have time for breakfast."

Again and again the cannon boomed and pecans rained down, and each time Bowie repeated his warning: "Keep low, boys. Keep low. Hold your fire."

The Texas guns remained silent.

At last the Mexicans moved forward, bringing their cannon with them. When they came within range of Fannin's men on the right arm of the bend, the Texans opened fire. Halting, the enemy began to form for a charge.

"Coleman! Send some of your men around and give Fannin support," Bowie yelled. The order was unnecessary. Coleman's men, seeing the attack forming, had already broken for Fannin's position. A few foolhardy souls, excited and eager to get in a shot, mounted the bank and cut across the open plain, exposing themselves to enemy fire instead of running around the riverbed. Conn cursed as he saw a Texan go down, but there was no time for feelings. The Mexicans, outnumbering them four to one, were charging.

"Fire!" rang out Bowie's steady voice, and the volunteers responded with a fervor. The sharp crack of long rifles drowned out the dull bang of muskets. Caught in a crossfire, the soldiers toppled in waves. Three times they charged, and each time they were halted by the crack marksmen. Three times the Texans picked off their gunners, and the cannon remained silent.

When the third assault met disaster, the soldiers panicked and broke for the ford. Some jumped on the mules hitched to the caisson, two and three on each animal. Without bothering to cut loose the empty caisson, they galloped for the fort, leaving the cannon in the field.

"C'mon, men, let's get 'um!"

The Texans let loose a rousing cheer and swarmed up out of the river bottom to give chase. Caught up in the excitement, Conn found himself running at the front of their men, his moccasined feet pounding across the open plain. To either side and behind, the volunteers whooped and yelled as they raced after the enemy. Pike raced just ahead, his muscled body stretched out.

When they reached the artillery piece, Conn signaled a halt and shouted, "Here, help me turn the cannon!"

Within seconds the gun was repositioned. Conn picked up the torch dropped by the last gunner and touched it to the fuse. The cannon roared with a bouncing recoil, and the fleeing soldiers dropped their muskets and splashed across the river as though the hounds of hell were after them. The cavalry units waiting at the ford had taken no part in the battle, but they spurred their mounts and joined the race for the fort as well.

A cheer went up from the volunteers. Conn and Jim thumped one another on the back and grinned like fools.

A count showed that one Texan had been killed and one wounded. The Mexicans left sixty dead and dozens wounded on the field.

The men were still jubilant an hour later when Austin came up with the main body of the army. The Texans who missed out on the battle, however, were bitterly disappointed and groused long and loud about the course of fate that had deprived them of their share of the glory.

Austin and Conn and several others thought they should attack while the Mexicans were demoralized, but the few men among them who had seen military service argued that without artillery they could not take the city. By his own admission, Stephen Austin was not a military man, and he bowed to the will of the others.

The Texas volunteer army swarmed around the city like a horde of angry army ants and settled in for a siege.

It took almost no time to discern that siege warfare did not set well with the frontier spirit. The men had come to fight, not hole up behind barricades and take an occasional potshot at a careless enemy. They wanted action.

Within a matter of days the volunteers were bored and grousing. Some, dissatisfied with the delay, and there being no power to stop them, returned home.

Further dampening spirits, the weather turned cold. Many men who had left their homes in late September in the scorching heat had not even brought a coat. Food was not only poor, but irregular, since there was no organized commissary or service support of any kind.

Barely two weeks after the siege began Stephen Austin called Conn into his tent.

"Something has to be done, Mr. Cavanaugh. We need supplies and ammunition if we're to hold this army together. To that end, I have drafted a letter to the delegates in San Felipe requesting aid. I would like for you to take it personally to Sam Houston and enlist his support in convincing the others to take action. Sam is a military man. He understands these things. Will you do it?"

Conn's heart leapt, but he hid his jubilation behind a stern face. San Felipe was only a few hours' ride from Riverbend.

Chapter 21

The moment the railed fences of Riverbend came into view, Conn felt his spirits rise. Gripped by a sense of urgency, he had been pushing his horse ever since he'd left San Felipe. He had handed over Austin's letter to Sam, told him that when the delegates were ready to send a reply he could be reached at Riverbend, and took off for home with shameless haste.

Eleven weeks he'd been gone. Eleven long weeks of dodging Indians and Mexican patrols, of fighting and standing watch and waiting for something to happen, of sleeping on the ground and eating jerky and hardtack, and tough rabbit and squirrel when he could get it. Hell, it felt like eleven years.

Since leaving home in September he'd ridden hard all over the southwest section of Texas, crisscrossing that harsh border country so many times, he felt like he knew every rock and gully. And since Cibolo Creek he'd either been fighting for his life or half bored to death.

Nothing had ever looked so good to his eyes as the rolling, fertile fields of Riverbend.

From the looks of things, Harper had been doing a damned fine job, Conn thought with satisfaction. In the fields on either side of the road, only the tattered remnants of cotton remained on the dry stalks. Far in the distance he could see the hands in the cane and sorghum fields, and as he drew closer to the house the sweet smell hanging in the air grew stronger, a sure

341

sign that sugar and syrup making had begun.

Conn tried to subdue the excitement and anticipation building in his chest, but at the gate he put his heels to his horse, and as they raced up the drive his heart began to pound in time with the galloping hoofbeats. Pike raced along beside, his big, muscled body stretching out eagerly.

When they rounded the bend Conn drew the big bay up to a sedate trot, his excitement collapsing like a deflating bellows. On the rise ahead, the big white house sat with stately calm in the weak November sunshine, somnolent and tranquil. Except for the distant screech of machinery, all was quiet and still. There was not a soul in sight.

Feeling foolish, Conn realized that he'd been expecting to see Elizabeth running to greet him as she had the last time. Unconsciously he'd been looking forward to the moment, to seeing the joy in her eyes, to absorbing her eagerness and wallowing in her openhearted welcome.

Which was silly, he told himself, but that did not keep disappointment from creating a painful wedge in his chest, or his eyes from searching the yard as he swung out of the saddle and hitched his horse to the post before the veranda.

He poked his head in the front door and called, "Anybody home?" but the words echoed unanswered through the empty house. Following his nose and the sounds of activity, he walked to the side veranda, vaulted over the rail, and headed for the sugarcane press out back.

The wide yard between the back of the house and the outbuildings was a whirlwind of activity. Old Mose and Pearlie tended the kettles while others moved back and forth between them and the sugarcane press, carrying buckets of juice. Older children fetched armloads of wood to feed the fires and toted the buckets of sugar crystals skimmed from the boiling juice to the kitchen. Over all the hubbub, the smell of woodsmoke and sweet syrup hung thick in the air.

Conn's gaze searched among the workers for Elizabeth, but

there was no sign of her. As he crossed the yard, Dulcie looked up from adding wood to one of the fires and spotted him.

"Mastah Conn! You're back!"

Her shout drew the attention of the others, and he was besieged with greetings, but one stood out from the rest. Conn swung toward the sound of Taw's booming voice, but after only one step he pulled up short. "What in hell . . . ?"

He stared in disbelief at the old man propped up on a daybed in the dappled sunshine beneath an oak tree. Pike approached the bed with a cautious whine.

"Well, don't jist stand there gawkin'," Taw grumbled, tucking the blanket more securely under his armpits. Above the blanket, flannel underwear covered his arms and shoulders. "Act like you ain't never seen a feller laid up afore."

Conn walked to Taw's side, his narrowed gaze taking in his friend's pallor and the stiff leg elevated beneath the blanket. Taw looked thinner than he had eleven weeks ago. Older. "What the devil happened to you?"

The old man shifted his wad of tobacco and spit. He swiped his mouth with the back of his hand and shot Conn a sheepish look. "Fell off'n the loadin' platform down t' the gin. Busted my leg up good."

"When did this happen?"

"Couple o' weeks after you left. After Harper took off, the little missy needed help, so I was—"

"Hold it! Wait a minute! Harper quit?"

"Yep. You hadn't been gone no time when he lit out. Soon as he heerd 'bout that little skirmish down t' Gonzales when them soldiers tried t' take the cannon, why, that lily-livered coward took off fer the Sabine like a cat with his tail afire."

Conn cursed roundly. He yanked off his broad-brimmed hat and slapped it against his thigh, his jaw bulging, but after a moment an arrested look came over his furious face. Puzzled, he looked around at the bustle of activity and beyond the yard and surrounding trees to the harvested fields. "If Harper took off, who's been directing the work around here? Oh, hell, don't tell me she got Ben to come back?"

"Shoot, no! Not after the way you lit into her. 'Sides, last we heerd, Ben an' Liam an' his two oldest boys is all fighting in the siege on San Antone. Rachel's near 'bout worryin' herself sick that Johnny'll git shot."

"So who *has* been doing the overseeing?"

"The little missy, that's who."

"Elizabeth? How? She doesn't know anything about running a place like this."

"Well, sir, what she don't know, she learns. Pesters the fool out o' me fer what little I know 'bout farming an' sech, an' she's done made two trips down t' Groce's t' ast his advice. Ain't too proud t' ast Ebon an' the hands 'bout things, neither."

Taw smiled fondly, his faded old eyes softening. "That little gal, she purely is a wonder. Got the pickin' done an' been keepin' that gin goin' from first light till dark ever' day. Sent the first shipment downriver over a month ago, an' she'll have the rest ready soon. Got all the neighbors' crops ginned, too. She's done seen t' chinkin' up the cabins an' gittin' the wood cut' fer winter, an' she's issued new clothes. She's made soap an' candles, an' got all the foodstuff in an' stored an' preserved. She even set the young'uns t' gathering pecans down in the bottoms. They's down there now. An' as you kin see, she's busy now harvesting cane an' making sugar. Done tole me that soon as that's done she's gonna start the hog killing." Taw paused to spit again and grinned. "She's even put Miss Rachel t' work. Turned over the little ones' schoolin' t' her. Yessiree, that little gal may look like a good puff of wind could blow her away, but she's pure hickory."

Enjoying Conn's astonished look, Taw grinned, but after only a moment his expression sobered. "'Course, t' tell the truth, I'm plumb worried 'bout her. She's workin' herself right down t' a nubbin. Ever'body else, too."

Conn frowned, tipping his head toward the workers. "Have they given her any trouble?"

"Trouble? Shoot, no. Why, son, ever' livin' soul on this place'd walk through fire for that gal."

"Where is she now?"

"Down by the cane press, I 'spect. Or mebbe the gin."

Conn headed in that direction, his long strides eating up the ground. Leaving Taw with a whine, Pike went with him and trotted ahead, stopping here and there to sniff the familiar territory.

As Conn neared the area where the press was located, his steps faltered and he came to a halt and stared. A wagon driver coming in from the fields with a load of cane hailed him, but he didn't answer. He didn't even hear the man. Directly ahead stood Elizabeth. Despite all that Taw had said, he wasn't prepared for the sight of her.

Wearing a worn dress with the sleeves rolled up to her elbows, a bandanna tied over her hair and knotted at her nape beneath the thick coiled braid, she moved among the workers directing the entire operation, from unloading the wagons to stripping and cutting to grinding. At one point, to Conn's amazement, she picked up an armload of cut cane and fed it into the hopper herself. When done, she stopped to flex her shoulders and arch her back before stuffing in another bunch.

That was too much. Dodging the pair of mules circling the press, Conn ducked beneath the long drive spoke harnessed to their backs and bore down on his wife. Several of the workers noticed him, but Elizabeth didn't hear their calls above the grinding screech of the rollers. As she shoved another handful of cane into the hopper, Conn hooked an arm around her waist. Ignoring her shriek, he hauled her back a step and growled into her ear, "What in the name of all that's holy do you think you're doing, woman?"

The cane tumbled from her grasp and she twisted her head around, her face lighting up. "Conn!" She turned within his embrace and flung herself against his chest, her arms locking around him. Her hands clutched his back as though she would never let him go. "Oh, Conn."

The feel of her soft body pressed against his drove every other thought out of his mind. Holding her close, he laid his cheek against the top of her head and rocked her. His nose twitched as the scent of violets rose from her hair and mingled with the heavy sweetness in the air. His hands moved over her shoulders and back, and he frowned as he felt the new sharpness of her shoulder blades.

Leaning back, he framed her face with his hands and lifted it for his inspection. Slowly, as though weighted with lead, her eyelids lifted and she smiled up at him mistily. "Oh, Conn, I'm so glad you're home." The words came out on a sigh, heartfelt and quavery with emotion. Looking into those luminous gray eyes and that beautiful, exhausted face, Conn felt as though someone had tied a half hitch around his heart.

He bent his head and kissed her, unmindful of the grinning servants or the screeching press or the mules that powered it, plodding around them in an endless circle. Had the entire Mexican army come marching into the yard at that moment, he still could not have resisted those trembling lips.

The kiss was soft, savoring, a slow meeting of lips, a mingle of breaths, the barest touch of tongues, a sweetly restrained hello that made their throats ache and their hearts pound and their bodies clamor for more. When at last Conn raised his head, the small hands that clasped the sides of his waist were trembling and he felt as though all the air had been knocked out of his lungs.

She sagged against him, and looking down into her face, he noted the faint violet smudges beneath her eyes and the weariness that not even her smile could hide. There was a sharp chill in the air, yet a sheen of perspiration lay across her forehead and upper lip. It also dampened the back of her dress and formed dark circles beneath her sleeves. Numerous stains marked the old brown linsey-woolsey and the worn apron, and dirt streaked her pale face.

"You're exhausted. You've been working too hard."

"Conn!" she said with mild rebuke. "Is that any way to greet your wife after being gone so long? Besides, I'm fine."

"No, you're not fine, you're worn out. I want you to go back to the house right now and get some rest. I'll take over here."

"But that's silly. There's too much left to do for me to stop—Oh!" she squeaked as he swept her up in his arms. "Conn, what are you doing?"

"I'm taking you to the house so I can put you to bed where you belong. Ebon!" he called, marching away with Elizabeth in his arms. "Take over here."

"Yes-*suh*!"

Elizabeth looped her arm around his neck and gave in to the inevitable with a tired little sigh. With Pike trotting ahead as though clearing a path, Conn strode swiftly back the way he'd come. A strange welter of emotions swelled in his chest, lodging beneath his breastbone like a tight fist.

"Wouldn't listen t' you none either, huh?" Taw chortled as Conn marched past the daybed with Elizabeth. "Heh, heh, heh. Tole you she was a wonder!"

Conn ignored the old man's delighted guffaws and the smiles of the others in the yard. Elizabeth felt like a feather in his arms, and already her head dropped against his shoulder like a wilted flower. Spotting the housekeeper standing in the kitchen doorway beaming at them, Conn yelled, "Jemma, get Isaac and whoever else you need. I want a warm bath prepared for Mrs. Cavanaugh at once."

Conn had barely deposited Elizabeth on the fainting couch in their bedroom and knelt to unbutton her shoes when Jemma entered lugging the slipper tub. She placed it before the hearth and built up the fire as Isaac and several strapping young men filled the copper bath with steaming water.

When the men left Jemma bustled over to take charge of her mistress, but Conn shooed her away. "That's all right,

Jemma. I can manage. You run along now."

"I think you shocked poor Jemma," Elizabeth murmured
with a tired giggle as the tiny housekeeper bustled out.

"She'll get over it." Conn pulled off her shoes and peeled
down her stockings, then went to work on the row of hidden
hooks down the front of her gown.

"Conn, I can undress myself, you know," Elizabeth protested weakly.

He shot her a sardonic look and kept right on stripping
her. As docile as a lamb, she raised her arms when he yanked
the dress off over her head. He lifted her to her feet and, with
an arm around her waist to steady her, untied the strings of
her petticoats and let them fall in a billowing circle about her
ankles. "Well, at least you have the good sense not to wear
stays when you're working like a field hand," he muttered,
grasping the hem of her chemise and whipping off the thin
garment.

"Conn?" Elizabeth asked in a small, uncertain voice. "Are
you angry with me?"

He looked up from untying the drawstring on her drawers,
straight into those troubled gray eyes, and felt a stab of remorse. She stood there swaying on her feet, clad in only the
thin pantalets, her white, pink-tipped breasts bare, looking
worried and apprehensive, like a beautiful, exhausted waif.

Conn drew a deep breath and released a heavy sigh, and the
tight knot in his chest eased somewhat. "No. Of course I'm
not angry with you, sweetheart," he assured her gently. He
pushed the drawers down over her hips, scooped her up in his
arms, and strode to the tub. Elizabeth moaned in ecstasy as
he eased her down into the steaming water.

Relaxing against the high curved back of the tub, she rested
her head against the rim and closed her eyes. "Mmm, this
feels heavenly."

"Good. You just lie there and let me do the rest." Conn
plucked the pins out of her hair, and the heavy coiled braid

unwound. At once he released it.

Slowly, over and over, he drew a brush through the silky strands. Elizabeth made a soft, purring sound and rolled her head from side to side on the rim of the tub. Behind her, Conn smiled. When he finished, the soft locks trailed down the outside of the tub like a golden waterfall, the ends lying in a tumble of soft curls on the polished pine floor.

Conn knelt on one knee beside her and worked up a lather with the violet-scented soap she preferred. He applied the sudsy cloth to Elizabeth's chest, and immediately her eyes popped open. "Wh—"

"Sssh. Just take it easy." The hand flattened against her chest pushed her back against the tub, and she obeyed, though this time she kept her eyes open, watching him drowsily as he lifted first one arm, then the other, and lathered it from shoulder to fingertips. Conn smiled at the look of sensual pleasure on her face.

When finished with her arms, he bathed each long, shapely leg, holding the delicate ankle in one hand as he glided the sudsy cloth over the wet limb in long, slow strokes. All the time his gaze remained locked with hers, his eyes smoldering blue flame.

Even as weary as she felt, Elizabeth's heart began to pound and her blood began to heat beneath that searing look. Taking both her hands, he pulled her upright and onto her knees. Water sheeted down her body and dripped from the tips of her breasts, rejoining that sloshing around her thighs. The bottom portion of her heavy, unbound hair still lay draped over the high back of the tub, holding it away from her body. She knelt in front of him, gripping the sides, her glistening skin reflecting the dancing oranges and reds of the fire. A delicious shiver rippled through her as he methodically washed her shoulders and back and buttocks.

Abandoning the washcloth, he rubbed the bar of soap between his hands. When each palm was filled with creamy lather he stared into her eyes and tenderly cupped her breasts. Elizabeth sucked in her breath, her back arching.

His big hands circled the pliant flesh, kneaded, lifted, squeezed, stroked. Her nipples grew achingly taut and tender, and his thumbs swept back and forth over the sensitive nubs. A delicious shiver rippled through Elizabeth.

"Look at me, Beth," Conn commanded in a velvety tone when her eyelids began to drift shut. She obeyed, her gray eyes slumberous and smoky with passion beneath the curl of dark lashes.

"Oh, Conn, I've missed you so."

"I've missed you, too, little one," he murmured.

Mounds of lather slithered down her body. Like a master sculptor, Conn glided his hands over her, moving in slow circles over her sides, her midriff, her abdomen, the tops of her thighs. His finger delved into her navel. The heel of his hand rotated against the triangle of gilt curls.

Then one hand slipped between her legs.

Elizabeth moaned and gripped the sides of the tub so tightly, her fingers whitened. "Oh . . . Conn, I . . . oh." The delicious torment of those stroking fingers snapped her last bit of strength, and her quivering muscles went lax. As she sagged, Conn eased her back into the water and hurriedly rinsed away the mounds of soap.

Hooking his hands beneath her arms, he lifted her from the tub as though she weighed no more than a child and stood her on the towel he'd spread on the floor. He dried her quickly, noting grimly as he wiped the moisture from her skin that she'd lost weight she hadn't needed to lose. Even so he found himself admiring the graceful, delicate lines of her body. Her legs were gorgeous, so long and slender and shapely. And her firm, rounded little bottom drove him crazy. For the sake of his own sanity he moved the towel up to her back, and frowned when he felt the fragility of her ribs. Dammit! She'd been working too hard.

Standing, Conn tossed the towel aside and picked her up again, and Elizabeth slipped her arms around his neck as he carried her to the bed. He managed to toss back the counterpane, but when he placed her on the mattress she kept her hands locked behind his head. "Come to bed with me, Conn," she whispered, and to his delight, she blushed the instant the bold invitation left her lips.

He barely stifled a grin. "You're tired. You need to rest."

"I need you more."

He caught his breath at the simple declaration. "Elizabeth . . ."

"Please."

He bent and kissed her, intending to keep it light and quick, but she held on tight and kissed him back with a passion that sent heat streaking to his loins. When he raised his head she looked at him pleadingly. "Please, Conn. I've missed you so."

He knew he should let her sleep; she was so tired she could barely move. But he was not strong enough to resist those sweet entreaties. His mouth twitched in a rueful grimace. "All right," he surrendered, but when she tried to pull him down to the bed, he grasped her wrists and pulled her arms from around his neck. "But first I need a bath, too. I've got enough trail dust on me to start a good-size cotton field."

"But I don't care. I—"

"Sssh." He placed four fingertips over her mouth. "I won't be long."

To save time, he used Elizabeth's bath. He scrubbed himself with haste, a hot heaviness in his loins and an eagerness in his heart that not even the now chilled water could subdue. Within moments he emerged, smelling slightly of violets. After a few cursory swipes with a towel he hurried to the bed. He reached to pull back the quilts, but his hand halted in midair.

Elizabeth was sound asleep.

He stood immobile and looked at her, his chest tight with conflicting feelings; frustration warred with satisfaction, disappointment with pleasure, anger with overwhelming tenderness.

Elizabeth lay on her back, one hand resting atop the quilt, the other, palm up, on the pillow beside her face, her glorious hair spread out around her. A reluctant smile tugged Conn's mouth. Elizabeth. Beth.

Taw was right; she was a wonder. Lord, would she ever stop surprising him? A mixture of pride, concern, and amazement filled him at the thought of how hard she'd worked to keep the plantation running, how much she'd accomplished. He felt foolish recalling how he'd worried about taking her west. He'd doubted her ability not only to cope, but even to survive.

Cope? Conn shook his head. She'd done a hell of a lot more than cope. Elizabeth—genteel, soft-spoken Elizabeth—had faced it all squarely and done what needed doing, taking the complete running of Riverbend on her delicate shoulders, doing the work of three men, and doing it well.

But the tremendous burden had taken its toll, Conn thought, studying the bruised look about her eyes. Her lashes were dark against her pale cheeks. Unable to resist, he reached out and ran his forefinger over the curling tips. She was exhausted, and she'd lost weight. Her cheekbones stood out prominently, and the wrist that lay against the pillow looked so small and fragile, as though the least pressure would snap it in two.

Conn tried to imagine Millie doing the things Elizabeth had done, but the very idea was ludicrous. She would not have even tried. She would not have cared.

Life was strange; Elizabeth was his wife only because of a cruel twist of fate and the narrow-minded interference of a bunch of sanctimonious old busybodies coupled with his own selfishness. And yet, he could not imagine a more perfect mate.

Outside, darkness had fallen. The fire had died down and a chill had invaded the room. Conn could hear the sound of voices below. For a moment he considered getting dressed and going down to have dinner with the family. Instead he lifted the cover and slid into bed beside Elizabeth. Giving a little shuddering sigh, she snuggled close but did not awaken as he pulled her into his arms and settled her head on his shoulder. He lifted a heavy swath of golden hair and brought it to his nose, inhaling the sweet scent of it deep into his lungs, then he spread the pale strands over their bare shoulders. He placed a soft kiss on Elizabeth's temple and laid his cheek against the top of her head.

Friendship. That was the key to a happy marriage, not love, he told himself. Love was overrated. It got in the way, blinded you to the truth and made you vulnerable. You were better off without it. It had taken him most of his life to learn that lesson, but it wasn't one he was likely to forget.

Stroking Elizabeth's hair, he set his jaw and ignored the sweet, aching feelings she stirred in his heart.

Elizabeth awoke slowly, blinking as she looked around. She was alone. Had she merely dreamed that Conn had returned? No. There were his buckskins draped over a chair.

She flung back the thick quilts, snatched up her robe, and dashed over to the windows, her toes curling against the cold wood floor. To the west the sky was purple and orange as the last sliver of sun slid below the horizon. She'd dozed off for only a moment. Why had he left?

Deflated, she trudged back to the bed and pulled the chamber pot from underneath to answer nature's urgent call. When done, she poured water from the pitcher atop the dresser into the matching bowl and washed her face and hands. As she turned from drying them, the bedroom door opened and Conn walked in.

"Ah, you're awake."

"Of course I'm awake. I just closed my eyes for a moment. Where have you been?"

Conn's brows rose at the rare note of petulance in her voice, but a slow grin followed. "Down at the press, finishing up the last of the sugarcane. And, sweetheart, you didn't just close your eyes for a moment, you slept the clock around."

"What? Why, I—I couldn't have. I wasn't that tired," she protested, but her voice faltered toward the end under Conn's sardonic stare. She looked at him sheepishly. "Did I really?"

" 'Fraid so. Dinner'll be ready soon. I came up to roust you out of bed and help you dress."

"Oh. All right," she said, but she just stood there, gazing at him with such longing that Conn's face altered subtly and he crossed the room to stand in front of her.

"Or"—he bracketed her face with his rough hands—"if there's something you'd rather do, I'm sure dinner will wait."

She looked up into his eyes, her heart fluttering so rapidly that she could barely breathe. With great daring she placed her hands on his chest and slid them upward over his shoulders until her fingers laced together behind his neck, and as she went up on tiptoes and lifted her face, she tugged his head down.

He let her control the kiss for only a moment before taking charge. With a low groan, he wrapped his arms around her and deepened the kiss, his mouth rocking over hers as their tongues swirled and their hands moved in restless urgency.

His arms tightened, and with their mouths still fused, he lifted her and walked to the bed with Elizabeth hanging in his arms, her feet dangling a foot above the floor. Even as they collapsed together on the bed their hands were busy, frantically working open buttons, snatching at ties, shoving aside unwanted clothing. Within seconds they were naked, their clothes lying in crumpled heaps about the bed where they'd been tossed. They reached for one another, their soft groans of pleasure blending as their warm flesh met, silky smooth to hair-roughened hardness.

There was no time and no need for foreplay. The loneliness of the last eleven weeks, the worry and need that had bedeviled them both, had built their desire for one another to a fever pitch. They kissed deeply, and as Conn rolled Elizabeth to her back, her legs curved around his hips in a move as instinctive as breathing, each desperately seeking that special joy and peace only their oneness could bring.

Their joining was swift and smooth and deeply satisfying, a homecoming, a reassurance, a balm for two hearts not yet secure. For a moment they savored it in stillness. Eyes closed. Hearts pounded. Straining muscles quivered.

Then the movement began.

The age-old rhythm carried them quickly to their goal, and together they reached a tumultuous completion. As they held one another in fierce possession, their cries echoed through the rapidly darkening room.

For long moments after, sated, too replete to move, they lay fused together, pale flesh to dark, soft gentle curves to sinewed strength. Only the flickering fire in the hearth lit the room, gilding their entwined limbs and sleek, sweat-sheened bodies with its dancing red-and-orange light.

Finally Conn stirred and rolled to his side. Propping up on one elbow, he looked down at her, his blue eyes intent as they roamed her flushed face. She gazed up at him so sweetly, so openly, her eyes full of emotion. Oh, God, could it possibly be love he saw?

His chest tightened at the thought, and his heart began to bang. "Beth . . ." He smoothed her arched eyebrows with his thumb and trailed the backs of his knuckles down her cheek. She smiled and curved her fingers around his wrists. Absently she raked her nails through the crisp hairs there.

"You're an amazing woman," he managed as his heart seemed to swell to twice its normal size. "I . . ."

"Yes?" Elizabeth prompted, her eyes growing wide and luminous with hope.

"I . . . I care for you very much, Beth. You're very important to me."

The light in her eyes dimmed, but before the full weight of disappointment hit her, a knock sounded on the door.

"Mastah Conn? There's a man downstairs to see you. Says Mr. Houston sent him."

Conn and Elizabeth exchanged a tense look and scrambled for their clothes, their personal feelings put aside for the moment in favor of more urgent matters.

The rider was, indeed, a courier from Sam Houston.

"The convention meeting in San Felipe has established a provisional government. They've made Sam commander of all the troops, except the volunteers laying siege to San Antonio," Conn said when he'd read Sam's message. "They've sending Austin to the States to appeal for war funds and volunteers. I'm to deliver that message to the militia in San Antonio and tell them that we're fighting for our rights under the constitution, not independence."

Less than an hour later Elizabeth once again stood on the veranda and watched Conn ride away. This time he would stay with the troops until the battle was either won or lost.

"Come back to me," she whispered as he disappeared around the bend in the drive. "Please. Come back to me."

Chapter 22

When Conn returned to the troops at San Antonio, he found the morale of the men had worsened. A vast discouragement pervaded the Texan army. They lacked artillery, and few of the officers were willing to assault San Antonio and the presidio of the Alamo without it.

Stephen Austin, on receiving his new assignment from the Convention, left immediately for the States. The man was a diplomat, not a soldier, and Conn had the feeling that he was relieved to be free of his military command.

True to their independent spirit, and contrary to every rule of military procedure, the troops held an election and made Colonel Edward Burleson commander.

As the days wore on men began leaving by the score, and the ones who stayed groused incessantly about the worsening conditions and the lack of action. Finally, a week after he took over, Colonel Burleson called a consultation of his officers, and they agreed to abandon the siege.

"Dammit, Colonel, you can't do that," Conn argued. "If we give up now, we'll destroy the entire army. The only common goal the fighting men of Texas had was to take control of San Antonio and drive Cos out."

Colonel Frank Johnson, the adjutant general, and several other officers agreed with Conn, but their arguments could not sway the new commander and the rest of his staff. The next day, on the fourth of December, the men were called in and orders were issued to retreat to Gonzales.

The order was met with even less enthusiasm by the troops. As miserable as they were, they had come to San Antonio to fight.

"This is a grave mistake," Jim Bowie grumbled to Conn as they saw to the packing of the baggage wagons. "If we abandon this mission, we all might as well pack up our belongings and head for the Sabine River, because that little tyrant in Mexico won't rest until he's driven every last Anglo out."

"Yes, I know." Conn tightened a rope around a keg of gunpowder, the muscles in his jaw working. Worry gnawed at his gut. He could almost feel Riverbend slipping through his grasp.

"What this army needs—"

A commotion down the way interrupted Jim. Looking around to discover its cause, Conn saw two Texans leading a Mexican officer into camp.

They marched the enemy officer to Colonel Burleson, and every man in camp, Conn and Jim included, hurried over. When they pushed to the front of the crowd, the Mexican lieutenant was speaking in rapid Spanish, much to Burleson's frustration.

Spotting Jim, the commander ordered, "Bowie! Get over here and tell me what the devil he's saying. All we know is he's a deserter. Find out why he left."

Jim Bowie had married into a wealthy Mexican family and spoke fluent Spanish. After listening to the man for a few minutes, his face lit with excitement. "He's says that all of Cos's army is discouraged. Worse, they're hungry. With their supply lines cut off, they're running out of food. The lieutenant here seems to think that, the way things are now, San Antonio could be taken."

Wild excitement spread through the troops, and suddenly Colonel Ben Milam raised a shout:

"Who will go with old Ben Milam into San Antonio? Who

will go with old Ben Milam into San Antonio?"

Conn looked around, his heart beginning to pound as a great cry went up.

"Then fall in line!" Milam roared.

The men could not comply fast enough. Pushing and shoving, two hundred volunteers stepped forward. Conn was one of them.

The men who gathered at the Old Mill north of town at three the next morning, waiting for orders to storm the city, numbered over three hundred. They talked in whispers, when they talked at all. For the most part they just waited, their faces hard, expressionless, eyes aglitter.

"Men, when I give the signal be ready to move out fast," Ben Milam instructed in a low voice. "We'll go through the picket line in small groups. Keep low and keep quiet. You men under Colonel Johnson enter town on Soledad Street. The men with me and Colonel Cavanaugh will enter on the second street, Calle de Acequia. Our objective is to flush out the Mexican troops quartered in the buildings around the main plaza and the military plaza.

"To divert General Cos's attention, Colonel Neill is going to open fire on the Alamo with the cannon we took from the Mexican's at Concepción. When we hear the cannonade, we'll move out.

"Colonel Burleson will remain here with the reserve force, which will be committed when and where needed."

The men nodded and shifted their feet, eager to begin.

The distant boom of the cannon sounded. Colonel Milam signaled and took off at a lope. Conn commanded Pike to stay, signaled to the men under his command, and fell in behind.

Near the Mexican picket line, they halted and crouched low. Each time the sentry passed by, more men filtered through, until finally they were all sprinting through the darkness.

The men under Johnson's battalion broke off at the edge of town and headed down the first street running north and south. Following Milam's group, Conn and his men pelted for the next one. As they came around the corner onto Calle de Acequia, from over on Soledad Street the dull boom of a Mexican *escopeta* broke the quiet of the night. Immediately a line of Mexican soldiers came streaming around the next corner toward them.

"Take cover!" Conn shouted.

The Texans scattered. They flattened against the sides of buildings, crouched behind stoops, darted into alleys and doorways, hunters blending into the adobe city as easily as they blended into the forest.

They returned the soldiers' musket fire, their long rifles spitting flame and lead with deadly precision. The baggy pale gray uniform of the Mexican infantry made an easy nighttime target, and they crumpled one after another like rag dolls. Those who survived the first volley retreated into the stone houses on the corner.

All along the street shutters cracked open and gun barrels appeared. From windows and alleyways, roofs, around corners, the soldiers opened fire.

"We'll have to break in to get to them!" Milam shouted over the staccato gunfire when Conn flattened himself against a wall beside the commander. Conn nodded, checked the street, and tore across to an alley where ten volunteers had taken cover and were returning enemy fire.

Conn sent a detail back to the mill for logs to use as battering rams. When they returned he instructed a group to cover him and led the assault on the first house. Texans on both sides of the street kept up a barrage of gunfire, and chips of wood flew like rain from the shutters and doors all along the block as four men pounded the plank door with a section of log and Conn stood ready beside it with his rifle.

A musket ball thwacked the adobe wall a couple of inches

to the right of Conn's head. He ducked and whirled in time to see a flared musket barrel retract at a corner. The men kept pounding. Conn waited and watched. A moment later the gun barrel eased out again, then an arm and shoulder. Conn fired. A faint cry, and a gray-clad form collapsed onto the dirt street. The musket clattered against the adobe wall and bounced on the ground. As he turned back Conn was already reloading. He had barely rammed the ball home when the door crashed back on its leather hinges.

Conn charged inside as a soldier rushed in from the next room, his musket raised. Conn fired, and the front of the man's uniform blossomed red as he fell back. Two more followed, and with a brutal slashing motion Conn smashed his rifle butt into one face, then the next.

The battering detail dropped the log and rushed inside as more soldiers swarmed down the stairs in the corner. In rapid fire, muskets boomed and pistols banged. The acrid smell of gunpowder hung in the air as metal struck metal and a hand-to-hand struggle began.

Conn dispatched two more men, one with his rifle butt, another with his pistol. One of the men on battering detail took a bayonet in the leg, but he kept on fighting until they had cleared the house. Then Conn tied a bandanna around the man's thigh and sent him back to get medical attention from one of the doctors with Burleson's unit.

Without pause, he drafted another man for the battering detail, shouted to them to retrieve the log and follow him, and moved on to the next house.

The hot and bloody battle raged on without letup. The Texans fought their way toward the plazas in the center of town, inch by inch. They fought man to man, house to house, sometimes room to room, driving the Mexicans back.

It was the kind of warfare frontiersmen had been taught all their lives: take cover, shoot to kill, keep moving.

Building after building, plaza after plaza, were cleared by

deadly sniping and hand-to-hand combat. The Mexicans responded with heavy cannon fire but succeeded only in knocking down walls.

The assault went on all the remainder of that night, all the next day and night, and the next.

On the third day of bitter, close-in combat, Conn and his men had just cleared another house when he saw Ben Milam lead a charge into the courtyard of the Veramendis mansion. The stone house, which had belonged to Jim Bowie's late in-laws, was just half a block off the main plaza. It and the de la Garza house one street over, were their primary objectives, for from those two points of vantage they could launch their attack on the main plazas.

Conn signaled to his men, and they darted into the Veramendis courtyard behind Milam and his small detail. Inside the walls, the men spread out and took cover. A musket ball whizzed past Conn's head. He made a diving roll across the flagstone floor and came up against the tiered fountain in the center of the enclosure.

Milam hunkered down behind a stone bench a few yards away to reload his long gun. When done, he lunged to his feet and ran toward Conn, but halfway across he stopped cold, as though he had hit a wall, and his eyes glazed. He fell just feet from where Conn knelt, blood pouring from a small, obscene hole in his temple.

"They got Ben!" one of the men yelled.

For a full minute Conn stared with horror at the lifeless body of the man who had led them this far. Milam was lying on his back, his sightless eyes fixed on the sky.

Fury boiled. Conn raised his gun and shouted, "Let's get them, men! For Ben!"

"For Ben!"

"For Ben!"

"For old Ben Milam!"

The cry swelled through the courtyard, until it was a roar

of rage that spurred the men into an all-out, head-on charge at the house. Under heavy fire they broke down the door and swarmed inside like an unleashed fury, shooting and bashing without mercy.

Spurred by the loss of the man who had inspired them, the Texas troops fought on like demons for two more days. They brought up their single cannon and mercilessly battered Cos at the Alamo, and fought the soldiers back from the plazas in deadly man-to-man combat.

The Mexicans were not used to street fighting, nor such blazing determination. By the fifth day Cos had had enough and sent out a white flag. The Texans, barely more than three hundred strong, had routed the entrenched enemy, who outnumbered them more than four to one.

After months of anxiety and worry, December brought Elizabeth two reasons for rejoicing.

The first occurred midmonth when a neighbor brought the news that the volunteers had taken San Antonio. General Cos had surrendered, and after signing a pledge to uphold the constitution and never fight against the colonists again, he and his men had been provided with enough weapons and powder to protect themselves against the Indians and sent marching back across the Rio Grande.

Elizabeth was so relieved that she sat down in the parlor and cried. All the battles had been fought one hundred and fifty miles away along the western frontier, but for months she'd lived with the fear of the war spreading eastward. Now, it was over.

The second cause for joy occurred a week later when Hester and her three youngest children arrived to spend Christmas. Hester took one look at Elizabeth, and her keen hazel eyes narrowed shrewdly. "So. You're breeding, are you. 'Bout time."

Shock reverberated through Elizabeth, and her eyes widened. She had suspected for weeks, since before Conn's brief return the previous month, but suspecting was one thing; having your best friend pronounce it as fact was quite another. "How . . . why do you say that?"

"Lord, woman, it's plain as the nose on your face." Hester laughed when Elizabeth's hand went to her still flat belly. "No, not that way. You've got that look about you. You know, kinda pasty and green around the gills. I'd wager you've been chucking up your breakfast lately, haven't you?"

"Some," Elizabeth admitted weakly.

"Well, don't worry. That'll soon pass." Hester eyed her again. "When do you figure you're due?"

Elizabeth blinked at the question. She was still coming to grips with the whole idea. She'd missed two monthly cycles—soon it would be three—and she'd been tired and sick, but she'd put all that down to worry and overwork. She hadn't dared to believe she could possibly be with child.

"Well?" Hester prodded.

"Uh . . ." Elizabeth made a quick mental calculation. "June, I think. Around the middle."

Just saying the words aloud made it all suddenly real. Elizabeth's expression grew dreamy. A baby. A child of her own. She couldn't believe it. She was thirty-three years old and had long ago given up hope of ever becoming a mother. And now . . . Elizabeth placed both palms flat against her stomach. Her throat ached. The back of her nose burned. She was going to have a baby! Conn's baby.

Overcome, she closed her eyes against the sting of tears and pressed her quivering lips together.

"Have you told Conn?"

Elizabeth's eyes snapped open. Conn! She had no idea how he would take the news. "No, not yet. I'll tell him as soon as he gets home. I expect him any day, now that the fighting is over."

The next afternoon Johnny and Daniel Grimes rode in,

looking tired and battle worn but flush with triumph over their part in the victory at San Antonio. Rachel was beside herself with joy. The young lovers were so absorbed in each other, it was several minutes before Johnny remembered the letters he was to give his mother and Elizabeth.

"They're from Paw and Mr. Cavanaugh," he said, handing them over.

A brief look of apprehension passed between the women, and Elizabeth's heart began to pound as she opened the letter.

Dearest Elizabeth,

By now, you have heard of our victory, and I'm sure you are expecting me to return in time for Christmas. I wish with all my heart that were possible, but I'm afraid it isn't to be.

The men are jubilant over Cos's surrender and believe the war won, as does our provisional government. They believe that our courtesy to Santa Anna's commander in sending him and his men back across the border is ample proof of our unwillingness to break ties with Mexico and all that remains to be done is for them to establish statehood within the Mexican Republic. To that end, they have called for a new convention to meet at Washington-on-the-Brazos on the first of March to form a more effective state government.

General Houston does not share this optimistic view. He has tried to rally them and make them see that Santa Anna's pride is sure to be stung by the defeat and that he will try to exact reprisals. Foolishly, most of the men are returning to their homes, leaving only a hundred or so to defend the Alamo, should that happen.

I tend to agree with General Houston, and would have stayed at the Alamo myself, but he has assigned me another duty. The Indians are taking advantage of the unsettled conditions to raid and plunder along the frontier. Because of my experience, General Houston wants me to command a group of rangers and patrol that area to give what protection we can.

We are also to hold ourselves in readiness in case the Mexican army returns. There are twelve good men in my command, Liam being one. Tell Hester I will do my best to see that no harm comes to him.

I have no idea how long this conflict will last or when I will see you again, but I pray it will be soon. Take care of yourself and the children and say hello to Taw for me. Dad, too, if he has returned.

As ever,
Conn

That was it—nothing of missing her, no word of affection, not so much as a casual endearment. Elizabeth read the letter through twice, just in case she'd missed something, but the result was the same. Struggling against the tears that seemed to come so easily these days, she refolded the letter and tucked it into her pocket.

For the sake of the family and their guests, she put on a pleasant face, but she went through the happy rituals of Christmas with a heavy heart.

As winter continued Elizabeth blamed her low spirits on her condition. After all, women got melancholy when they were expecting. After one bout of prolonged weeping in her solitary bed the night she received Conn's letter, she flatly refused to give in to the despondency that weighted her soul. She hadn't time for such foolishness. Too many people were depending on her, including her unborn child. For Conn's sake, for all their sakes, she had to keep the plantation running. She had the children to look after. And Taw.

The fall he had suffered had been a bad one, breaking his leg in three places, and his old bones were not knitting well. Elizabeth suspected it would be months before he could put any weight on his leg.

Work helped her keep her mind off Conn and the constant, niggling worry of war, and God knew there was plenty to do. Throughout the long, cold winter, as the lonely days mounted and Elizabeth grew heavy with child, she worked ceaselessly. Under her direction the sugarcane was planted, gardens were readied and spread with manure, fences and buildings were repaired, the seed corn was tarred. As long as the cold weather held, the hog butchering continued until the smokehouse was full and hogsheads of rendered fat were stacked high in the storage sheds. When freezing rains and bitter cold drove them indoors, there were tools and instruments that needed repairs; harnesses and shoes that needed mending; spinning, weaving, basket making, and corn shelling to be done. Whenever weather permitted, Elizabeth kept the plows moving.

Through it all, her eyes searched the road for a big, buck-skin-clad man and a mongrel dog.

Elizabeth missed Conn desperately, but as one peaceful day followed another, her fear of the war starting up again began to recede. They had obviously won. Conn would be home soon.

In mid-February, a hard-riding courier shattered that hope.

As the man came splashing up the drive through the winter mud and sleet, waving his hat and shouting, Elizabeth snatched up a shawl and hurried out onto the veranda, her heart in her throat. Hard on her heels came Taw, thumping along awkwardly on his crutches, with Rachel following behind him, along with Johnny, who had arrived for a visit only an hour before.

"What is it? What's happened?"

"We got word that Santa Anna's on his way!" the excited man exclaimed as his lathered horse sidestepped under him. "Our spies say he left Saltillo two weeks ago with over six thousand men. And General Urrea crossed at Matamoros with another thousand men to protect Santa Anna's left flank. He's slashing his way north from San Patricio right now."

"Oh, my Lord," Elizabeth gasped. One hand flew to her throat, the other unconsciously splayed over her swollen belly. Around her rose a chorus of outcries and questions from the others, but she scarcely heard them over the thunderous booming of her heart. Her gaze turned westward. *Conn.*

Had he heard the call and gone to the Alamo? Dear God, there were only a hundred or so defenders there, and Santa Anna was marching on it with over six thousand.

"Davey Crockett and twelve Tennessee volunteers arrived at the Alamo a few days ago, but we're still undermanned. Colonel Travis is calling for every able-bodied man to come to our aid. We've got to stop the Mexicans there, or nobody'll be safe."

The words galvanized Johnny into action. Before the man finished speaking he grabbed Rachel and gave her a hard kiss.

"Johnny, wh—"

"I've got to go, honey. But I'll be back. Don't you worry."

"Johnny, no!" Rachel cried, but he was already racing for the barn.

"There's troops in Gonzales and Goliad," the courier shouted after him. "You can join up with them!"

He wheeled his horse and raced back down the drive. Moments later, mounted on a piebald mare, Johnny came galloping from the barn and tore off after him, waving his hat and shouting as he went by, "Don't worry! We'll give 'em hell!"

As the hoofbeats died away, the three on the veranda stood stunned; only the sound of Rachel's soft sobbing filled the silence.

"What're you gonna do, Missy?"

Elizabeth turned at Taw's gently worded question, and his old heart squeezed at the dazed look of fear in her eyes. But even as he watched, she squared her shoulders and lifted her chin. "I'm going to get ready to run, in case it comes to that. But in the meantime"—with a determined stride, she headed around the veranda toward the back of the house—"I've got corn and cotton to plant."

Conn and his group of twelve rangers rode into Gonzales at sunset on the eleventh of March and found the town in chaos. Everywhere, people were scurrying about in panic. Many were packing to flee eastward; wagons, handcarts, donkeys—anything that would move was being pressed into service. Patience was in short supply, and tempers were high.

"Sorta reminds you of an anthill that's been stirred with a stick, don't it?" Liam remarked as they cantered through town on their tired mounts.

"Everyone's heard about Santa Anna's march," Conn replied with a trace of bitterness. "Sam tried to tell them three months ago that this would happen. If they'd paid attention, we'd be better prepared to meet him."

At Sam Houston's camp they found the same frenetic rush of activity. Men tore about, loading supplies, striking tents, packing belongings. In the middle of the hubbub, three-inch rowels jingling on his spurs, a long feather in his hat, his six-foot-two-inch, powerfully muscled frame standing out from the rest, Sam cut an impressive figure, striding about barking orders. He looked every inch the commanding general.

Leaving his men with orders to get some rest, Conn dismounted and went to report. Sam greeted his arrival with obvious relief.

"Conn! You made it! Good man."

"Sorry for the delay, General. I received your recall order a few days ago in Bastrop when we brought in a boy the Comanches had captured. We headed out as soon as we could. When we left the town was in an uproar. Pretty much like here."

"Yes," Sam said gravely. "There is a general panic, I'm afraid. And who can blame them, with Santa Anna on a rampage?"

Sam surveyed the bustle of activity in the camp, his rugged face hard. "But at least this crisis has opened the eyes of the provisional government and stirred them into action. Santa Anna's intentions are known to everyone now. The convention met two weeks ago at Washington-on-the-Brazos, and the first order of business was to draft a Declaration of Independence. We also drafted a constitution and set up an interim government until after our fight for independence is won."

"Who are our leaders?"

Houston grinned at the unvarnished skepticism in Conn's voice. "David Burnet is president; Lorenzo de Zavala, vice-president; and Thomas Rusk is secretary of war," he supplied succinctly. "I remain commander in chief of the army, only now I command all armed men in Texas, regulars and volunteers."

"Well, thank God for that."

"General! General!"

Conn and Sam turned at the interruption and spotted Sam's aide, Colonel George Hockley, approaching at a run with two Mexican peasants in tow.

"General, these two men say that the Alamo has fallen!"

"*What!*"

Conn stared, speechless. He felt as though he'd received a solid blow to the chest.

"*Sí, señor,* eet ees true!" one of the men insisted.

"*Sí, sí!*" the other agreed.

Crossing themselves, they both began to speak at once, lapsing into rapid-fire Spanish in their excitement. An interpreter was sent for, and the three Texans listened in stony silence as the terrible news was repeated at length.

After an initial burst of fury, General Houston responded with quick, cool-headed authority.

"Colonel Hockley, Fannin and his troops are still at Fort Defiance in Goliad. Send word that he's to blow up the fort and fall back to Victoria and await my orders."

"Yes, sir, General." Colonel Hockley snapped a salute and spun away.

"Conn, find yourself a fresh horse, round up Deaf Smith and one more scout, and the three of you ride to San Antonio. I want confirmation of this tragedy before I inform the wives of those men."

Within minutes Conn, Deaf Smith, and a man named Hadley, whom Conn had never met, were galloping west down the San Antonio road. They pushed hard all night, talking little, stopping only when they had to rest their mounts. Each man's face was set in grim foreboding of what they would find.

The next day, after covering only a third of the distance, they spotted two riders coming toward them and pulled up.

"What the devil . . . ? That looks like a woman."

"It is. A woman carrying a child." Conn stood high in his stirrups and squinted his eyes. "There's a Negro man with her."

"Well, that's sure as hell odd," Hadley commented. "What do you suppose she's doing out here?"

Conn spurred his mount forward. "C'mon. Let's go find out."

When they drew near and the woman saw that they were Texans, she reined in her horse and burst into tears. At a loss, the three men looked to her escort, but the black man just rolled his eyes. The woman, a pretty, plump young female of somewhere around eighteen or nineteen, clutched her baby to her breast and continued to cry piteously.

"Ma'am, we're scouts with General Houston's army," Deaf said in his usual booming voice. He was so hard of hearing, even when he tried to be gentle he almost shouted. "What're you doing out on the road, ma'am? It's not safe, what with the Mexicans attackin' an' all."

The woman gulped and sobbed and struggled to gain control. "Th . . . they're dead. They're all . . . d-dead."

"Who, ma'am?"

"The m-men at . . . the Alamo. Jim Bo-Bowie, Davey Crockett, Colonel Tra-Travis . . . all of them. I was th-there. I saw it happen. They killed and . . . mu . . . mu . . . mutilated them all. Every last man. Even the ones . . . wh-who tried to surrender. I was in the room when they . . . they shot Jim Bowie on his sickbed. And then . . . and then four of them . . . they lifted him on their bayonets," she wailed.

"Good God!"

"Why, those dirty—" Hadley bit off the curse and looked away, his jaw bulging.

Conn closed his eyes. Jim . . . his old friend . . . dead. Swallowing the bile that rose in his throat, he looked at the woman again. "What's your name, ma'am?"

"Su-Susannah Dickerson." The woman brushed her wet cheeks and lifted her chin, though her lips still quivered. "My husband . . ." She squeezed her eyes shut and fought back more tears. "My husband was Almeron Dickerson. They . . . killed him, too. They killed them all," she said forlornly.

"Ma'am? How did you get away?"

"Santa Anna spared me only because he wanted me to spread the word to the Texans that all who opposed him would receive the same treatment."

Later that evening when they returned to Gonzales, Susannah Dickerson repeated her horrifying story to General Houston and an assembled crowd that included at least thirty wives whose husbands had perished in the siege. The cries of those women were something Conn knew he would never forget.

The mood of the crowd went from shock to rage, and when Susannah Dickerson also told of Santa Anna's plans to drive every Anglo out of Texas, that rage melded into a furious determination.

"All right, men! Strike camp and prepare to move out!" General Houston shouted when Mrs. Dickerson was led away. "We retreat tonight for the Navidad!"

What had begun as shouts of approval turned to protests.

"Retreat!"

"Retreat, hell! I say we march to San Antonio and whip those bastards!"

"We can't turn tail and run!"

"We want to fight!"

"Gonzales is in immediate danger," Sam bellowed back. "There are probably troops marching on us now. We haven't the numbers to fight them here! We'll pick up more volunteers if we fall back into Anglo Texas."

"What do numbers matter?" a soldier yelled. "We've whupped 'um before when we were outnumbered. I say we fight!"

"We will," Sam assured them. "But I will pick the time and the place. Now, strike camp and get ready to move!"

The men grumbled and cursed, but they obeyed.

Houston gave orders to evacuate the town. He shot off another message to Fannin and sent Conn and Deaf Smith in different directions to scout Mexican troop movements. Hardly pausing to draw breath, he detached a rear guard to escort the civilians out of Gonzales, with orders to set fire to the town on their way out.

At eleven that night the small Texas army marched east.

In the early hours of the morning, the second day following the evacuation, Conn caught up with the retreating Texas army and the pitiful horde of refugees camped at the ford of the Navidad River, some thirty miles east of Gonzales.

"Halt! Who goes there?"

"Conn Cavanaugh. Scout for General Houston."

The picket guard waved Conn past, and he walked his horse through the pouring rain into the sleeping camp. The big, barrel-chested sorrel plodded, head down, at the end of his endurance. Conn was in no better shape. Except for a couple of naps he'd snatched along the way, he'd been in the saddle almost continually for the past four days.

Rain pelted his slicker and poured from the rolled brim of his hat like water gushing from a drain spout. A trickle inched down his spine, and his buckskins were wet from the knees down, his legs numb from the cold. He was too tired to notice.

He headed straight for General Houston's tent. Feeling every one of his thirty-eight years, he dismounted and hitched his horse to a tent guy rope. Without ceremony he ducked inside.

Sam came awake instantly. "Who's there?"

"It's me. Conn."

A match flared, and Sam touched it to the stubby candle stuck to a tin plate beside his bedroll. He reached for his breeches, but Conn stopped him.

"Don't bother getting dressed, Sam. I haven't much to report. Besides, I not going to be awake much longer, anyway."

"What did you find?"

"I rode about halfway down the road to San Antonio before I ran into troops. Santa Anna is still there, mopping up. He's sent General Sesma with about fourteen hundred men to Gonzales. I rode hard all the way back. Unless he force-marches, which I don't think he'll do, he's two to three days behind you. That's all I can tell you."

"That's enough. My thanks to you, Conn. Now you go get some rest before you fall down. I'll give you new orders in the morning before we pull out."

Conn didn't need any encouragement. He located Liam's tent, crawled inside, and rolled in a blanket. He was asleep the instant his head touched the ground.

Four hours later, at dawn, he woke to shouts and curses. "What the—" He bolted up, grabbing for his rifle, but Liam stayed his hand.

"Take it easy, Conn. It's just the men."

"What the devil's going on?"

"They're angry is all. Sam has issued orders to gather our gear and break camp. We're retreating again."

Conn noticed then that Liam's bedroll was gone. Except for packing the tent, he was ready to move out.

Given the situation, the decision was the right one, Conn knew, but none of the men saw it that way. No Texan had ever run from a fight, and a lust for revenge for their slaughtered friends burned in them all.

When the men fell into line a few minutes later, they were close to mutiny. Sitting astride his horse, Conn watched, concerned, as staff officers rode along the column shouting, "Close rank! Close up! Close up!"

The troops moved out, cursing and complaining, and Conn shook his head. How long, he wondered, could Sam hold his independent, makeshift army together?

Chapter 23

What followed after those at Riverbend received the news of Santa Anna's invasion made their labors of the past months look like child's play.

Every day it didn't rain Elizabeth kept the plowboys and drillers working in the fields from first light till full dark. Furniture and valuables were taken down to the river and stashed in the bottoms or in shallow caves along the steep banks of the Brazos. Under her instructions, the blacksmith labored to ready the wagons and mules for travel, while she and the other women gathered supplies, clothing, arms, and ammunition.

Elizabeth made a solemn vow that she would not leave her home unless she knew with absolute certainty that the Mexican army was advancing on them, but she was determined to be ready. With Taw laid up and Conn and Joseph gone, it was up to her to keep the family and all their people safe.

Rachel was almost hysterical with worry over Johnny's fate, and her fear transmitted itself to Ian and Faith, as well as to those in the quarters. It fell to Elizabeth to calm and reassure everyone, leaving her with no choice but to keep a tight rein on her own terror.

She was merely taking precautions, she told them. They were probably going to a lot of trouble for nothing. Everything was going to be fine, and in a few weeks they would no doubt be putting everything back. She repeated the assurances so many times that she almost believed them herself, but in mid-March, almost a month after the first courier had come, another arrived with a dispatch from Sam Houston.

"What's it say?" Taw asked as Elizabeth read the letter.

She looked up, her face pale. "That . . . that everyone is to leave with all possible haste." She licked her dry lips and swallowed hard. "Oh, Taw, the Alamo has fallen, and all the defenders have been put to the sword. Santa Anna is on the march."

Rain pelted Conn's back and streamed from the broad brim of his hat as he bent to duck under the tent flap. Inside, he straightened in time to see Sam Houston leap to his feet.

"Conn! Thank God you caught up with us. I was beginning to get worried, my friend." He hurried forward and clapped Conn's shoulder.

"Sorry for the delay, General. I've been kept pretty busy dodging Mexican patrols. Santa Anna is still in San Antonio resting his men."

"Hmmm. I suppose that's why General Sesma hasn't attacked. He's camped right across the Colorado, about two miles above us," Sam said, nodding toward the river just to the west of camp.

"Yeah, I know. I almost ran into one of his patrols when I swam my horse across."

"According to a dispatch I received from President Burnet, Santa Anna sent Gaona and his division northeast to Bastrop as well. When he got word that the Mexicans were in Bastrop, just sixty miles from Washington-on-the-Brazos, he and the rest of the provisional government hightailed it east to Harrisburg. He wants me to abandon my plans and proceed there to protect the government personnel."

Conn grimaced. He had never liked David Burnet. He was a dour, straitlaced man who carried a Bible in one pocket of his black coat and a pistol in the other. Burnet made no bones about his dislike for Sam or his hard-drinking, hard-swearing ways, but in Conn's opinion, even dead drunk, Sam was ten times the man Burnet was.

He cocked a brow at his friend and commanding officer. "Are you going to?"

"I think not. I have more pressing concerns than saving David Burnet's hide. Such as winning this war." With a wry smile he dismissed President Burnet as easily as he would a pesky mosquito.

General Houston's expression turned grim. "The men are expecting to stand and fight Sesma here, you know."

"You can't blame then, Sam. Not after the Alamo."

"Yes, I know. But I can't allow it. We'll have to keep retreating and wait for the right opportunity."

"What if the men won't do it?"

"They'll retreat, by God, if I tell them to!" Sam blustered. "I'll personally shoot the first man who refuses."

Both men knew it might come to that, but neither voiced the thought. "Dammit, Conn, we're not ready," Sam continued with only slightly less heat. "We're picking up more men all the time. We have over seven hundred now. But they're untrained and undisciplined, and we're still woefully outnumbered. If we fight now, we'll lose, and the men of the Alamo will have died for nothing."

Sam rubbed his neck tiredly and gazed into the distance. "One hundred and eighty-three brave men against an enemy of more than four thousand." He shook his head, a look of respectful awe on his worn face. "They fought the Mexicans off for twelve days, Conn, but they never stood a chance. Yet from the first, Santa Anna refused them quarter. With that barbaric act he has made one thing clear. We Texans are no longer fighting for our rights as citizens of Mexico. This struggle has become a matter of independence, or extinction."

In taut silence the two big men regarded each other, absorbing the dark implications of their situation. The lone candle on the camp table flickered and cast wavering shadows. Outside, the rain fell in blowing gusts, pelting the canvas shelter like pea gravel. The dank, cold air inside the tent smelled of mud and candle wax and wet wool and buckskin.

After a moment Conn nodded. "What do you want me to do, General?"

Sam Houston sighed. "To tell you the truth, my friend, I had intended, despite our army's shortcomings, to make a stand here. But then I was counting on Fannin to arrive with his four hundred men. I've recently received word that General Urrea has him surrounded and cut off from water, six miles out of Goliad on an open plain. He's being battered by a force of fourteen hundred. I want you to go down there and assess the situation. Find out what's happened to him and his men and report back to me. I know I've been pushing you hard, Conn, and I wouldn't ask it if I had anyone else to send, but all the other scouts are out."

"That's all right, I'll go. Anything else?"

"When you get back I want you to return to exactly what you've been doing. What you did last fall." General Houston moved back to the camp table that served as his desk and thumped the map spread out there with his meaty fist. "I need to know Santa Anna's every move and those of his generals commanding other divisions. We're outnumbered and out-gunned. We can't let them outmaneuver us. It's looking more and more as though those men out there are all we've got, Conn," he said with a sweeping gesture toward the dismal, waterlogged camp outside the tent. "We won't be able to lose a battle, then fall back and regroup and fight again. This war is going to be won or lost in the next battle. When that time comes, I intend to choose when and where we fight.

"When the conflict is joined you can rest assured that Santa Anna will be leading the attack. His ego will demand it. I want you to watch him closely and keep me informed whenever he makes a move."

Sam sighed heavily. "But first, I must know what has happened to Fannin."

Conn nodded. "I'll leave for Goliad this evening, General, as soon as I've had a few hours sleep."

"Good, good. I knew I could count on you. Now you go and get some rest. Oh, by the way," he added when Conn turned to go. "Your father is here. He and a small group of men joined us when we came across the Colorado at Burnham's Crossing. Since December he's been down in Victoria, helping to treat an outbreak of cholera. I just thought you'd like to know."

Relief flooded Conn. Since hearing the awful news he'd carried deep within him a fear that his father might have returned to the Alamo in response to Travis's impassioned appeal for reinforcements. Flashing the general one of his rare smiles, Conn murmured, "Thanks," and ducked out into the steady downpour.

He found his father in a small tent, made from one of the canvas wagon tops they'd used coming west. The two embraced enthusiastically and thumped one another on the back, grinning like fools and saying with their eyes what neither could put into words. When at last they settled down to talk, sitting cross-legged on their bedrolls, each voiced the same concern simultaneously.

"I hope Elizabeth—"

"Have you seen Eliza—"

Self-conscious, they chuckled, then fell silent. Joseph cocked his head to one side and studied his son, but Conn did not meet his eyes.

"You love her, don't you?" he asked quietly.

Conn shifted. "Of course I love Elizabeth," he said with a too casual shrug. "I've always loved her."

"That's not what I mean, and you know it."

That earned him an annoyed look, but Joseph persisted. "Before this trouble started you were happier and more at peace than I've ever seen you. I think the reason was that little slip of a female you're trying so hard not to love. What I want to know is, why?"

"Dammit! How can I love her so soon after Millie?"

"Soon?" Joseph looked puzzled. "My boy, it's been over a year and a half since Millie died."

"But you don't understand! These . . . these *feelings* I have for Elizabeth have been there from the beginning. I loved Millie. I did!" he insisted furiously. "So how the hell could I fall in love with another woman that quickly? What's more, a woman who's nothing at all like her?"

"Ahhh, so that's it. Son, you have no reason to feel guilty—about Millie's death, or about your feelings for Elizabeth. You loved Millie with the hot passion of youth. What you feel for Elizabeth is a man's love. That's deeper, truer. It's something that'll last right through your rocking chair days. Enjoy it. You're cheating yourself, and Elizabeth, too, if you don't."

"Are you all right?"

Elizabeth swallowed hard and tore her eyes away from the swift-running waters of the Brazos. Shifting in the saddle, she peered at Hester from the depths of her enveloping slicker. "Yes. I—I'm fine."

It was a lie, and they both knew it. Her back ached abominably, she was chilled to the bone and terrified of crossing that rain-swollen river. The only thing that terrified her more was the enemy pursuing them.

"Don't you at least want to get into the wagon to cross?"

"I will when we board the ferry." She had to shout to be heard. All around them animals shifted restlessly and people clamored and cursed and tried to crowd into the line of rigs waiting to board the ferry. Adding to the din was the freezing rain, which came down in sheets, splattering in the puddles and the mud and drumming against the canvas wagon tops and her slicker with a deafening racket.

Elizabeth forced herself to look at the river again. She shivered and clenched her jaw. She had to do this. She had to. These people were depending on her.

She glanced worriedly back at the six wagons following Hester's and the pitiful bunch of people slogging along beside them through the mud and wet. There hadn't been enough time to get the rest of the wagons ready and packed. Of these, only four contained provisions. The other two were being used primarily to carry the old folks and the small children. Everyone else had to walk.

The decision to leave the rest of their good riding and work stock behind had been a difficult one, but in early spring forage on the road was sparse, and Elizabeth didn't feel she'd had any choice. With so many people streaming eastward, it was going to be difficult enough just to feed the mules they were using and her horse.

Elizabeth prayed she would be able to feed the people as well. All together they numbered sixty-four, not counting Hester and her three children. At the rate they were traveling, what she'd managed to bring wouldn't last until they could get across the Sabine. It had been a week since she'd read General Houston's dispatch, and they hadn't even crossed the Brazos yet.

She and Hester had agreed weeks ago that if it turned out they had to flee, they would travel together, and Elizabeth had delayed a day and a half, waiting for her. The rains had turned the ground into a sea of mud, and it had taken them another three days just to reach the ferry crossing at San Felipe. There they'd found a throng of refugees trying to get across, and they'd had to wait another two days for their turn.

At least now they were next in line, Elizabeth thought as the oxcart ahead of them rumbled onto the ferry. Her heart thrummed and her stomach knotted. She watched the log craft bob and lurch across the swollen river. All too soon it was back.

Determined to set an example for the frightened women and children in her care, instead of huddling inside one of the wagons as she had done on the trip from Charleston, Elizabeth made the crossing standing next to her lead rig, holding on to the front wheel with a death grip. Despite the cold, perspiration ran down her spine in rivulets, and she was so numb with terror that she could not move. When they reached the other side she promptly lost the contents of her stomach, but she didn't care. For once she had crossed a river without cringing, and without hysterics.

Intent on putting as many miles behind them as they could before dark, they pushed on across the prairie, struggling at a snail's pace through the mud and mire and icy rain. Ahead and behind them, an unending stream of refugees did the same. Mostly they were women and children and a few men too old or too crippled to fight.

By unspoken agreement, after an hour or so they began to break up into smaller groups, and as darkness came Elizabeth and Hester found themselves guiding their wagons into a protective camp circle with eight or nine other rigs beside a small stream.

"I wonder if we know any of these people?" Hester mused as Ebon lifted Elizabeth down from her horse.

"Mmm, maybe." Rubbing the small of her back, Elizabeth fell into step beside her friend. They had barely gone six paces when a man stepped out from behind one of the wagons into their path.

"Evening, ladies."

Both women jerked to a halt.

"Garth! What are you doing here?" Elizabeth gasped.

"I'd like to know that, too," Hester added aggressively, taking a protective step closer to Elizabeth. "You don't look old or infirm to me, so why aren't you with the troops?"

Garth smiled, not in the least ruffled. "Ah, well, you see, Mrs. Grimes, I don't happen to be a sucker for a lost cause.

And at the moment I'm busy escorting the Guettermans to safety. I'm their overseer now." He gestured toward a wagon on the opposite side of the small circle, where a familiar stout figure minced through the mud with her skirts held aloft. Lisa followed behind her mother, doing the same. Even from that distance they could hear the two women's whining complaints.

Garth observed Elizabeth's and Hester's appalled expressions, and his smile stretched into a grin. "Looks like we'll be traveling together, ladies. It'll be just like old times."

A sick sensation settled in the pit of Elizabeth's stomach. An instant later it turned to fury when she noticed Garth staring at one of the women in their group and the fair-skinned toddler she carried on her hip.

"Well, I see Latice dropped her brat," he noted callously. Showing no more interest in the child he had fathered than if the little boy had been a stray dog, Garth switched his attention to Lottie, and his black eyes glittered between narrowed lids.

Elizabeth saw red. "I'm warning you, Mr. Lathom," she bit out through clenched teeth. "You stay away from me and my people. If you lay a hand on any of us, so help me I'll shoot you." Throwing open the front of her slicker, she made a show of thrusting her hand into the deep pocket of her apron and gripping the bottle of peppermint tea she carried to relieve her heartburn, praying he would think it was a pistol.

It wasn't the contents of her pocket that riveted Garth's attention, however, but the swollen mound beneath the apron. Elizabeth hadn't thought it was possible, but his grin grew nastier. "Well, well, well. So Cavanaugh managed to plant one in your belly before he took off to play soldier."

Hester took a threatening step toward him. "You shut your filthy mouth and get on outta here, you polecat, before I take Elizabeth's gun and shoot you myself. Now git!"

"All right, all right. I'm going. But you ladies just remember, I'm here if you need me for anything." Smiling, he tipped his hat and sauntered off, leaving Elizabeth and Hester gritting their teeth.

"Of all the rotten luck," Hester spat. "We're stuck not only with that wretch, but with Agatha and Lisa Guetterman, too."

Elizabeth remained quiet, watching the arrogant man stroll to the other side of the circle, and Hester looked at her curiously. "Tell me, are you really carrying a gun in your pocket?"

"No," Elizabeth said in a quiet, determined voice. "But I will be from now on."

He waited patiently. From within the concealing clump of mesquite he wasn't visible even to someone traveling on the road winding around the base of the hill, a hundred yards below. It was impossible for anyone in Goliad to spot him. Nevertheless, he stood as still as stone. His sorrel was hidden in a cedar break farther around the hillside and about twenty yards below.

With their weight braced on a low branch, Conn kept the field glasses trained on the fort entrance a mile and a quarter away. The Mexican farmer had told him that General Urrea was to march Fannin and his men to Copano Bay that morning and put them on ships bound for the States.

A week before, the same day Conn had left the Colorado for Goliad, Fannin had surrendered to the Mexican general on the promise that he and his men would be treated with honor and sent to the States. According to what Conn had learned, Fannin and his officers had done so only to save his wounded.

After looking over the battle site, Conn felt he'd had no choice, surrounded out in the open that way, with no water and no chance of escape. What he couldn't figure out was why the devil Fannin had allowed himself to get in that situation in the first place. If he had obeyed Sam's orders promptly, he wouldn't have.

The front gate of the fort swung open, and Conn tensed. He pressed the field glasses tighter against his face. A platoon of soldiers marched out at the head of a two-abreast column of buckskin-clad men. On either side, at barely four-foot intervals, marched a guard.

They're not taking any chances, Conn thought as the column headed his way.

Whoa, what was this?

After a hundred and twenty or so men had emerged, the column broke off and the second group headed in a different direction, toward the lower ford of the river. After a while another group broke off and marched for the San Patricio road.

Conn frowned. He didn't like it. If they were all going to Copano, why take three different routes?

The last two columns quickly disappeared from sight. Conn trained the field glasses on the group approaching his position on the road to San Antonio. He gradually began to make out individuals. Slowly he scanned down the length of the column. His search moved past a young man dressed in homespun, then he stopped and swung the glasses back, and his heart leaped. My God! It was Johnny Grimes!

Conn kept the glasses trained on the boy. As the column came closer he could see Johnny's face. He was dirty and disheveled, and scraggly peach fuzz grew along his jaw, but he looked happy. He laughed at something the man next to him said and marched along jauntily. Conn grinned. Ah, the resilience of youth; the boy was already smelling salt sea air and freedom.

A quarter of a mile before they drew even with Conn's position, the officer in front of the column called a halt. Immediately the guards on the far side of the column, next to the river, filed around to the near side and formed an almost solid line facing the men. Conn frowned. What the—

Heavy musketry sounded in the distance from the direction the other two columns had taken. One of the Texans yelled something. At once the line of Mexican guards raised their weapons and fired.

Conn jerked back. *Jesus!*

His heart clubbed. He lowered the field glasses and stared, his mouth open, his face drained of color.

The column of men lay crumpled, their life's blood pouring into the dirt road. A few men on the back side of the column who had miraculously escaped serious injury bolted for the river. The Mexicans took off after them, running right over the fallen Texans. Conn could not take his eyes from Johnny.

Get up. Get up, dammit! Get up and run!

He screamed the words in his mind, but Johnny did not move. Neither did Conn. He stood there, gasping for air, his chest heaving as if he'd just run five miles, unable to look away from the gory sight. Vaguely he heard the distant shouts of the soldiers, the musket fire, the screams of the fleeing men they bayoneted and shot. He was aware that a few of the men managed to jump into the river and swim to the other side, but little registered other than that long line of crumpled bodies.

Conn had no idea how long he stood there. It could have been hours. It could have been minutes. He gradually became aware that the soldiers were returning from the river. Then they began to stack the bodies, working in pairs, grabbing arms and legs and slinging them into piles like cordwood. When they broke out shovels and started digging a trench, Conn turned and stumbled away toward his horse.

He didn't bother to be careful; it didn't occur to him. He skirted around the hillside and staggered and stumbled down the incline to where his horse was tethered to a cedar tree. He unlooped the reins and grasped the saddle horn to mount, but instead he leaned his forehead against the saddle.

God in heaven, how was he going to tell Liam? And Hester? How was he going to tell Rachel?

An enormous shudder rippled through him. Then he turned away and retched.

A steady drizzle fell. Elizabeth rode with her head lowered, trying to keep the rain out of her eyes. The tiny beads of moisture gathered in rivulets and streamed down her slicker.

Drops fell in a steady *plop-plop* off her visor and from around her face. Her back hurt. Her bottom hurt. Her ankles were swollen. She was cold, and miserable, and frightened. *Oh, Conn. Where are you?*

Had he perished at the Alamo? Elizabeth shivered and squeezed her eyes shut. No. She couldn't think about that. She'd go mad if she did. For her child's sake, she had to believe he was alive. She turned her head and looked to the rear through the gray mist. He had to be back there somewhere. He had to be.

But so was Santa Anna. The day before, during a brief time of no rain, they'd seen black smoke rising on the western horizon. Garth had said it was the Mexicans burning homesteads. Taw had not disputed him, so she knew it was probably true. She wondered if Riverbend was still standing.

The wagons rocked along beside her, the wheels squishing and splashing across the soggy prairie. The mules strained to pull the load, sinking into the mud. Even Thistle's hooves made a sucking sound with each dainty step.

"Elizabeth! Elizabeth! You'd better come see about Taw," Rachel called from the back of the lead wagon. "I think his fever is up again."

"Ebon, stop the wagon," Elizabeth ordered as she drew in her horse. Abram, one of the field hands, rushed forward to help her from the saddle, and when she waddled over to the tailgate, he lowered it and gave her a boost up. As she climbed awkwardly to her feet and stepped into the wagon, thunder rolled in the southwest.

Rachel stood beside Taw's bed, looking worried. She already had Elizabeth's doctor bag in her hand. Elizabeth smiled and patted the girl's shoulder as she took it from her.

The change in Rachel was truly amazing. She had been wonderful ever since they had left Riverbend, pitching in to help with whatever was needed without even being asked, never complaining, looking after the children and the sick ones.

And there had been plenty of those. Besides Taw, seven others in the group they were traveling with were down with a fever.

Taw's brow was hot and dry when she laid the back of her hand on it. He opened his eyes at her touch.

"Now, Missy, don't be fussin'."

"It's time for another dose of medicine, Taw."

"Oh, Lord a' mercy, not more quinine," he complained weakly.

"I'm afraid so. Now be a good boy, and take it without a fuss this time."

She poured a cup of water from the jug and stirred in the powder. Slipping her arm beneath his shoulders, she lifted him up and held the cup to his lips. He drank it down in two big gulps and made a horrible face. As Elizabeth lowered him gently she paused and cocked her head.

"My goodness. I've never heard thunder rumble on that way before."

Taw opened his eyes and listened for a moment. The sound rolled on and on without stopping, a low roar, growing gradually louder. "Missy, that ain't thunder," he said, and something in his tone sent alarm streaking through her.

Elizabeth looked at him, her heart picking up speed. "Then what is it?"

"Buffalo."

"What?"

"That's a herd o' buffalo. A big 'un. An' it's comin' this'a way."

"Oh, my Lord!"

Rachel let out a little scream, and Elizabeth hurried out onto the tailgate. She looked southwest toward the sound and sucked in her breath. Coming through the distant haze was an undulating dark blob, growing ever larger and wider.

Elizabeth put her hand over her mouth and stared. Behind her, Rachel began to cry.

"Get the wagons in a circle, Missy," Taw called weakly. "Hurry, now."

Elizabeth scrambled to obey. "Abram, bring me my horse! Ebon! Form a circle! Form a circle!" she cried as she remounted Thistle. She dug her heel into the mare's flank and took off down the line of wagons at a gallop, shouting, "Form a circle! Buffalo are coming! Form a circle, and everybody get inside! Hurry!"

All those on foot started to run, shrieking and crying, their eyes wild with panic. The drivers slapped the reins and startled the mules into a run. In the lead, Ebon hauled back on the left rein and started around in a curve. The other five Riverbend wagons and Hester's one followed, lurching and swaying over the spongy earth, and drew up into a tight circle. "Now everyone get inside!" Elizabeth shouted. "Quickly, quickly."

Elizabeth's group had been lagging behind when she'd stopped to doctor Taw, and now the Guettermans and the others were far ahead. She didn't stop to see how they were faring but guided Thistle in between two rigs into the circle and slipped from the saddle before anyone could assist her. When her feet hit the ground she stumbled to her knees but quickly picked herself up and ran for Taw's wagon.

The roar was growing louder. Beneath her feet, the earth vibrated. As she scrambled onto the tailgate she paused to look southwest, and her eyes dilated. The herd raced toward them, like a black sea spreading over the land. She could make out the lead animals, great shaggy beasts pounding toward them with their peculiar up-and-down gait.

"Taw! They're heading straight for us! What can we do?"

"They spook easy, Missy. Git out some blankets an' wave 'um as hard as you can."

She turned and shouted to the others, "Everyone get a blanket and shake it at them! Hurry! You drivers hold those teams steady!"

Elizabeth snatched blankets from a trunk. She thrust one

into Rachel's hands. "Here, go stand up there with Ebon and flap this thing."

"Me! But, Elizabeth, I'm scared! What if—"

"Just *go!*" Elizabeth yelled, and gave the girl a shove. Taking another blanket, she rushed back out onto the tailgate. The buffalo were within fifty yards. All around, women and children screamed, but all that could be heard was the deafening pound of thousands of hooves. The ground shook and the wagons vibrated and swayed. Elizabeth popped the blanket with all her might. All around the south side of the circle men and women followed her lead, waving blankets, sheets, aprons, petticoats, whatever they could get their hands on.

The buffalo kept coming. Elizabeth was sure they would all be trampled to death, but about twenty yards from the wagons the great beast leading the herd veered off, and the others followed, flowing around them like water seeking its course.

The mules brayed and danced in the traces, eyes rolling. The drivers fought to keep them from bolting.

Elizabeth went right on waving and flapping the blanket. Strung out to the south as far as the eye could see and about a mile wide, there was nothing but dark, shaggy bodies . . . running . . . running . . . running. They came by for almost two hours, never slackening the pace. By the time the last straggler pounded past, Elizabeth felt as though her arms were about to fall off.

As the rumbling roar receded into the distance, her shoulders drooped and she sagged against the back wagon bow, leaning her forehead against the slat of oak. The sodden blanket slipped from her grasp. All around it grew quiet, except for the keening wail of a baby and the soft whimpers of small children. Elizabeth wanted to curl up and go to sleep and forget there was a world and people depending on her. Oh, God, she was so tired.

"Mama! Mama!" Ian cried as he and Faith scrambled up onto the wagon and threw their arms around her.

Elizabeth put an arm around each child and pressed their tear-streaked faces against her body. She could feel the tremors that quaked through them and held them tight.

"I thought we was gonna die," Faith gulped.

So had Elizabeth, but she would not tell them that. She stroked the top of Faith's head. "No, sweetheart. It was just scary, that's all."

"Lawd a' mercy, jist lookit that," someone murmured in an awe struck voice.

Wearily Elizabeth raised her head, and what she saw made her heart sink.

Where the buffalo had passed, the prairie looked as though it had been plowed. Thousands of hooves had churned up the soggy ground until not a blade of grass could be seen over a mile-wide swath that angled across their path.

On the other side, huddled together in a bunch, were the rest of their party. Many were standing outside their wagons, looking back and waving their arms. Elizabeth had no fear that they would go on without them. Too many were sick, and she was the closest they had to a doctor.

Elizabeth stared at the bare earth. Even as she watched, the clods grew shiny and turned to mud in the drizzle. Weeks of rain had saturated the ground. The going had been difficult before, but at least the prairie grass had provided some support for the wagons. They would sink down to the axles in that mire.

"What're we gonna do, Miz Liz'beth?" Ebon asked.

Elizabeth closed her eyes briefly. How many times had she heard that question in the last few months? She allowed herself one deep sigh, then squared her shoulders. There was nothing for it; they had to keep going. To the rear, black smoke billowed on the horizon again.

"You children go stay with Taw," she said, and shooed them inside. She got down from the wagon and remounted Thistle. Then she looked at Ebon and ordered, "I want you to get some men to help you and knock eight boards off each wagon."

"Miz Liz'beth! What for you—"

"We're going to wedge them under the wheels and use them for support runners," she told him.

His eyes widened. "You mean . . . all the way acrost that mushy prairie?"

"That's right."

Mumbling and looking at her askance, the men obeyed.

When the boards were ready, at Elizabeth's instructions the line of wagons moved up to the torn-up strip of prairie. There the men wedged a board under the front of each wheel, and the wagon moved forward onto them. Then they positioned the second set of boards in front of the first, and the procedure was repeated.

The six wagons behind did the same.

Slowly, a few feet at a time, they began to make their way across the mire.

Chapter 24

Conn rounded the bend at full gallop. Ahead, through the driving rain, he could see that the house was dark, but he urged his horse on at the same reckless speed, pulling up at the last possible instant.

"Elizabeth!" Conn flung himself from the saddle while the lathered horse was still in motion and raced for the veranda. He took the steps in one leap and burst through the double front doors, sending them crashing back against the wall on either side.

"Elizabeth! Where are you!" he yelled, but the words bounced back at him. He stood in the dark, his chest heaving, water streaming from his soaked buckskins onto the polished wood floor of the entry hall, straining for some sound, some word of reply; but all he heard was his own harsh breathing.

He fumbled for the candle table that stood to the right of the door, but his hand encountered only air where it should have been. Cursing, he finally located a wall sconce and removed the tall taper, lighting it with a match from the small tin he carried inside his shirt.

Holding the candle high, he walked through the house, a feeling of despair and amazement filling him as he moved from room to room. Except for the piano in the front parlor and a few small, unimportant items—a rickety table, a couple of footstools, some bric-a-brac—the house was empty.

Elizabeth must have hidden it all, he realized. She couldn't have taken everything with her.

Conn thought of the sights he'd seen in the past weeks while galloping back and forth across Texas. He'd passed scores of abandoned homesteads. The houses had been left standing open, the beds unmade, food still on the tables, pails of milk molding in the dairies. The frightened civilians had left cribs full of corn, smokehouses full of bacon, yards full of chickens that had run after him, clucking for food. There had been nests of eggs in every fence corner, young corn and gardens full of vegetables . . . all abandoned.

But his plucky little wife, the woman he'd thought helpless, had not let herself be caught unawares. Pride swelled within him, but it did nothing to ease his fear.

Houston and the Texas troops had not been camped on the east bank of the Colorado River, where he'd left them two weeks before. He had not really expected them to be. When he'd ridden eastward looking for them, he'd begun to encounter the legions of frightened refugees. They trudged eastward in a solid, sodden stream, most of them women and children, struggling through the mud and rain, many of them ill, almost all poorly equipped for travel. Their suffering had been enough to bring tears to a man's eyes.

Now his wife was out there somewhere among them, with three children and a crippled-up old man and almost sixty blacks—all depending on her.

Conn blew out the candle and walked out into the rainy night. Astride his horse, he paused and stared eastward. He thought of how far it was to the Sabine. He thought of how many dangers there were. Then he thought about all the rivers there were to cross. *Oh, Elizabeth.*

Conn made it back to the Texas camp, across the Brazos from Jared Groce's plantation, around eleven. Several men were still up, huddled around the sputtering fires, grumbling among themselves.

Joseph looked up as Conn ducked into the tent, but he

merely nodded and dumped his bedroll and wet saddle on the ground cloth. Conn wasn't surprised to find his father awake, reading by the light of a single stubby candle.

"Well? What did you find?" Joseph asked as Conn stretched out on his blanket and rested his head on his clasped hands.

"They're gone."

"I told you they would be. So did General Houston. He sent out the warning weeks ago." When Conn made no comment Joseph added, "Sam wasn't pleased with the way you hightailed it out of here."

"Too bad. I gave him the information." By the time he'd found the Texas camp, late in the afternoon, his gut had been eaten up with worry. The scene he'd witnessed at Goliad had driven home to him just what kind of monster they were dealing with. It terrified him to think of Elizabeth and his family out there, alone, at the mercy of the Mexicans and God alone knew what else. Whether or not he held on to Riverbend no longer seemed important. All he cared about now was keeping his wife and family safe.

He'd galloped into camp and stopped only long enough to report the massacre and to break the sad news about Johnny to Liam. Then he had informed Sam that he was riding to Riverbend. Sam and his father had shouted after him that he was wasting his time, but he'd ignored them. He'd had to see for himself.

The two men fell silent, and there was only the sound of the rain pattering on the canvas. "I went over to see Liam after you rode off," he father said finally. "He's taking Johnny's death hard."

"I know." Conn stared at the canvas overhead. Telling Liam had been the hardest thing he'd ever done. At first he wouldn't accept that Johnny was gone.

"But . . . maybe he got away." Frantic, Liam had grabbed Conn's shirtfront, his eyes desperate, pleading. "You said yourself that some ran and swam the river, didn't you? One of them could have been my Johnny."

"No, Liam." He'd gripped his friend's shoulders and given him a small shake. "Listen, to me. I saw Johnny. I saw him get shot and fall. He never got up again."

Conn closed his eyes, remembering the awful pain on Liam's face as belief had come. He'd looked like an old, broken man. Liam and Hester loved all of their children equally, but Johnny had been special—their firstborn, the sort of son to make you proud—kind, hardworking, honest, dependable. He would have made a fine man.

Liam's grief had been a terrible thing to see, and after his initial breakdown he had asked to be left alone, and Conn had respected his wishes.

Joseph shook his head sadly. "First the senseless slaughter at the Alamo, and now a massacre. The men are hopping mad, and they're sick of retreating. They want to stand and fight. Some are even openly doubting Sam's courage."

Conn snorted. "Sam's no coward. He knows what he's doing."

"I hope you're right." Joseph sent his son a worried look. "Because I'm not sure how much farther he can push those men out there. They volunteered to fight, not retreat."

Conn said nothing, and after a moment his father added, "There's a feeling growing that Sam should be ousted from command. A man named Mirabeau Lamar arrived in camp a few days ago with a plan to rally men to himself and march off to fight the Mexicans."

"What!" Conn came up off his back in one fluid roll, his expression thunderstruck. "Does Sam know about this?"

Conn never got a chance to find out. The next morning Sam promptly sent him back out to look for Santa Anna.

Two days later Conn watched from a stand of trees as the general arrived at the west bank of the Brazos River, across from the ashes that had been the town of San Felipe.

Conn smiled as, time after time, Santa Anna's attempts to cross the river were thwarted.

When General Houston had come through San Felipe a little over a week before on his way to camp at Groce's plantation, he had left Captain Moseley Baker and one hundred and twenty men to take up defensive positions on the river at San Felipe.

Baker and his men had burned the town to keep it from enemy hands, then retreated across to the east side of the river and taken every boat with them. Every time the Mexicans tried to launch a raft, old Moseley and his men picked them off with their long rifles like birds on a fence rail.

Santa Anna soon got impatient, and with about seven hundred and fifty men and a cavalry detachment, he turned south. Conn followed along on the east bank for another day, then doubled back to report to General Houston.

When he rode into camp two days later, he found a crowd of subdued men gathered. Curious, Conn rode closer and saw three fresh-dug, open graves. Spotting his father among the men, he nudged his horse over to his side and leaned down. "Who died?" he asked, keeping his voice low out of respect.

"No one, that I know of. General Houston ordered them dug."

At that moment Sam Houston emerged from his tent and stalked to the gaping holes. His steely gaze swept the crowd. "Men, I am told that evil-disposed persons have spread the rumor that I am going to march you clear to Louisiana. Some are doubting my honor and my courage. I have even heard that some would take over my command." His gaze locked on Mirabeau Lamar for a full thirty seconds. "Be warned, gentlemen. Anyone who attempts to beat for volunteers in my camp will be shot forthwith." He looked at the graves, looked back at the silent crowd, and turned on his heel and stalked into his tent.

Conn grinned down at his father, and as the stunned crowd drifted away, he nudged his horse and went to make his report.

* * *

Elizabeth had graves dug that day as well. A pitifully small one for Latice's baby and another for old Zena. They were shallow and water-filled, and there was not so much as a pine box for either. It broke Elizabeth's heart to lower them into the cold, wet ground wrapped only in threadbare blankets, but she had no choice.

The rain poured down as the men shoveled the muddy soil over the shrouds. As the women wailed and moaned Elizabeth stared at the two graves. The very young and the very old. The sickness that had swept through their number, the hardships they had to endure, took their harshest toll on both.

Which was why she'd been so worried about Taw. If she lost him, she didn't know how she would bear it. Thank God his fever had broken several days before. He was still weak, but he seemed to be on the mend.

When the graves were filled, they all walked back to the waiting wagons to resume their trek. Neither Elizabeth nor Hester talked. Her friend climbed back into the driver's seat of her rig and took up the reins, and the men and women of Riverbend took their places, but instead of mounting her horse, Elizabeth climbed into the wagon where Taw lay.

He was asleep, but she didn't care. She simply needed to be with someone. Tired and heartsick to the marrow of her bones, Elizabeth sank down on the floor of the wagon beside Taw's cot as Ebon clucked the mules into motion. The deaths ate at her. She felt that she had let Conn down, that somehow she should have been able to save them, done something different.

"Oh, Taw," she whispered, and leaned her forehead against the edge of his cot. "I'm so scared."

Then the tears came, silent and soul deep. Her shoulders shook and the scalding moisture flowed as fear and despair and utter weariness overwhelmed her.

Taw's huge hand cupped the crown of her head and rubbed gently. "You jist go 'head an' cry, Missy. God knows you gotta right."

* * *

The evening following the grave-digging episode a young boy came galloping into the Texans' camp "General Houston! General Houston! It's Santa Anna!"

From everywhere men came running, guns in hand, crowding around the boy as he leaped from his horse.

"Here, let me through! Move aside! Move aside, I say!" Sam's booming voice preceded him as he pushed his way through the crowd to the boy's side. "Here I am, son. Now calm down and give it to me slow. What's this about Santa Anna?"

"He crossed the Brazos down south at Fort Bend two days ago, sir. He's heading for Harrisburg to capture President Burnet and his cabinet. Then he plans to head back here and attack you."

"You sure about this, boy?"

"Yessir. My name's Joseph Powell. My maw's got a tavern down by Fort Bend, and she refused to leave it. Santa Anna rested his troops there, and I overheard him myself while I was serving him and his officers." The boy grinned slyly. "I didn't let on that I spoke Spanish."

Sam clapped the lad on the back. "Thank you, boy. You've done your country a great service."

When Conn had reported on Santa Anna's movements and the two scouts he'd sent north and south to General Gaona and General Urrea, he and Sam had figured the Mexican leader was going to concentrate his forces, then come after them. The move east with an army no larger than their own came as a surprise, a welcome one, for it was, Conn knew, the opportunity Sam had been waiting for.

General Houston looked around at his troops. "Get your gear together, men. We're pulling out."

No one moved.

"Where're we marching to?" one surly man asked.

Sam Houston's piercing gaze stabbed into the man. Several

tense seconds passed. "Southeast," he snapped, and stalked away without another word.

The men were not happy. They groused and cursed and speculated every step of the way. The rumor that Sam Houston was going to march them all the way to the Redlands in Louisiana persisted. "Southeast," many of the Texans grumbled, didn't necessarily mean they were marching to Harrisburg.

"We all joined up to fight for our rights and avenge our friends who died at the Alamo," one farmer griped loudly. "And all we've done for over five weeks is retreat. And drill," he added in outright disgust.

Riding alongside the marching men, Conn had to stifle a laugh. During the nine days the army had camped on the Colorado and the two weeks on the Brazos, Sam had worked desperately to instill discipline into his motley forces and train them in military tactics. He had kept patrols moving through the woods around the clock. He had maintained a strict sentry watch. He had drilled and redrilled the men, then drilled them some more.

No one but General Houston and a few officers had ever fought in formal warfare before. The rugged frontiersmen knew nothing of forming columns, or fighting in lines, or even obeying the commands of the officers. These men thought for themselves, acted on their own, and fought to win. All the foolish marching up and down and letting someone else tell you when to walk and when to stop and when to fire your gun stuck in their craw.

Besides, what good did it do to train if all you were going to do was retreat?

Several men swore aloud that if Houston did not stand and fight soon, they were leaving. They would follow no coward.

Conn knew that General Houston heard the comments and complaints. The men were so disgusted, they did not bother to keep their voices down. But Sam ignored them. He rode

at the head of the column on the big white stallion named
Saracen that he'd picked up on Groce's plantation, his expression unconcerned.

The road they were taking forked about forty-five miles
from Harrisburg; one branch led to Louisiana, the other to
Harrisburg and the enemy. As they approached the fork, one
of the general's own officers, Captain Moseley Baker, demanded
to know which one he planned to take. Sam ignored him as
well.

The dispositions of the troops worsened. Their grumbling
increased as they marched on sullenly, and almost to a man
they threatened to rebel if he attempted to lead them to the
Redlands. The tension mounted as they drew near the fork.
They were scarcely a mile from the spot where the road divided
when General Houston ordered a halt. All night the men
complained and wondered. By morning tempers and tension
were stretched tight. They fell in line to march the mile to
the fork, and every man watched Houston.

He mounted Saracen and led them out. He explained nothing, confided in no one. At the last moment he simply ordered,
"Company, ri-ight!" and sent his army down the Harrisburg
road.

The men hurried on, grumbling still but fired with renewed
spirit and anticipation. At last they were going to fight.

The screaming awoke Elizabeth. She jerked upright, the
hair on the back of her neck rising as the bloodcurdling sound
came again.

"What in the world!" Hester exclaimed.

"It sounds like a woman," Rachel said shakily from the
pallet she shared with Faith and Annabelle. At the front of
the wagon, Ian, who was bunking with Jeremy, began to
whimper.

"Elizabeth! You're not going out there!"

"Yes, I am. Someone's in trouble. You stay here, Rachel,

and look after the children." She was exhausted from her pregnancy, from five miserable weeks of travel, from nursing all the sick people in their group, but nevertheless she hauled her awkward, aching body from the bed. Hurriedly she pulled on her robe and snatched up the rifle she kept loaded by her side.

"Well, hold on. I'm coming with you," Hester muttered, but Elizabeth had already eased her ungainly body down from the wagon.

The hysterical screams continued as people tumbled from their wagons and carts or whatever shelter they had, in various stages of dress. "Oh, my Lord," Elizabeth gasped as Hester came running up behind her.

At the edge of the camp, an alligator waddled for the river, dragging a young Negro woman by the arm. He had obviously snatched her from the blankets where she slept, beneath one of the wagons.

"For God's sake! Do something!" Elizabeth shouted at Karl Guetterman and Garth, but the two men just stood staring, their jaws agape while around them women screamed and children cried.

"Help me! Help me! Oh, please, Lawd, somebody help me!" the terrified woman screamed.

"Elizabeth! Come back here! Are you crazy?"

It wasn't a conscious decision on Elizabeth's part. One moment she was standing watching the helpless woman being dragged away to her death and the next she was going after her. Her pregnancy made running difficult and ungainly, but the alligator was hampered by his victim's weight and frantic resistance. Elizabeth caught up with the beast a few yards from Buffalo Bayou. In midstride, as she lumbered alongside, she placed the muzzle of her rifle against the reptile's great head and pulled the trigger.

The powerful tail lashed, catching Elizabeth in the back of the legs and knocking them out from under her. The beast released the woman and cut loose with a deafening roar as it twisted toward Elizabeth. She screamed, expecting at any second to feel those monstrous jaw snap around her leg, but after only one step in her direction the beast collapsed. The long snout had barely hit the ground when Ebon came running up. Without hesitation he fired another ball into the massive head.

"You awright, Miz Liz'beth?" he asked worriedly, dropping down beside her.

Elizabeth nodded. She was shaking so hard, she couldn't speak. On the other side of the lifeless carcass Isaac and Jemma and several others were kneeling over the sobbing woman. Hester pushed her way through the gawking people and rushed to Elizabeth's side. Right behind her, Taw struggled along on his crutches.

"Oh, God, Elizabeth, are you hurt?"

She tried to reassure Hester with a smile, but she couldn't seem to make her lips work. "I . . . I'm fine."

"What about the baby?"

A look of horror flashed across Elizabeth's face, and she cradled her swollen abdomen with both arms. Her heart hammered so hard, it took a moment to realize that nothing felt amiss. "I . . . I don't think there's any problem."

Taw sagged on his crutches. "Tarnation, Missy, you scart me outta ten years' growth."

Hester would have preferred that someone carry Elizabeth back to the wagon, but she wouldn't hear of it. She'd no sooner gained her feet, with the help of her friend and Ebon, than Agatha came rushing forward.

"Elizabeth, I must protest. Don't you have any better sense than to allow this man to carry a weapon!" she huffed, casting an outraged glance at Ebon. "Why, he could kill us all in our beds!"

"You have nothing to fear, I assure you, Agatha," Elizabeth said wearily, and started for the wagon on decidedly shaky legs.

"Nevertheless, I must insist that you disarm your Negroes at once."

"Shoot, woman. Who you think shot the game you been eatin' this past week?" Taw demanded. "That man o' yorn is too lazy t' hunt, an' that polecat you call a overseer couldn't hit a bull in the rump with a shovel."

Agatha gasped and huffed, her ponderous bosom heaving like a smithy's bellows. "How dare you talk to me that way, you . . . you uncouth old ruffian!"

Elizabeth's nerves were raw, and over the past five wretched weeks she'd had all she could take of Agatha Guetterman. She rounded on the overbearing woman in a rare blaze of temper. "That is quite enough, Agatha! I trust Ebon and the other men from Riverbend a lot more than some others around here," she declared with a meaningful look toward Garth. "If that bothers you, then I suggest that you move on without us."

"Wh-why . . . you know we can't do that," Agatha sputtered. "My poor Lisa is sick! She needs your help! You know she can't be moved yet."

"Well, I'm glad you at least have the decency to admit that much," Hester snapped. "Elizabeth's been working herself into the ground nursing everyone who's took sick. Anyone else would have gone off and left you, but she wouldn't do that. If it hadn't been for your precious Lisa and a few others, we could be almost to the border by now. Instead here we sit, helpless as lambs with that monster Santa Anna and his butcher army just ten or so miles away on the other side of that bayou. If his patrols discover our camp, we're all gonna be buzzard bait."

Chapter 25

The Texans waited in the woods that lined the south bank of Buffalo Bayou. They looked out with hard eyes across the open plain of San Jacinto at the enemy's camp, their impatience building. Their two cannon, the ones the men had dubbed the *Twin Sisters,* were in place about ten yards out on the prairie.

The line of foot soldiers, two men deep, stretched nine hundred yards along the front of the woods. In the center of the line, the fledgling republic's flag fluttered: a plain white silk with a five-pointed blue star and the words *Ubi Libertas Habitat, Ibi Nostra Patria Est*—"Where Liberty Lives, There Is Our Homeland."

A mile away the Mexican soldiers rested behind the breast-works that they had labored all night to build, water-blocked on their right and to the rear by the San Jacinto River. Their only escape lay to the southwest, over Vince's Bridge, and the Texas cavalry had moved into position to block that route.

The sun arced high and warm toward the western horizon. A light breeze stirred the ghostly strands of Spanish moss in the live oak trees. It was a good day for a battle, Conn thought.

He looked around at his fellow Texans, and a hard smile curved his mouth. They were all unwashed and unshaved, their long hair and beards matted, their clothes in tatters and plastered with mud. A more savage-looking band he'd never seen.

General Houston, mounted on Saracen, rode out onto the plain in front of the woods. In silence he cantered the length of the line. Every man tensed. In front of the first regiment he stopped.

"Trail arms! Forward!" he called in his big, booming voice, and turned his horse toward the enemy.

They marched out silently, with the stealth of death. Save for the grunted oaths of the gunners dragging the heavy cannon across the rain-softened ground, and Houston's voice, held low, exhorting, "Hold your fire, men, hold your fire!" all was quiet.

Two hundred yards from the Mexican barricade, Houston signaled with a sweep of his battered campaign hat. The gunners wheeled the cannon and fired, shattering the somnolent quiet of the still afternoon.

Drums rolled. The fifers broke into a rousing tune. All down the line a roar went up as the dirty, ragged, enraged Texans broke into a run.

"Remember the Alamo! Remember Goliad!"

The cry spread down the lines until every Texan was pounding for the Mexican camp, shrieking the words at the enemy. The fury and frustration that had been building for weeks had reached fever pitch during the cautious stalk across the field, and the roar of the cannon had been like striking a spark to gunpowder.

Running full tilt with the screaming infantrymen, Conn tore across the plain for the pile of breastwork. His own blood-curdling war cry rose above the rest. Though one of only sixty-five or so men with a horse, Conn had elected to go in on foot with the first attack rather than wait on the right flank with the cavalry.

As he ran he thought of the abandoned homesteads. He thought of the years of toil and sweat every Texan had poured into the land. He thought of the suffering women, children, and old folks he'd seen on the roads. He thought of Jim Bowie being lifted on the bayonets of four Mexican soldiers . . . and a red rage filled him.

A bugle finally sounded in the Mexican camp, and the soldiers leaped up from their siesta, confused and groggy, horrified to find the howling Texas horde almost upon them.

"Halt! Halt and fire! Then charge!" Sam Houston bellowed. "If they're waiting, they'll cut you down like wheat unless you press them with rifle fire!"

But the Texans were not soldiers. Many, Conn included, felt they were too far away for their shots to be effective, and the rage boiling inside them demanded that every lead ball find a mark. They continued to run forward screaming their battle cry: *"Remember the Alamo! Remember Goliad! Remember the Alamo!"*

The Mexican gunners fired too late and too quickly. Grape screamed over the volunteers' heads. The Texas line wavered and spread, but the men kept running. Some of the enemy were firing on them now, but the main body of soldiers was trying desperately to assemble into disciplined order.

Suddenly Deaf Smith galloped down the length of the Texas line shouting, "Vince's Bridge is down! Fight for your lives! Vince's Bridge is down!"

Only hours before, General Cos had marched his men over that bridge, adding four hundred to Santa Anna's ranks. By destroying it, General Houston had made sure that no more reinforcements would be arriving and that the Mexicans' only means of escape was gone.

So, however, was the Texans', and the knowledge that they must now win, or die, fired the men even more. Every last trace of discipline vanished.

Before the Mexican bugler could sound the *Centinela Alerto*, the Texans were within range. Long rifles began to blaze, a tremendous staccato barrage. Eight hundred deadly marksmen left the ground littered with pale gray uniformed dead and dying. They fired as rapidly as they could, and as soon as a man reloaded he moved on without waiting for orders.

Conn was out in front, running, his heart pounding, in his mind the picture of Johnny Grimes's face when the musket balls struck him. Off to his right, Moseley Baker jerked to a halt in midstride and fell with his arms flung wide, a musket ball in his chest. Dr. William Mottley gave a groan and collapsed. Conn took aim and fired. He poured powder, dropped a ball, rammed it home, and took off again.

A few yards ahead, General Houston pointed toward the barricades with his saber. An instant later a volley of musket balls struck Saracen in the chest. As the big stallion collapsed beneath him, Sam stepped off.

Out on their right, Maribeau Lamar's cavalry had successfully routed the dragoons, and many riderless Mexican mounts caromed through the melee. A Texas man quickly caught one, and Houston remounted.

They hit the barricades headlong, smashing the flimsy fortifications apart. The Texans swarmed into the Mexican camp in a frenzy, rifles spitting death. Panicked, the Mexicans could not reload, could not regroup. The enraged Texans tore into their ranks with rifle butts and long knives and tomahawks.

Wild with fear, the Mexicans turned and ran.

The Texans ran after them.

Conn saw a Mexican colonel jerk one of his own men from a horse and climb aboard. Halting, he raised his Hawkin and took aim. The rifle boomed, and the colonel fell to the ground.

Conn reached for his powder horn, but as his hand touched it a searing pain struck his temple. He let out a sharp cry, and the Hawkin slipped from his hands. Groaning, he staggered to his knees, clutching his head. Men ran past. Shots rang out. Screams and shouts reverberated through his head.

The smell of blood filled his nostrils. As the world began to tilt and whirl, he realized it was his own.

Then everything went black.

Elizabeth heard a sound like thunder. Stepping down from the Guettermans' wagon, she paused to rub the small of her back and cast a puzzled glance at the sunny sky. She heard the sound again and realized it had come from across the bayou.

She froze, her hands still pressed against her arched back, and stared in that direction. A distant popping noise carried across the water. Elizabeth's heart began to slam against her ribs as though trying to beat its way out of her body.

Taw came hobbling up and stopped beside her. "That's a battle fer sure," he said somberly, confirming what she had already surmised but hadn't wanted to accept. He leaned on one crutch and lifted the other high, shaking it. "Give 'um hell, men! Give 'um hell!"

Elizabeth was more frightened than she'd ever been in her life. She'd had no idea the Texas troops were nearby. The group they were traveling with was camped on the north bank of Buffalo Bayou, near where it joined the San Jacinto River. Only two days before a man had crossed the bayou in a skiff with the bad news that Santa Anna was at Morgan's plantation, ten miles or so to the south.

She bit her lip and gazed worriedly across the sluggish water. Conn might be over there somewhere, fighting for his life. She hadn't seen him in five months, not since his brief return last November. Every day since, she'd wondered if she would ever see him again. If he's over there, please keep him safe, she prayed. Oh, please, God. Please.

Everyone came running. They stood together, staring across the bayou, their faces drawn and anxious, but all they could see were the trees lining the opposite bank. After scarcely twenty minutes, as suddenly as it had started, the cannonade stopped.

"Well, that's it. The Mexicans must have beat them. The Texans are too outnumbered to win that quickly." Garth smirked at Elizabeth. "I told you it was a lost cause."

A chorus of wails went up from the other women, but Elizabeth refused to accept his opinion. She turned to the old man at her side, her eyes beseeching. "Taw . . . ?"

Taw spit into the tall grass. His lips flattened into a grim line, disappearing within the white beard. "Well, Missy . . ." Hunched on his crutches, he hung his head, and when he finally met her gaze his faded old eyes held a forlorn look that tore at her heart.

"Oh, Taw, no. No!"

"We've got to get out of here!" Breaking away from the group, Garth raced toward where the animals were picketed, calling over his shoulder, "The mopping up won't take long, and then the Mexicans will be after us!"

The remark had the impact of a direct cannon shot. In a panic, the women and children scattered. Sobbing, they scrambled to gather their belongings and catch their stock and hitch them to whatever vehicle they had. Fires were doused. Children were tossed into wagons and carts like sacks of meal or taken up behind their mothers on trail-weary horses. The sick were offered curt apologies and told to hang on. In minutes they were on their way, whips cracking, urging the animals across a plain still covered with water and mud from the spring rains.

The animals could not keep up the frantic pace, nor could the people on foot, and before long they were forced to slow to a plodding walk. Still they kept going.

A cold numbness enveloped Elizabeth. She sat in the saddle staring straight ahead, her body swaying with the horse's rhythmic gait, a hollow ache where her heart should be.

They had been traveling a little over an hour when Isaac shouted a warning. "There's riders comin', Miz Liz'beth!"

Everyone craned around and saw two men galloping up behind them, shouting and waving their hats. Alarmed, they

whipped up their animals again, and the people on foot started
to run. But as the men drew nearer their words became dis-
tinguishable.

"Turn back! Turn back! The Texas army won! Turn back!"

"Whoa! Dammit, I said whoa!" Taw bellowed from the
back of one of the wagons. "Stop this thing! Cain't you people
hear? Our men have won!"

Shock, disbelief, and joy slammed through Elizabeth in
rapid succession. All around her people began drawing to a
halt. They tumbled from their rigs and ran back toward the
two men with glad cries on their lips and tears of happiness
streaming from their eyes. Even Taw joined the stampede,
thumping across the uneven ground at a reckless pace, his
body swinging between the crutches like a church bell on
Sunday morning. After a moment of stunned hesitation, Elizabeth nudged her horse and took off after them.

She reached the men just ahead of the crowd. Her eyes lit
up when she recognized one of them.

"Ben! Oh, Ben, is it really you?" she cried as he jumped
from the saddle and raced to her side.

"Elizabeth! Sweet Jesus, it's good to find you safe!" Laughing
exultantly, he lifted her from her horse and swung her in a
circle. "We won, Elizabeth! We won! The war is over!"

Her laughter blended with his, and when at last he sat her
on her feet she gripped his hands and looked up at him with
shining eyes, her expression brimming with eagerness. "Ben,
what about Conn? Have you seen him? Is he all right?"

The light in Ben's eyes faded a bit, but he smiled at her
with sad acceptance. "I haven't seen him since before the
fighting began. But don't worry. I'm sure he's all right. We
didn't have many casualties."

"Then he is with the army? You're sure?"

"Yeah. He's been scouting for General Houston. Why—
Elizabeth? What's wrong? Are you all right?" he asked quickly
when she closed her eyes and sagged with relief.

She looked up and gave him a fluttery smile, blinking back tears. "Yes. I'm fine. It's just that . . . I . . . I was afraid that . . . well, that maybe he'd been at the Alamo."

"Oh, Elizabeth," he said with heartfelt sympathy. "All this time you've been worried about that?"

"But not any more, thanks to you. Oh, Ben, I'm so glad to see you. Thank God you're all right."

"You too."

Ben stood back to look her over, and his attention was caught at once by the protruding mound beneath the loose folds of her wrapper. He looked up, his wistful smile tender. "Ah, Elizabeth. I knew you'd look beautiful like this. Does Conn know about the baby?"

"Not yet," she murmured, blushing.

"Ben Whitelaw! You scamp! I should've known you were too ornery for them Mexicans to kill," Hester yelled as she pounded toward them with her skirt held high. Laughing, Ben turned just in time to catch his sister up in his arms. Elizabeth stepped back and watched their joyful reunion with a shaky smile.

"How is Liam? And Johnny and Daniel?" Hester asked the instant they broke apart.

At once Ben's expression changed from joyous to somber, and Elizabeth's heart squeezed as a look of dawning horror came over her friend's face.

"Oh, dear God. It's Liam, isn't it?"

"No, no. Liam is fine. So is Daniel. But, Hes . . ." Ben gripped his sister's shoulders and grimaced. "Hes, Johnny was with Fannin at Goliad." Gasps went up all around, and Hester's face drained of color; they had heard about the massacre a few days before. "I'm sorry, Hes, but Johnny's dead."

With a groan, Hester burst into tears and collapsed against Ben's chest.

A few feet away, Rachel gave a single cry and crumpled to the wet ground.

* * *

Only two dead and twenty-six wounded. It was a miracle, Conn thought, watching his father and three other doctors move among the injured men. Especially when you considered that the enemy had lost six hundred. And at least that many more had been captured.

Even with their superior numbers and all their discipline and training, the Mexican soldiers had been no match for the ragtag band of enraged Texans. *Diablos Tejanos*. Devil Texans, the Mexicans had begun calling them after Travis and his men fought so ferociously at the Alamo. After today, Conn thought with grim satisfaction, they'd never doubt it.

Conn sat with his back against a stump, one forearm resting on his updrawn knee. Pike lay a few feet away with his snout on his paws, watching him. Hunger gnawed at Conn, but he was too exhausted to move. He fingered the bandage tied around his head. The wound on his temple wasn't much; the ball had only grazed him, but it sure made his head hurt like hell.

Conn's gaze switched to where Sam Houston lay stretched out beneath a tree, conferring with his officers. That he was one of their injured was not surprising. The man'd had two horses shot out from under him leading the attack. He'd promptly gotten off the second slain mount, climbed on another captured runaway Mexican horse, and kept right on fighting, while his boot filled with blood from the wound in his ankle. Conn's hard smile appeared. No one was accusing Sam of being a coward now.

"Hey, Cavanaugh!"

Conn turned his head and saw Thomas Purdy bearing down on him. He frowned; there was something about the man that rubbed him the wrong way. Still, he'd fought well. Conn nodded when he halted before him. "Tom."

"Glad I found you, Cavanaugh. I just came back from across the bayou. Thought you ought to know, your wife is over there."

"Elizabeth!" Conn came to his feet like an uncoiling spring. "Where?"

"Camped out on the plain over yonder. Me'n Ben Whitelaw took the general's dispatch to the civilians. Had to run her group down to give 'um the news. We escorted them back as far as their camp." He grinned and elbowed Conn in the ribs. "If I were you, I'd hightail it over there. Ben stayed—to comfort his sister, he said. But myself, I think he's sweet on your wife. She sure was powerful glad to see him, too."

The man's chuckle died in a choking sound under Conn's hard stare. "I'm grateful to know where Elizabeth is, Purdy," he said in a low, dangerous voice that had Pike rising to his feet. "But if you ever say anything like that about her again, I'll beat the living hell out of you."

Leaving the man gulping, Conn stalked away. The big dog growled at Purdy and trotted after him.

Conn ground his teeth. He trusted Elizabeth completely. She liked Ben, and she probably had been happy to see him. Whatever had passed between them, he knew that it had been perfectly innocent. But he didn't like the idea of a man—any man—mooning around after his wife. Elizabeth was *his,* dammit!

Conn cooled his heels for over an hour before he got to talk to Sam and get permission for him and his father to leave camp. Then it took another half hour to locate a canoe and paddle across the bayou, swimming his horse alongside. Two-thirds of the way across the animal balked and tipped them over. Joseph nearly lost his medical bag, and Conn hit his head on the paddle and scraped his shin on a submerged log. By the time he waded ashore, tired, dripping wet, limping, his head throbbing like hell, his dark mood had worsened.

"Has anyone seen Rachel?" Elizabeth asked.

"Nope. Ain't seen hide her hair o' her sinct Ben carried her t' the wagon."

"Me neither," Ben replied.

Hester shook her head and stared numbly into the fire.

"That's funny. I stopped by the wagon on my way back from looking in on Lisa and she wasn't there."

Elizabeth had tried to comfort Rachel when she recovered consciousness, hours earlier, but the girl had curled into a ball on her pallet and screamed that she wanted to be left alone. They all had honored her wishes for the past few hours, allowing her time to regain her composure, but Elizabeth felt it was time they had a talk; it wasn't healthy to grieve alone.

"She's at the dance."

The statement was muttered so softly, Elizabeth wasn't sure she'd heard right. She looked at Faith. "What did you say?"

The child sat on a box before the fire, her lowered gaze fixed on her fingers as they creased tiny pleats in her sprigged muslin skirt. At Elizabeth's question she shrugged her slender shoulders. "Rachel's at the dance," she repeated, only slightly more audibly.

The sound of boisterous music carried across the plain, and Elizabeth's horrified gaze snapped toward the torchlit area a few hundred yards away, where everyone had gathered to celebrate.

"At the *dance*!" Hester gasped.

"But . . . but that can't be! Not four hours ago she was crying her eyes out. She's devastated by Johnny's death!" Elizabeth knelt down beside Faith and took her hands, stopping the nervous pleating. "Sweetheart, you must be mistaken," she said gently. "What makes you think Rachel went to the dance?"

Faith raised her head and looked at Elizabeth, her big green eyes solemn and filled with reluctance. "I saw her leave the wagon wearing her best dress, with her hair done up all fancy, so I followed her." Her mouth worked, and tears gathered against her lower eyelids. "I was worried about her, Elizabeth. Truly I was! I wasn't trying to get her in trouble."

"I know, sweetheart. I know. And don't worry, Rachel isn't in trouble. I'm glad you told me."

"How could that girl do such a thing?" Hester raged. "I thought she loved my son. How can she sashay off to a dance just a few hours after hearing of his death?"

"Rachel doesn't know how to deal with grief, Hester. Remember how she reacted when her mother died? I imagine she's trying to escape the pain by pretending not to care." Rising clumsily, Elizabeth gave a weary sigh and started toward the music. "I'll go get her."

On the way, Elizabeth fluffed out the generous folds of her wrapper. A woman wasn't supposed to appear in public when she was increasing, and no doubt if Agatha spotted her, she would be scandalized, but the loose garment hid her condition fairly well. After the past five weeks it was a bit late to worry about that particular taboo anyway. Besides, she didn't intend to stay any longer than it took to find Rachel.

Elizabeth spotted her immediately. She had expected to find Rachel dancing. She hadn't expected to find her dancing with Garth.

As her stepdaughter whirled by, laughing up gaily into his leering face, Elizabeth saw red. She didn't wait for the music to stop. Jaw set, she marched out among the dancing couples.

Rachel let out a shriek when Elizabeth grabbed her wrist and snatched her out of Garth's arms, but she ignored the protest and gave the girl a shake for good measure. "What on earth do you think you're doing? Have you completely lost your mind? It's bad enough that you're even here, but to dance with this . . . this . . . vermin is inexcusable!" She tugged on the girl's arm. "Come on."

"Let go of me!"

"Oh, no. You're coming with me, young lady. Right now."

"No! I won't go. You have no right—"

"No right?" Elizabeth whirled on the girl, full of righteous anger, the temper she hadn't known she possessed bursting

forth like water through a breaking dam. "I have every right!
You are a minor, and until your father returns you are in my
care. You may think you're grown-up, but your behavior tonight proves otherwise."

"Now wait—"

"Shut up, Garth! You're lucky I haven't put a bullet in you.
I will yet if you come near this girl again."

Grinning, Garth assumed a cocky stance. "What's the matter, Elizabeth? Jealous?"

Elizabeth barely restrained herself from hauling off and driving her fist into his smirking face. Her gaze raked him con-
temptuously. "I'd rather lie down with swine than be touched
by the likes of you."

Garth stiffened. His black eyes narrowed coldly, but Elizabeth ignored him and turned back to Rachel. "You have two
choices. You can come with me now, or I'll send Ben with
orders to pick you up and carry you back if he has to."

"You wouldn't!"

"Oh, yes, I would. You've made a spectacle of yourself
simply by being here. If you don't care about your reputation,
why should I?"

Fuming, Rachel darted a look around. Already they were
drawing stares from the other dancers. "Oh, all right!" she
snapped, snatching her wrist free. "I'll go. But my papa's
going to hear about this!"

Elizabeth struggled for patience. For the last year or so
things had improved between her and Rachel. Rachel had even
accepted the coming baby without a fuss, and on this trip
she'd been a model of cooperation, pitching in to help without
complaint. Elizabeth didn't want to do anything to jeopardize
their tenuous new relationship, but she couldn't just ignore
the incident.

There was no talking to the girl, however. Every step of
the way back to their camp Rachel vented her outrage, heaping
insults and complaints on Elizabeth.

"Don't you understand? Tonight you hurt not just yourself, but Hester, too. I know you think that by denying Johnny—"

"I told you I don't want to talk about Johnny!" Rachel shrieked, turning on Elizabeth as they reached the camp. "Not now! Not ever! So just leave me alone!"

Only Taw and Faith remained by the fire. The old man spat and shook his shaggy head. Faith scuttled into the shadows and tried to make herself invisible.

"Rachel, dear, listen to—"

"No! I won't listen! I hate you!"

Conn's mood turned from black to livid when he and his father walked up on the scene. It was the last straw. Flinging down the reins, he ground-hitched his horse and strode into the firelight. "What in hell is going on here?"

Chapter 26

Elizabeth whirled, her face lighting. "Conn!"

She started toward him, but Rachel got there first and flung herself into her father's arms. "Oh, Papa! Papa, I'm so glad you're back. Elizabeth is being so mean to me!"

"Rachel, stop this. You know that's not tr—"

"That's enough! Quiet! Both of you!"

Elizabeth jumped at Conn's angry shout. Turning reproachful eyes up at him, Rachel let out an anguished cry, spun away, and raced for the wagon, sobbing piteously.

"Goddammit!" Conn thundered. "Why the hell did I listen when everyone said marriage to you would solve all our problems?" He swung on Elizabeth, his expression wrathful. "I've nearly gone crazy worrying about you. At the very least I assumed you would comfort Rachel. Instead I find you screaming at one another like a couple of shrews. Hell! I've got problems now I never dreamed of having. What next?"

Elizabeth merely looked at him, too stunned and hurt to reply. After a moment he made an aggravated sound and took off after his daughter, stalking away with long, furious strides. Pike, who had positioned himself at Elizabeth's side, gave her a mournful look and padded after Conn.

"Elizabeth, dearest, he didn't mean it," Joseph said, stepping toward her from the shadows. Elizabeth had been so overjoyed at seeing Conn, she hadn't even known he was there, and now she could only look at him with desolate, tear-

420

drenched eyes. "He's just tired and out of sorts."

"Please . . . don't." She stepped back, shaking her head, and held up her hands to ward him off when he would have taken her in his arms. "Just . . . don't."

"Joseph's right, Missy. Now mind, I ain't sayin' the boy don't deserve a good kick in the rump, but he didn't mean it. He's jist lettin' off steam is all."

Their compassion, their concern, were more than she could take. She turned away blindly and stumbled a few feet to where Conn's horse stood quietly munching grass and leaned her forehead against the saddle. Oh, God, she'd been a fool to think that Conn would ever love her. A hopeless, romantic fool.

Despair welled up inside her, so intense it wrung a silent cry of agony from her soul. In an unconscious, protective gesture, Elizabeth hunched her shoulders and placed one hand on her abdomen. Her chin trembled and her throat worked as she fought to hold back tears. One after another they seeped through her tightly closed eyelids and trickled down her cheeks.

Suddenly it all became too much—her condition, the flight, the terror of endless river crossings, battling alligators and buffalo, having to put up with Garth's smirking and Agatha's carping, the months of work and worry, looking after everyone, fighting with Rachel. And now . . . Conn. She couldn't take any more. She had to get away.

Impulsively she put her foot in the stirrup and lifted herself aboard Conn's horse. It wasn't a sidesaddle, but she hooked her knee over the horn and kicked the animal into a run.

"Missy! Missy, you come back here!" Taw bellowed, but she gave the horse its head and rode away into the darkness with no thought to where she was heading, too blinded by tears to even notice . . . or care.

All she could think of was the mess she had made of everything. You were a fool to be happy about this baby, she told herself scathingly. Conn married you to help raise the children he has—Millie's children—not saddle him with more. And you're not doing a very good job of that. You should never have married him. Face it, you don't belong in this family. You're nothing but an intruder.

A low limb slapped her in the face, almost unseating her. She swiped at the tears that blurred her vision and realized she was in a stand of trees by the river. When she came to a spot where she could maneuver, she attempted to turn the animal around. Before she could, two men leaped out of the darkness into the moonlit clearing.

Letting loose a stream of rapid-fire Spanish, they danced around her, waving their arms and grabbing for the horse's bridle. Instinctively Elizabeth pulled back on the reins, and the frightened animal gave a shrill whinny and reared. Elizabeth screamed.

"Mr. Cavanaugh! Mr. Cavanaugh!"

Conn turned from talking to Rachel and scowled at Faith, who skidded to a halt beside him, her chest heaving. "Dammit! What is it now?"

Faith quailed at his angry tone, but for once she held her ground. "It's . . . Mi . . . Miss . . . Elizabeth!" she gasped. "Sh-she rode off into . . . into the woods on your hor . . . horse!"

"*What!* My God! Those woods could be full of Mexican deserters! We haven't even found Santa Anna yet!"

Before the words were out of his mouth he was running for the stock picketed a few yards out on the prairie. He grabbed the mane of the first horse he found, swung up onto the animal's bare back, and kicked him into a gallop. He entered the trees at a pace only slightly slower and crashed through the underbrush. Just as he opened his mouth to call her name, he heard a scream.

The hair on the back of his neck stood on end. "Oh, God, Elizabeth!" She screamed again, and he turned his horse toward the sound.

When he broke into the clearing his heart leapt right up into his throat. Gripping the saddle horn and a handful of mane, Elizabeth clung precariously to the rearing horse's back and at the same time fought two men for possession of the beast. Both men were dressed in the baggy pale gray uniform of a Mexican private.

As Conn drew his pistol she caught one of the men with a kick to the head that sent him reeling. Before he could recover, Conn fired. The soldier stumbled back and collapsed, a dark stain spreading on the front of his uniform. Conn jumped from the horse and pounded toward Elizabeth, reaching for his knife, but the other man prudently dashed away into the woods.

"Elizabeth! Oh, God! Are you all right?" He snatched her from the horse's back before she could answer and gathered her close.

"Oh, C-Conn," she sobbed against his chest. "I was so fri . . . frightened."

"Shhh. I know. I know." He laid his cheek against the top of her head and rocked her tenderly, while his heart hammered and his muscles turned to quivering jelly. "It's all right. You're safe now, sweetheart," he crooned. "I won't let anyone hurt you."

"Well, well, well. Isn't this cozy?"

The cynical voice snapped Conn's head up. Every muscle in his body tensed. Elizabeth turned within his embrace and gasped. Just a few yards away stood Garth, pointing a pair of pistols directly at them.

"What the hell do you think you're doing, Lathom?"

"Me?" Garth's teeth flashed white in the moonlight as his oily smile appeared. "Why, I'm about to become the new owner of Riverbend."

"Oh, really? Just how do you figure that?"

"I'm going to shoot the two of you and tell everyone the Mexicans did it. I'll say I heard the shots and came running, but I arrived as they were riding away on your horses." He waved one of the pistols at the dead Mexican soldier. "Unfortunately, I only managed to get one of the bastards."

"How do you figure killing us will get you Riverbend?" Conn's keen blue eyes remained trained on the man as he eased Elizabeth to his side and shifted slightly to shield her with his body.

"Why, I'll be on hand to comfort the bereaved daughter, of course," Garth said with an ironic lift of his eyebrows, as though that should have been obvious. "I already have Rachel eating out of my hand. It should be a simple matter to talk her into marriage. After all, she'll need a strong man to lean on, someone who can run the plantation for her." He shrugged, and his grin widened. "Who better than me?"

"Almost anyone!" Elizabeth spat, and to her fury, Garth chuckled.

"Ah, Elizabeth, you are a treasure. Actually, you're my only regret in this whole thing. I had hoped you and I could spend a few pleasurable hours in bed together before I had to dispose of you. You've turned from a docile kitten into a tigress, but I'm sure I could make you purr."

"Why, you—"

"Conn, no!" Elizabeth cried, and grabbed his arm as he took a threatening step forward. Conn halted at the sharp click of a pistol being cocked.

"What's the matter, Cavanaugh? Don't you like the idea of me having your wife? Well, too bad. I've already had the first one."

Conn's head jerked back as though he'd received a punch to the jaw, and Garth chuckled.

"That's a lie!" Elizabeth cried. But even as she voiced the denial, Millie's dying words, the halting confession that she had refused to think of all this time, whispered through her mind. Looking up at Conn's taut face, she felt sick. She would have given anything to spare him this.

"Oh, really? Well, just to prove it's not . . . your precious cousin had a cute little mole on her left breast. And another one next to her navel."

She felt Conn stiffen, and she knew with sickening certainty that it was true; Millie had betrayed Conn with this awful man.

"Actually, Elizabeth, my original plan was to make you a widow and marry you, but you turned downright unfriendly on me. So, I'll just have to settle for Rachel." He looked at Conn with hatred in his eyes and sneered, "How does it feel, big man? To know that I screwed your wife, and that when you're gone I'll be screwing your daughter?" He laughed as Conn's fists clenched and his jaws bulged.

"You bastard!"

"Maybe. But I'll soon be a rich bastard."

Garth slapped the horses on their rumps and sent them running in the opposite direction of the camp. Grinning evilly, he leveled the gun in his right hand at Conn's heart.

"*Nooo!*" Elizabeth screamed and threw herself in front of Conn at the same instant the gun's explosive report sounded.

"*Elizabeth!*"

The ball struck her shoulder and slammed her back against Conn. She felt the stinging pain, and her eyes widened. Then blackness closed in, and she knew no more.

"Oh, God, Elizabeth!" Conn caught her and eased her to the ground as she crumpled. He looked at her pale face and the spreading stain just above her heart, and a blind rage gushed up inside him. With a roar like a wounded beast, he charged.

Thrusting the empty pistol into his belt, Garth fumbled to switch the other one to his right hand, but Conn rammed him with his head and shoulder, catching him in the midsection and slamming him back against a tree.

Garth's breath *whooshed* out, and the pistol dropped from his hand. Grabbing his shirt, Conn jerked him upright and slammed his fist into his face. Garth staggered back against the tree again and slid down the trunk in a limp heap. Blood spurted from his mouth, and his eyes drooped shut.

Conn rushed to Elizabeth's side and dropped to his knees. "Beth . . . Oh, my darling, talk to me. Oh, God, sweetheart, don't die. Please don't die," he murmured over and over as he searched frantically for a pulse. His relief was so great when he found one, his head sagged forward.

Quickly he ran his hands over her to check for further injuries. When he encountered her swollen belly his heart lurched. He froze and stared. She was with child! Elizabeth was going to have a baby! As that truth soaked in, his horror and fright increased tenfold.

She was still breathing, but the wound was bleeding heavily. Frantic, he tossed back her loose wrapper and tore two wide strips from the bottom of one of her petticoats. He folded one strip into a thick pad and pressed it against the wound, then used the other to tie it in place.

He slid his arms beneath her and stood up. A slight sound alerted him. Conn whirled with Elizabeth in his arms and saw Garth scrambling for the pistol, but as his hand reached for the weapon Pike sprang out of the darkness.

Snarling and growling, the dog went for Garth's throat. Pike knocked him to his back, and for a moment it appeared as though the man had no chance. Then Garth's groping hand closed around the pistol. He raised the weapon, pressed the muzzle against the rough fur on Pike's side, and hooked his thumb over the hammer.

Powder flashed and the boom of a rifle exploded in the small clearing. Garth's body jerked beneath the furious dog, and the hand holding the gun dropped to the ground. The weapon slipped from his lifeless grasp.

At the side of the clearing Conn saw Ebon lower the butt of a smoking rifle from his shoulder. Ben stood beside him, his gun still trained on the man Pike continued to savage.

"Enough, Pike!" Conn barked as he hurried across the clearing with Elizabeth in his arms. "Garth shot Elizabeth. Do you have a horse? I have to get her back to camp. Fast."

Ben's startled gaze went to the bandage on Elizabeth's shoulder. Already blood had soaked through the white pad. Without a word he darted back into the woods and returned in only seconds leading two horses.

Minutes later Conn relinquished Elizabeth to his father's care. He wanted to stay with her, but Joseph ran him out of the wagon; there was barely room for three people beside the bed, and he needed Hester and Jemma there to assist him.

Conn paced up and down next to the wagon, his fists clenching and unclenching. *Oh, God, please let her live. Please.*

He loved her. He suspected that he had all along, but it wasn't until he'd ridden into that clearing and seen her struggling with those two deserters that it really hit him just how much he loved Elizabeth. He loved her more than he'd ever loved anyone or anything in his life. He loved her more than life. If he lost her now, he didn't think he could bear it.

The casual, undemanding love he'd always felt for Elizabeth had deepened and grown into something vital and all-consuming without his knowing quite how or when, though he suspected it had begun even before he'd asked her to marry him.

The thought of the time he'd wasted filled him with sadness. And anger. Ever since they'd married he had fought against his feelings for Elizabeth, unable to escape the niggling thought that if he let himself love her, it would be a betrayal of Millie. Yet all along it had been Millie who had betrayed him.

He thought about Millie and Garth and felt nothing. That part of his life was over. Finished. All that mattered to him now was the slender, golden-haired woman who lay in the wagon, hovering between life and death.

All around, others kept the vigil with him. Looking guilty and worried, Rachel sat on a box between Ian and Faith, doing her best to reassure the frightened children. Taw sat on a log with his injured leg stretched out in front of him, and Ben leaned against a wagon wheel nearby. Isaac shuttled back and forth between the fire and the wagon, keeping Joseph supplied with boiling water and clean bandages. Hovering just beyond the firelight was Ebon and Lottie and every other person from Riverbend. Pike lay beneath her wagon.

"Come light fer a spell, boy." Taw thumped the log beside him. "You ain't doin' no good wearin' a rut in the ground."

Conn didn't feel like sitting, but rather than argue he lowered himself to the log. Leaning forward, he rested his elbows on his knees and clasped his hands together in a fisted prayer. *Let her be all right. Please, God. I beg you.*

Taw put his hand on Conn's shoulder. "Take it easy, son," he said kindly. "That little gal's a lot tougher'n you think."

"Dammit, Taw. I just don't understand. Lots of men get angry and say things they don't mean without their wives running off and taking risks like that."

"Mebbe so." Taw pulled a cake of tobacco out of his shirt pocket and cut off a big plug. "But then, most wives know they is loved."

Conn's shoulders hunched even more, and he hung his head. "And I never said those words to Elizabeth," he murmured guiltily. Now he wondered if he would ever get the chance.

The children fell asleep sometime after midnight and had to be carried to their beds, but not another soul left. Dawn was breaking before Joseph stepped down from the wagon. He looked weary beyond words.

Conn lurched to his feet. "How is she? Will she be all right?"

"Calm down, son. I can't promise you anything at this point, but I think she's going to make it. The baby, too."

"Thank God." Conn closed his eyes and released a long breath as a shudder rippled through him.

"I removed the ball from her shoulder, and she's stable now.

The next twenty-four hours should tell the tale."

Elizabeth did not regain consciousness until late that evening.

When Conn was finally allowed into the wagon, his heart reeled at the sight of her, so small and still in the bed. She lay with her eyes closed, her hands folded atop the covers over the swell of her abdomen. Her nightgown was unfastened almost to her waist to allow access to the bandage on her shoulder, which seemed very little whiter than her pale skin. Her golden hair lay draped across her other shoulder in a neat braid.

Conn swallowed hard. Love swelled in his chest. He bent over her and with an unsteady hand reached out and tenderly stroked her cheek.

Elizabeth's eyes fluttered open. "Co-Conn?"

Gently he slipped his hand beneath one of hers and brought it to his mouth. He kissed each fingertip and pressed his lips to the center of her palm. Elizabeth watched, bewilderment in her eyes. When she opened her mouth to speak, Conn placed two fingers against her lips.

"Shh. Before you say anything, there's something I have to tell you." He pressed her hand to his whisker-stubbled cheek. "I love you, Beth," he said softly. "I love you more than anything in this world. More than life itself."

The astounding statement caught Elizabeth completely by surprise and seemed to set off an explosion in the region of her heart. She caught her breath, her eyes widening.

"I should have told you long before this," Conn continued as she stared at him. "But, fool that I am, I didn't realize it myself until I thought I'd lost you."

Tears welled up in Elizabeth's eyes and spilled over. "Oh, Conn," she managed in a voice that quavered with emotion. "Do you really mean that?"

"I mean it."

"Oh, Conn." Her chin wobbled, and more tears followed,

streaming down her cheeks unheeded. She touched his cheek with trembling fingertips. "I love you, too," she declared tearfully. "So very much. I always have."

Conn bent over and kissed her with such tenderness that Elizabeth thought her heart would surely burst. For long, breathless moments his lips caressed hers lovingly, sweetly, while her heart thrummed and the world outside ceased to be.

When at last he raised his head, his blue eyes were dark with love and concern. "Forgive me for the things I said, Beth. I behaved like an ass. I'd been missing you something awful, and when someone told me how happy you were to see Ben, I was so eaten up with jealousy I couldn't think straight. Hell, I didn't even give you a chance to tell me about the baby. Or even notice."

A touch of alarm entered her eyes. "Do . . . do you mind very much? About the baby?"

"I was surprised." He gave a shaky laugh. "No, *surprised* isn't the word. I was stunned. And scared out of my wits, since at the time I made the discovery you'd already been shot." He pulled a chair up close to the bed and sat down. Bending forward, he laid his cheek against her stomach. "But mind? No. God, no." He rocked his head forward, and she felt him kiss her rounded belly. "The thought of you having my baby makes me the happiest man alive." He slid his hand up over the mound and cupped her breast. "And you? How do you feel about it? Do you mind? Are you worried about having children?"

Elizabeth heard the concern in his voice, the doubt, and she knew he was thinking of how much Millie had hated bearing children and all that motherhood entailed. Her heart ached with the need to reassure him. She ran her hands though his hair and smiled, luxuriating in the slight weight of his head against her, the moist warmth of his breath filtering through the cotton gown, dewing her skin. "I've loved you, wanted you, wanted to have your babies, ever since I can remember. How could I be anything but happy?"

Conn raised his head and looked at her, his stunned expression filled with wonder. "Oh, Beth," he whispered. He reached out and touched her cheek with his fingertips. "My sweet, sweet, Beth."

Chapter 27

Two months later, on a sunny day in the middle of June, Conn brought Elizabeth home to Riverbend.

When he guided the wagon into the drive, Pike took off for the house like a streak. By the time they came around the curve the veranda and yard were filled with people waiting to greet them, their faces eager and smiling, and more were rushing in from the fields and the quarters.

As soon as Joseph had pronounced Elizabeth out of danger, Conn had sent everyone except Jemma and Isaac home to salvage what they could of the crops and put the plantation in order. He and Elizabeth and the two servants had remained camped out on the prairie until she could begin the journey home. For the last few weeks Elizabeth had been up and about and feeling as chipper as ever, but Conn had continued to fuss and pamper. She had been anxious to return to Riverbend, but he had insisted on making the trip in slow stages.

Awash with feelings of happiness and homecoming, Elizabeth beamed and waved from her perch on the wagon seat. From the moment the railed fences and the rolling fields had come into view, she had been consumed with excitement.

"Mama! Mama!" Ian cried, jumping up and down on the veranda. Faith tried to calm him, but even she, who hid her emotions so well, fidgeted anxiously. The instant the wagon stopped in the circular drive, the children came bounding down the steps like a pair of boisterous puppies.

"Here now, you two. Be careful! Elizabeth hasn't been well." Rachel, who had been hovering uncertainly in the background, rushed forward to overtake them and grabbed each child by the arm. "At least let Papa help her down from the wagon before you pounce on her."

Due to Elizabeth's now enormous girth, the task was not easily accomplished, but at last she had both feet on the ground. Released, Ian and Faith surged forward and tried to clasp their arms around her middle as they had in the past, but their efforts were thwarted by the bulge of her belly.

Laughing, Elizabeth bent as best she could and hugged and kissed their hot, freckled faces. They smelled of sweat and sunshine, and their mouths were ringed with purple stains. She smiled, knowing that their arrival had caught the children in the blackberry patch behind the carriage house.

As she straightened she was at once caught up in Joseph's embrace. "Welcome home, daughter," he whispered in her ear. Elizabeth hugged him back, her throat tight, her eyes misty.

"Well, it's 'bout time you two got home." Leaning on his cane, Taw stumped down the steps, his white beard bisected by a huge grin that belied his querulous tone. He snatched Elizabeth against his chest in a one-armed bear hug, his rough voice wobbling with emotion. "Ah, Missy, Missy. Yore shore 'nuff a sight fer these tired old eyes. The place jist ain't the same without you, honey."

"Hey! Wait a second," Conn said with feigned indignation. "Isn't anyone glad to see me?"

"Shoot, boy. Why would anyone be wantin' t' look at that ugly face o' yorn?" Taw said with a grin, thumping him on the back.

One by one, Ebon and Lottie and Dulcie and the others pressed forward, grinning, their joy at Elizabeth's return gleaming in their eyes. They squeezed her hands or patted her shoulder awkwardly and murmured words of welcome that filled her heart with gladness. The only person who held back was Rachel, and Elizabeth did not press her. Before leaving for home with the others, the girl had visited Elizabeth a few times, but never for long and never alone. There had been no chance to make peace, and the strain of their last quarrel still hovered between them.

When at last the greetings were done, Elizabeth looked around, her eyes drinking in sights that had become so dear to her. Riverbend. Smiling, she released a long sigh. It was heaven to be home at last.

"Come on, let's get you inside." Conn hooked an arm around Elizabeth's waist, but as she turned toward the house she gave a cry and bent nearly double, clutching her stomach.

Conn blanched. "What is it? What's wrong?"

Elizabeth gritted her teeth and grimaced, unable to answer for a moment as the grinding pain worked around from back to front. When it passed she drew a gasping breath and tried to reassure him. "Don't . . . don't look so worried," she panted. "It was just a contraction."

"*What!*"

"When did the pains start, Elizabeth?" Joseph calmly moved to her other side and grasped her arm to assist her up the veranda steps.

"A few hours ago."

"*What!*" Conn yelped again, and with a muttered curse he swooped her up into his arms and took the steps in two leaps.

"Are you crazy, woman? Why didn't you tell me your time had come?" he raged. "I would have stopped and sent Isaac ahead to fetch Dad." He strode in through the double doors, held wide by the anxious servants, and stormed up the stairs with his precious burden, his face white and set as stone.

Elizabeth smiled lovingly and combed her fingers through his raven hair. "Darling, I was homesick. Besides, I wanted our child to be born at Riverbend. I was afraid you'd stop if I told you about the pains."

"Damn right!"

He laid her down on their bed as though she were made of fragile glass, but before he could straighten up she took his face between her palms and gazed at him lovingly. "Don't be angry, darling," she pleaded. "I knew we would make it in time, and we di—"

She caught her breath, and her eyes widened. Alarm tightened Conn's face as she clutched his arms. "But . . ." She threw back her head, and her body arched. "You'd better g-get your father now," she gasped between clenched teeth. "And tell him to *hurry*!"

The last came out on a scream that sent Conn tearing out of the room at a dead run.

In less than fifteen minutes, while Conn paced the hallway outside the door and Taw tossed back more whiskey than he'd consumed at one time in over thirty years, Seth Joseph Taw Cavanaugh made his entrance into the world. The strapping babe announced his arrival with a lusty cry that put a smile on his mother's lips and nearly brought his father to his knees.

As Conn sagged against the wall, Taw tossed back another shot of whiskey. "Lord a'mighty."

It seemed to Conn that an eternity passed before Jemma stepped out into the hall with the swaddled infant in her arms. The tiny black woman beamed as she introduced father and son. Conn was thrilled with his child, but his main concern was Elizabeth, and after a brief look he left Taw standing in the hallway, inspecting tiny fingers and toes in awestruck silence, and hurried into the bedroom.

"How is she?" he demanded of his father in a voice that wasn't quite steady.

"She's fine. See for yourself."

She looked more than fine; she looked like an angel. Wearing a lace-trimmed nightgown, her freshly brushed hair spread out around her like a golden cape, Elizabeth lay propped up on a pile of pillows with her eyes closed, a tired but contented smile curving her lips.

Joseph discreetly slipped out of the room, but Conn didn't notice. He stared down at his wife, his heart aching with love. Elizabeth. Beth. She was his heart, his life, his dearest treasure in all the world.

To think that all those years ago she had been there within reach. And for his entire life she had been secretly loving him with her quiet fire and her gentle strength, and he'd never even noticed. When he thought of all the years wasted, all the happiness his blindness had cost them both, he felt like a fool.

And when he thought of all she'd done, all she'd faced, all she'd endured, all the courage and valiant spirit in that delicate body, he felt humbled.

He knew he didn't deserve her, but she was his now—truly his—and as God was his witness, no power on earth would ever take her from him.

Her eyes fluttered open, and she smiled. "Hi."

The soft sleepiness of her voice set off a fresh wave of emotion that rolled through him like a hot tide. He bent over, bracing his hands on the mattress on either side of her, and looked deep into her luminous gray eyes. His heart clubbed. His throat grew so tight, he wasn't sure he could speak. "Hi," he managed huskily, and her smile widened.

"Have you seen him?"

"Yes."

"Isn't he beautiful?"

"You're beautiful."

Her eyes softened. "Oh, Conn. I do love you so."

Unable to resist, he bent his elbows and kissed her, a whispery caress that spoke of feelings too deep and too profound to express. It was homage. It was exultation. It was a pledge of devotion and love never-ending.

When Conn lifted away from her, one corner of his mouth tipped upward. "I love you, too. But if you ever, *ever* scare me like that again, I swear I'll paddle your cute little backside."

"Yes, Conn," she said demurely, without an ounce of contrition or concern in her eyes.

Two months of being the focus of Conn's undivided and lavish attention had given Elizabeth a new confidence, that special inner glow of a woman who knew she was loved. If she had been lovely before, now she was breathtaking, and the look in her husband's eyes proclaimed that fact more eloquently than words ever could.

Later that evening, after Elizabeth had rested, Conn tugged off his boots and propped up on the bed beside her. They talked together quietly, admiring their son, who lay sleeping peacefully in the cradle beside the bed, exchanging looks and touches, basking in the pleasure of being home at last, and of being in love.

A light tapping drew their attention to the door as it opened and the children stuck their heads inside. "May we come in?" Rachel asked, and when they received a nod from Conn, the three tiptoed inside.

They knelt beside the cradle and admired the baby. Seth Cavanaugh was a robust infant who had his father's black hair and strong features. Folding back the light blanket, the children inspected him closely, marveling at how tiny he was, how perfect—at least, the girls did. Ian eyed the infant with suspicion, not quite sure whether to be pleased or resentful of this new person in their lives.

As Faith lifted the baby's hand to show Ian the tiny fingernails, Rachel looked up at her stepmother.

"Elizabeth," she began hesitantly. "I just want you to know that . . . well . . . I'm glad you're home. And . . ." Her gaze darted away again and fixed on her own hand, which rested on the edge of the bed. "And I've, uh . . . I've been thinking. After . . . well . . . what happened, it's probably going to be a while before you get your strength back. So . . ." Rachel's fingers plucked at the cotton sheet. "If you'd like, I'd be glad to help you with the baby."

Elizabeth knew an olive branch when one was offered. She laid her own hand over Rachel's. "I'd appreciate that, dear. Very much."

Rachel turned her hand over and gripped Elizabeth's tightly. A deep sadness still clouded her blue eyes, and Elizabeth knew it would take time for her to get over Johnny, but perhaps having the baby to look after would help.

"And . . ." Rachel glanced at her cautiously and licked her lips. "Well . . . we, uh . . . the three of us talked it over and decided that, uh—so Seth won't grow up confused and all— that . . . well . . . it would be best if from now on we all called you Mama."

Conn's arm tightened around Elizabeth's shoulders, but she didn't dare look at him or she would break down and cry. Her chest grew so tight that she could barely breathe. Her lips trembled as she murmured over the lump in her throat, "I would love that. Truly."

Uncomfortable with the emotion-charged conversation, Rachel nodded and quickly returned her attention to the baby.

Conn leaned close and whispered in Elizabeth's ear, "Welcome home, my love."

With her heart in her eyes, she reached up and kissed him softly. "Yes. Welcome home."

A warm summer breeze stirred the lace curtains at the windows. Outside, the velvet dark night was alive with the croak of bullfrogs and the cicadas' whir. Inside, two old men played checkers and toasted the birth of their grandson while two small children and a sad-eyed girl chattered over him.

Her heart overflowing, Elizabeth snuggled back against Conn's chest and watched them through eyes grown blurry with tears.

Together they had struggled through terrible loss and hardship and strife, and it had somehow made them stronger, drawn them closer. It had made of them what she had long hoped they would someday be. It had made them a family.

Author's Note

In the 1820s and 1830s settlers flocked to Texas. The land was cheap, plentiful, and rich, and the government, first of Spain, then of Mexico, encouraged settlement. After the Mexican Revolution, under the Constitution of 1824, Mexico was ostensibly a democracy, and the settlers, with their predominantly American heritage, were comfortable with this system.

When power-hungry Mexican leaders began to chip away at their freedoms, the Texans reacted in a fashion typical of their background: they sent elected representatives to meetings to discuss matters and draw up petitions stating their grievances and wishes. To them this was the obvious, peaceful means of settling differences.

However, this concept was foreign to Mexico's leaders. In that country only insurrection and riot resulted from initiative taken by the people; therefore they viewed the peaceful assembly, so natural to the Anglo settlers, as a threat and countered with more oppression. The result was, inevitably, open confrontation.

I have tried faithfully to incorporate into my story the events that led up to the decisive battle of San Jacinto. There, on April 21, 1836, despite formidable odds, the enraged Texans, in a bloody clash that lasted barely eighteen minutes, won their independence. For the next ten years, until the citizens voted to join the United States, Texas was a sovereign nation, the only state in the Union that can claim that distinction.

With the exception of the people listed below, all the characters in this book are fictional. The historical events mentioned, however, are factual.

Stephen F. Austin

William Barret Travis

Jim Bowie

Joseph Powell

Hosea N. League

David Burnet

Lorenzo de Zavala

Dr. William Mottley

Ben Milam

Frank W. Johnson

Sidney Sherman

Wiley Martin

General Santa Anna

Colonel Ugartechea

General Sesma

General Urrea

Samuel Houston

Davey Crockett

Jared Groce

Patrick Jack

Susannah Dickerson

Almeron Dickerson

Thomas Rusk

Erastus "Deaf" Smith

Edward Burleson

George Hockley

Moseley Baker

Mirabeau B. Lamar

General Martin Perfecto de Cos

Captain Tenorio

Captain Castañeda

General Gaona

GINNA GRAY is a best-selling author with fourteen published books, to date. Her two passions are writing and painting. She lives with her husband in Houston, Texas.